Credits

Written & Designed by: Shane Lacy Hensley

Additional Material by: John Hopler & Matt Forbeck

Editing: Matt Forbeck   **Layout:** Matt Forbeck & Shane Lacy Hensley

Front Cover Art: Paolo Parente   **Back Cover Art:** Brian Snoddy

Logos: Ron "Voice o' Death" Spencer & Charles Ryan

Graphic Design: Hal Mangold & Charles Ryan

Interior Art: Thomas Biondolillo, Mike Chen, Jim Crabtree, Kim DeMulder, Paul Daly, Marcus Falk, Mark Dos Santos, Tom Fowler, James Francis, Darren Friedendahl, Tanner Goldbeck, Norman Lao, Ashe Marler, MUTT Studios, Posse Parente, Matt Roach, Jacob Rosen, Mike Sellers, Kevin Sharpe, Jan Michael Sutton, Matt Tice, George Vasilakos & Loston Wallace

Advice & Suggestions: Paul Beakley, Barry Doyle, Keith & Ana Eichenlaub, John & Joyce Goff, Michelle Hensley, Christy Hopler, Jay Kyle, Steven Long, Ashe Marler, Jason Nichols, Charles Ryan, Dave Seay, Matt Tice, Maureen Yates, Dave "Coach" Wilson & John Zinser

Special Thanks to: All the folks who supported *Deadlands:* our fans, our friends, and our families.

Pinnacle Entertainment Group, Inc.
P.O. Box 10908
Blacksburg, VA 24062-0908
www.peginc.com or deadlands@aol.com
(800) 214-5645 (orders only)

Dedicated to:
Caden.
Who's raised a little Hell on Earth of his own.

Table o' Contents

Table o' Contents

Posse: 4

Chapter One:
The Prospector's Story

Get up, Ranger. I know you're groggy from yer dirt nap, but I ain't got time to wetnurse a 200-year-old piece o' meat.

Yeah, I look a little different than the last time you laid eyes on my ugly puss, but it's me, Coot Jenkins. The Prospector. Ringin' any bells, wormfood? I'm the one who stuck you in that hole 200 years ago. June 8th, 1876, if memory an' that tombstone behind you serves. Kind of a "contingency plan," y'see. In case my other little scheme didn't work.

Well, guess what? It didn't.

If your brainpan ain't too full o' bugs from all them years in the ground, you might remember I put together a couple score of your kind back then to fight the Reckoners, the monsters responsible for all the stuff that happened in the "Weird West," as the papers used to call it.

For that, me and my little undead army had to go into the spirit world—the Hunting Grounds as the Injuns say—where the Reckoners lived.

We had no problem gettin' there. It was that army o' demons waitin' on us that gave us a few problems. Worst part of it was the demons took control o' most of my stiffs and turned 'em against me. I shoulda known the same demons that keep corpses like you movin' would have an easier time gettin' control on their home turf.

We still won—the battle at least—but we lost the war. Me 'n' what was left o' the meat put down the bad ones.

Then we got "lost" somehow.

The last dozen o' my soldiers and I wandered around the Hunting Grounds for a long time before we found our way out again. I didn't know how long we was gone 'til a few weeks back. You'll see what I mean if you turn your sorry sack o' bones around and look at some o' them other tombstones.

Brace yourself, friend. It's 2094.

No use cleanin' that dirt outta yer ears, son. You heard me right. I've been back about a month. Now I'm diggin' up my reserves, and you're the first o' the lot to see the light o' day. I just hope it ain't too late fer us ta do somethin' about all o' this.

I don't know what we're gonna' do yet, but I ain't goin' back in the damn Huntin' Grounds, that's for sure! I shoulda realized the demons would have more control over your kind in their own stompin' grounds.

Worst part is, I reckon my mistake cost us pretty dear. I think they done gone and blowed the world up while we was away.

I walked a couple hundred miles to get here, and there ain't much left o' the world. The cities have been blasted, and there's hardly a tree between here and Deadwood.

It gets even worse. Y'sure you wanna hear it? Maybe you oughta wait a while and catch your breath. Don't give me that look! It's a figure o' speech.

All right, smart-ass. You wanted to know.

The Prospector's Story

The Weird West

I'll have to start from the beginnin'. You remember when the Reckoning started? It was July 3, 1863, right when we was fightin' the Battle o' Gettysburg. No? What's been crawlin' through yer brain?

Anyhow, it actually all started a while afore that when an angry shaman by the name o' Raven led a bunch of other angry shamans into the Hunting Grounds. They had an idea about lettin' these demons called manitous loose on the world, and you know what? They did it.

How's not important. The fact is that these demons spurted back into our world and started causing trouble right away. Some folks even managed to harness the power of these filthy things. Funnier yet, some of 'em didn't even know they were doin' it.

Anyhow, these manitous set straight out to fill the world with mischief an' fear, and they did a damn good job of it. They got some help from all sorts o' critters from legend, plus some all-new things straight from the depths o' some twisted sicko's mind.

Worse yet, they got help from us by means of this stuff called ghost rock. Folks found it in the walls of the Great Maze after Raven tossed most o' California into the sea.

The Secret o' Ghost Rock

Lookin' back on it now, I see ghost rock was the Reckoners' secret weapon. I know you was dead before it got discovered in 1868 or so, but it was this "superfuel" that boomed bigger than gold. We shoulda known the stuff was evil the way it screams when burnt. And that smoke that looked like damned souls? It was. I know that now. Those were manitous, sealed in the stuff just waiting for—well, I'll get to that in a minute.

The Reckoners put ghost rock here on Earth. Anywhere there was coal, gold, silver, or other ores, folks was likely to find ghost rock as well. Funny thing is I don't remember a soul ever askin' why this stuff had never been discovered before. Makes you feel kinda stupid, don't it? That the stuff would just appear overnight like that, an' none of us even questioned it.

Huh? No, I don't know how they did it. They just did. They *are* freakin' supernatural. An' I reckon any kinda monsters that can make a corpse like you wake up and ask stupid questions can make a few billion tons o' rock. Now shut up and lemme finish.

Anyway, the Reckoners put the stuff here for several reasons, though the last one's the clincher.

The first reason was to get us to fight over it. We sure did plenty o' that. Who can say how many died in the Great Rail Wars, the War Between the States, and God-knows how many claim jumpings, holdups, and robberies?

The second reason was to get us fightin' each other with weapons sure to kill lotsa folks in real painful ways. Even better, I 'spect ghost rock moved us along a little faster than we prob'ly shoulda gone. Most o' the gadgets the "mad scientists" made were one-of-a-kind. They couldn't be made on an assembly line like Peacemakers. They was harmless enough in total, though not if you were one of the unlucky ones that got torched by a flamethrower or run over by a steam tank.

Still, enough real progress got made that all that stuff got deadlier faster than we could learn how to use it. I guess you might say technology grew faster than diplomacy. Don't look at me like that, Ranger! Just 'cause I got a bit of an accent don't mean I'm an idjit!

That's better. Anyhow, the real reason the Reckoners gave us ghost rock was because of those damned manitous inside.

Y'see, there was this thing called the "Last War" in 2081. I'll tell you more about it later on, but it ended with every nation on Earth droppin' bombs on every other. The "Apocalypse." Not a city was spared as far as I've heard.

Sure, we had ghost-rock bombs back in '76, but the ones they got here had been "irradiated." I still don't know 'xactly what that means, but the effect is to make the stuff a hundred times more powerful than it was before. Scary, ain't it?

So those bombs blew things up real good, but they did somethin' else too. Somethin' none o' them deluded scientists who invented 'em ever counted on. Y'see, that 'radiated ghost rock full o' damned spirits did more than just blow folks up. It also created "Deadlands."

In case your memory's rottin' like your face, a Deadland's a place so full o' fear it actually warps the land and gives birth to monsters drawn right out o' folk's nightmares.

And that's what the Reckoners had been waitin' on: for the whole stinkin' planet to turn into one giant Deadland. The bastards need that sorta fear to survive, kinda like a fish needs water or a prospector needs gold—or in my case, stinkin' corpses. Speakin' o' which, we gotta roll you around in a flower patch or somethin', Ranger. You're a little gamey after 200 years.

The Reckoners Revealed

So with the world all warm like a nice hot bath, the sons o' bitches stepped on outta the Huntin' Grounds and onto Mother Earth. The Reckoners tore through the survivors of the Last War like foxes in a henhouse. And you'da never guessed who—or what—they are.

The Four freakin' Horsemen of the Apocalypse.

That's right! Just like it says in the Bible! That feller I talked to says War popped up in Kansas, Famine in the Maze, Death in Death Valley, and Plague somewhere in Texas. They killed a mess o' folks, then raised an army o' their own demons outta the bodies. Then they each tore a swath of destruction across the West and vanished across the Mississippi into the East—which I hear is even more blasted and ruined than it is out here. If you can believe it.

Does that mean it's the End Times? Judgment Day? I dunno. We're still here, so either we're the meek and we've inherited this chunk o' rock or the Reckoners jumped the gun on God's little plan. Personally, I gotta believe the latter. Most folks around here think God forgot about 'em. I don't even think they got many preachers anymore. I guess most of 'em gave up or died.

In the end, I don't reckon it much matters. We're here, and we gotta survive. An' the only way to do it is to dry up all that fear that's keepin' the Reckoners alive.

Hell on Earth

Best I can figure, the bombs dropped in 2081, 13 years ago. Now most every place is still a Deadland. You can feel it. This spot we're in right now is one. Feel them evil spirits watchin' from on high? I do. An' I'd swear some of 'em was the same one's I whooped back in Hell!

BLAM!

I know that was a waste of good buckshot, damn you! But it sure made me feel better. I been staggerin' aroun' a place that'd make most men mad for 200 years! Well I'm mad, all right, just not that kinda mad. I'm mad 'cause these damn monsters took away my life. An' I'm mad 'cause they ruint my world. An' most of all I'm mad 'cause I'm a sore loser. An' we lost, friend.

All right. I'll simmer down. I gotta watch my ammo anyway. Bullets and buckshot are real scarce here. I reckon there's a lot to shoot at.

That's the kind o' thing you need to know now that you're seein' sunlight again. Maybe I'd better tell you everything I've learned so far.

A History Lesson

No one I talked to knows much about what happened back in our time. I don't think knowin' the date the Civil War ended or who won the Great Rail Wars is too important when you're eatin' a glowin' rat for dinner. Yeah, I said glowin'. It has somethin' to do with that radiation stuff.

What folks do know about is recent history. Let's start with goin' into the stars. You heard me right, son. I said the stars.

The Faraway War

From what I understand—an' I've only been here a month, understand—our old buddy Darius Hellstromme, the most famous mad scientist from our time, is still around. Don't ask me how, but I reckon a man who can invent a dang-blasted automaton can figure out how to keep hisself alive a couple o' centuries. Harrowed? No. I don't think so. I get a feelin' about those things these days and that just don't sound right.

Anyway, folks had been goin' to the moon for a long time. No one I talked to remembers 'xactly since when. That was about as far as they got, though, 'cause them other planets was just too durn far. Around 2044, Hellstromme invented somethin' they call the "Tunnel." It hung up in space between us and the moon and allowed space machines—they call 'em "ships" for some reason—to fly out to a whole 'nother place.

In this place, they found a "system" of planets called "Faraway." On one of 'em—a rock they called "Banshee" 'cause of the winds—was a race o' aliens! Y'know, space ferners! They called themselves "anouks" and proved to be mostly friendly. They was a primitive sort, so when we found out there was ghost rock on Banshee, we did 'em just like we did the Injuns: traded 'em some beads and claimed most of it fer ourselves.

Just like the Injuns, they eventually got fed up with us takin' everything from 'em. Around 2074 or so, most of the aliens rose up and started fightin' back. At first, the humans was winnin'. See, all the nations were fairly friendly at that point, so the settlers was protected by marines from somethin' they called the "United Nations." (I guess they gotta call 'em marines if they're gonna call their flyin' machines "ships.") Those boys were tough hombres. They had all kinds o' guns and bombs, and the anouks didn't have much of a chance.

Sykers

So the anouks turned to raidin' 'steada fightin', and they brought out their own kinda witch doctors. The marines called 'em "skinnies," and I reckon they could take over folks' minds, blow things up, and cause all kinds o' Hell. Remind you of anything? Yup. Sittin' Bull and his shamans whupped Custer's ass the same way. Maybe somebody remembered, 'cause the United Nations asked all its members to send 'em some special troops they call "sykers."

Best I can tell, the governments and war departments of a whole mess of countries learned how to make soldiers into somethin' like hucksters from our time. Only these boys and girls got their power kinda like them Oriental folks they useta have out in Shan Fan in our day. They drew it right outta the Hunting Grounds without the aid o' manitous, animal spirits, or even the blessings of the Almighty hisself. It took years of training, and most who tried to become "sykers" couldn't cut it. Those who did were perfect for fightin' the skinnies, so a couple thousand trekked out to Banshee to show 'em what for.

Things got bloody in a hurry, just like the Injun Wars in our time. Both sides did things that would make their mommas cry. A lot of them anouks didn't have nothin' to do with the raids, but they knew where the others was hidin', so the sykers had pretty much become cold-blooded killin' machines by the time it was all over.

Then the war back on Earth started up, and all the armies wanted their troops back. It was a big enough fight that they took their regular troops first. It was almost a year afore they got a ship to haul the sykers home. In the meantime, they was the only army left to protect millions o' colonists. The last few months on Banshee was worse than anything they'd gone through before.

Eventually they all got on a ship named *Unity* and headed home. By the time they got there, everything had already been blown to Hell. Helluva homecoming, huh, Ranger?

You can spot these folks from a country mile away by their heads. They're balder'n the tops o' the Rockies. (I think their magic makes their hair fall out.) Steer clear of 'em, though. After what happened to 'em on Banshee, they're ornery sons o' bitches.

HELLSTROMME INDUSTRIES, LTD.
SGT. J. STRYKER

FARAWAY TACTICAL FOOTAGE
RENAISSANCE SECTOR 937-0L105
BATTLE OF REAGAN'S BLUFF
NATIVES "PACIFIED" WITH HELP OF RIVAL TRIBE.
CASUALTIES WITHIN TOLERANT LEVELS.

17:35:47

The Last War

So how'd the Last War begin? You can prob'ly guess. It started in the Maze over ghost rock.

Huh? You don't even remember when California was tossed into the sea in '68? Yer more worm-addled than I thought. To backtrack a bit, what was left after the Great Quake was a maze of sea canyons and the richest veins o' ghost rock ever known. That's what triggered the whole Great Rail Wars later on, a race to build a transcontinental railroad and supply the North and South with ghost rock for their war toys.

I don't know what good it did 'em besides gettin' lots o' folks killed. In the end, the Confederacy was its own nation.

It was pretty much the same story 200 years later. The Maze was still boomin' in 2080, and everybody still wanted the ghost rock for themselves. I ain't figured out exactly how it got started, but in 2081, the US and a whole passel o' countries from around the world formed the "Northern Alliance" and claimed the Maze, which had been split between the US and the Rebs.

Fights broke out, and the Rebs did the best they could, but it was just too much too soon. They formed the Southern Alliance, and soon half the countries on Earth were fightin' in what was left o' California.

The war spread all over the world and went on for the better part of three years. I doubt me an' you can imagine the kind of carnage it caused. Flyin' machines, tanks, artillery that could fire across oceans, and Harrowed soldiers sewed full o' contraptions like automatons.

At the last, one o' the armies musta thought they was losin'. New York City vanished under the skull-shaped cloud of a ghost-rock bomb in 2081. No one knows who dropped that first one, but within hours, thousands more fell on every city or fort in the world. There were lotsa Deadlands already, places where some critter or madman had been workin' for years. But the ones caused by the bombs came complete with big, swirlin', black storms full o' manitous.

That's when the Reckoners came through and did their Texas two-step on the survivors. What was left o' the Northern and Southern Alliances here in the West did their best to fight back, but what good do bombs do against hunger and disease? And the unholy critters the Horsemen made to fight for 'em could whip most anything thrown at 'em anyway. The brave fighters died tryin' to make a last stand. The smart ones hid 'til the Reckoners eventually stalked off east.

The Combine

There warn't much left after that. Not a city was left standin'. Towns that weren't too near the blast sites or in the path of the Reckoners survived, but they didn't have much food left, and no way to defend themselves against the marauding bands of deserters and other scum that come out of the woodwork when somethin' bad happens.

The worst of that scum was a Southern Alliance general named Throckmorton. He ran a prison camp with hundreds o' captured Northerners and their equipment, as well as some of his own. When the bombs started falling, he hid 'em all in a huge cave somewhere and offered 'em a deal: their freedom in exchange for joining his "American Combine." There would be no more North and South, he claimed. Instead, there would be one nation of strong, fit, warriors who could resettle the land and fight the Reckoners.

It sounds good, but Throckmorton's goons kill the leaders of any village that don't support 'em with crops, ghost rock, or whatever else they may have that's worth spit. The Combine also kills whole tribes o' what they call "mutants," folks who get all diseased and warped by radiation. They don't fit in with that whole "strong and fit" part o' Throckmorton's new world.

Now it seems the general's somehow taken over what was left o' Hellstromme Industries in the ruins o' Denver. Throckmorton's got all o' Hellstromme's toys, includin' legions of automatons that fly, swim, crawl underground, and God-knows-what-else.

Hellstromme

You're prob'ly wonderin' why Hellstromme don't run his own business no more. That's a question I can answer, Ranger.

You 'member he'd taken up with the Mormons in Deseret back in our time? They finally kicked him out when he wouldn't play nice, so he set up shop in Denver with nothin' but automatons for workers.

Hellstromme disappeared when the bombs fell, and no one's seen him since, even though his labs survived well enough that Throckmorton could move in. Either he got hisself killed, or he finally realized what a rotten egg he is and ran off to sulk. Why Hellstromme's automatons work with Throckmorton is just a mystery.

The Prospector's Story

The Law Dogs

What with all the bandits and monsters after the Apocalypse, it was only a matter of time 'til some do-gooder stepped up to do what he felt was his duty. 'Cept in this case it was a "her." This'll make you proud, Ranger.

Y'see, there was this lady Texas Ranger—yup, I said "lady." I guess a lot changed while we was gone. Anyway, this Ranger was named Jane Swindall. After the bombs, she gathered up all the other Rangers and lawmen she could find: sheriffs, deputies, US Marshals, Pinkertons, firemen, whatever. She knew the only way to beat the Reckoners was to give folks hope, and the only way to do that was to restore some law and order to the folks who were still kickin'.

Swindall called 'em all "Law Dogs," and the name stuck. Those who stuck with her swore their loyalty and ventured off into the wastes to bring back the law by their actions, their fists, and—if needed—their guns. They don't have no written laws, and they don't recognize no court they don't think is fair.

If you run into one of these Law Dogs, make sure he or she's on your side. You can imagine what kind o' person it takes to bring the law to a place like this.

The Templars

The Law Dogs ain't the only ones fightin' to make things right again. There's another group that calls themselves the "Templars," after the knights of the Crusades.

These Templars ain't quite as bright and shiny as you might want 'em to be, though. They was founded by a fella named Simon Mercer. Like a lotta folks, Simon lost his family in the war and wandered around lost for a while tryin' to get over it. While he was wanderin', he watched Law Dogs and other do-gooders tryin' to protect the rest of the folks from terrors and marauders like Throckmorton. I reckon it made him sick to watch these good men and women throwin' their lives away for a town fulla ingrates who begged for help when Throckmorton was around, and then double-crossed the Law Dogs and strung 'em up afterwards.

A few years later, he did somethin' about it. He started up the Templars in Boise, Idaho. Simon calls hisself the Grandmaster, and he managed to recruit a bunch of others he felt was worthy o' wearin' the white shirt and red cross of the old knights. God must love 'em, 'cause the Templars can heal like the preachers learned to do back in our time. Templars also make their own swords that can cut through a zombie like a hot knife through butter.

In some ways, Templars are a lot like the Law Dogs. They travel around the West protectin' the innocent, healing the sick, and all that other hero stuff. The difference is they don't throw their lives away for just anyone. If a town's in danger of being overrun by raiders, a Templar might disguise himself and listen to the folks to see if they're "worthy" of saving. If they are, the Templar'll whip off his disguise and show them their uniform and sword. If the Templars don't deem your sorry hide worth their sacrifice, they keep right on goin', and you never even know they were there. Once they're committed, though, Templars fight to the death.

One other thing I've heard about 'em. It ain't easy to become a Templar, and those that betray the rest are in for a sorry fate.

Doomsayers

Templars are a stingy lot, and Law Dogs are few and far between. Neither one of 'em has much to do with mutants poisoned by that radiation stuff I told you about. Most of the time it just makes 'em sick and ugly as sin, but a lot go loco as well. Most all of 'em get thrown out of towns full of "norms" to live in the nearest rat-infested ruins with other mutants.

Law Dogs an' Templars don't go out of their way to defend muties, but there's a group who does. They call themselves "Doomsayers." If you can believe it, these loonies actually think the Apocalypse was a good thing! Their leader's a crackpot named Silas Rasmussen. He preaches mutants are the next evolution o' mankind, and it's the "Cult o' Doom's" job to protect 'em!

The way they do it is to whip up muties into armies and then lead 'em against norms. The muties are tough enough, but the Doomsayers got "radiation magic" they use to blow stuff up and make norms into deranged muties.

Fortunately, some of the Doomsayers have turned against Silas. You'll know 'em by their purple robes. These "heretics" run around healin' and helpin' folks to prove the cult is good—it's just Silas who's all wrong. They still believe norms are doomed (that's where they get their name), but they ain't our enemies.

Oh, and they're lookin' for a particular mutant they call the "Harbinger." That one's s'posed to replace Silas and lead us all to a new age. God, I hope they're right, 'cause this one stinks.

Junkers & Ghost Rock

While I'm talkin' about all these weird types, I might as well mention the junkers.

You might already know how mad scientists back in our time made all those crazy gadgets. They thought they was geniuses—Hell, I'm sure they were—but their ideas didn't come without help from the manitous. 'Course most o' the mad scientists didn't know it and woulda laughed at you if'n you'd said so.

I'm just guessin' at this next part, so I could be wrong, but I think once the ghost-rock bombs got built, the manitous stopped volunteerin' information. It took a while for the mad scientists to realize their "muse" was gone. Before they could do much about it, most of 'em died when the bombs fell. But there's always a few who survive. Those who did couldn't deny there were spooks in the world when the Reckoners appeared and started stompin' on folks like ants. Once that happened, the old mad scientists started lookin' for ways to make the manitous talk again. Only this time, they had to beat the truth out of the little buggers.

An' I hope it hurts 'em like Hell.

You'll see these old codgers pokin' through ruins lookin' for parts for their gizmos. That's why folks call 'em "junkers."

You can tell a junker from some other fellow 'cause they power all their gadgets with these things called "spirit batteries." They take ghost rock an' do somethin' to it to draw out the manitous inside. I don't know this for sure, but I think they run the little bastards like rats in a wheel and suck off their juice 'til they escape. I can't really explain it, but it does my heart good to think o' those demons sufferin' like that!

The downside o' messin' with evil spirits is folks tend to shy away from you. Everyone knows junkers mess with demons—the same ones that ended the world—so they don't make friends too easy. Still, if we can round a few up and get 'em to help out, their gizmos oughta help us put down more than a few o' the Reckoners' critters.

Oh, an' junkers ain't the only ones who use ghost rock. Folks use it to light their homes, power their buggies, and so on, so there's still a fortune to be made in minin' it. An' if you can 'radiate it, it can even run them big, ol' tanks an' even flyin' machines.

The Prospector's Story

The Wasted West

You 'member how the *Epitaph* used to call home the "Weird West?" Now I reckon folks call it the "Wasted West." Shame, ain't it? You'll see why when we get movin'. I'm anxious to see more of it myself. I've heard a few things about some of our old haunts that I just gotta see for myself. Lemme tell you about a few.

The Maze

I reckon all the fightin' in the Maze durn near emptied it out during the war, but folks have moved back in since then. Yup, they're still after ghost rock. Only trouble comes from all the monsters. Two hundred years o' fightin'—and a Deadland to boot—makes for a whole lotta evil.

I hear parts of it are overrun with some kinda bizarre fish-folk. The Doomsayers say they're just mutants, but the stories I hear make 'em sound like monsters to me.

Deseret

You might remember the Mormons set up their own country—Deseret—back in our day. They musta held on to it, 'cause it still exists.

They ran off Hellstromme before the Last War started, but I reckon he left some kinda shield in place to protect his home and factories, 'cause the bombs hit all around the City o' Gloom but didn't go off.

Unfortunately for the Mormons, they didn't know about Hellstromme's shield or they coulda gathered up the flock. Only a quarter or so of those who lived in the city when the bombs hit were of the faith.

Now Salt Lake City's about the only city left in the West, and you can bet it's got walls and a whole lotta armed folks keepin' out all those who want in.

Denver

It ain't no surprise that Hellstromme had the same kinda shield in place over his factories in Denver. There mighta been some folks survive there, too, but by now they're all slaves of General Throckmorton and his automatons.

No one gets within a couple hundred miles o' Denver these days.

The Indians

I ain't been able to figure out what happened to the Coyote Confederation yet. The folks I've talked to look at me like I'm crazy when I ask about 'em. Yeah, I may be a little crazy, but 200 years in Hell can do that to a man. Now shut up, and lemme talk.

The Sioux I know about. They split in two a long time ago. Half stuck with that Old Ways business that was goin' around back in our day. They fared pretty well. I guess it wasn't worth droppin' bombs on a bunch of buffalo herds and teepees that move around constantly anyway. They're gettin' by just like they always have and sayin' "we told you so" to the rest of us.

The other half of the Sioux call themselves "Ravenites," and I can't tell you how scary that is. I reckon Raven, the damned shaman that started this whole Reckoning mess, started some kinda movement that got all the young braves to forget the Old Ways. It was good for 'em for a while, 'cause the Ravenites took over Deadwood and controlled the rich ghost-rock mines in the Black Hills.

Deadwood was big, I hear. It had a mess o' saloons, casinos, and arms factories. In the end, the city was valuable enough to get blasted back to the stone age with everyone else. The Ravenites who survived learned a hard lesson, but they still can't stand their southern brothers thumbin' their noses at 'em.

Posse: 12

Stone

We're bein' watched. I can feel somethin's beady eyes borin' into the back o' my neck. We'd best get outta here soon, so I'll stop with the lecture and get to the big story.

This is the strangest part yet.

While I was in the Huntin' Grounds, I ran into the spirit of an old shaman who told me the world was not right. I already knew that, but somethin' about the way he said it made me listen. He took me to a strange path made o' black rocks cut right through the land itself. He said this was the "path of stone," and that it was a bridge to my time and another. I said "whoopee" and hopped on it, but he told me it was not the path of stone, it was the Path of Stone. Confused? So was I. Then he explained it.

The shaman said the whole world had been betrayed by two men. One was Raven. The other was a dead man named Stone. Right, he's Harrowed like you. Only, according to the shaman, this one's so mean his manitou gets nightmares. Stone was from our time, and he survived all those years into the future, but here's the real shocker.

We won. Me and my stiffs never returned, but enough heroes on Earth fought back against the Reckoners that they'd all but dried up 'n died! Then those sons o' bitches cheated. They sent Stone into the Hunting Grounds and gave him the power to rip through time itself. They can't do it again, I'm told, but once was enough.

Stone went back to our time and started huntin' down heroes. Every one he killed meant some horror continued to live. The Reckoners grew more powerful, Hellstromme built his bombs, and the whole thing went boom in 2081.

This time, the Reckoners won. I ain't afraid to admit I bawled like a baby, what with wanderin' and fightin' all that time just to find out we'd lost. When I finally came around, that ol' shaman was gone.

I knew I had to go back and warn someone, so we could stop Stone and change things again, but I didn't know which way to go on that damn path. As you can guess, I chose poorly and ended up here. It's already taken me one Hell of a month to figure out what's happened here, and it'll take me a few more to dig up the rest o' your kind.

Once I do, I'm gonna try to find a way back into the Hunting Grounds. But I ain't doin' it without someone to guide me this time! I ain't wanderin' around in Hell for 200 years again!

Our Job

That's why I'm diggin' you up now, Ranger. I figure someone as mean as Stone and as powerful as the Reckoners won't let just anyone slip back and forth between worlds, so I might not make it back. If'n I don't, you and the others gotta fight the good fight here. I know it seems like a lost cause, but there's a lotta folks still sufferin' here, and you got the power to save a whole mess of 'em. If you can just keep that demon o' yours locked down, you might be able to do enough good to rebuild this blasted place.

How? Look around you. Looks a lot like it did back in our day, don't it? There's more rubble, but the desert's the same, and the folks are the same. Sure they got sykers, Doomsayers, Templars, and junkers where we used to have hucksters, priests, and mad scientists, but they all do pretty much the same thing. The towns also look a lot like they did back in our day. They're days apart and pieced together from whatever folks can get their hands on, though maybe with a little more metal and glass. The only real difference out here is there's a whole lot more bad guys and hordes o' critters. That's okay, though, 'cause the good guys have bigger guns to shoot 'em with.

Most importantly, the Reckoners are the same as well. Sure, they're here instead o' the Huntin' Grounds, but they still live off everyone else's misery just like they used to. Just like 200 years ago, the Reckoners wanna keep things in a constant state of fuss. An' just like then, there ain't much government out here to give people security, there's monsters in the wastes, and gangs o' outlaws rapin' and ravagin' everything in their path. It's Hell on Earth, buster, and that's just the way the Reckoners wanna keep it.

An' that's why we gotta fight 'em the way we did it back in 1876. The hard way. Only this time, there won't be no showdown 'til we've crippled 'em first. That means goin' around and bringin' some hope back to folks. That means fightin' monsters, savin' villages, and rescuin' damsels in distress. Yep, hero stuff. Then we gotta tell everyone we meet about it. Spread every last bit o' hope as far as it'll go. And maybe, just maybe, we got an advantage this time. Maybe now that the Reckoners are stompin' around in the flesh, we can kill 'em.

So crawl on outta that hole 'n' clean off those old six-guns. We got work to do.

Veterans o' the Weird West

Those of you who have been playing *Deadlands: The Weird West* may wonder if *Deadlands: Hell on Earth* means the efforts of your group are in vain. Absolutely not. In fact, the good guys won once, but then the Reckoners cheated and changed the past. *They* can't do it again, but *you* can!

Hell on Earth is currently what history has in store for the *Weird West*, but the Reckoners can still be defeated. The world of 2094 depends on 200 years of mayhem and fear. Your posse can still change that.

Officially, we'll continue to explore both game settings (and even a third which we'll tell you about later on in this book!). You'll see products and major story events such as the end of the Civil War in the *Weird West* and the return of Hellstromme in *Hell on Earth*.

Your group can adventure in *both* settings. You can play one without ever looking at the other, or you can travel back and forth with the goal of eventually preventing the Reckoners' victory and avoiding *Hell on Earth*, though that should take a long time!

For now, those of you who are fans of both settings should know that both stories will keep developing. You can still play *Hell on Earth* as a future your group is trying to change, and the *Weird West* as a battleground where the prize is humanity's future itself! As you can see, those crafty Pinkertons and wily Texas Rangers weren't kidding around about what was at stake.

Of course, you can also play *Hell on Earth* as just a really cool, post-Apocalyptic roleplaying game and use all this Reckoner business as background. Think of it as just a neat way for the Marshal to create whatever kind of monster he wants without worrying about chemistry, biology, and reality in general.

If you're not interested in such a grand storyline, you can still shoot flesh-eating muties, race biker gangs, and skulk through ruined cities to your heart's content without ever worrying about what caused such a dark and deadly place.

The Clues

When we first hinted at *Hell on Earth* in the *Deadlands: The Weird West* rulebook, we told you there would be clues scattered throughout our sourcebooks. There were lots of little hints, but here are some of the big ones.

The Quick & the Dead: We told you the true identity of the Reckoners in our worldbook, but you really had to be looking for it! The Four Horsemen (War, Famine, Death, and Pestilence) of the Apocalypse were used as headers on pages 82, 54, 58, and 64, respectively. (Yeah, Death was listed as Death Valley, but "Death" alone makes a really lousy header.)

Smith & Robards: We told you ghost rock was actually full of "damned souls," just as some superstitious Weird Westerners suspected. Manitous are once-damned humans (those folks who went to Hell) who have now graduated to being full-fledged demons.

The City o' Gloom: Brigham Young's vision about Hellstromme destroying the world was correct. Was he correct about converting him? Not in Brigham's time, and not before he destroyed the world. But Hellstromme's sudden disappearance and his current fate is one of the little secrets we'll reveal as this story continues.

Thanks!

For those of you who stayed with us, kept poking and prodding us for the secret via letters and e-mail or by stopping by to visit with us at conventions, we can't tell you how much we appreciate your enthusiasm. Our fans are some of the brightest, nicest folks in the world. We know, 'cause we talk to them every day.

Thanks for that, and for sticking with us through thick and thin.

For those of you just joining our ride, hang on! We usually know where we're going, but we never follow the map!

Posse Territory

Chapter Two:
Welcome to Hell

Deadlands™: Hell on Earth™ is one possible chapter in a story that begins in the year 1863 with an event called the "Reckoning." That tale was told in our sister game, *Deadlands: The Weird West™*. If you aren't familiar with it, here's a quick summary of the story so far.

The Reckoning began when a vengeful Indian shaman named Raven released long-imprisoned evil spirits back into the world. The Indians call them manitous; Westerners call them demons. Their purpose is to carry fear and other negative energy to the Hunting Grounds, where the forces of destruction, in the form of the Four Horsemen, feed upon it. The Reckoners regularly reinvest some of their precious energy to create new horrors, which in turn create even more fear.

Unfortunately, the return of the Reckoners occurred during one of the most violent times in human history, especially in America, where the Civil War raged. (The Reckoning began July 3, 1863.) That war eventually ended and established the Confederacy as a new nation. The two countries even mended their wounds and fought side-by-side in World War I, World War II, Vietnam, and even a war in space.

During this time, a secret war was taking place between the Reckoners and those who had learned of their existence. Pinkertons, Texas Rangers, other national security forces around the world, and independent heroes battled the horrible creations of the Reckoners until they had nearly been banished from the Earth.

Because of their efforts, the forces of evil were nearly defeated. But the vanishing Reckoners did not give up easily. They broke the cosmic rules and cheated. The Four Horsemen used the last of their power in a one-shot effort to make a rift in the Hunting Grounds. Through this they sent their most deadly agent, Stone, back to the Weird West. The undead gunslinger hunted down heroes and helped create Deadlands until the Reckoners won the next time around through history's timeline.

The combined efforts of Stone and his dark masters culminated in the "Last War" of 2081, a massive, worldwide conflict that ended in an incredible conflagration of irradiated ghost-rock bombs. Billions died. Worse, the bombs created Deadlands, areas where fear was so strong it actually warped the landscape and gave life to obscene horrors drawn from humanity's worst nightmares. With most of the world one vast Deadland, the Reckoners had "terrorformed" the Earth in fear and could walk upon it as physical beings.

The Four Horsemen first appeared in the American West. There they slaughtered thousands, then stalked off across the Mississippi and haven't been heard from in nearly 13 years. Rumors persist they are "touring" the world, reveling in the destruction they've caused. If true, they will inevitably return to the Wasted West. And soon.

Welcome to Hell

A Western in Post-Apocalyptic Clothing

Hell on Earth combines four great genres in one big glowing package: post-apocalyptic, fantasy, horror, and western.

It's a world in ruins, and that means lofty goals are distant dreams. Most folks are concerned with simple survival. There are treasures to find, people to save, and monsters to slay, but by and large, a hero's number-one concern is keeping his skin out of the mouth of some sharp-toothed mutie.

Where's the horror in a world like this? What could be more fearful than the end of the world? Plenty. Your character is still alive (well, maybe not, but we'll get to that later). He might have heard of the walkin' dead before, but that doesn't mean he won't pee green when he gets rushed by a pack of groaning zombies.

What kind of lunatic goes looking for trouble in a world like this? Westerners, that's who! Heroes in *Hell on Earth* are like those of the Wild West. They're bigger, bolder, and badder than life. They wear cowboy hats and dusters not just because they keep off the fallout, but also because they reflect their attitude.

What Kind of Book is This?

Deadlands: Hell on Earth is a roleplaying game. This is the rulebook. The next book you'll want is the worldbook, *The Wasted West™*.

These books describe the rules and setting of the game. In the game, you and a group of your friends take on the roles of characters from a post-apocalyptic future. One player, the Marshal, describes a situation, and the rest of you (the posse) decide how your characters respond.

The rules are used to resolve tests of strength, who acts first in a fight, or how much "fate" is on your side. The worldbook describes the setting these scenes take place in.

We know what you're thinking. This looks cool, but you want more info on the world and you have to buy a second book to get it.

That's absolutely true. The *Wasted West* is chock full of backstory for our creepy new setting, and you need to pick it up to get the most out of *Deadlands: Hell on Earth.*

On the plus side, these are the only two books you really need. We have a lot of other sourcebooks planned, and we hope you'll want them, but all the vital stuff comes in the core two books.

How to Use This Book

The first section of this book, **Posse Territory,** teaches you the basic rules of the game, how to make a character, and how to blow chunks out of creepy crawlers. Every player, including the Marshal, should read through this part.

(Chapter) The **No Man's Land** section features material only certain players need to (or should) know about. If the Marshal says you can read it, usually because you want to play a Doomsayer, Templar or some other weirdo, the warning sign points you to the chapter in question. This keeps your character mysterious to those player characters who shouldn't understand his strange ways.

(Page) **The Marshal's Handbook** is for the Marshal's eyes only. Whenever you see the Marshal's badge like the one here, it means there's some secret tidbit or table hidden away in the "Marshal's Handbook." The number underneath tells you what page to look at. If you're a player-type, stay out, or we'll toss you in the nearest toxic pond.

Using Other Deadlands Books

Many of the special characters particular to our companion game, *Deadlands: The Weird West,* aren't around in any real numbers in the Wasted West, but *your* hero might be. You want to play a huckster or a blessed? Feel free! There aren't many of those types left in this devastated world, but there are some. We won't be putting out *Hell on Earth* books for these types of characters because there aren't that many of them running around, and we don't want to make those of you who already have the *Weird West* character books buy a new one full of mostly the same information.

All that said, here's a list of the *Weird West* character books you can use in *Hell on Earth* if you want.

Hucksters & Hexes: Card-using magicians.
Fire & Brimstone: Priests and the blessed.
Law Dogs: Old fashioned gunslingers.
City o' Gloom: Huckster spells that use metal or machinery—very useful here!
The Great Maze: Early martial arts.
River o' Blood: Voodoo.

Tools o' the Trade

Besides some pencils, paper, and an overactive imagination, there are three things you need to play *Deadlands:* dice, cards, and poker chips.

Dice

Because *Deadlands* is a game, we need some way of randomizing certain actions such as determining whether or not your Law Dog hears the mutie creeping up behind her. We pull off this neat little trick with dice.

Deadlands uses 4-, 6-, 8-, 10-, 12- and sometimes 20-sided dice. These are abbreviated as d4, d6, d8, d10, d12 and d20. If there's a number in front of the type of die, such as 2d6, it means you should roll that many dice. If you see "5d8," for example, you should roll 5 eight-sided dice.

With skill checks, you roll all the dice and take the highest. Damage rolls are added. We'll explain all this later in the book. Sometimes there's a number added to or taken away from the roll, like "2d12+2." That means to add 2 to the total, whether it's the highest number rolled or the sum, depending on the type of roll.

A d10's got a "0" in the 10s place, so if you roll a "0," be sure to read that as a "10."

If you need some dice, you should be able to scavenge them where you got this book or in any good game store.

Cards

Deadlands also uses a standard deck of playing cards with the Jokers left in (54 cards total). If your deck comes with identical Jokers, you need to come up with some way to distinguish between them. Official *Deadlands* card decks are available wherever you purchased this book, and they have distinctively separate Jokers. But if you're using other cards, make sure you designate one Joker red and the other black. The easiest way to do this is to simply mark one of the Jokers with a red marker. That way you can never forget which is which.

In combat, the cards are used as "Action Decks." You need one deck for the posse and one for the Marshal. We'll tell you how these work in Chapter Five.

It's good to have decks with different backings in case they get mixed together. If you don't have different backings, you can color the edges with markers. That way cards from the wrong deck stick out like radiation burns.

Chips

Deadlands uses poker chips to represent how a hero might control fate. We'll get into how this works in Chapter 6. If you can't find poker chips, you can use gaming stones, pennies, nickels, and dimes, or any other tokens you can divide up into at least three types or colors.

Your group needs 50 white chips, 25 red chips, and 10 blue chips to play. Put all of these into a big, opaque cup or "Fate Pot" so you can draw them out without looking at them. A big plastic cup, cowboy hat, or even a spittoon work great as Fate Pots. (Don't throw away the extra chips, by the way! They have other uses for the Marshal, as we'll show her in Chapter 14.)

Once you've set up the Fate Pot, put unused chips away. Whenever you spend a chip (more later), toss it back into pot.

Six

Only at special times do you ever add new chips to the pot. These are called "Legend Chips," and should be a different color from the others if possible. If not, mark the chip with a marker. We'll tell you more about them in Chapter Six.

The Stuff Heroes Are Made Of

Traits

Characters, varmints, and other horrors of the Apocalypse are mostly made up of Traits and Aptitudes. Traits are things like *Strength*, *Quickness* and *Smarts*. These are always written in *Capitalized Italics* and expressed as a type of die. A really strong critter might have a d12 *Strength*, while an elderly schoolmarm probably has a d4. Here's a quick table to give you an idea of the relative differences.

Trait Descriptions

Die Type	Description
d4	Sorry
d6	Average
d8	Good
d10	Amazing
d12	Incredible

Teller, a legendary tale-teller of the Wasted West, has better than average hand-eye coordination. His *Deftness* Trait is a d8.

Aptitudes

Aptitudes are skills, talents, or trades learned during life (or sometimes unlife, but we'll get into that later). These are rated from 1 up and tell you how many Trait dice to roll when using that Aptitude. Their names are always written in *lowercase italics*.

Most characters have Aptitudes of 1-5. Higher Aptitudes are possible, and they mean a character is one of the best at that particular skill. Your character cannot start the game with an Aptitude higher than 5, as we'll tell you about in the next chapter.

Aptitude Level

Level	Description
1	Beginner
2	Amateur
3	Apprentice
4	Professional
5	Expert

Teller's *shootin'* Aptitude is 3. Since his *Deftness* Trait is a d8, he rolls 3d8 when blasting at drooling scavvies.

Coordination

When you are asked to make a test of one of your character's basic Traits, you roll a number of that Trait's dice equal to its "Coordination." Coordinations function just like Aptitudes—they tell you how many of your Trait dice to roll whenever you need to test that Trait.

Trait tests are usually called for when the Marshal wants to test your character's raw abilities, such as his *Strength* or *Smarts*. *Quickness* is another Trait you use often, especially in combat.

Starting characters have Coordinations of 1-4, but they can be raised beyond that later on.

Teller's *Deftness* Trait of d8 has a Coordination of 3, so he rolls 3d8 to make a *Deftness* test. He ignores his Coordination when making a skill test, such as *shootin'*, and uses that Aptitude level instead.

Concentrations

Deadlands uses broad Aptitude descriptions, so you often need to choose a "concentration." If your character has the *fightin'* Aptitude, for example, he also needs to choose a concentration such as *knives* or *swords*. The same is true for an Aptitude like *science*. He needs to specialize in *biology, chemistry, engineering*, or some other field.

Concentrations within most Aptitudes are "related"—such as *shootin': pistols, shotguns*, and *rifles*. Other Aptitudes may be related depending on the situation. The list of Aptitudes later in this chapter tells you if certain concentrations within an Aptitude are not related. *Search* and *trackin'* are good examples of Aptitudes that are usually related, as are *persuasion* and *bluff*.

It's much easier to learn a new concentration of an Aptitude than it is to learn a whole new Aptitude from scratch. For that reason, your character can learn additional concentrations without having to raise each one as a whole new skill. We'll show you how in the next chapter.

Teller used to be an officer in the Southern Alliance. In the military he was taught *shootin': pistol* as well as *shootin': rifle*. Later on, he may want to pick up concentrations in *shootin': MG, SMG,* or *shotgun*.

The Stuff Heroes Are Made Of

Mixing Aptitudes

Aptitudes are normally associated with a particular Trait, but sometimes another Trait might be more appropriate. Say the Marshal asks for a *climbin'/Knowledge* roll. *Climbin'* is normally based on *Nimbleness,* but in this case, she wants to see how much your character knows about *climbin',* not how well he can actually scale a cliff.

When this happens, just substitute your character's *Nimbleness* die with his *Knowledge* die.

Later on, when your character falls through the wall of a ruined building, the Marshal might ask for a *climbin'/Strength* roll to see if your hero is strong enough to hold on, not how "good" a climber she normally is.

Aptitudes are listed under the Trait they're normally associated with on your character sheet (see pages 62 and 63 for this).

Teller is in a firefight when his pistol jams. Normally, *shootin'* is a *Deftness*-based Trait, but the Marshal wants to see if Teller can clear the jam, she asks for a *shootin'/Knowledge* roll instead.

Rollin' the Bones

A character's Trait tells you what kind of dice to roll, and the Aptitude or Coordination tells you how many dice to roll.

A character with a *Deftness* of d8 and a Coordination of 3, for example, would roll 3d8 when asked to make *Deftness* checks. When making skill rolls, substitute the Aptitude level for the Trait's Coordination.

So how do you read the die roll? Easy. Your result is the highest single die result you get when you roll all your dice together. So if you roll 3d6 and get 2, 3, and 5, your total is a 5.

If there are any modifiers, they are applied after the dice are rolled. Negative modifiers are penalties of some sort, and positive modifiers are bonuses.

Tasha, a "savage" who grew up after the bomb, hurls a sharpened hubcap at a sand serpent. The Marshal wants a *throwin'* roll, which is a *Deftness*-based Aptitude. Tasha's *throwin'* is 4, and her *Deftness* is a d10. She rolls and gets a 1, 3, 3, 5. Her highest die is a 5. That's a pretty lousy roll.

Unskilled Checks

Sometimes you have to make an Aptitude check when you discover your hero doesn't have the Aptitude. Are you hosed? A little, but not completely.

In these cases, you can roll your character's Trait dice (using the Coordination as the missing Aptitude level), but you must subtract -8 from the total.

If your character has a different concentration of an Aptitude, it's called a "related skill." You can roll that instead, and you only have to subtract -4 from the total.

Unskilled Attempts

Condition	Modifier
Related skill	-4
Unskilled	-8

Teller drives hummers just fine, but he's never set his kiester on a hovercycle. The Marshal lets him drive around slow without making a skill check, but when a wormling comes bounding out of the ruins and Teller guns the throttle, it's time for a roll.

Teller's *drivin': cars* is 3d6. Since it's a related skill, he has to subtract -4 from his total. If he rolls a 2, 2, and 4, his total is 0. That's bad news for him.

Aces

Trait and Aptitude rolls are open-ended. This means if you roll the maximum number on any of your dice, you can roll that die again and add the next roll to *that* die's current total. The maximum number on a die is called the "Ace." You can keep rolling the die and adding it to the running total as long as you keep getting Aces.

If you get Aces on several of your individual dice, you need to keep track of each die separately. When you're done, the single die that got the highest total is the result.

Teller takes a shot at the wormling bounding at him. His *shootin'* is 3d8, so he rolls and gets 3, 8, and 8. He rolls the two 8s again and gets 3 and 8. These dice are hot! He rolls the 8 again and gets 5 for a grand total of 21. He plugs the wormling smack between the eyes.

The Stuff Heroes Are Made Of

Target Numbers

Okay, you've got your result. How do you know exactly how well you've done? Just look on the standard Difficulty Table below.

The "difficulty" is a rough estimation of how hard a particular task is. The "TN," or Target Number, is the number you need to meet or beat on your dice roll to succeed at that task.

Difficulty

Difficulty	Target Number
Foolproof	3
Fair	5
Onerous	7
Hard	9
Incredible	11

Teller must make a Hard (9) *persuasion* roll to get inside a walled village. He rolls his 5d10 *persuasion* and, after a lucky Ace, gets a 13. The gate swings wide.

Raises

Every time you beat your Target Number by 5 points, you get an extra success. This is called a "raise." Raises are "extra successes" sometimes used to show your character has done exceedingly well at whatever it was she was trying to accomplish.

Every raise over the base Target Number means your character did that much better at a task.

If you're told to draw an extra card for every raise and the TN is Fair (5), you draw one card for every 5 points you roll over the TN of 5. If the text says you get an extra card for every success, you draw a card for getting a 5, and another card for every 5 points over and above that.

Raises are just "extra" successes (and are sometimes called just that). Basically, the better you roll, the better your character does at whatever task she was attempting.

Tasha is trying to hear over the storm that surrounds a blasted city. The Marshal asks her to make a Fair (5) *Cognition* roll. She gets a 10. She not only hears the danger coming at her, but she also realizes the noise is a horde of radrats heading her way.

Opposed Rolls

Occasionally, someone your character is bamboozling, wrestling, or staring down might have the audacity to fight back. If this is the case, both characters roll against a Fair (5) difficulty. The character who beats the TN *and* his opponent is winning, but she needs a raise to decide the struggle (see the table below).

Raises are always used in opposed rolls, though they are counted from the opponent's total, not the base TN of 5.

When a cowpoke is forced to make an opposed mental roll against a group, use the Aptitude or Trait of the group's "leader." The rest usually follow his example. If it's a physical contest, such as a tug-of-war, add +2 to the roll for every assisting friendly character who makes a Fair (5) roll in the Trait or Aptitude in question.

One last time because you'll see this a lot—beating someone by 1-4 points on an opposed roll has no effect. You have to get a raise to make something happen.

Opposed Rolls

Result	Effect
Success	There is no clear victor. Both characters can continue to struggle on later actions.
One Raise	The winner manages to accomplish his goal with room to spare. The opponent loses or surrenders until he can find another way to recover his loss.
Two Raises	You make it look easy. Your opponent surrenders and no longer resists without a major change in the situation.
Three Raises	You get your way, and your opponent suffers some minor disadvantage as well. If wrestling, you reverse the hold. If debating, he puts his foot in his mouth.

Tasha is rummaging through the ruins of Fresno when the hand of a walkin' dead reaches up and grabs her ankle! She and the zombie roll *Strength* totals. The zombie gets a 2; Tasha gets a 17. That's 3 raises over her undead foe! The withered zombie's arm breaks like a brittle twig as she rips free.

The Stuff Heroes Are Made Of

Going Bust

There's a bad side to all this dice-rolling business. If the majority of your dice come up 1s, you've "gone bust." A roll of 1, 1, 3 is a bust, but a roll of 1, 1, 3, and 5 isn't. Get it?

When your character goes bust, it means a setback of some sort has occurred. The Marshal determines how bad the catastrophe is, based on the situation.

Busts are relative. Most of the time, your hero drops his weapon, says something he shouldn't have, or drives his hoverbike into a tree. Busts are usually embarrassing, but not catastrophic.

If your hero goes bust while doing something dangerous, say trying to put the pin back in a grenade or climbing a high cliff, he's got real problems.

Teller must talk a handful of villagers into defending their homes against an attack by General Throckmorton's goons. He makes an opposed *persuasion* roll and uncharacteristically goes bust. The locals decide discretion is the better part of valor and abandon their homes.

Dice-Rolling Summary

The Trait tells you what kind of dice to roll.

The Aptitude or Coordination tells you how many of those dice to roll.

The total is the highest die that you rolled, plus or minus any modifiers.

An Ace lets you roll that die again and add it to the current total.

The final total is compared to the Target Number (TN) to determine if the roll is successful.

Game Terms & Slang

Ace: The maximum number on a die, like the 6 on a d6, or the 0 on a 10. When you get an Ace on a Trait, Aptitude, or damage roll, roll the die again and add it to the previous roll. Aces are good things.

Aptitudes: Skills, talents, and trades a character has learned or developed.

Automaton: A mechanical soldier powered by irradiated ghost rock and controlled by a zombie brain wired into the suit's electronics. Very nasty.

Big Bang: The Apocalypse.

Black Hat: One of Throckmorton's soldiers. They wear scavenged black hats.

Brainer: As in "no brainer." Sarcastic but not insulting enough to get you blasted.

Bust: You go bust when you roll more 1s than anything else. This means something bad happens. How bad depends on what your hero was doing when you screwed him over with such a lousy die roll.

Deader: One of the Harrowed.

The Glows: Radiation sickness.

Marshal: The boss. The Big Cheese. Other games call her the "Game Master." She's the one who sets up the adventures and throws all those bad guys at you!

Milrats: Military rations. There's still some of these left after the Last War.

Mutie: A mutant warped by irradiated ghost rock. Most are deranged, violent, and not much fun at parties.

Posse: The player characters and any extras who happen to be tagging along for the ride.

Raise: Every 5 points over the TN is an extra success, also called a raise.

Savage: A person too young to remember what the world was like before the Apocalypse.

Scavvie: Scavenger.

Target Number: The number you're trying to meet or beat with a Trait or Aptitude roll.

Chapter Three:
The Stuff Heroes
Are Made Of

Now it's time to learn how to make a *Deadlands* character. Don't worry, it's not hard. Just copy the character sheet found on pages 62–63 and follow along as we explain how to fill it in.

If you're in a hurry or want to try the game out before making your own character from scratch, there are several pregenerated "archetypes" at the end of this chapter (check out that pretty color section). If you want to use one of these, you need to give the hero a proper name, but other than that, these survivors are ready to hop off of the pages and into the world of *Hell on Earth*.

Roll Your Own

Archetypes are cool, but when you're ready to make your own hero, just follow these seven easy steps:

1. Concept
2. Traits
3. Aptitudes
4. Hindrances
5. Edges
6. Background
7. Gear

One: Concept

The first step in making your hero is to have some kind of idea who you want your character to be. There are thousands of heroes, and every one of them is different. Let your imagination run wild.

If you don't already have a good idea for the type of hero you'd like to play, we have a few "sketches" here that might spark an idea. These sketches are broad generalizations. You can alter them to fit your own ideas any way you choose. Not all Templars are brave and honorable, and there's no reason why a three-eyed mutant can't be a gifted gunslinger.

Adventurers are folks who have no real profession, at least not anymore. They simply wander the Wasted West looking for something better. Some might have been waitresses; others were lawyers. Whatever their trade, they find little use for it now.

Your character is an "adventurer" if he's a common man or woman who just happens to wind up in incredible adventures. His skills are entirely up to you, but he shouldn't be too good at combat or survival, at least not yet.

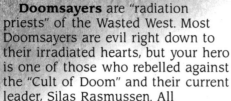

The Stuff Heroes Are Made Of

Doomsayers are "radiation priests" of the Wasted West. Most Doomsayers are evil right down to their irradiated hearts, but your hero is one of those who rebelled against the "Cult of Doom" and their current leader, Silas Rasmussen. All Doomsayers believe norms are "doomed," hence their name, but Silas slaughters them to hurry things along. Your character is far more noble than that. He knows norms are going to be around a good long while, and he wants to ensure they don't rise up and destroy the true watchers of humanity's destiny.

Chapter Seven tells you everything you need to know about these heroic heretics.

Gunslingers sell their guns to the highest bidder or those in need, depending on their personal codes. Duels are still fairly common in the Wasted West, so gunslingers are quick-draws and deadly shots.

Your gunslinger needs a high *Quickness* and several levels in *quick draw* and *shootin'*.

Indian Braves are Native Americans who followed the "Old Ways." They sensed long ago that technology was leading humanity to a bitter fall, and so they use only natural, handmade tools and weapons.

Indian braves should be good with some sort of hand-to-hand weapon, and a bow is handy as well. Most are excellent trackers and can survive in the outdoors with ease, so high *trackin'* and *survival* levels are a must.

Junkers are the Wasted West's version of "mad scientists." They wander the wastelands, collecting junk with which to build incredible machines. The inspiration for their infernal gizmos, some say, comes from the very evil spirits who destroyed the world.

Check out Chapter Eight if you think you want to play one of these strange outsiders.

Law Dogs have taken a solemn oath to bring law and order to the ruined world. They have no real authority, just common sense and their own incredible wills. Their enemies are many, and their rewards are few, but someone must bring justice to the wastes.

Like gunslingers, Law Dogs need a decent *Quickness, quick draw,* and *shootin'*, but they also need a high *Mien* and *overawe* to make foes back down before lead starts flying. It's just too expensive to kill every lawless heathen on the Irradiated Plains, and the best Law Dogs aren't crazy enough to try.

Ravenites are Indians who laughed at the "Old Ways" movement. They embraced technology and became incredibly rich before the Big Bang, selling ghost rock from the once-sacred Black Hills. Now these once-proud tycoons are well-armed wanderers scattered when Deadwood was destroyed by ghost-rock bombs. Some refuse to acknowledge their part in the Apocalypse. Others seek retribution.

Ravenites usually have lots of top-quality equipment, so it's good to take the *dinero* Edge and grab some extra equipment like body armor, a high-quality machine gun, and lots of ammo.

Road Warriors travel the ruined highways of the Wasted West looking for fuel to sustain their wanderlust. They often help towns plagued by other highway marauders in exchange for precious ghost rock or gas. The odds are often overwhelming, so road warriors outfit their rigs with salvaged armor and heavy guns.

Road warriors need several levels in *drivin'*, as well as a good *artillery* skill to fire their heavy weapons. The *belongin's* Edge can set you up with a beat-up rig as well.

Savages are younger survivors who have little or no memory of the world before the bombs. Some have built their own communities where "elders" are reviled for destroying the world. Others are simply idealistic youths looking to become a great hero or heroine.

Savages don't have much experience with technology, so most have the *all thumbs* Hindrance. They're also usually very young, so the *kid* Hindrance is common. Guns are tough for them to repair, so most use hand weapons.

Scavengers are those desperate enough to enter the ruins of the blasted cities. They must brave ghost-rock storms, irradiated battlefields, and the creatures of the outlands in search of treasures left intact after the Last War. Most end their days violently, but a lucky few become wealthy traders.

Search, scroungin', and *survival* are important skills for these wasteland wanderers.

Soldiers are hardy survivors of the Last War. Some lived because they were deserters or cowards, others because fate made them the sole survivors of units annihilated in the final days of blood. Now they wander the wastes, offering their grim services to those who feed them—or pay them just enough bullets to fight the next job.

Soldiers should have reasonable *Strength, Deftness,* and *Quickness* scores. Some might still have their heavy armor and weapons as well, which you can buy with the *belongin's* Edge.

The Stuff Heroes Are Made Of

Nine

Sykers are former soldiers with incredible mental powers. They learned their amazing trade in government academies where they were made into commandos, spies, and assassins. In the years before the Apocalypse, most sykers served on an alien planet named Banshee, though those that did are loathe to talk about the atrocities they were forced to commit there. Now they travel from town to town, drawn to trouble like moths to flames and using their incredible powers to fight the horrors of the Reckoning.

See Chapter Nine if you think you might want to play one of these grim veterans of the psychic wars.

Tale-Tellers know the Reckoners can only be defeated by spreading hope and eroding their precious fear. They join with other heroes in defeating those evils and then make sure the locals hear the story of their victory. Other taletellers may not be so noble, or perhaps they don't know of the Reckoners' weakness. They perform for pay, for food, or simply for a warm bed for the night.

For taletellers, high *Mien* and *tale-tellin'* are a must.

Ten

Templars travel the Wasted West in disguise, looking for those worthy of protecting. Once they discover a worthy cause, they reveal themselves as modern-day knights and pledge themselves to see the trouble through to the end.

Once revealed, Templars are heroic figures with white tabards adorned with a red Maltese Cross, and swords enchanted by their own acts and deeds.

Templars are a stingy lot however. They don't hesitate to desert those who prove immoral.

They are also cautious and, unlike the chivalric knights of old, have no qualms about backstabbing or tricking a foe if it wins the day.

Chapter Ten tells you how to play one of these odd heroes.

Traders are merchants who have discovered, earned, or stolen great treasures to sell and barter with others. They often command squads of loyal bodyguards or war beasts to protect their valuable wares.

High *Mien* and *persuasion* skills are critical to ensuring you get the best deal possible from both buyers and sellers.

The Stuff Heroes Are Made Of

Two: Traits

Now it's time to determine just how strong, smart, or charismatic your hero is. In *Deadlands*, we call your characters' raw physical and mental abilities "Traits."

Look on your character sheet. There you'll see that each character has 10 Traits—five corporeal (physical) and five mental. These are rated on a scale from 4 to 12, with the average being a 6. Average Coordination is 2-3.

Corporeal Traits

Deftness: Hand-eye coordination and manual dexterity.
Nimbleness: Agility and overall physical prowess.
Quickness: Reflexes, speed, and the ability to concentrate during stressful situations.
Strength: Raw muscle, brawn, and how well a character uses it.
Vigor: Endurance and constitution.

Mental Traits

Cognition: Perception and general alertness.
Knowledge: Education from book-learning and experience.
Mien: Presence and influence, as well as charisma and how the character is regarded by others.
Smarts: Wits and deduction. This is the ability to figure things out or piece together clues.
Spirit: Psyche and spiritual presence.

Luck o' the Draw

To generate your character's Traits, you need a standard card deck. Make sure to include the Jokers (all 54 cards). Of course, you'd do better with an official *Deadlands* poker deck, but you can always take chances with "lesser" decks if you don't have ours. (Just kidding!)

Now deal yourself 12 cards and throw away any two except deuces (2s) and Jokers—you're stuck with those.

The 10 cards you have left are then assigned to each of your character's 10 Traits any way you want. The card you assign to each Trait determines the type of die you get to roll when making rolls with that Trait, and the suit determines that Trait's Coordination (remember we told you about all this in Chapter One). See the Traits & Coordinations Table for how this works.

Traits & Coordinations

Card	Trait
2	d4
3-8	d6
9-Jack	d8
Queen-King	d10
Ace-Joker	d12

Suit	Coordination
Clubs	1
Diamonds	2
Hearts	3
Spades	4

Jokers

Jokers are wild cards. If you draw a Joker (which has no suit of its own), draw another card and use its suit to determine the Joker's Coordination. If this one's a Joker too, your Coordination is 5. Congratulations, sparky!

Jokers count as d12s, but they also mean there's something strange about your survivor. A red Joker means your character has a "mysterious past." A black Joker means your character has been mutated by the supernatural *and* radioactive energies of the Apocalypse.

195-201

In either case, we'll tell the Marshal how to resolve your mysterious past or mutation in the Marshal's Handbook.

More than Human

Sometimes you're going to run into people or creatures that are more than human. With a little luck, you might even survive the encounter. And if you're *really* lucky, magic or technology might even give *your* character a supernatural boost.

After reaching a d12 in a Trait, the Trait's value rises in steps of 2. The next highest Trait after d12 is d12+2, then d12+4, and so on. Roll all the dice and then add the bonus to the total.

You can't raise a Trait above a d12 without a supernatural advantage of some kind. You can raise Coordinations to any level.

Tasha loses an arm and somehow gets a cybernetic replacement that raises her *Strength* 2 steps. She already had 3d10, so with this one arm, Tasha's *Strength* is now 3d12+2. The first step raised it to 3d12, and the second to 3d12+2.

The Stuff Heroes Are Made Of

Secondary Traits

Now that you've figured out your hero's Traits, we can derive a few others to give us a little more information. Secondary Traits are Grit, Pace, Size, Strain, and Wind.

Grit

Six

As your hero survives the terrors of the Wasted West, he slowly gains Grit. He doesn't start with any, so put a goose-egg here now. Later on, the Marshal might award you Grit for defeating particularly nasty varmints. Mark it here, and add every point of Grit to your hero's *guts* checks whenever he's forced to make one.

Pace

Your character's Pace is how far he can walk and run in a combat round. We'll tell you all about it in Chapter Five. For now, write down your hero's *Nimbleness* die type. A hero with d8 *Nimbleness* has a Pace of 8. When you get to picking Edges and Hindrances later in this chapter, modify your hero's Pace accordingly and change the number you entered here.

Size

Your survivor's Size is a measure of just how big he is. Unless he has a special Edge or Hindrance that modifies it, his Size is 6.

When the hero takes damage, every increment of his Size causes a wound. (This is another one of those things that makes more sense when you get to Chapter Five.)

Strain

Strain is only used if your hero is a Doomsayer or syker. Ignore it if your survivor isn't one of these.

All supernatural abilities in the world of *Deadlands* are fueled by mystical energy from the Hunting Grounds. When your hero uses his powers, he opens a channel to the Hunting Grounds and draws forth this eldritch energy. This is powerful stuff, and it burns going down.

This causes a certain amount of Strain. When your hero reaches his maximum Strain, he can't handle any more for a while. This is called his "breaking point."

Your hero's Strain is equal to his *Vigor* die type. This is the maximum amount of Strain his poor mind can handle without him taking some time out to recuperate.

Wind

Wind is a special Trait derived from your character's *Vigor* plus *Spirit* die types. This is the amount of shock, fatigue, or trauma your character can take before he keels over. Wind is represented only by a number. It has no die type. If your character has a d8 *Vigor* and a d10 *Spirit*, her Wind is (8+10=) 18.

When his *Wind* is reduced to 0 or less, the character is effectively out of the action. It doesn't necessarily mean your hombre is unconscious. It just means he's out of breath, tending to a really painful wound, or maybe just in shock from the horror that surrounds him.

Characters can't normally take actions when they're Winded, but sometimes the Marshal might cut you some slack. At his discretion, the Marshal might allow a Winded hero to crawl or conduct very simple actions, depending on the circumstances. In general though, Winded heroes are tuckered out, able only to bleed freely and whimper for momma.

We'll explain more in Chapter Five. For now, circle your Wind number on the bottom of your character sheet.

The Stuff Heroes Are Made Of

Three: Aptitudes

Aptitudes are skills, talents, or trades a character has learned during his life. For most people, these skills range from 1 to 5.

Aptitude levels of 6 or more are the mark of a true professional, someone who's not only trained hard at a particular skill, but has a special talent for it as well. You can't buy a skill higher than level 5 when you create your hero, but you can raise it as high as you want later on, as we'll explain to you in Chapter Six.

Aptitude Points

The sum of your character's *Knowledge*, *Smarts*, and *Cognition* die types is the number of points you have for Aptitudes and Edges (see the next step) when you first make your character. If your survivor has a d8 *Knowledge*, d6 *Smarts*, and d12 *Cognition*, you have (8+6+12=) 26 points to spend on Aptitudes.

During character creation, each Aptitude level costs 1 point, so a 1-point skill costs 1 point, and a 4-point skill costs 4 points. Remember, your hero can't start with an Aptitude higher than 5.

The next few pages list the standard Aptitudes available in *Deadlands*, grouped by the Trait they're normally associated with. Feel free to make up new ones as needed.

Concentrations

"Concentrations" are listed in italics below some Aptitudes. These help narrow down just what your character is good at. Just because he knows how to swing an iron pipe (*fightin': brawlin'*) doesn't mean he knows how to properly wield a sword (*fightin': sword*).

If a concentration is listed, one must be chosen. *Shootin'*, for instance, must be followed by *pistol, rifle*, or some other concentration.

You always have the same score in each of your concentrations for a skill. If you want more than one concentration for a skill, extras costs 3 character points each. That might seem expensive if the first concentration is only at level 1 or 2, but in the long run, it's far cheaper than having to buy extra concentrations from the ground up.

Teller buys *shootin': pistol* at level 3 for 3 points. He also needs to know how to fire a rifle, so he buys *shootin': rifle* for an additional 3 points. Now he has both concentrations at level 3.

Basic Skills

Every character starts with a few basic skills. These are free and aren't taken out of your Aptitude points. They're listed below here and in parentheses next to each of these skills on the character sheet.

If you want to increase any of these skills beyond their initial levels, you may add +1 level for +1 point, +2 levels for +2 points, and so on, up to the normal limit of 5.

Basic Skills	Level
Climb	1
Search	1
Sneak	1
Language: native	2
Area knowledge: home county	2

Cognition

Artillery

Missile/Grenade launchers, Rockets, Howitzers

There are a lot of nasty creatures lumbering through the wastelands. Some of them are big as houses. Others eat houses. For either kind of varmint, you're going to need a really big gun.

Artillery is the skill to use when firing them. Heavy machine guns and the like use the *shootin'* Aptitude.

Arts

Painting, Sculpting, Sketching, Others

Artists can be found even in the most desolate wasteland. If they're any good, people love 'em. If not, the locals think they're slackers who should get a real job.

An artist should make an Aptitude check whenever he completes a performance or a work of art. This is the quality of the work, and it doesn't change unless the work is later altered in some way. If it's important, the Marshal can determine the "value" of the piece based on the material it's made of and the artist's skill.

The Stuff Heroes Are Made Of

Scrutinize

Any gambler worth his salt can tell when an opponent is lying through his teeth. *Scrutinizing* someone might not tell you everything, but it could tell you when the buffalo chips are starting to get thick.

Scrutinize is the ability to judge another's character, penetrate disguises, or detect lies. When used "passively," the TN is Fair (5). Each success tells the hero a little more about the target based solely on his appearance. Used against another skill, like *disguise*, *bluff*, or *persuasion*, it's an opposed roll, with each success providing a little more insight.

Search

Any fool can find a crossbow bolt sticking in his backside, but a character with a good eye can find the proverbial needle in a haystack.

Search is used when a hero's looking for items, clues, or evidence. It's also used to detect movement, ambushes, and *sneaking* enemies. The latter is an opposed roll versus the opponent's *sneak* Aptitude. Check the *sneak* Aptitude (under *Nimbleness*) for details.

Search rolls can be used to find obvious footprints, but to actually read and follow anything but an obvious trail requires the *trackin'* Aptitude.

Trackin'

Good trackers usually find whoever or whatever they're looking for. Of course, that's not always a good thing in *Deadlands*. Track a wormling to its lair, and you'll see why—just before you become the next carcass for its squirmy young. (Blech.)

A successful *trackin'* roll helps a character find a trail and stay on it. The difficulty for following tracks is shown on the Trackin' Table.

A character trying to hide his tracks can use this skill too. He simply makes a *trackin'* roll for the number of tracks he's trying to hide (use the same table as for finding tracks.) If he's successful, he's done a moderately good job. Only someone specifically looking for the trail can detect it. When that happens, the tracker and the character who hid the tracks should make an opposed *trackin'* roll. Add any modifiers to the tracker's roll; don't apply them twice. A single success lets the tracker realize a trail has been covered, but a raise is needed to follow it. The two should usually roll once per mile, but the Marshal can change the interval, depending on the terrain.

Trackin'

Number of People Trailed	TN
1–2	11
3–4	9
5–8	7
9–15	5
16+	3

Trackin' Roll Modifiers

Condition	Modifier
Snow	+4
Night	-4
Rain since tracks were made	-4
Rain before tracks were made	+4
High-traffic area	-4

Carlos Whitefeather tracks a band of 10 muties to an old mall. The base TN is Fair (5) for the group's size. It's night (-4) and it's rained too (-4), so Carlos needs 13 or better.

The Stuff Heroes Are Made Of

Deftness

Filchin'

Sometimes it's best to let others scavenge for you, especially if you're unscrupulous and light-fingered enough to take their treasures from them when they're not looking.

Thieves can make an opposed *filchin'* roll versus a target's *Cognition* to lift objects from pockets, purses, holsters, and the like. The Marshal should modify either character's roll based on the size of the object lifted, the situation, and whether or not the thief managed to distract his prey first.

Lockpickin'

A lot of folks locked things up tight before the bombs fell. A good lockpicker can get at treasures beyond imagining: toothpaste, milrats, maybe even a gun or two.

A character with this skill and a set of lockpicks can try to open any mechanical lock. Electronic locks use this skill as well, but a character must have at least one level in *science: electronics* before he can try to pick electronic locks.

A character can attempt a failed *lockpick* roll multiple times, but each try after the first incurs a cumulative -2 penalty, up to -6. After that, she's stumped until she earns another *lockpicking* level.

The difficulty depends on the lock itself. For safes, some sort of listening device, like a stethoscope, is required. A simple glass or even the *big ears* Edge might count as "improvised lockpicks."

For electronic locks, the character must have some sort of electronic lockpicks. He can't simply wedge a penny into the crack of a keypad and expect it to open (unless it's a really old or poor system).

Lock Difficulty

Type of Lock	TN
Interior household door	3
Desk drawer	5
Front household door	7
Padlock	9
Safe	11
Bank vault	13 or higher
Improvised lockpicks	-2
Darkness	-4

Shootin'

Bow, Pistol, MG, Rifle (includes carbines), Shotgun, SMG

There's an old saying about there being only two types of gunslingers: the quick and the dead. In *Deadlands*, some characters are quick *and* dead.

Shootin' is the ability to fire pistols, rifles, shotguns and the like quickly and accurately in stressful situations—such as when some ungrateful mutie's shooting back. We're not talking target practice here. Anyone can hit the side of a barn given all day to aim. (Okay, maybe not everyone, but you get the point.)

Special weapons default to the closest weapon type. A dart-gun, for instance, would likely fall under pistols or rifles, depending on how much it looked and handled like one kind of gun or the other. Truly unusual weapons like junkguns are their own concentration.

For those of you not up on your gun abbreviations, an MG is a machine-gun, and an SMG is a submachine-gun. Automatics, and bullets to run through them are expensive in the Wasted West, but are a whole lot of fun if your brainer has one.

Sleight o' Hand

Cheating at cards can get you plugged—if you're dumb enough to get caught at it. If you're going to take your life into your hands and cheat, you'd better make sure you're good at it—or at least a heap faster on the draw or the hoof than the people you're playing with. No one likes being cheated. Not even other cheats.

Sleight o' hand allows a character to draw small items out of his sleeve or pockets quickly and without notice.

In a pinch, *sleight o' hand* can sometimes (Marshal's call) be used like the *quick draw* Aptitude on derringers (a traditional weapon of a professional gambler), small knives, or any other weapons smaller than a standard pistol. Treat this as a related skill, applying the standard -4 penalty to the attempt.

Speed-Load

Bow, Pistol, MGs, Rifle (includes carbines), Shotgun, SMG

There's nothing worse than the feeling you get in the pit of your stomach when your hammer falls on an empty cylinder and you're left fumbling for bullets. Regular reloading is for brainers looking to become meat. *Speed-loading* is the mark of a true gunslinger.

The Stuff Heroes Are Made Of

In weapons in which each bullet is placed in the magazine separately (like many rifles and most shotguns), reloading a single bullet is a short task and takes an entire action. A successful *speed-load* check allows a character to slam up to three rounds into such a weapon as a short action (just look up the difficulty on that nifty Speed-Load Table below). Do yourself a favor, and check the weapon's maximum shots before you start shoving those bullets home. Your hero would look pretty darn silly trying to load more rounds into a gun than it's able to hold.

Revolvers with speed-loading cylinders (a spare cylinder already loaded with bullets) are much easier to handle. A Fair (5) *speed-load* roll pops out the empty cylinder and slaps the full one into place in a single action. Otherwise, it takes two actions: one to unload the spent cylinder and another to pop the fresh one back in. Anyone carrying a revolver had best scrounge up a few of these babies if she wants to keep her skin.

Clip-fed weapons are even faster and easier to work with. A character can easily change clips in one action normally. On a Fair (5) *speed-load* roll, she can even change clips as a simple task and then still fire in the same action without so much more than a pregnant pause in the gunfire. Greased lightning, baby.

Failing a *speed-loading* roll is embarrassing enough, but it could get your hero planted six feet under as well. If you fail at a *speed-load* roll with a magazine-fed weapon, your character still gets one bullet into the gun, but that's it. If you fail with a speed-load cylinder or clip, he fumbles the thing entirely, although he can try again on his next action.

Should your hombre go bust on a *speed-load* roll, well, you guessed it: It's nothing but bad news. Your embarrassed cowpoke drops the bullets, cylinder, or clip at his feet. Better hope he can talk his way out of the grave, because few badlands banditos are considerate enough to wait politely while he bends over to pick that ammo up.

Speed-Load

Rounds Loaded	TN
2 rounds	9
3 rounds	11
Clip	5
Spare cylinder	5

Throwin'

Balanced, Unbalanced

In a world where bullets are as scarce as good teeth, throwing things is often a cheap way to off your foes. Besides, there are few things more fun than throwing things at people—unless it's throwing *exploding* things at people.

This Aptitude covers everything you can chuck at someone. We'll show you how it works in Chapter Five. For now, you just need to realize that things you can throw are divided into balanced objects (like throwing knives and axes) and unbalanced objects (like grenades, rocks, and skulls—there are lots of those lying about these days). If your survivor can chuck a rock, he can chuck a grenade, and if he can flip a knife point-first into some mutie's glowing third eye, he can do it with a hatchet too.

Again, we'll explain how combat works later on (including where things "deviate" when you miss), but just so you can easily find this information later on, your survivor can throw most weapons up to 5 times his *Strength* in yards. Also, unbalanced weapons like rocks, hand grenades, and other 1 to 2 pound objects have a Range Increment of 5.

Knowledge

Academia

Philosophy, History, Occult, Others

Bookworms are rarely appreciated until the conclusion of some epic adventure. That's when their obscure knowledge about what kills a critter that's already gobbled up half the posse tends to come in handy.

The *academia* skill provides a character with information about his chosen subject. The more obscure the question, the harder the roll.

A scholar might also choose a concentration within a more narrow field, such as *military history* instead of just *history*. The Marshal should take this into account when asking for any *academia* Aptitude checks and modify the difficulty level accordingly.

A note about historians: Even the most knowledgeable old coots seem confused about events and dates of the last 200 years. Even some of the books that survived the Apocalypse don't agree on when the American Civil War ended, who won the Great Rail Wars, and a few other key issues. Strange, huh?

Academia: Occult

Academia: occult tells how much your hero knows about legendary creatures and (as this table shows) the Reckoning.

Level	Knowledge
1	After the bombs fell, it triggered the Reckoning. The Reckoners are the Four Horsemen.
2	Evil spirits called manitous carry fear to the Reckoners.
3	The Reckoners feed off fear and would die without it. The hero knows of the Harrowed.
4	A shaman named Raven started the Reckoning, freeing the manitous.
5	The Reckoners lost, but they sent a man named Stone into the past to kill the world's heroes. This time, the Reckoners won.

Area Knowledge

By Region

Area knowledge is a measure of how much a character knows about a place.

A character always knows the basics of an area he's traveled to or through before, but any kind of specific information requires the *area knowledge* skill. Your hero can concentrate in any size region, but the bigger the region, the less specific the information the Marshal gives you when you need it.

Demolition

Sometimes you just have to blow the snot out of some giant creepy crawler. It's usually best if you don't catch your posse in the blast.

A character with this skill knows how much explosive material is needed for the job at hand and how far away to stand. This is the skill used to make and plant charges like Molotov cocktails, pipe bombs, and so forth.

Disguise

Only actors and spies are actually trained in the art of *disguise*. Sometimes an outlaw has to learn on the fly, however, and knowing a fake beard from a hairpiece might save him some embarrassment.

Whenever a disguised character is spotted by someone who might catch on, he makes an opposed *disguise* roll versus the observer's *scrutinize*. One success makes the observer suspicious, but a raise is required to see through the *disguise*.

Language

Any

Knowledge in foreign languages can mean the difference between life and death. If you're in Mexico and a sign reads "peligro biológico," you'd better know it means "biological hazard."

All characters are fluent in their native language and start with a 2 in this Aptitude. That's just how well they can write or speak—they're still fluent. A character with 1 point in another language can communicate common verbs and nouns with little difficulty. At skill level 2 and higher, the character can read and write the language and has a larger vocabulary. Different languages are not related skills.

A character trying to understand a language (other than his native tongue) gets about half the words (usually nouns and verbs) on a Fair (5) *language* roll. Each raise gets him another 25% or so of the message.

The Stuff Heroes Are Made Of

Medicine

General, Surgery, Veterinary

Some folks think of "sawbones" as butchers, but a good one knows when to cut your leg off and when to let it be.

A *general* concentration in *medicine* means the doc can make herbs and poultices, stop bleeding, set broken bones, and perform simple surgery such as lancing boils or digging out a shallow bullet. This concentration lets a character heal up to heavy wounds. He can do nothing for serious and critical wounds and maimed limbs other than stop bleeding.

A surgeon has had formal training in cutting people open. Your character must first have 3 levels of *medicine: general* before you can take the *surgery* concentration.

Surgeons can stop internal bleeding, perform operations, and dig bullets out of the deepest holes, so they can treat any level of wound (though maiming wounds to the head or guts area mean your hombre's past saving and is now an ex-survivor).

Vets take care of animals. If pressed, a vet can treat a human as if he had *medicine: general* as a related skill. Regular doctors can also treat animals, but the wide variety of critters adds an additional –4 penalty to any unskilled attempt.

See Chapter Five to find out how your hero can use these valuable skills to keep his companions from dying on him.

Professional

Accounting, Computer Programming, Journalism, Law, Military, Photography, Politics, Stock Broker, Theology, Others

There's not much call for lawyers or journalists these days, but there is some, and there are lots of folks who had normal jobs before the bombs fell. That mutant warlord you just took down might have been Al the accountant 15 years ago, before his "number" came up.

The *professional* Aptitude is a catchall category for jobs that require formal education or training of some sort, such as law, journalism, or theology.

A character can use this Aptitude whenever he needs to recount a law or battle, write a news story, compose a sermon on the evils of the nuclear age, or do whatever task calls for his particular concentration.

Use *Knowledge* whenever the character is rolling to know something about his craft. When actually applying it, other Traits might be appropriate. A former lawyer trying to talk a Law Dog out of hanging him should make a *professional: law/Mien* roll, for example. (Although since the character was once a low-life lawyer, the Law Dog might just hang him on principal.)

Due to the grab-bag nature of this Aptitude, concentrations in the *professional* Aptitude are *never* considered related unless the Marshal says otherwise.

Science

General, Biology, Chemistry, Electronics, Engineering, Occult Engineering, Physics

The discovery of ghost rock changed the face of the world forever. Scientists used it to better humanity and, in the end, blow it to Hell. Science is a dual-edged sword with rusty, jagged blades, but man, does it cut.

This Aptitude covers book-learning, experience, and skill in all sorts of scientific pursuits. Most scientific concentrations are related to each other to varying degrees. In each case, it's the Marshal's call if a particular concentration is related to another. A *science* concentration is often related to *tinkerin'*, depending on what the hero is trying to repair.

Trade

Blacksmithing, Carpentry, Electrician, Seamanship, Mining, Undertaking, Others

Life as an adventurer can be a real kick in the pants, but somebody's got to actually do all the work. The hard jobs are done by the folks with the practical skills.

Trade is a catchall skill like the *professional* Aptitude. It covers hands-on jobs like blacksmithing and undertaking.

Each *trade* is fairly inclusive. If your survivor knows *trade: mining*, he knows a decent amount about geography, the history of the big strikes, how to swing a pick, and just how nasty ghost rock can be.

Use *Knowledge* when the character needs to know something about his trade. *Deftness* or *Nimbleness* might be more appropriate when actually applying it.

Trade: weaponsmithing is a very important skill. A character can make some of the items listed on the Gear Table (see Chapter Four), and bullets can be reloaded (given the right materials, see *scroungin'*) on a Foolproof (3) roll.

Like its counterpart the *professional* Aptitude, *trade* concentrations are never related unless the Marshal thinks otherwise.

The Stuff Heroes Are Made Of

Mien

Animal Wranglin'

Life in the Wasted West sometimes depends on the obedience of a good mount. This is the skill a character needs to handle wild beasts or teach an animal who's boss.

Animal wranglin' skill checks are opposed rolls versus the animal's *Mien*. Teaching most animals a simple command takes four or five days, with each raise reducing the time by a day or so. The wrangler shouldn't roll more than once per day, and he can only teach his critter one trick at a time.

Leadership

There are lots of folks barking orders in the Wasted West. Bark them loudly enough, and someone might even listen.

In a combat situation, a *leadership* roll can keep people from being surprised. Whenever an ally fails a surprise roll (explained more in Chapter Five), your hero can attempt to make the roll for her instead, as long as he is not surprised as well. This counts as an action for your character. Every raise you get on your *leadership* check allows the leader to affect one other individual.

You can also use your *leadership* Aptitude to switch Action Cards between friendly characters during combat. When it's your survivor's turn to take an action, make a Fair (5) *leadership* roll. For every success you get, you can let any two players (including yourself) trade one Action Card in each of their hands (though the one used to make the *leadership* roll is spent first). The only catch is that in each trade, both players must first agree to make the trade.

That last bit can be a little confusing, so here's an example. (Oh, and if you haven't read Chapter Five yet, skip this and come back later.)

Teller is dealt a King and Queen of spades in combat—great cards! Tasha gets a Ten and a Deuce. Teller wants Tasha to hurl her killer hubcaps before he wastes his ammo, so he points to a mutie, quietly directing the young savage to attack. She agrees, and Teller makes his *leadership* roll. He trades her his Queen (his King was discarded) for her Deuce. Tasha goes first and makes mutie pâté.

Overawe

The most successful gunslingers can back down their opponents before anyone slaps leather. An *overawe* attack might come in the form of a surly stare, a deadly threat, or the feel of cold iron in someone's back.

An *overawe* attack is an opposed roll versus a character's *guts*. The Marshal should modify your roll based on the circumstances. If your survivor has a minigun and he's trying to *overawe* a savage with a knife, he's very likely got an edge. The exact modifier is up to the Marshal, but the maximum penalty or bonus is ±6.

See Chapter Five for information on tests of will.

Performin'
Acting, Singing

There isn't a lot of entertainment in the outlands, so most people appreciate a good actor or a sexy singer. Crowds are rough on the acts they don't like, but they treat a good performer like gold.

A good performance against a Fair (5) TN can net the character the cost of a good meal per success. Better wages can be earned, of course, but this rate works for impromptu performances and average-sized crowds.

Persuasion

Scavengers had best be able to fast-talk the local warlord when they get caught trespassing. And heroes looking to lead had best be able to talk some of the locals into backing them up.

Persuasion attempts are opposed rolls versus the target's *scrutinize* Aptitude. The more raises achieved, the more the other character is likely to do for you. See the **Opposed Rolls** section in Chapter One for some examples.

Tale-Tellin'

Besides letting your hero earn a meal or a drink by spinning a good yarn, this skill has another use. Spreading the word of your posse's deeds is vital to defeating the Reckoners.

Twelve

Your character may have some idea that spreading hope is the best way to defeat the Reckoners, but that doesn't mean she knows how. If your character has *academia: occult* 3 or better, the Marshal should let you read Chapter Twelve. Otherwise, she should just tell your hero how to better use his *tale-tellin'* as the game goes on.

Nimbleness

Climbin'

Most times when a hero has to climb something, he's trying to get away from some angry varmint on the ground. That works fine unless the varmint's a better climber than he is.

Climbin' is especially useful when exploring ruined cities. Find your hero crossing twisted beams several stories up, and you may regret not having a few levels in it.

See the Gitalong Table on page 84 for movement rates for *climbin'*.

Dodge

No, we aren't talking about the ruins in Kansas (as in "get the Hell out of"). We're talking about the ability to use cover and be where the bullets aren't.

The *dodge* skill is used as an "active" defense when your character is about to get drilled by any type of ranged attack. It doesn't mean your hero's actually dodging bullets—it means he's alert enough to jump for cover a split second before some loser takes a shot at him. We'll tell you exactly how to use this skill in Chapter Five.

Don't use *dodge* in hand-to-hand. Use the character's *fightin'* instead.

Drivin'

By Specific Type

There are lots of vehicles out there, from hover bikes to jet packs. This is the skill a character needs to drive them. (Driving a rig pulled by animals uses the *teamster* Aptitude, and riding an animal is covered under *ridin'*.)

The Marshal must decide which concentrations of this skill are related. A hover bike is about the same as a hover car, but neither one is anything like a fighter jet.

The Marshal should make exceptions when it makes sense. Someone who knows how to fly an F-18 Hornet could fly a Cessna, but the Cessna pilot would be lucky to get the Hornet started! Once he did, of course, he could maneuver fairly well (as a related Aptitude), but he probably wouldn't know how to use the weapon systems or automatic landing system. You'll have to "wing" this one.

The Stuff Heroes Are Made Of

When your character wants to sneak past someone, make an opposed *sneak* roll against the best *search* Aptitude of those who might detect her. A single success on the spotter's part means he's suspicious but not alarmed. One raise means he hears the sneaker, but doesn't know *exactly* where he is. Two raises means the creeper is spotted dead-to-rights.

Here are some common modifiers to the character's *sneak* roll.

Sneakin'

Modifier	Condition
+4	Lots of cover
+4	Pitch Dark
+2	Wearing dark or camouflaged clothing
+2	Rain
+2	Twilight
–4	No cover
–4	Moving over gravel, dry leaves, etc.

Swimmin'

Heroes who can't swim sink like stones, even when they're just taking their annual baths.

See your local toxic pond or Chapter Five to find out about drowning (not swimming).

Teamster

This skill lets your character drive wagons, stagecoaches, buggies, and carts and control the ornery animals that pull them.

Quickness

Quick Draw

Drawing a weapon takes an action, as does cocking and firing. What if you don't have that kind of time?

Easy. The *quick draw* skill not only lets you draw a weapon as a simple task, it also lets you cock it if needed as well. The TN to draw or draw and/or cock a weapon as a simple task is shown on the table below.

Quick Draw

Task	TN
Draw	5
Cock	5
Draw & cock	7

Fightin'

Ax, Brawlin', Club, Knife, Sword, Others

Bullets are scarce in the Wasted West. When you run out of ammo, it's time to whip out the old Bowie knife and start slicing.

A character uses this Aptitude to make hand-to-hand attacks. All *fightin'* Aptitudes are related.

Ridin'

There are lots of critters a hero might ride through the Wasted West. He'd best know how to handle these ornery beasts before he crawls on one's backside.

The Marshal shouldn't call for *ridin'* rolls to ride in a slow, flat line across the High Plains. If your hero tries to ride fast, avoid rocks, or anything dramatic, however, he'd best have a few levels in *ridin'* or expect to take a spill.

Falling off a mount usually causes from 1–3d6 damage, depending on the speed (Marshal's call).

Sneak

Sometimes charging into the face of death doesn't make a lot of sense. Subtler tactics are occasionally called for.

The Stuff Heroes Are Made Of

Smarts

Bluff

Poker is still a common game in the Wasted West, and a good *bluff* can win a pot full of bullets on a pair of Deuces. Telling lies, spinning tall tales, or making someone look behind them so you can get in a cheap shot is all part of the game.

Bluff is a test of wills versus an opponent's *scrutinize*. The more raises you get, the more the opponent falls for your crafty lies.

Gamblin'

Most folks can hold their own in poker and other games of chance. Professional gamblers roam the surviving towns and can turn a few bullets into an armory.

Here's a quick way to handle things when the posse wants to gamble for a bit.

First, the gamblers decide on the average pot per hand. One to six bucks worth of goods is common.

Next each character involved makes a Fair (5) *gamblin'* roll. Every success lets a gambler draw a card from a standard card deck.

Now each player flips over her highest card. The player with the lowest card pays the difference between her card and the highest, times the stake. The next lowest player pays the second highest player the difference times the stake, and so forth. An odd "middle" man breaks even.

Count red Jokers as 15, Aces as 14, Kings as 13, Queens as 12, Jacks as 11, and all other cards as their number value. Black Jokers count as 1.

This accounts for about 1 hour of gambling.

A character who loses more than he has pays as much as he can.

Most gamblers in the Wasted West play for bullets, whiskey, or other items they're sure to need someday.

Ridicule

There's a fine art to making fun of someone in a world where trigger fingers are itchier than radiation sores. Knowing when and just how far to push your opponent is the real skill.

Using the *ridicule* Aptitude is an opposed roll versus an opponent's *ridicule*. Someone with a good sense of humor can take a joke better. (Other types usually just grimace and switch to full-auto.) Tests of wills are covered in Chapter Five.

Scroungin'

Scroungin' is the ability to find life's little necessities in a hurry. In *Hell on Earth*, this skill is second in importance only to breathing.

The TN to find particular items depends on the item and the location (Marshal's call). Finding food works just like the *survival* skill (see below), your scavenger just finds his grub a little differently. The TN is 5 if near cities or towns and 11 out in the wastes.

For bullets, 2 hours and a Hard (9) *scroungin'* roll in a ruined city or town nets 1d6 bullets of assorted types for each success and raise. With 2 hours and a Fair (5) roll, the scavenger can find primers, powder, and lead to make 1d6 bullets for each success and raise. Once found, the bullets have to be loaded in a bullet-press. This requires a *trade: weaponsmithing* roll of Foolproof (3).

The rolls above assume a character is searching for 50¢ bullets. Halve the number of bullets found if searching for $1 bullets, quarter it for $5 bullets, and so on (see Chapter Four for bullet prices).

Streetwise

A *streetwise* character knows how to work the streets and get information from the seedier elements of settlements.

This Aptitude is most often used to get illegal items or restricted information. The difficulty depends on the prize and the steps the character takes to secure it.

Survival

City, Desert, Mountain, Other

A veteran wastelander knows which bugs to eat and which ones to step on.

A successful *survival* roll feeds a person for one day. Each raise provides the bare necessities for one other person. The TN depends on the environment. An area with plentiful game and water has a difficulty of Foolproof (3), while it's an Incredible (11) task to find vittles in a barren desert. You can normally make only one *survival* roll per day.

Tinkerin'

There are lots of artifacts lying about the Wasted West. A fellow good with tools can make a fortune fixing them up.

Tinkerin' is the ability to repair stuff. This Aptitude is a must for junkers who want to make or repair the infernal devices they devise.

Posse: 39

Spirit

Faith

Faith is a rare commodity these days. A lot of folks believe Judgment Day has come and gone, so there's little point in praying anymore. Many others aren't convinced and retain their faith. A few (like the Doomsayers) have placed their faith in strange new gods and truly wild beliefs.

The only thing for sure is that *faith* is strong medicine against certain creatures of the Reckoners. Perhaps it's more a measure of faith in one's own goodness. That would explain why a Christian's *faith* is just as powerful against creatures of darkness as someone else with *faith* in a new religion that just sprang up since the Apocalypse.

In any case, this Aptitude is a must for Doomsayers, and a few levels are handy for most anyone else. It's best to figure out exactly who or what your character has faith in when you choose this ability, but you don't have to. Even an atheist or agnostic could have *faith*. It's just her own morality and deeds she believes to be good and righteous.

Guts

Even a hardened veteran of the wastelands might wet his pants when charged by a slobbering wormling. When your character sees a hideous creature or a gruesome scene, you need to make sure he's got *guts*.

187

When a hero fails a *guts* check, the Marshal rolls on the Scart Table to find out what happens to the poor slob. The more you miss the roll by—and the greater the source of fear—the worse the result is. On the low end, your hero might just hesitate. In the middle, she develops quirks and phobias that may hinder her in the future. At the extreme, she just might suffer a heart attack and keel over dead.

Let's talk about this whole *guts* thing. Even though your hero has certainly seen his share of corpses and probably a few mutated beasties of the wastelands as well, he's still going to be shocked when he sees a friend gutted like a fish or when a walkin' dead bursts up out of the dirt and grabs his ankles.

Eventually, your survivor is going to become more accustomed to such horrors and gain Grit. (We told you about it in Chapter Two, remember?) If your hero has Grit, add it to your *guts* total whenever you're forced to roll.

Strength

Strength is not usually tied to particular Aptitudes. The Marshal might call for certain Aptitudes to use the *Strength* Trait, however. For example, if two characters are wrestling for a gun, the Marshal might ask for *fightin': brawlin'/ Strength* checks.

Strength is also used to determine your damage when your character hits someone in hand-to-hand combat. You'll see how this works in the fabled Chapter Five we keep hinting at.

Vigor

Vigor is another Trait that has no particular Aptitudes associated with it. The Marshal might use *Vigor* whenever your character's endurance could determine the success of a particular Aptitude test, however. For example, a long arduous climb up the twisted scaffold of a ruined building might call for a *climbin'/Vigor* check. Also, a long ride to get help for a wounded comrade might be a *ridin'/Vigor* roll.

Four: Hindrances

Hindrances are physical or mental handicaps. You can take up to 10 points in Hindrances during character creation. These can be used for Edges or more Aptitudes.

The number of points each Hindrance is worth is listed next to its title. Ranges of numbers or numbers with slashes indicate the Hindrance comes in more than one level of severity. The higher the number, the worse the Hindrance affects your survivor.

While you get points for Hindrances now, they're far more important in helping you earn Fate Chips (more on that later). If you choose a Hindrance, you'd best be willing to roleplay it. That's how you earn rewards (Fate Chips) that can be used to save your hombre's skin and improve his abilities.

Ailin' 1/3/5

If your arm sloughs off after your last trip into a blasted city, you can bet you've got radiation poisoning.

Ailin' characters are affected by their ailments, depending on the severity and the symptoms of their affliction.

It's assumed these ailments aren't temporary. Your hero has tried conventional cures, and they just didn't take. Even supernatural cures like those administered by Templars or Doomsayers don't do any good.

Furthermore, if a character contracts an ailment during play and attempts to have it cured by supernatural means, he only gets one chance. Once the cure is attempted and failed, no other supernatural power can heal it, even if it's from a different source. If your character takes this Hindrance, it means he's already attempted to heal the illness by supernatural means and failed. He's stuck with it, buddy.

At the start of each game session, roll *Vigor* against the TN listed with each type of ailment on the Ailin' Table. Add +2 if a sawbones is treating your hero and makes a *medicine* roll against the same TN.

If the roll is failed, your character suffers the associated penalty to all Trait and Aptitude checks for the rest of this game session.

If you go bust on the roll, your character's affliction increases to the next level of severity. Going bust at the *fatal* level means he's dead.

An ailment that's gone above its original level, can be reduced by getting 2 raises on your hero's *Vigor* roll at the start of a session.

Ailin'

Value	TN	Penalty	Ailment
1	5	-1	**Minor:** (Recurrent allergies, asthma, cold, or hives) Your character has a minor but incurable ailment that causes him to cough, get the squirts, etc.
3	7	-3	**Chronic:** (Early stages of fatal diseases, ghost rock fever, or radiation sickness) Your hero has a chronic illness that causes constant agony and may someday kill her.
5	9	-5	**Fatal:** (AIDS, cancer, or tummy twisters) Your hero is in the final stages of a chronic illness that can kill him at any time.

The Stuff Heroes Are Made Of

All Thumbs 2

You don't like machines, and they don't care for you. This is a great Hindrance for "savages," adventurers too young to remember before the bombs, when tech was common.

All rolls made to use complex machinery or repair any mechanical device are made at -4.

Bad Ears 3/5

What? Your hero's lost some hearing. Maybe a gun went off near his ear, maybe a high fever cooked it, or maybe he was just born that way.

Choose how bad it is from the table below.

Bad Ears

Value	Status
3	**Mild:** Subtract -2 from all *Cognition* tests based on hearing.
5	**Stone Deaf:** Your character can't hear at all.

Bad Eyes 3/5

Huh? Who said that?

Choose how bad your eyes are from the table below. The Marshal might allow you to use your *bad eyes* as a bonus to *guts* checks made when viewing gruesome horrors at long range.

Bad Eyes

Value	Status
3	**Myopic:** Subtract -2 from your rolls made to see or affect things at greater than 20 yards. If your character wears glasses, reduce the value of the Hindrance by -1.
5	**Near Blind:** As above, but take -4.

Bad Luck 5

Don't even think about playing with high explosives. If you go bust, whatever your hero is doing has the worst effect possible. The Marshal should be creative and spread the effects of your calamity to your friends too!

Big Britches 3

It's good to be confident, but only a fool charges into a den of mutants armed with only a Swiss army knife.

Your character is severely overconfident. He believes he can do anything and never turns down a challenge.

Big Mouth 3

A little lip-flapping can cause a whole passel of trouble. Loose lips sink more than just ships in the Wasted West.

Your hombre's lips are looser than mutant wrinkles. He always speaks before he thinks. Worse, he's constantly blurting out the posse's plans or telling the bad guys (or one of their informants) what they want to know. The hero also manages to put his boot in his mouth fairly often. No one ever trusts this habitual gossip twice.

Big 'Un 1/2

Your scavvie had best hope he can find the ruins of a "Big and Tall" store. Fortunately, it's pretty hard to bust up someone this big.

The effects of a character's size depend on whether he is merely husky or truly obese. Increasing your character's Size has an effect on the damage he can take. See Chapter Five for details.

A hero can't be a *big 'un* and *brawny* (an Edge), by the way.

Big 'Un

Value	Status
1	**Husky:** Add +1 to your hero's Size and reduce his movement by one step (minimum is 4). His maximum *Nimbleness* is a d10.
2	**Obese:** Add +2 to your hero's Size and reduce her movement by two steps (minimum is 4). Her maximum *Nimbleness* is a d8.

Bloodthirsty 2

Some folks are just plain mean. Others don't believe in leaving their enemies alive to come back and haunt them later.

Your character's a warmonger. Worse, she actually revels in carnage and violence. If she's forced to take prisoners, they don't tend to outlive their usefulness.

Cautious 3

A good plan can turn a posse into an army, but no army won a war sitting on its tuckus.

Your character is a planner. He likes to plot things out long before any action is taken, often to the chagrin of his impulsive, gun-toting companions. Of course, sometimes this can be a lifesaver.

The Stuff Heroes Are Made Of

Clueless   3

If everyone calls you a brainer and laughs at most everything you say—even though you weren't trying to be funny—the odds are you're a clueless wonder.

Your survivor is about as alert as toxic goo (which actually *is* alert sometimes, but you get the idea). Whenever the Marshal asks for *Cognition* checks to notice things, you must subtract -2 from your roll. Yes, this includes surprise checks.

Curious   3

If it killed the cat, think what it can do to you.

Your hero wants to know all he can about just about everything he comes across. Anytime a mystery presents itself, he must do everything in his power to try to solve it, no matter how dangerous the situation might be.

Death Wish   5

Sometimes a fellow just doesn't want to go on. Maybe his family has fallen victim to some heinous creature. Maybe he's got some plague set loose by Pestilence and wants to go out in style instead of wasting away like a feeb. Or maybe he's a young upstart who knows just enough about the Harrowed to be dangerous.

Your character wants to die for some reason (secret or otherwise), but only under certain circumstances. Most want to go out in a blaze of glory, such as saving a town or taking some major villain or critter to Hell with them. Your survivor isn't going to throw his life away for nothing (suicide is easy, after all).

The Marshal should reward your character for taking extreme chances, but only when they help him attain his most important goal.

Doubting Thomas   3

Everyone's heard the old joke about "denial ain't just a river in Egypt." Real *doubting Thomases* probably swam the damn thing and still don't believe it exists.

Doubting Thomases are skeptics. They don't believe in the supernatural and try to rationalize weird events regardless of circumstances.

Some are simply in shock (the end of the world can do that to you). Others just insist all this Reckoning business is some sort of mass hallucination brought on by the nuclear holocaust.

Needless to say, this Hindrance doesn't last long. Be prepared to buy it off after a few adventures (see Chapter Six).

Enemy   1-5

Every foe you put down likely has someone who might come looking for you later.

Your character has an enemy or enemies of some sort. You and the Marshal should determine their value based on their relative power level and frequency of appearance.

Geezer   5

Your teeth may have all fallen out, but your scattergun's got more than enough bite for a passel o' nursing home rejects. You reminisce a lot about how things were "before the war" and how many feet of snow you had to ride your hover bike over to get to the academy.

Your hero's practically a fossil. Most cowpokes call you "old timer."

You can determine his age yourself. Some folks are old at 40, while others are still young at 90. Regardless, he's got one foot in the grave and the other in Hell.

Reduce your hero's *Vigor* (minimum of d4) and Pace (minimum of 2) by a step and act like an old coot. You might also want to take the *bad eyes* and *bad ears* Hindrances.

Greedy   2

It's one of the seven deadly sins. But while your soul might be damned to Hell, you'll sure have a good time here on Earth rolling in loot.

Money and power mean everything to your scoundrel, and she's willing to do most anything to get more of it. Things that belong to other folks are especially valuable!

Grim Servant o' Death   5

"And I looked, and behold a pale horse: and his name that sat on him was Death, and Hell followed with him."

– Revelations 6:8

Well, maybe that's a bit much, but folks do seem to get dead around you—a lot. Maybe you look like a loser, and all the other losers like to pick on you—at least until you pick back.

Whatever the story, your hombre gets picked on a lot, even when he isn't looking for trouble. He might not even be mean-tempered. He's just trouble looking for a place to happen. Most of his troubles end up buried in Boot Hill while he runs from the local Law Dog.

For obvious reasons, once folks start dying, other folks don't like your hero much. Forget about peaceful negotiations. Your hombre's enemies are just dying to put him six feet under.

Habit   1-3

Folks aren't much on cleanliness in the Wasted West, but that doesn't mean they like to watch some mutant picking his scabs.

Your character has a habit others find annoying or revolting. Besides putting off other characters, this Hindrance subtracts a number of points from your character's *persuasion* rolls equal to the value of the Hindrance. The value of the Hindrance depends on the frequency of the habit and just how gross and disgusting it is.

Hankerin'   1/3

If you just can't think without a stogie in your pie-hole, you've got yourself a habit. If it's alcohol or some drug you're craving, welcome to Addiction City, population: you.

For the record, there are no "illegal" drugs in the Wasted West. There just aren't enough left to make it a problem. Still, on those rare occasions when some loser hauls out an old case of something potent, the town militia or the Law Dogs won't hesitate to put down someone acting dangerous.

A mild *hankerin'* means the character is highly addicted to some mildly harmful substance (such as tobacco), or slightly addicted to a more dangerous substance. These days, though, even finding that kind of stuff can be hard.

A severe *hankerin'* means the character is addicted to alcohol, opium, laudanum, peyote, or some other dangerous drug. In those cases, he'd best know how to make the stuff himself because he'll rarely find it in the wastelands.

Hankerin'

Value	Status
1	**Mild:** Subtract -2 from Mental skills if the substance is not available after 24 hours.
3	**Severe:** Your character suffers the same as above and also subtracts -4 (total) from Mental and Corporeal skills if the substance is not available every 48 hours.

Heavy Sleeper   1

Logs wake up faster than you.

You must subtract -2 from your hero's *Cognition* rolls made to wake up in an emergency or when some critter is sneaking up on him. He usually oversleeps.

Heroic   5

You're a sucker for someone in trouble. Ever hear of nice guys finishing last? Heroes who go chasing down wild critters aren't likely to finish at all.

Your character can't turn down a plea for help. She doesn't have to be cheery about it, but she always helps those in need—eventually.

Note that *heroic* is worth a little more in the Wasted West than in the Weird West of 1876. In a world of survivors, heroes are just a little more rare.

High-Falutin'   2

High-falutin' snobs turn their noses so high they usually drown when it rains. And the rain these days burns, friend.

Your character has no tolerance for those of a lesser class, or who seem less "worthy" than him. Those who notice your hero's upturned nose don't like him. Subtract -2 from any *persuasion* rolls you make toward those your hombre thinks are beneath him in social stature.

Illiterate 3

It's a terrible thing to come back from the dead and not be able to read the words on your own tombstone.

Illiterates cannot read even the most basic words of their own language or any other language they happen to speak. This Hindrance is pretty rare in folks over age 20. They grew up in public schools where some busty schoolmarm made them learn. *Illiteracy* is rampant among "savages" and children under 20. Reading isn't fundamental anymore, but learning how to fight sure is.

Intolerance 1-3

There are some folks you just can't stand. They don't cotton to you, either, and given a chance, you'd like to push them off a tall cliff.

Your character does not get along with certain kinds of people (mutants, Doomsayers, Law Dogs, savages, and so on) and has nothing to do with them if possible. If forced to work with them, he insults and provokes them whenever he gets the chance. The value of the Hindrance depends on the frequency of encounters your character has with those he is intolerant of and just how violent he gets.

Kid 2

Don't let that face fool you. A kid with a gun can still blow your guts out. And kids in the wastelands grow up a little faster than they used to.

Your character is a kid 8-14 years of age. Most people don't take him seriously, his maximum *Strength* is a d10, and his maximum *Knowledge* is a d8. You must buy off this Hindrance with Bounty Points (see Chapter Six) by the time the kid hits 16. Oh, and if your *kid* lives that long, congratulations. He's either one tough son-of-a-gun, or he hides really well.

Lame 3/5

There's an old chestnut that says when something's chasing you and your friends, you've only got to outrun one person. Unfortunately, you're usually the big loser in any kind of footrace.

There are a lot of *lame* folks in the Wasted West. Some lost their legs in the war, others to disease, and some to simple infections. If you take this Hindrance, take a moment and figure out just how your hero got his wound or lost his leg. You might find answering this question ties in with some of his other Hindrances as well.

Lame affects a character's Pace and certain other skills as shown on the table below. Whenever you modify Pace, be sure to round down. No matter what kinds of modifiers your hero winds up with, his Pace can never drop below 1.

Lame

Value	Status
3	**Limp:** Your hero's Pace falls by 25%. Subtract -2 from active *dodge* rolls and other tests requiring mobility.
5	**Crippled:** One leg is missing or maimed. Your hero's Pace is reduced to 25%. Subtract -4 from active *dodge* rolls and other tests needing mobility.

Max busted his leg in a high-speed car crash while chasing road warriors. His *Nimbleness* is 8, so his Pace starts at 8, and then is reduced to one quarter by his crippling injury. Max's Pace is now 2.

The Stuff Heroes Are Made Of

suffering from phobias, delusions, depression, or schizophrenia. The illness is always present, and it rules your hero's actions most of the time. The value of the Hindrance depends on the severity of the illness and its effects on your survivor.

Loyal   3

You may not be everyone's hero, but your friends know they can count on you when the chips are down.

The character is extremely loyal to his friends. He's willing to risk his life to defend them. Obligations to nations, villages, or ideals are usually *oaths*, instead.

Lyin' Eyes   3

You can't hide those *lyin' eyes.*

Your character can't tell a lie to save his life. Because of this, he suffers a -4 to his *bluff* rolls whenever he tries to mislead, deceive, or even omit the truth from others. Maybe his eyes twitch or he wrings his hands. Whatever he does, it's a dead giveaway.

Miser   3

A miser knows the price of everything and the value of nothing. Miserly characters must always buy the "cheapest" goods available and haggle incessantly over everything. Because of this, they can only buy cheap gear. See Chapter Four for details.

Mean as a Rattler   2

You were *born* on the wrong side of the bed.

People tend not to like your hero. He's hateful and mean-spirited. Besides making it hard for others to be sociable, subtract -2 from friendly *persuasion* attempts. At the Marshal's discretion, you may occasionally be allowed to add +2 to hostile *persuasion* or *overawe* rolls.

Night Terrors   5

Anyone not having nightmares these days must be a little mad. Those folks who can't get away from their nightmares, however, are likely the victims of *night terrors*.

Your character's nightmares are far worse than most, something that keeps her from sleeping much. Coffee is her best friend, and she usually only gets three or four hours sleep at night.

Some say those who suffer *night terrors* are the playthings of manitous. That may well be true, because there's a chance your hero will lose more than just a few nights' sleep to her horrible predicament.

Law o' the West   3

Even in the Wasted West, there are a few good-hearted fools who don't know when to shoot their enemies in the back.

Your hero lives by a code of honor that hardly anyone else subscribes to. He refuses to kill unless provoked, never draws first in a duel, and refuses to shoot someone at a significant disadvantage (such as in the back).

Even these throwbacks don't apply their strange rules to hordes of walkin' dead, deranged mutants, or others they deem unworthy of the code. Still, your hero is only rewarded by the Marshal when he does obey the *law o' the West*, so it's your call.

On the plus side, you can add +2 to *persuasion* attempts when your character's honorable reputation is known and might make a difference. Folks love do-gooders.

Loco   1-5

You don't have to be crazy to fight some of the critters of the wastes, but it helps.

Your hero has a mental illness of some sort. This can range from being absentminded to being a compulsive liar or

The Stuff Heroes Are Made Of

Make an Onerous (7) *Spirit* check every time your character beds down. If you fail, your hero gets no sleep and must subtract -1 from all her Aptitude and Trait rolls the following day. These effects are cumulative to a maximum of -5, so if your character can't sleep for five nights, she has to subtract -5 from everything she does. After that day, she collapses around sacktime into a deep, dreamless sleep. This fresh start entirely eliminates the penalty on the following day.

Anytime your character can't sleep, you should roleplay her sluggish delirium the next day. The Marshal should reward you with Fate Chips appropriately.

If you ever go bust on the sleep roll, your character's dream self is actually transported into the Hunting Grounds. There she experiences a horrible nightmare scenario that lends insight into her current predicament but risks her mortal soul.

The Marshal should construct this nightmare as a short solo adventure for your character. In it, she is given vague hints about whatever is going on in the current adventure. If she "dies" in the nightmare, her Wind is permanently reduced by -1.

Oath   1-5

A person is only as good as his word. Go back on it, and people aren't ever going to trust you—if you ever come back after they run you out of town on a rail. Once bitten, twice shy, as they say.

Your hero has an oath to perform some important task or defend certain values, people, or ideals. The value of the *oath* depends on how often it might come into play and the risk it involves.

Law Dogs, Templars, and Doomsayers all have different kinds of *oaths*. For Law Dogs, see their Edge later in this chapter. Templar and Doomsayer *oaths* are described in their chapters.

Obligation   1-5

A hero's got to do what a hero's got to do, and so do you.

Your character is obligated to his family, his job, the military, a town, or a duty of some sort. The value of the Hindrance depends on how far and how often your character can leave his area.

A good 1-2 point *obligation* might suit a regional messenger or mail carrier. His job is important, but he can carry it out however he sees fit, so it's only a minor responsibility.

An example of a 3-4 point *obligation* is a hero tasked with finding something of importance for someone, and with only a few weeks or months to do it in. Maybe his village is dying of typhoid and needs medicine, or the water hole has gone bad, and the villagers need a new home.

The sheriff of a small village has a 5-point *obligation*. She can't leave the area to go off on some wild adventure, and she's always "on duty." A character with a child or sickly spouse who can't take care of themselves is another good example of a 5-point *obligation*.

Note that an *obligation* is not the same as an *oath*. The hero doesn't actually have to care about his job, he just has to do it, and he usually can't get away from his home base or some other attachment for long. Law Dogs, Templars, and Doomsayers usually have *oaths* instead of *obligations*.

Outlaw   1-5

Times are hard, so make your own rules. If the Law Dogs get in the way, it's their problem.

Outlaws are lawbreakers by nature. They have little respect for the law and are likely wanted for anything from petty larceny in a single town to being a renowned killer throughout the West.

Of course, some *outlaws* are branded as such for crimes they didn't commit. Or maybe they did commit a crime, but for a good reason. These types don't hate Law Dogs, but they're certainly wary of them.

One-Armed Bandit   3

There's lots of folks who have lost an arm in the Wasted West, but it only takes one finger to yank a trigger.

Your character has only one hand or arm. You must subtract -4 from any skills that require the use of two hands.

Pacifist   3/5

Being a pacifist doesn't mean a survivor is afraid of a fight. It's just that he'd rather find a different way. Or maybe he knows all that violence only feeds the Reckoners.

Pacifists range from those who simply don't like to kill until it's absolutely (in their judgment) unavoidable (3 points) to those who refuse to kill under any circumstances (5 points). Pacifists kill animals for food, but not for sport. Monsters and other strangeness are fair game regardless of how "peaceful" a person is.

Poverty   3

A fool and his money are soon parted, and the bullets you've got in your pocket are burning a hole straight through your jeans.

Your character has a hard time saving, and he spends bullets (the currency of the Wasted West) like water. Anything he buys eventually falls into disuse and is lost or discarded. He also starts with only $50 in starting funds.

Randy   3

If it moves...

Your character wants sex and lots of it. He or she hits on every reasonably good-looking member of the opposite gender in sight, usually more than once. Like it or not, men and women suffer this Hindrance differently.

If your hero is a man, he's well-known in every local bordello. Polite society thinks he's a pig, and "respectable" women avoid him like the plague. The lecherous hero has a -4 to any *persuasion* rolls made to influence these types.

If your character is a woman, all other women, respectable or not, call her all sorts of unpleasant names. She suffers the same modifier as a man around polite society (rare as that may

be), but other men might treat her differently, especially if the two of them are alone. Your heroine may never gain any real respect from "respectable folk" or be able to hold a position of authority if her sordid past becomes known. It may not be fair, but that's just how it is in the Wasted West.

On the plus side, a female with this Hindrance actually gains +4 to any *persuasion* rolls she makes to seduce a fellow. This can have its own consequences, of course, but it can be really handy in distracting guards and the like.

Scrawny   5

"Faminites" are victims of a particular type of plague loosed on the world by Pestilence. They're skinny and rabid, and folks mistake your bag o' bones for them all the time.

Scrawny survivors are slight and weak and must subtract -1 from their Size (see Chapter Five). Their maximum *Strength* is a d10. A character's slight frame might benefit him in certain situations, like crawling through a small cave or window, but usually it just gets him picked on or mistaken for a faminite.

Self-Righteous   3

If you're not always right, then you're at least sure the ignorant masses are always wrong. Given a chance, you're sure you can prove it.

Your character believes everything she does serves some greater cause (such as protecting mutants, upholding the law, etc.). She never backs down from her beliefs.

Slowpoke   2

You'd better learn to fight, 'cause you ain't gonna get away from anything that's chasing you.

Your hombre is faster than a dead turtle—but just barely. His Pace is reduced a step, down to a minimum base Pace of 2.

Don't take this Hindrance if your hero is also *lame: crippled*. You can only get so slow before you're just downright immobile, brainer.

Squeaky   2

Your voice is high-pitched, painful, and annoying as Hell. Needless to say, that's not a good quality in the Wasted West (or anywhere else, really).

Your character suffers -2 to any test of wills rolls he initiates (he can defend normally) that involve his voice. Folks don't tend to take him very seriously.

The Stuff Heroes Are Made Of

Squeamish
3

You can't hold your chow when you see blood and gore. It's a little embarrassing compared to your friends who don't flinch when rifling through corpses for bullets or milrats.

Guts checks caused by blood, gore, or other grotesque spectacles are made at -2. Your hero isn't necessarily more afraid of monsters or even carnage, he just has a weak stomach that wants to get in on the action and spew some food at the scene.

Stubborn
2

It's your way or not at all. If the rest of the world is too stupid to realize you're right, they can go hang themselves with an itchy rope.

Your hero is pigheaded and as *stubborn* as a mule. He always wants to do things his way and holds out until everyone agrees or some major concession to his idea has been made.

Superstitious
2

Owls never hoot "just for the Hell of it," and black cats should be shot before they cross your path. You keep a rabbit's foot in your pocket, and you rarely wonder why it didn't seem to do the rabbit any kind of good.

Your character believes in superstitions and tries to live his life by signs and omens of portent. You should check out a book of superstitions from your local library to help you roleplay this Hindrance.

Tinhorn
2

The hardened veterans who live in the wastes don't think much of overeducated, fancy-talking types. You can spot tinhorns a mile away. They're the ones who use big words and brag a lot about their careers before the war.

Subtract -2 from *persuasion*, *overawe*, and *bluff* rolls.

Thin-Skinned
3

You get splinters from your own pistol grip and don't quit whining about it until you see a sawbones.

Increase your character's wound penalty by 1.

Tuckered
1-5

A strong man can run a mile without getting winded. Others get tuckered out just getting up in the morning.

Reduce your character's Wind by -2 for each point of *tuckered* you take, down to a minimum of 4.

Ugly as Sin
1/3

It's too bad the old saying about "stopping a bullet with your face" isn't true. If it was, you'd sure never have to worry about being shot.

For 1 point, your hero got a serious beating with an ugly stick. Maybe he's always dirty, or he dresses in lime-green leisure suits scavenged from a retro store. Whatever the case, looking at him is as painful as getting the squirts from a bad milrat. Subtract -2 from friendly *persuasion* rolls made whenever your character's looks might intervene. On the plus side, you can add +2 whenever his looks might actually help, such as when making *overawe* or hostile *persuasion* attempts.

For 3 points, your hero is an obvious mutant. He's got pustulant sores, scales for skin, rotting digits, a third eye, or whatever. Most norms don't want his kind in their towns. Double the usual modifiers whenever another character knows or can see your hero is a mutie.

Vengeful
3

The world needs to be taught a lesson, and you're the professor.

Your character must always attempt to right a wrong committed against him. Whether this revenge is violent or not depends on his nature.

Yearnin'
1-5

Be careful what you wish for. You might get it.

Your character has a dream or goal of some sort. Maybe he wants to restore the old United States, become a Law Dog despite his age, or prove himself once and for all the fastest gun in the wastelands. The more difficult and dangerous the yearning, the more points the Hindrance is worth.

If the character ever actually attains his goal, he might have to buy off this Hindrance. The Marshal might forget about making you buy off the *yearnin'* if fulfilling your ambitions come with a whole new set of problems. Most dreams do.

Yeller
3

You usually get shot in the backside, and you've got the stitches to prove it.

Cowards don't have the heart for combat and try to avoid it whenever possible. Survivors don't like scaredy cats. Subtract -2 from *persuasion* rolls made against those with little respect for your character's cowardly ways.

Five: Edges

Edges are physical bonuses or background advantages you can purchase for your hero. Descriptions of each of the Edges and the effects they have on your character follow.

Arcane Background   3

Characters with this Edge have mastered some kind of supernatural power, something well beyond the pale of what most folks would consider standard, scientific knowledge. If your hero has this Edge, she's either a Doomsayer, junker, syker, or Templar. In *Hell on Earth*, no hero can *ever* have more than one *arcane background*. One person can only serve so many masters, so to speak.

Seven

Doomsayers are heretical radiation priests who have rebelled against Silas Mercer's murderous Cult of Doom. They use radiation magic to scour the wastes, protecting the world from their misguided brothers (who want to kill every unmutated human) and searching for a prophesied mutant they call the "Harbinger."

Eight

Junkers are far more than tinkerers and mechanics. They knowingly consort with evil spirits for inspiration and assistance in designing their amazing contraptions. Then they build their infernal devices and power them with the incredible fury of ghost rock and their own mortal souls. Many do not trust them. Most everyone fears them.

Nine

Sykers were trained by the military and spent years in intensive training academies, learning incredible powers of the mind. Most fought in a horrible psychic war on the distant planet of Banshee before returning to a ruined Earth. They don't talk much about the atrocities they were forced to commit there in the names of their governments.

Ten

Templars are the both noble and selfish knights of the Wasted West. They live by their swords, and they pledge them only to those survivors whom they deem worthy of their efforts. Their powers aren't as spectacular as those of the sykers or the Doomsayers, but they're also not nearly as costly. There is a religious fervor about them, but it's tempered with practicality.

The Stuff Heroes Are Made Of

Belongin's
1–5

Some heroes claim they need nothing more than a trusty sidearm to get them through the Wasted West. If an opponent has a bigger sidearm, a wise hero might think differently.

This Edge covers all the unusual equipment you might want for your character. You need to work out the specific point cost of any given item with the Marshal, but the table below should give you a rough guide.

Anything really incredible, such as a fighter jet or a legendary weapon like Excalibur, can't be bought with this Edge. Those are prizes your hero must find during the game. Don't be too disappointed. Part of the fun of a game like *Hell on Earth* is finding these kinds of goodies.

Lesser magical items (relics) can be bought with this Edge, but be reasonable. Relics usually add a +1 per level of *belongin's* bonus to their user's skill roll when used. Weapons add +1 per level to their damage totals as well.

Other magical effects must be approved by the Marshal, though even a level 5 *belongin'* shouldn't be quite as spectacular as a legendary weapon.

Finally, check out the *dinero* Edge if your hero is well-equipped and has a way of getting more bullets and other necessities when he needs to, whether it's through contacts or trading savvy.

Belongin's

Cost	Item
1	Item worth up to $1000
2	Item worth up to $2000
3	Item worth up to $3000
4	Item worth up to $4000
5	Item worth up to $5000

Big Ears
1

Some folks got "head handles" as big as a donkey's. Those that do can usually hear a soft-toed critter creeping over stone at 100 yards.

A character with the *big ears* Edge adds +2 to *Cognition* rolls involving hearing things.

Brave
2

Most folks aren't really brave—they're just too stupid to know better. Either way, they're often the last to run and the first to die.

Characters with this Edge add +2 to their *guts* checks. This is in addition to any bonuses for *Grit*, so brave *and* experienced heroes don't usually run until they want to.

Brawny
3

Some folks think a fellow as big as you is dumb as a post. They sometimes change their minds when your 21-inch biceps let them know what it feels like to *be* a post.

Your character is big—not obese, just big and chock full o' muscles. He must have at least a 2d8 *Strength* to take this Edge. If he does, you can add +1 to your hombre's Size.

Your hero can't be both *brawny* and a *big 'un.*

Dinero
1–5

Old money makes great toilet paper in the Wasted West. Paper money that is. Coins just hurt.

The real currency these days is in salvage (see Chapter Four). Your hero can usually come up with some sort of valuable goods for trade when he needs to.

A wealthy individual starts with additional funds and can come up with more when pressed. To do so, he simply makes a Hard (9) *bluff, persuasion, scroungin',* or *streetwise* roll. How much time this takes and exactly which skill your character uses depends on his background. *Bluff* means he's conned someone. *Persuasion* means he's talked others into giving or loaning him something of value. *Scroungin'* is for those who have a knack for finding something valuable to trade. *Streetwise* characters get goods by arranging deals, usually the shady type.

Certain *trades* or *professions* might also net the hero some found money.

If successful, your savvy hero gets the "found money" shown on the table below. The "money" is usually favors, milrats, a gun, fresh fruit, or maybe even healing by a traveling Doomsayer or Templar. Whatever, your survivor manages to salvage, weasel, con, or even steal it.

In any case, the hero can't "find money" with this Edge more than once a week in the same place. He could use other methods, of course, such as *scroungin'* or actual adventuring.

Dinero

Cost	Starting Funds	Found Money
1	300	25
2	400	50
3	500	100
4	1,000	200
5	2,000	400

The Stuff Heroes Are Made Of

Eagle Eyes
1

Sharp-eyed folks can spot a fly on a raisin cake at 20 paces. Others might just wonder what's so chewy. You may add +2 to any *Cognition* rolls made for your character to spot or notice things at a distance.

Fleet-Footed
2

There often comes a time when a hero needs to hightail it away from some angry varmint. If that's the case, remember the golden rule of skedaddling: You only have to outrun one person. Unless there's a lot of angry varmints, of course. Then you'd better be *fleet-footed* enough to outrun the whole posse!

Your character's base Pace is 2 more than his *Nimbleness*. A character with a *Nimbleness* of 12, for example, would have a base Pace of 14 and could run up to 28 yards in a single round.

Friends in High Places
1-5

It's not who you know—it's who knows you.

Your character has friends who occasionally help him out. The value of the friends depends on how powerful they are and how often they show up. A biker boss who shows up with the cavalry every other game or so is worth 3 points, or 1 if he usually shows up alone. A wealthy trader who buys your character's way out of trouble on occasion might be worth 2. There are many ways to use this Edge, so work out the details with your Marshal before you determine the final point cost.

Gift o' Gab
1

A lot of foreigners fought for the Northern and Southern Alliances. Most of them don't speak a lot of English. Sometimes the only way to talk to one of these grizzled veterans is in their own language.

This Edge allows your character to learn languages at half the normal cost (round down).

Keen
3

Veterans of the wastelands expect the unexpected. Other folks are just jumpy. The only thing they've got in common is that they can both sense a walkin' dead creeping up on them from 50 yards away.

A *keen* hero notices little details, sounds, and movements that others may ignore. She may add +2 to any *Cognition*-based rolls.

Law Dog
1/3

The badge of a lawman carries a lot of weight, mostly in the form of responsibility. The common folk depend on you to fight off marauders, bandits, and stranger things.

While this Edge grants your hero a great amount of authority, it also brings trouble.

For 1 point, your character is a local lawman of some sort. Most towns call them "sheriffs" these days. Folks do what you say in matters of justice and the defense (unless there's some other official with that job).

For 3 points, your hero is one of the Law Dogs. It's his job to travel the wastes and bring justice to the survivors. Remember that these days justice is more important than law. That means he's got a lot of room for personal judgment. Of course, a Law Dog who makes a lot of bad decisions is likely to be hated by even peace-loving folks.

Most villages obey the wishes of the Law Dogs, but are quick to turn on a lawman who doesn't live up to his reputation. How much authority your character can command depends on his deeds, his words, and lastly his gun.

All Law Dogs have a -5 point *oath* to bring justice to the Wasted West.

The Stuff Heroes Are Made Of

Level-Headed   5

Veteran gunmen claim speed and skill are vital, but they're overrated compared to keeping your cool, aiming at your target, and putting it down. A hothead who empties his hogleg too fast soon finds himself taking root in the local bone orchard.

Immediately after drawing Action Cards in combat, a character with this Edge can discard his lowest card and draw another. If the character draws a black Joker on the first draw, he's out of luck and can't draw again.

Light Sleeper   1

Sleep doesn't always come easy in *Deadlands*. While it might make you grouchy before your morning cup of java, being a light sleeper can be fairly handy when some critter tries to slither into bed with you.

A character with this Edge may add +2 to *Cognition* rolls made when he needs to wake up quickly. *Light sleepers* may also add +2 to their night terror *Spirit* rolls if they happen to have that Hindrance as well.

Luck o' the Irish   3

A survivor with luck like this might catch an incoming bullet on the new pistol he salvaged a few hours earlier. That's the way it works for these folks: Some minor bad luck winds up saving their butt in some genuinely freaky but ultimately fortunate way.

Whenever you spend a red or blue Fate Chip on a die roll (more about this in Chapter Six), you may reroll any 1s. Note that you can't spend anything but a Legend Chip if you've already gone bust, however (again, Chapter Six, friend).

Mechanically Inclined   1

Gadgets and gizmos lie strewn about the blasted battlefields and ruined cities. Those who know how to fix them can recover valuable tools.

A character with this Edge adds +2 to rolls involving fixing or understanding machinery. No good junker would be caught dead without this skill. Of course, those without it probably *are* already dead.

Nerves o' Steel   1

Some heroes are too darn stubborn to run, even when their boots are full of "liquid fear." Most of their skeletons lie glowing in the irradiated wastes, but a few are still fighting the horrors of the Reckoners.

When the hero fails a *guts* check and the Scart Table (the Marshal's got this) says he must flee, the character can stand his ground instead. He still suffers any penalties imposed by the Scart Table.

A hero with *nerves o' steel* isn't necessarily brave. Sometimes he's just more afraid of being branded a yellow-bellied coward than he is of death. Some folks are funny that way. Most don't live long.

Purty   1

Maybe he still has teeth. Or maybe he found a comb somewhere. Whatever, your hombre is one good-looking survivor.

A *purty* character may add +2 to most *persuasion* rolls or other situations where his attractiveness might come into play.

Renown   1/3/5

A reputation's a funny thing. The bigger it gets, the more most folks stay out of your way. But the fellows who don't get out of the way are most likely gunning for you.

Recognizing a famous person is a Fair (5) task for most—a Foolproof (3) task for those in the character's field, town, etc. Add +1 per point invested in this Edge to any *persuasion* rolls made on those who know your hero, assuming they actually *like* him that is!

Renown

Cost	Reputation
1	Well-known among a small group (town, junkers, Law Dogs, sykers, Templars, Doomsayers).
3	Well-known among a large group of people (county-sized region).
5	Known everywhere (war hero).

Sand   1-5

Sand, grit. You'd think folks in the Wasted West never take baths. Well, most don't, but that's what we're talking about. We're talking about the kind of hombre who keeps fighting even when his boots are full of his own blood. The kind of hero who can punch the Grim Reaper in the face and then ask him to dance. In short, a hero with fire in his eyes and spit in his belly.

Every level of *sand* allows the hero to add +1 to any stun and recovery checks he must make during combat.

The Stuff Heroes Are Made Of

Sense o' Direction   1

You can usually find north, smart guy. To determine direction, make a Fair (5) *Cognition* roll. With a Hard (9) *Smarts* roll, your hero also knows about what time it is.

Sidekick   5

Some of the greatest heroes have *sidekicks*, whether they're mutated allies, guy or gal pals, or gabby old geezers. If your character gains a sidekick during the course of the campaign, you don't need to use these rules. That's just one of the rewards of roleplaying. If you want to start with such a close companion, however, you need to buy this Edge.

The first thing you should do is write out a brief description of the companion and his relationship with your hero.

The Marshal then generates the character's game statistics based on your description. A *sidekick* should never be more powerful than your character. Otherwise your hombre would be *his* sidekick.

If your survivor's *sidekick* isn't around half the time, drop the cost by 1. If he only comes around when you call for him—and that takes some time—then you have *friends in high places* instead. *Sidekicks* are more or less always in your hair.

Before you imagine you've picked up a living shield, let's get something straight: *sidekicks* are strictly under the control of the Marshal. Neither you nor your character control them. Although they are very loyal, they probably won't throw themselves in front of bullets for you, even if you ask real nice. Got that, brainer?

To reflect the relationship with your ally, your hero automatically has an *obligation* (-2) to safeguard the companion's life. After all, your hero would be pretty broken up if his best friend became mutie kibble. Despite the listed cost, the *obligation* Hindrance is free to your character. It does not confer additional Hindrance points, nor does it bring you over the 10-point limit on Hindrances. No whining: It's the price of having another pair of hands to help out in a pinch.

One last thing. The world of *Deadlands* is a creepy place, and old friends make nasty enemies if left for dead. Imagine having an enemy that knows your every weakness and how to cause you the most grief possible. Now imagine having that enemy come back from the grave as one of the Harrowed. Keep that *sidekick* kicking, friend!

"The Stare"   1

There's something in your stare that makes others nervous. When your eye starts twitching, someone's about to meet his maker.

A character with "*the stare*" may add +2 to his *overawe* attacks, as long as the intended victim is close enough to look into his steely gaze (usually less than 30 feet or so).

Thick-Skinned   3

Whether he's tough-as-nails or just plain dumb, a fellow who can handle a little pain is a hombre that's hard to beat. Tinhorns cry over a splinter. *Thick-skinned* survivors blaze away with both guns even when they taste their own blood.

Thick-skinned characters may ignore 1 level of penalty modifiers per wounded area. Thus a character with light wounds in both arms has no modifiers (see Chapter Five).

Tough as Nails   1-5

Some folks keel over in a stiff wind, but you chew razor blades for breakfast. A real hero's got to persevere no matter how rough things get.

Every level of *tough as nails* adds +2 to your character's Wind. She can tough out losing blood and getting banged around when others are curling up like babies with their thumbs in their mouths.

Two-Fisted   3

A rare few are just as good with their left hand as they are their right. These folks make deadly gunfighters and better cheats.

A *two-fisted* character ignores the -4 penalty for using his off hand. Note that this doesn't negate any penalties for using a second weapon—just the additional -4 penalty for using the wrong paw.

Veteran o' the Wasted West   0

You can tell by the stare. Or the way her hand slowly eases down toward her SMG when there's trouble. Some folks have seen what humanity was not meant to know—in living color—and lived to tell the tale.

Your character has been around a while. She's encountered the denizens of *Deadlands* and said "howdy" to a few of its less-than-friendly types with her machine gun blazing.

Your character has an extra 15 points with which to buy Edges or Aptitudes or even improve her Traits or Coordinations (at the usual cost).

The Stuff Heroes Are Made Of

Sounds great, doesn't it? Don't think your hero's encounters with the occult come without a steep price, brainer.

202

If you decide to make your hero a *veteran o' the Wasted West,* the Marshal figures out what kind of Hell your hero's mind and body have gone through to get there.

Be warned. The cost for playing a *veteran* can be high. You might lose a limb, be stalked by a nefarious creature, or find yourself drawn into a struggle against evil far older than you could ever have imagined.

"The Voice"

When you speak, folks shush up and listen hard, whether you've got something worthwhile to say or not. It's the medium, not the message.

You can choose what kind of *voice* your character has. A *soothing voice* adds +2 to *persuasion* rolls made in calm, seductive, or otherwise peaceful situations. A *threatening voice* adds +2 to *overawe* rolls. A *grating voice* adds +2 to *ridicule* rolls. You can buy multiple *voices* as well.

Six: Background

Now it's time to add the "meat" to your hero's skeleton. You should now have some idea what he's like, so now you have to figure out where he comes from, and what happened to him in the past to give him all those Edges and Hindrances you just took. Write down a bit of your hero's story on the back of your character sheet. Don't forget to fill in your hero's worst nightmare too.

If you can't think of all the answers right away, play a session or two. Once you've gotten a feel for your hero's personality, you can probably figure out where he came from a little easier. Come back and fill in whatever you've left out as it comes to you. No pressure, friend.

Seven: Gear

Heroes in the Wasted West start with nothing but the clothes on their back and $250. The rest of your gear must be purchased. The next chapter tells you what kind of junk is available, and how much it costs.

Chapter Four:

Gear

The problem with a ruined world is that hardly anything works right. You can't just walk into S-Mart and buy a new shotgun. You have to find one, make sure it has all its parts, isn't full of mud, and isn't going to fall apart the first time you bank it off a wormling's slimy skull.

The stuff on the gear list on the next page is considered to be in good condition. Some other bozo has already cleaned it up, taped it together, and used it enough to know it probably isn't going to blow up.

Of course, good equipment is expensive, and the traders of the Wasted West know it, so the goods listed in this chapter are priced at top dollar. During character creation, this is the price you must pay. No haggling. You can buy "cheap gear," however. We'll get to that in a second.

So what's the currency? Well, there isn't any—at least not any standard form, though some communities might have their own currency. The folks in the City of Gloom, for instance, print bills and mint coins, though they're not much good outside the city limits.

Everything else is pure barter. Folks don't trade for things they don't need unless they can turn it around for a quick profit. Some items traded commonly are bullets, milrats, food, toothpaste, ghost rock, and things folks miss a lot—like soda or chocolate. Jewelry and other luxury items are worn, but a diamond ring is far less valuable (to most) than a bushel of corn. Even a computer is useless to most wastelanders, even with a generator. A scientist trying to find a cure for tummy twisters might pay dearly however. Special cases like this usually require a little roleplaying to sell properly.

If your hero carries "cash," it's in small luxury items. There's nothing useful in his "cash," but he can trade it easily for things he needs from most folks.

Cheap Gear

If your hero's on a budget, or he finds stuff lying about the wastelands, his gear may have a few problems. A Fair (5) *tinkerin'* roll tells him if equipment is in good order. If it's not, it doesn't work quite as well as he'd like.

Cheap gear can be bought during character creation or picked up once play begins. It either has a quirk determined by the Marshal (such as a Geiger counter that reads half the normal rads), or it subtracts directly from the skill needed to use it (such as a pistol that subtracts -2 from the firer's *shootin'*).

For quirks, the Marshal must determine the item's "discount." For goods with modifiers, reduce the base price by 10% for every point of penalty, up to -5 and 50% off the basic price.

Some things, like bullets, can't be bought cheap. They work or they don't.

Gear

Shootin' Irons

Weapon Type	Ammo	Shots	Speed	ROF	Range	Damage	Cost
Bows							
Bow	Arrow	1	2	1	10	STR+1d6	25
Compound bow	Arrow	1	2	1	10	STR+1d6+2	50
Crossbow	Bolt	1	2	1	10	2d6+2	50
Thrown Weapons							
Small knife	—	1	1	1	5	STR+1d4	10
Large knife	—	1	1	1	5	STR+1d6	20
Boomerang[1]	—	1	1	1	5	STR+1d4	10
Sharpened hubcap[1]	—	1	1	1	5	STR+1d6	5
Shuriken[1]	—	1	1	1	5	STR+1	10
Pistols							
Police Pistol[2]	10mm	9	1	1	10	3d6	100
NA officer's sidearm[3]	9mm	15	1	1	10	3d6	100
SA officer's sidearm[4]	.50	6	1	1	10	4d6	100
Rifles							
Lever-action	.30	15	2	1	20	4d8	100
Hunting rifle	.30–06	9	1	1	20	4d8	150
NA assault rifle[3]	5.56	30	1	9	10/20	3d8	200
SA assault rifle[4]	7.62	20	1	6	10/20	4d8	200
Shotguns							
Double-barreled scattergun	12 gauge	2	2	2	5	1–6d6	150
Double-barrel	12 gauge	2	2	2	10	1–6d6	150
Pump	12 gauge	8	2	1	10	1–6d6	150
Auto-shotgun	12 gauge	20	1	3	5/10	1–6d6	600
Submachine-Guns							
Police Hellfire[2]	10mm	20	1	6	5/10	3d6	150
NA Commando[3]	5.56	30	1	12	5/10	3d6	150
SA Commando[4]	.50	20	1	6	5/10	4d6	150
Heavy Machine-Guns							
NA SAW[3]	5.56	60	1	12	20	3d8	1000
SA SAW[4]	7.62	30	1	9	20	5d8	1000
Other							
Grenade[4]	—	1	2	1	5	4d12	100
Grenade launcher	40mm	3	1	1	20	By grenade	1500
Rocket launcher[4]	Rockets	1	2	1	20	5d20, AP 3	2000

1: Can be made with an Onerous (7) *trade: weaponsmithing* roll. 2: General police model used before the Last War. 3: General type used by the Northern Alliance. 4: General type used by the Southern Alliance. 5: One use only.

Armor

Type	Value	Cost	Covers	Notes
Thick winter coat	-2	100	Guts, arms	Also adds +4 to *survival* rolls to resist the effects of cold.
Boiled leather shirt	-4	100	Guts, arms	
Boiled leather pants	-4	100	Legs	
Motorcycle helmet	1	250	50% noggin	
Kevlar vest	2	750	Guts	AV 1 versus hand-to-hand attacks.
Armored duster	-4	500	Guts, arms, 50% legs	
Infantry battlesuit	*	1100	Guts, arms, legs	As Kevlar in Guts, -4 arms and legs.
Infantry helmet	2	500	Noggin	

Posse: 58

Gear

Hand Weapons

Weapon	Defensive Bonus	Speed	Damage	Cost
Brass knuckles	–	1	STR+1d4	20
Small club	–	1	STR+1d4	–
Big club	+1	2	STR+1d6	5
Knife	+1	1	STR+1d4	10
Big knife	+1	1	STR+1d6	25
Machete	+1	1	STR+2d6	75
Sword	+2	1	STR+2d8	100
Bayonet	+1	1	STR+2d6	75
Spear	+3	1	STR+2d6	25
Hand ax	+1	1	STR+2d6	75
Battle-ax	+1	2	STR+2d8	100
Great ax	+1	2	STR+2d10	200
Mini-chainsaw	+1	1	STR+2d8	400

Ammo

Per Bullet Cost	Caliber
.50	Arrow, .22, .38
$1	9mm, 10mm, .45, .30, .30–06, 5.56, 7.62
$2	.50 pistol, 12-gauge shotgun shell (can't be AP), other strange sizes
$5	Shotgun slug, .50 machine gun
$10	20mm round, military calibers
$20	Spare magazines for most guns

AP Level	Cost Multiplier
AP 1	x2
AP 2	x3
AP 3	x4
AP 4	x5

Vehicles

Vehicle	Durability	Passengers	Pace	Turn	M.P.G.	Size	Armor	Top Speed	Cost
Pickup truck	40/8	3+8*	216	5	30	+3	2	90 m.p.h.	5,000
Economy car	20/4	4	216	5	40	+2	1	90 m.p.h.	2,000
Sports car	30/6	5	288	5	30	+3	1	120 m.p.h.	3,000
Motorcycle	10/2	2	240	3	100	+1	1	100 m.p.h.	1,000
Hoverbike	10/2	2	336	3	50	+1	1	140 m.p.h.	4,000

* Three in the cab and eight in the bed. *Turn* is the basic TN for any *drivin'* rolls. See Chapter Five for information on Durability, Size, and Armor.

Other Gear

Food

	Cost
Dr. Pepper (removes all Wind lost to radiation exposure)	100
Coffee (pound)	20
Fresh fruit (piece)	5
Jerky (1 meal, 1 oz.)	1
Loaf of bread	10
Milrats (1 day's food)	20
Soda (not DP)	50
Veggies (1 serving, fresh)	55
Whiskey (old)	100+
Whiskey (new)	2

Fuel

Ghost rock (1 ounce)	10
Spook juice (per gallon)	10
Small battery (10)[1]	20
Medium battery (50)[1]	100
Large battery (100)[1]	200

Clothes

Bandolier	10
Boots (AV –2 to feet)	100
Cowboy hat	50
Duster	100
Holster	30
Jacket	50
Jeans	50
Pants (handmade)	10
Running shoes (+1 Pace)	100
Shoes	25
Shirt	25
Shirt (handmade)	10
Sneakers (+1 *sneak*)	100

Survival Gear

Backpack	30
Binoculars	100
Compass	100
Flashlight (1/hour)[2]	50

Geiger Counter (1/hour)[2]	100
Mess kit	15
Night-vision goggles (1/hour)[2]	1000
Rope (50')	25
Scope (for rifle)	200
Tent (sleeps two)	100
Water purification kit[2] (1/quart)	10
Water tester (1)[2]	100

Other

Handcuffs	20
Horse	300
Playing cards	5
Saddle	100
Soap	5
Sunglasses	10
Toothpaste	10
Watch (mechanical)	30

1: Number in parentheses is number of charges. All batteries can be attached to any normal-powered device. Small batteries weigh 1 oz., medium are 8 ounces, and large are 10 pounds. 2: Number of battery charges per use or per hour.

Creating a Hero

The rules for creating a hero are pretty simple, but there's a lot of stuff to remember. For your convenience, we've collected all of the major things you need to know about (Traits, Aptitudes, Edges, and Hindrances) in one easy-to-reference place.

Check out the facing page for an example of how to use the front of a character sheet. Blank sheets (front and back) are on pages 62-63.

Mental Aptitudes

Cognition
Artillery
Arts
Scrutinize
Search
Trackin'

Knowledge
Academia
Area Knowledge
Demolition
Disguise
Language
Medicine
Professional
Science
Trade

Mien
Animal Wranglin'
Leadership
Overawe
Performin'
Persuasion
Tale-Tellin'

Smarts
Bluff
Gamblin'
Ridicule
Scroungin'
Streetwise
Survival
Tinkerin'

Spirit
Faith
Guts

Corporeal Aptitudes

Deftness
Filchin'
Lockpickin'
Shootin'
Sleight o' Hand
Speed-Load
Throwin'

Nimbleness
Climbin'
Dodge
Drivin'
Fightin'
Ridin'
Sneak
Swimmin'
Teamster

Quickness
Quick Draw

Strength

Vigor

Edges

Edge	Cost
Arcane Background	3
Belongin's	1 to 5
Big Ears	1
Brave	2
Brawny	3
Dinero	1 to 5
Eagle Eyes	1
Fleet-Footed	2
Friends in High Places	1 to 5
Gift o' Gab	1
Keen	3
Law Dog	1/3
Level-Headed	5
Light Sleeper	1
Luck o' the Irish	3
Mechanically Inclined	1
Nerves o' Steel	1
Purty	1
Renown	1/3/5
Sand	1 to 5
Sense o' Direction	1
Sidekick	5
"The Stare"	1
Thick-Skinned	3
Tough as Nails	1 to 5
Two-Fisted	3
Veteran o' the Wasted West	0
"The Voice"	1

Hindrances

Edge	Cost
Ailin'	-1/-3/-5
All Thumbs	-2
Bad Ears	-3/-5
Bad Eyes	-3/-5
Bad Luck	-5
Big Britches	-3
Big Mouth	-3
Big 'Un	-1/-2
Bloodthirsty	-2
Cautious	-3
Clueless	-3
Curious	-3
Death Wish	-5
Doubting Thomas	-3
Enemy	-1 to -5
Geezer	-5
Greedy	-2
Grim Servant o' Death	-5
Habit	-1 to -3
Hankerin'	-1/-3
Heavy Sleeper	-1
Heroic	-5
High-Falutin'	-2
Illiterate	-3
Intolerance	-1 to -3
Kid	-2
Lame	-3/-5
Law o' the West	-3
Loco	-1 to -5
Loyal	-3
Lyin' Eyes	-3
Miser	-3
Mean as a Rattler	-2
Night Terrors	-5
Oath	-1 to -5
Obligation	-1 to -5
Outlaw	-1 to -5
One-Armed Bandit	-3
Pacifist	-3/-5
Poverty	-3
Randy	-3
Scrawny	-5
Self-Righteous	-3
Slowpoke	-2
Squeaky	-2
Squeamish	-3
Stubborn	-2
Superstitious	-2
Tinhorn	-2
Thin-Skinned	-3
Tuckered	-1 to -5
Ugly as Sin	-1/-3
Vengeful	-3
Yearnin'	-1 to -5
Yeller	-3

Creating a Hero

Name: Teller

Occupation: Tale-Teller

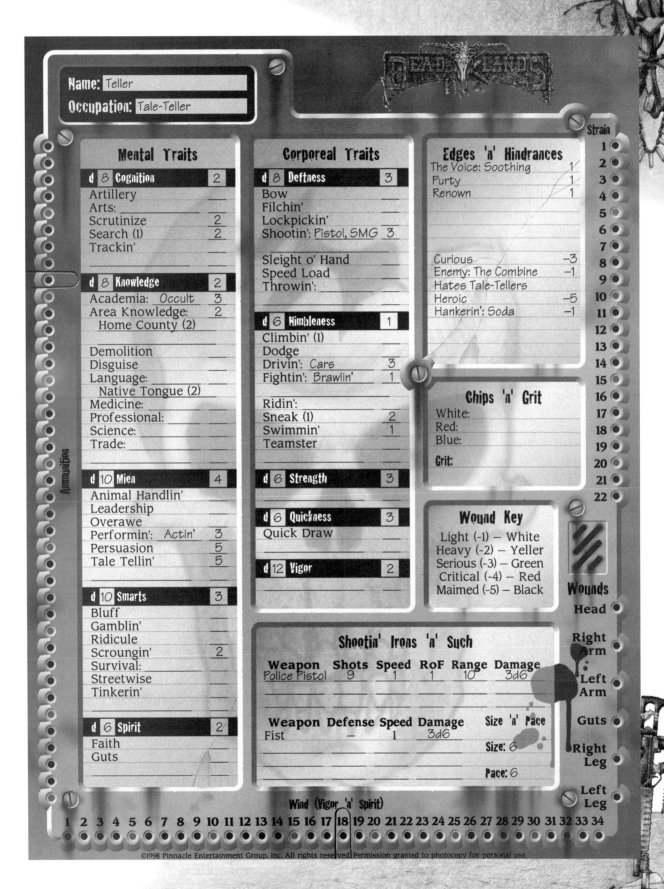

Mental Traits

d 8 Cognition — 2
Artillery ___
Arts: ___
Scrutinize 2
Search (1) 2
Trackin' ___

d 8 Knowledge — 2
Academia: Occult 3
Area Knowledge: 2
   Home County (2)

Demolition ___
Disguise ___
Language: ___
   Native Tongue (2)
Medicine: ___
Professional: ___
Science: ___
Trade: ___

d 10 Mien — 4
Animal Handlin' ___
Leadership ___
Overawe ___
Performin': Actin' 3
Persuasion 5
Tale Tellin' 5

d 10 Smarts — 3
Bluff ___
Gamblin' ___
Ridicule ___
Scroungin' 2
Survival: ___
Streetwise ___
Tinkerin' ___

d 6 Spirit — 2
Faith ___
Guts ___

Corporeal Traits

d 8 Deftness — 3
Bow ___
Filchin' ___
Lockpickin' ___
Shootin': Pistol, SMG 3

Sleight o' Hand ___
Speed Load ___
Throwin': ___

d 6 Nimbleness — 1
Climbin' (1) ___
Dodge ___
Drivin': Cars 3
Fightin': Brawlin' 1

Ridin': ___
Sneak (1) 2
Swimmin' 1
Teamster ___

d 6 Strength — 3

d 6 Quickness — 3
Quick Draw ___

d 12 Vigor — 2

Edges 'n' Hindrances
The Voice: Soothing 1
Purty 1
Renown 1

Curious –3
Enemy: The Combine –1
Hates Tale-Tellers
Heroic –5
Hankerin': Soda –1

Chips 'n' Grit
White: ___
Red: ___
Blue: ___

Grit: ___

Wound Key
Light (-1) — White
Heavy (-2) — Yeller
Serious (-3) — Green
Critical (-4) — Red
Maimed (-5) — Black

Shootin' Irons 'n' Such

Weapon	Shots	Speed	RoF	Range	Damage
Police Pistol	9	1	1	10	3d6

Weapon	Defense	Speed	Damage	Size 'n' Pace
Fist	—	1	3d6	Size: 6
				Pace: 6

Strain
1 2 3 4 5 6 7 8 9 10 11 12 13 14 15 16 17 18 19 20 21 22

Wounds
Head
Right Arm
Left Arm
Guts
Right Leg
Left Leg

Wind (Vigor 'n' Spirit)
1 2 3 4 5 6 7 8 9 10 11 12 13 14 15 16 17 18 19 20 21 22 23 24 25 26 27 28 29 30 31 32 33 34

Ammunition

Posse: 61

DEADLANDS

Name: _____

Occupation: _____

Mental Traits

d ☐ Cognition ▢
Artillery _____
Arts: _____
Scrutinize _____
Search (1) _____
Trackin' _____
_____

d ☐ Knowledge ▢
Academia: _____
Area Knowledge: _____
  Home County (2) _____
_____
Demolition _____
Disguise _____
Language: _____
  Native Tongue (2) _____
Medicine: _____
Professional: _____
Science: _____
Trade: _____

d ☐ Mien ▢
Animal Handlin' _____
Leadership _____
Overawe _____
Performin': _____
Persuasion _____
Tale Tellin' _____

d ☐ Smarts ▢
Bluff _____
Gamblin' _____
Ridicule _____
Scroungin' _____
Survival: _____
Streetwise _____
Tinkerin' _____

d ☐ Spirit ▢
Faith _____
Guts _____
_____

Corporeal Traits

d ☐ Deftness ▢
Bow _____
Filchin' _____
Lockpickin' _____
Shootin': _____
_____
Sleight o' Hand _____
Speed Load _____
Throwin': _____
_____

d ☐ Nimbleness ▢
Climbin' (1) _____
Dodge _____
Drivin': _____
Fightin': _____
_____
Ridin': _____
Sneak (1) _____
Swimmin' _____
Teamster _____

d ☐ Strength ▢

d ☐ Quickness ▢
Quick Draw _____

d ☐ Vigor ▢

Edges 'n' Hindrances

Chips 'n' Grit
White: _____
Red: _____
Blue: _____
Grit: _____

Wound Key
Light (-1) — White
Heavy (-2) — Yeller
Serious (-3) — Green
Critical (-4) — Red
Maimed (-5) — Black

Shootin' Irons 'n' Such

Weapon	Shots	Speed	RoF	Range	Damage

Weapon	Defense	Speed	Damage	Size 'n' Pace
Fist	—	1		

Size: _____

Pace: _____

Wind (Vigor 'n' Spirit)

1 2 3 4 5 6 7 8 9 10 11 12 13 14 15 16 17 18 19 20 21 22 23 24 25 26 27 28 29 30 31 32 33 34

Strain
1 2 3 4 5 6 7 8 9 10 11 12 13 14 15 16 17 18 19 20 21 22

Ammunition

Wounds
Head
Right Arm
Left Arm
Guts
Right Leg
Left Leg

Name:

Occupation:

Strain

1
2
3
4
5
6
7
8
9
10
11
12
13
14
15
16
17
18
19
20
21
22

Arcane Abilities

Ability	TN	Strain	Speed	Duration	Range	Notes

Your Worst Nightmare

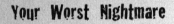

Gear

Ammunition

Wounds

Head

Right Arm

Left Arm

Guts

Right Leg

Left Leg

Wind (Vigor 'n' Spirit)

34 33 32 31 30 29 28 27 26 25 24 23 22 21 20 19 18 17 16 15 14 13 12 11 10 9 8 7 6 5 4 3 2 1

Using the Archetypes

The Archetypes

All of the archetypes on the following pages have been designed for you to photocopy and use right out of this book. (We prefer color photocopies ourselves—they show off all that beautiful artwork—but black-and-white ones work just fine). Each character has his Traits, Aptitudes, gear, leftover cash, Edges, and Hindrances all picked out for you.

The only things you really need to come up with are the character's history and name, which you can write right on the back of your photocopy. Be as creative as you like. Maybe your Templar actually was a Catholic priest at one time. He fell from his faith when the Four Horsemen came stomping through the Wasted West and then left. Now he's picked up a new faith—along with a really sharp sword—and he's ready to make a difference in peoples' lives—one cranium-cracked zombie at a time.

Pick a Name, Any Name

As for a name, go for something colorful. After all, who's going to want to tell your tales if she can't remember your name? Lots of heroes have ditched their old names and now go by something far more threatening. Which is more scary, Joe Marler, or Nemesis?

Just like in the Old West, a lot of folks have picked up nicknames as well. These usually reflect where a person is from, or some event they've become famous for, like the "Boise Kid" or "Black Hat Bill," a hero who fights the soldiers of the Combine.

Using a Character Sheet

You may still want to write your character down on a character sheet, even if you've got his information right there on the page in front of you. All you've got to do is transcribe all the particulars from the archetype page to a photocopy of the character sheet.

When you use a character sheet, you can keep track of wounds, Wind, weapons, and ammunition a little easier, as well as all the other bits of data, like what kinds of things your hero picks up in his adventures in the Wasted West. You can always keep a color photocopy of the original around, though, if for nothing more than the pretty picture.

Modifying the Archetypes

You can swap Traits and Aptitudes around if you want. Just make sure the numbers add up when you're done. This can be tricky if you start messing with your hero's *Cognition, Knowledge,* and *Smarts,* since they tell you how many points worth of Aptitudes your hero starts with. If you're new to the game, try staying away from messing around with these. Once you've got the hang of it though, feel free to switch those numbers around as much as you like.

You can also pick out new Edges and Hindrances that better suit your play style or your character concept. It's really all up to you.

All of the archetypes are balanced with the same numbers and types of dice. You might do a little better if you make your own character from scratch. Use the archetypes for your first foray into the Weird West or if you want to run a quick "pickup" game, or study them as an example of how you might build a *Deadlands* hero of your own.

If you plan on playing a campaign—we call them "sagas"—you're probably going to want to make your own character from scratch.

For the Lawyers

If your local copy center gives you grief over copying out of your book, show them this particular sentence:

We give you permission to photocopy the archetypes and character sheets in this book for your own personal use only.

Enjoy.

Archetypes

Doomsayer

Traits & Aptitudes

Deftness 3d6
  Climbin' 1
  Fightin': brawlin' 2
  Sneak 1
Strength 3d6
Quickness 3d8
Vigor 2d10
Cognition 4d6
  Scrutinize 3
  Search 3
Knowledge 4d10
  Academia: occult 3
  Area knowledge 2
  Language 2
  Medicine 2
  Science: physics 2
Mien 1d8
  Overawe 2
  Tale-tellin' 2
Smarts 1d6
  Scroungin' 2
  Survival 2
Spirit 2d12
  Faith 5
  Guts 2
Wind 20
Pace 6
Strain 10
Edges:
  Arcane background:
    Doomsayer 3
Hindrances:
  Enemy: Cult o' Doom −3
  Intolerance −1: Those
    intolerant of mutants
  Oath −3: The Pact
  Self-righteous −3
Powers: Atomic blast, nuke, powerup, tolerance, touch of the Doomsayers
Gear: Doomsayer robe (purple), knife, Geiger counter, and $140.

Personality

See the glowing rocks ahead, my friend? They mark the way into the future, a future in which altered humans rule the world with wisdom and foresight.

What? No, speak not of Silas and his misguided legions. He was good once, but he wandered too close to the core. Now his heart is twisted by the very energy he sought to control. One must embrace the power of the atom, not seek to control it.

Now trust in me. I will protect you from the mutant hordes. Why? Though I say you are doomed, I mean only that norms everywhere are at their half-life. A new species is being born from the ashes of the old. But do we throw out the eldest son when another is born? Of course not, and we heretics are here to make sure both the doomed norms and the new mutants live in harmony.

Quote: "Nuke 'em 'til they glow!"

Archetypes

Gunslinger

Traits & Aptitudes

Deftness 2d12
  Shootin': pistol, SMG 5
  Speed-load: pistol 3
Nimbleness 4d6
  Climbin' 1
  Dodge 3
  Sneak 1
Strength 3d6
Quickness 4d10
  Quick draw: pistol 3
Vigor 2d10
Cognition 3d8
  Search 1
Knowledge 1d6
  Area knowledge 2
  Language 2
Mien 3d6
  Overawe 3
Smarts 1d8
  Gamblin' 2
Spirit 2d6
  Guts 3
Wind 16
Pace 6
Edges:
  Sand 2 (+2 to recovery rolls)
  Thick-skinned 3
  Two-fisted 3
Hindrances:
  Grim servant o' Death –5
  Stubborn –2
  Vengeful –3
Gear: HI Hellfire, large knife, HI Damnation (cheap, –3 to hit), and 20 10mm bullets.

Personality

I hear this town's in need of some guns and someone to fire 'em. I'm your man. I can shoot all the eyes out of a two-headed rattler faster'n a five-legged hare in a sandstorm.

Pay? Bullets, friend. I'm runnin' low myself. How many? How many muties you want killed? One for each oughta do it. Plus a couple more for the really stubborn ones. 'Course, that's just expenses. I'll need a fistful or so after the job's done. A fellow's gotta have enough ammo left to make it to the next job.

Quote: "One shot, one kill. Anything else is a waste of ammo."

Posse: 66

Archetypes

Indian Brave

Traits & Aptitudes

Deftness 4d6
  Bow 3
Nimbleness 4d10
  Fightin': ax 5
  Ridin' 3
  Sneak 3
Strength 2d12
Quickness 2d10
Vigor 3d8
Cognition 3d6
  Search 1
  Trackin' 3
Knowledge 1d6
  Area knowledge 2
  Language 2 (All
    Indians speak
    English these
    days.)
Mien 1d8
  Overawe 3
Smarts 2d6
  Survival 2
Spirit 2d6
  Faith 2
  Guts 3
Wind 14
Pace 10
Edges:
  Keen 3
Hindrances:
  Big britches -3
  Intolerance -2: Ravenite
    "traitors"
  Oath -5: Old Ways (Refuses
    to use "modern"
    equipment.)
Gear: Battle-ax, bow and 10
  arrows, quiver, large knife,
  boiled leather pants, and $10.

Personality

For a thousand years we followed the Old Ways. That is why so many of my people survived the Apocalypse. No one wants to waste a bomb on a bunch of teepees.

The Ravenites forgot this lesson, and they were destroyed for their pride. Their great cities, casinos, mines, and other possessions did them little good when the Reckoners appeared.

Do you know that my people fought War itself? Yes, the Reckoner walked our lands, and we chased him across the Great River. I know you do not believe it, but I was there. I saw it ride in terror from our arrows. That is why I now roam the wastes. I can defeat the devils of this land with my bare hands. I do not need pay. The thrill of battle and the taste of wicked blood are all the reward I need.

Quote: "Arrows are cheap."

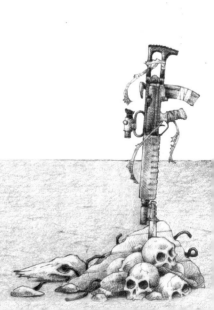

Junker

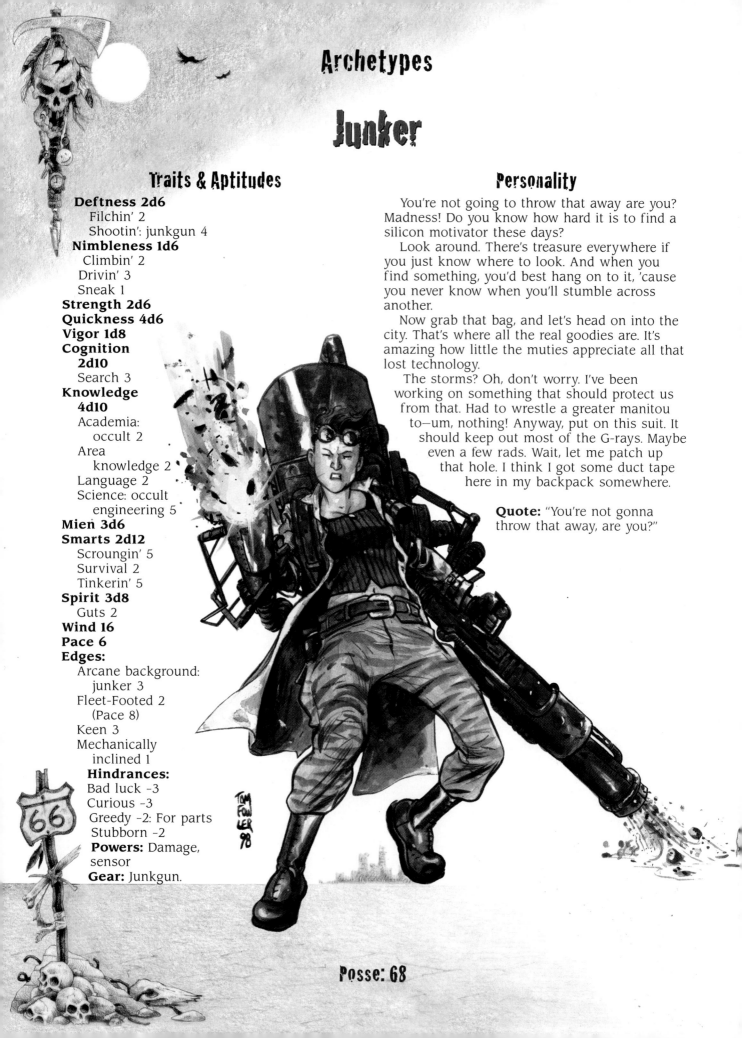

Traits & Aptitudes

Deftness 2d6
   Filchin' 2
   Shootin': junkgun 4
Nimbleness 1d6
   Climbin' 2
   Drivin' 3
   Sneak 1
Strength 2d6
Quickness 4d6
Vigor 1d8
Cognition 2d10
   Search 3
Knowledge 4d10
   Academia:
      occult 2
   Area
      knowledge 2
   Language 2
   Science: occult
      engineering 5
Mien 3d6
Smarts 2d12
   Scroungin' 5
   Survival 2
   Tinkerin' 5
Spirit 3d8
   Guts 2
Wind 16
Pace 6
Edges:
   Arcane background:
      junker 3
   Fleet-Footed 2
      (Pace 8)
   Keen 3
   Mechanically
      inclined 1
   Hindrances:
   Bad luck –3
   Curious –3
   Greedy –2: For parts
   Stubborn –2
   Powers: Damage,
   sensor
   Gear: Junkgun.

Personality

You're not going to throw that away are you? Madness! Do you know how hard it is to find a silicon motivator these days?

Look around. There's treasure everywhere if you just know where to look. And when you find something, you'd best hang on to it, 'cause you never know when you'll stumble across another.

Now grab that bag, and let's head on into the city. That's where all the real goodies are. It's amazing how little the muties appreciate all that lost technology.

The storms? Oh, don't worry. I've been working on something that should protect us from that. Had to wrestle a greater manitou to—um, nothing! Anyway, put on this suit. It should keep out most of the G-rays. Maybe even a few rads. Wait, let me patch up that hole. I think I got some duct tape here in my backpack somewhere.

Quote: "You're not gonna throw that away, are you?"

Archetypes

Law Dog

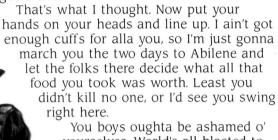

Traits & Aptitudes

Deftness 2d12
  Shootin': pistol, rifle 3
Nimbleness 2d6
  Climbin' 1
  Fightin': brawlin' 3
  Sneak 1
Strength 2d10
Quickness 4d10
  Quick draw 2
Vigor 3d8
Cognition 4d6
  Scrutinize 3
  Search 3
Knowledge 1d6
  Area knowledge 2
  Language 2
  Medicine: general 2
Mien 1d8
  Leadership 3
  Overawe 5
  Persuasion 3
Smarts 2d6
  Survival 2
  Streetwise 2
Spirit 3d6
  Guts 3
Wind 14
Pace 6
Edges:
  Law Dog 3
  Belongin's 1: Father's
    Peacemaker
  Thick-skinned 3
  Veteran o' the Wasted West
    (Tell the Marshal to draw a
    card for this Edge.)
Hindrances:
  Enemy –2: Throckmorton
  Oath –5: Bring law to the West
  Vengeful –3
Gear: Armored duster, Colt
  Peacemaker, 10 gallon hat,
  water-purification kit, 20
  bullets, and $95

Personality

Every last one o' you sons-a-bitches is under arrest. Throw down those rifles afore I give you a third eye.

I don't give a radrat's ass if there's 20 o' you. You try somethin', and I'm gonna put six o' you Black Hats in the ground before I go. Try it if you got the sand!

That's what I thought. Now put your hands on your heads and line up. I ain't got enough cuffs for alla you, so I'm just gonna march you the two days to Abilene and let the folks there decide what all that food you took was worth. Least you didn't kill no one, or I'd see you swing right here.

You boys oughta be ashamed o' yourselves. World's all blasted to Hell, and you're out here like common looters, stealin' folks' taters an' grabbin' at their daughters. Why my pappy used ta say...

Quote: "I am the Law!"

Old Soldier

Traits & Aptitudes

Deftness 2d12
  Shootin': rifle 5
  Throwin': unbalanced 3
Nimbleness 4d6
  Climbin' 1
  Dodge 3
  Fightin': knife 3
  Sneak 3
Strength 3d8
Quickness 2d10
Vigor 4d10
Cognition 1d8
  Artillery 3
  Search 1
Knowledge 1d6
  Area knowledge 2
  Language 2
Mien 2d6
Smarts 1d6
  Scroungin' 2
  Survival 2
Spirit 3d6
  Guts 2
Wind 24 (*tough as nails*)
Pace 6
Edges:
  Belongin's 3: Soldier's
    gear
  Tough as nails 4
Hindrances:
  Deathwish –5
  Greedy –2
  Loyal –3
Gear: NA Assault rifle, infantry
  battlesuit, large knife, 50 10mm
  bullets, and one frag grenade.

Personality

What's the plan, Mayor? Flank attack, diversion, frontal assault. I don't care. I'll survive. I always do. An' if I don't, nobody's gonna shed any tears.

Those muties got Doomsayers with 'em. The bad kind. That's gonna take some thinkin' if you really want to win this battle. I understand you got an old mortar, right? I know how to use it. A few rounds of HE oughta get most of the muties runnin' for cover. That won't last long, but me and these kids you're gettin' killed should be able to take out those damn rad priests before they start nukin' us.

Don't look at me like that. They are kids. I bet most of 'em ain't had their first kiss yet, let alone make babies or realize how hopeless all this is.

All right. I'll shut up. I know I'm a downer. I just seen a lotta killin' in my time, and it makes you old. But it's the only thing I'm good at.

Quote: "Yessir."

Archetypes

Ravenite

Traits & Aptitudes

Deftness 2d10
  Shootin': auto-shotgun, pistol 4
Nimbleness 4d10
  Climbin' 1
  Drivin': cars 3
  Fightin': brawlin' 2
  Sneak 1
Strength 1d8
Quickness 3d8
Vigor 2d12
Cognition 4d6
  Search 1
Knowledge 3d6
  Area knowledge 2
  Language 2
  Professional: business 2
Mien 2d6
Smarts 2d6
  Bluff 2
  Survival 2
Spirit 1d6
  Guts 2
Wind 18
Pace 10
Edges:
  Belongin's 3: Pickup truck
  Dinero 5
Hindrances:
  Cautious –3
  Greedy –2
  Habit –3: You only buy the "best" gear, keep your equipment clean, and so on.
  Intolerance –2: Old Ways Indians annoy you. Maybe because you know they were right.
Gear: Infantry battlesuit, night vision goggles, auto-shotgun, and 30 shells.

Personality

The Old Ways? No, cracker, that's my savage brothers and sisters. You know, the ones who blame the rest of us for "selling out." Hey, we weren't the only ones who sold ghost rock.

The difference? Man, you are white. The Old Wayers don't believe in "material things." Me? I used to own a casino in Deadwood. Made a lot of money. Even built me a fallout shelter when things looked bad there at the end. Yeah, the Old Wayers tipped us off. One last attempt to make us "see the light," I guess. At least those miserable wanderers served some kinda purpose.

Anyway, I got more ammo than one of Throckmorton's goons. And see these boots? The best money could buy before the war. Same as my armor. And these night-vision goggles are worth more than most folks make in a year.

It's true what they say about the Old Wayers fighting War. I wasn't *actually* in the fight, but I traded them some guns and ammo. Yeah, maybe I should have done more, but I had to protect my cache, see. Sure, it got overrun by wormlings a few weeks later, but how was I supposed to know?

Quote: "I'm not that kind of Indian."

Posse: 71

Road Warrior

Traits & Aptitudes

Deftness 2d10
  Shootin': shotgun 3
Nimbleness 2d12
  Climbin' 1
  Drivin': rig 5
  Fightin': brawlin' 3
  Sneak 1
Strength 3d8
Quickness 2d8
Vigor 2d10
Cognition 2d6
  Search 1
Knowledge 1d6
  Area knowledge 2
  Area knowledge: Old highways 3
  Language 2
Mien 3d6
Smarts 2d6
  Gamblin' 2
  Survival 2
  Tinkerin' 3
Spirit 2d6
  Guts 3
Wind 16
Pace 12
Edges:
  Belongin's 4: Semi-truck
Hindrances:
  Big britches –3
  Greedy –2
  Lame –3
  Stubborn –2
Gear: Leather jacket and pants (–1),
  pump shotgun (cheap, –3 to hit),
  10 12-gauge shells, and 3 slugs.

Personality

You want gas, you talk to me. You want your stuff hauled to Salt Lake for trade, you talk to me. My truck's the only thing connecting this Hellhole to all the other Hellholes out there. An' I'm one of the few who knows the way.

Maybe you can read a map, genius. But do you know which roads are still mined? Which ones Throckmorton patrols? How to get around the "S-Mart Overlord?" Didn't think so.

And what if you get attacked by road gangs. There's a lot of 'em out there. I know, 'cause I used to be one of 'em. Then I wised up. Saw they wasn't doin' anyone any good. They're mostly just a bunch of murderers and rapists, and no, I don't wanna talk about it.

Now load up my truck, fill my tank, and gimme five or 10 good fighters. We'll get your load up through and be in back before the weekend.

Quote: "Keep on truckin'."

Savage

Traits & Aptitudes

Deftness 2d10
  Throwin': balanced 4
Nimbleness 4d10
  Climbin' 2
  Fightin' 4
  Sneak 3
Strength 2d12
Quickness 3d8
Vigor 4d6
Cognition 3d6
  Search 1
Knowledge 1d6
  Area knowledge 2
  Language 2
Mien 1d8
  Overawe 3
Smarts 2d6
  Scroungin' 2
  Survival 3
Spirit 2d6
  Guts 3
Wind 12
Pace 10
Edges:
  Brawny 3 (Size +1)
  Thick-skinned 3
Hindrances:
  All thumbs -2
  Curious -3
  Illiterate -3
  Intolerance -2: Those
    who rely on
    technology
Gear: Spear, boiled leather
  shirt and pants, sharpened
  hubcap, and $50.

Personality

I don't care if you call me a savage. It's true I grew up after the bomb, but it was you old ones who destroyed our world with your guns and computers and cars!

I don't trust any of that stuff. I once watched a woman get eaten by wormlings because her gun jammed. You won't see my knife jam. Or my hubcaps. And yeah, that's worm-skin I'm wearing. They ain't so tough if you don't rely on that garbage you're carrying.

What's that? I never saw a music box before. It probably blows up if you touch it, right? No? Ooh. That is pretty. I think I used to have something like that—before the war. What do you want for it?

You want me to help kill wormlings? Sucker. I woulda done that for free.

Quote: "What's a (computer, car, accountant, calculator, etc.)?"

Archetypes

Syker

Traits & Aptitudes

Deftness 1d8
Shootin': SMG 3
Nimbleness 3d6
Climbin' 1
Fightin': brawlin' 2
Sneak 3
Strength 1d6
Quickness 3d8
Vigor 4d10
Cognition 4d6
Scrutinize 2
Search 2
Knowledge 2d12
Academia: occult 2
Area knowledge 2
Blastin' 5
Language 2
Medicine: general 2
Mien 2d6
Overawe 2
Smarts 2d10
Scroungin' 2
Survival 2
Spirit 2d6
Guts 3
Wind 26
Pace 10
Strain 6
Edges:
Arcane background: syker 3
Fortitude 2
Tough as nails 5 (+10 Wind)
Hindrances:
Intolerance: Authority –1
Night terrors –5 (The things you did
on Faraway still haunt you.)
Oath of *Unity* –1
Vengeful –3
Powers: Brain blast, chameleon,
fleshknit, mindwipe,
skinwalker
Gear: SA Commando SMG, 25
.50 bullets, and $25.

Personality

Get outta my face or I'll fry your brain. I told you I don't wanna join your "army." No, I don't want the muties overrunning the town, I just don't think your half-assed plan is gonna work. Probably just get a bunch of boys killed, just like on Banshee.

Want a better plan? Then sit down and shut up, brainer. Let me do it alone. I'll get inside their base and take out the leader. How? You payin' attention? You see my bald head? With my powers, I can get past anybody. A bunch of disorganized muties are dumber than anouks and twice as ugly.

My price? Glad you asked. I want that jeep and as many cans of gas as I can load on it. Sure it's high, but it's that or get half your town killed.

Yeah, you can think about it. But don't take too long. I got a killer headache.

Quote: "Don't mess with a man who can think you to death."

Archetypes

Tale-Teller

Traits & Aptitudes

Deftness 1d6
  Shootin': pistol 3
Nimbleness 3d6
  Climbin' 1
  Drivin' 3
  Sneak 3
Strength 2d6
Quickness 4d6
Vigor 2d6
Cognition 2d10
  Scrutinize 3
  Search 3
Knowledge 3d8
  Academia: occult 3
  Academia: history 2
  Area knowledge 2
  Language 2
Mien 2d12
  Performin' 3
  Persuasion 3
  Tale-tellin' 5
Smarts 4d10
  Streetwise 2
  Survival 2
Spirit 3d8
  Faith 2
  Guts 2
Wind 14
Pace 6
Edges:
  "The voice" 1
Hindrances:
  Curious -3
  Hankerin' -1: You've
    got a major
    sweet tooth
  Heroic -5
  Yearnin' -1: To
    be famous
Gear: SA
  Officer's
  sidearm, 25 .50
  shells, and a Geiger
  counter.

Personality

Get those wounds bandaged. We gotta get to town and tell everyone what happened. Why? We've been out here fighting monsters for a year, and you gotta ask why? Because it hurts the Reckoners, brainer! Every time we give the people a little hope, I can feel it eating away at those bastards! And I like to feel their pain. Makes me feel a little better about—well, what I lost. Of course, you gotta come. The kids wanna see a war hero, and you're all I got. It won't be so bad. Besides, you know they're gonna feed us afterwards, and I saw real cows outside the town. You know how long it's been since I've had a real steak? And milk? God, wouldn't that be good.

Hey, you think we can cut that trog's head off? That would really get their attention. Just make sure it ain't playin' dead. I'd feel real bad if I caused you to lose another hand.

Quote: "It all began when..."

Posse: 75

Archetypes

Templar

Traits & Aptitudes

Deftness 1d8
  Shootin': SMG 3
  Speed-load 2
Nimbleness 4d6
  Climbin' 1
  Dodge 3
  Fightin': sword 4
  Sneak 3
Strength 4d10
Quickness 2d10
Vigor 2d6
Cognition 3d6
  Scrutinize 2
  Search 2
Knowledge 1d6
  Academia: occult 2
  Area knowledge 2
  Disguise 4
  Language 2
Mien 3d8
  Leadership 2
  Overawe 2
Smarts 2d6
  Streetwise 2
  Survival 2
Spirit 2d12
  Faith 3
  Guts 3
Wind 18
Pace 6
Edges:
  Level-headed 5
  Veteran o' the Wasted West
    (Tell your Marshal to
    draw a card for this
    Edge.)
  "The voice" 1
Hindrances:
  Templar's Oath -5
  Heroic -5
  Powers: Lay on hands 3,
  inner strength 2
  Gear: NA Commando SMG,
  50 bullets, Templar's sword,
  and $50.

Personality

Now that you all know what I really am, let me tell you why I'm going to help fight off that road gang. It isn't because this town deserves my help. When I was disguised as a beggar and I asked for work, the guard kicked me. Later on, I begged scraps out back of that roach-infested-deathtrap you call an inn. The owner threw me out. To beat it all, your children threw rocks at me! Look at them: Now the little brats can't even sit after I paddled them with my sword.

So why am I still here? Let me tell you why. Just up the road is another town, a good place with good people. And this same gang is causing as much trouble there as they are here. So you're going to assault the biker camp with me while the other town prepares for its defense.

Many of you won't come back, but every last one of you is going, except the children. They're going to the other town to dig a moat.

Now gather whatever weapons you can. If we're lucky, we'll take the gang by surprise and wipe them out. If not, we'll take enough with us to save one town, but it certainly won't be yours.

Quote: "I'll find the killer, but there's something you must do for me as well."

Scenes from the Wasted West

Three adventurers prepare for the fight of their lives.

Posse: 77

Scenes from the Wasted West

A Harrowed claws his way out of his grave.

Posse: 78

Scenes from the Wasted West

Wormlings descend on an ornery meal.

Blowin' Things All to Hell

Things to do in Denver before you're dead: run and hide!

Posse: 80

Chapter Five:
Blowin' Things
All to Hell

Now you've got your character, and you know how to make Trait and Aptitude checks. If you're like most gamers, you're wondering how to blow things all to Hell (and back—this is *Deadlands* after all).

Rounds

When a firefight or a brawl erupts, the Marshal breaks the game down into "rounds" of about five seconds each.

Each round is further broken down into "segments." Your character gets to act on certain segments and not others. How do you know which ones? That's where the Action Deck comes in.

Each card (from Ace down to Deuce) represents a segment. The King is a segment, the Queen is a segment, and so on, all the way down to a Deuce. Let's dig into the Action Deck and see exactly how it works.

The Action Deck

You've heard the expression "the quick and the dead." There's a lot of truth to it. It doesn't matter how good a shot you are if you're slower than a one-legged mutie on a cold day.

Once a fight starts, each side (the players and the Marshal) needs an Action Deck. Using the Action Deck lets us have all the action, detail, and tension of a gunfight in an orderly way that everyone can understand.

Once the Marshal says the game is in rounds (a fight has started or is about to), each player makes a *Quickness* roll for his hero and compares it to a TN of Fair (5). You draw one card "for free" from the Action Deck, plus one for every success. If you go bust, you get no cards this round, though you might still use a card from up your sleeve (we'll explain later).

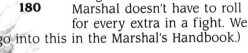

Then the Marshal counts down from Ace to Deuce. As players' cards come up, their characters get to take actions. (The bad guys get Action Cards too, but they do things a bit different so the Marshal doesn't have to roll for every extra in a fight. We go into this in the Marshal's Handbook.)

180

Teller rolls a *Quickness* of 7. He gets one card "for free" plus another for one success. On a 17, he'd get four cards (one freebie plus one for each success).

Posse: 81

Blowin' Things All to Hell

Maximum Cards

No matter how high your *Quickness* total is, you can never have more than five cards (without supernatural aid).

Reshuffling

If your Action Deck runs out, reshuffle it immediately. If someone draws a black Joker, finish the round, then reshuffle.

Surprise

Most folks don't just whip out their pistols and start blasting when some monster comes jumping out of the bushes at them. Some run, some cry for momma, and some just stand there drooling like idiots.

Anytime there's a good chance your character might be surprised, the Marshal is going to ask you to make a *Cognition* check. The difficulty is Fair (5) if your character is expecting some sort of danger—Incredible (11) if she's not.

If you fail the roll, you don't get any cards, and your character can't act that round. She can act normally in the next round as long as she makes a Fair (5) *guts* check.

Actions

Once everyone has their cards, the Marshal starts counting down from an Ace. When one of your cards is called, toss it into the discard pile and tell the Marshal what your character is doing that segment.

Suits

Compare suits to break ties with other characters who have the same cards. The ranking of suits is:

Suit Ranks

Suit	Rank
Spades	First
Hearts	Second
Diamonds	Third
Clubs	Fourth

Since the Marshal has his own Action Deck, it's possible for each side to have an action on the same card and suit. If so, these actions are simultaneous.

Speed

Action segments are very short periods of time. That means everything your hombre does is broken up into simple, short, and long tasks.

Simple Tasks (Speed 0)

A character can perform a simple task in coordination with any other rolled task. A simple task is one that doesn't require much concentration, such as saying a few quick words, resisting a test of wills, or moving.

Short Tasks (Speed 1)

Short tasks are things like drawing or cocking a gun, firing a gun, making a test of wills, or concentrating on a supernatural ability of some sort. Short tasks are declared and resolved on a single Action Card.

Long Tasks (Speed 2+)

Long tasks are things like searching through a backpack, reading a long, arcane text, or firing up a gizmo of some sort. Long tasks are strung out over two or more Action Cards. When you start a long task, declare the task your character is beginning and use the cards as they're called out by the Marshal. Resolve the task as you spend the last card required.

Blowin' Things All to Hell

If the Marshal doesn't have a good idea of how long something like this should take, roll 1d6. It takes that many Action Cards to complete the task.

Below is a table that summarizes all this business about tasks. Some of the things on there might not make sense to you now (like recovery checks). These things are explained later in this chapter.

Task Speeds

Type	Speed	Example Actions
Simple	0	Saying a single short sentence, moving, making a stun check, resisting a power or test of wills.
Short	1	Saying a few short sentences, drawing a weapon, cocking a weapon, making a recovery check, making a test of wills, reloading a single shell or clip, climbing, jumping, or any kind of movement that requires an Aptitude roll.
Long	2+	Relating complex information, short speeches, some powers and spells, searching a pack, or readying a gizmo.

Cheatin'

Sometimes you might want to wait until some hombre does something before you take your action. Say you know some slavering beastie is about to burst into your fallout shelter and you want to blast a hole in it the moment it comes crashing through.

The way to do this is by "cheating" and keeping a single card "up your sleeve." When the card you want to put up your sleeve would normally be played, tell the Marshal you're going to put it up your sleeve instead. Now place it face down under your Fate Chips.

You can only ever have one card up your sleeve, but you can hold onto it over subsequent rounds, saving it until you need to use it.

Once a card has been designated a cheat card, its value no longer matters. A Deuce up the sleeve can beat an Ace in the next round.

When you're ready to play the "cheat" card, whip it out, show it to the Marshal, take your action, and discard it. If you want to interrupt someone else's action with a cheat card, you have to beat him in an opposed *Quickness* match. A success means the actions are simultaneous. A raise means that character goes first. This way you're never guaranteed to beat someone just because you've got a cheat card, but at least you've got a chance.

Assuming you don't use it, you can hold on to your cheat card until the fight is over, you draw a black Joker, or an opponent forces you to discard it through a test of wills (which we'll discuss later in this chapter).

Jokers

Jokers can never be hidden up your sleeve, they're just too wily to get that close to a survivor's armpit. They do have a few special effects, however. The big thing to remember is red Joker good, black Joker bad.

Red Jokers

The red Joker allows your character to go at any time during the round. He can even interrupt another character's action without having to make a *Quickness* check. In a nutshell, your survivor can go whenever he wants this round.

The downside is that, since you can't put Jokers up your sleeve, you only get this advantage for one round. If you don't use it before the round is over, you have to discard it. You can still have a normal card up your sleeve, however, and you can even use them both at once if you like.

The second advantage to drawing a red Joker is that you get to draw a random chip from the Fate Pot. Congratulations, bunkie!

The Marshal doesn't get a draw from the Fate Pot by drawing a red Joker for the bad guys, but he does when the posse draws a black Joker.

Black Jokers

The black Joker is bad news. It means your character hesitates for some reason. Maybe he's starting to feel his wounds or he's distracted by the bad guys. Whatever the reason, the Joker is discarded, and you have to discard any card up your sleeve as well.

The other downside is the black Joker gives the bad guys (run by the Marshal) a draw from the Fate Pot. Your side doesn't get a draw when the Marshal gets a black Joker though. Who said life was fair?

There's one last side-effect to a black Joker. Your side's Action Deck is reshuffled at the end of the current round. This counts for both the posse and the Marshal.

Blowin' Things All to Hell

Movement

The number of yards a character can move each round is his "Pace." The Pace of characters and most critters is their *Nimbleness* in yards. A vehicle or really fast varmint's Pace is listed in its profile.

Because characters in *Deadlands* have different numbers of actions each round, movement is broken up over each segment.

Divide your character's normal Pace by his total number of actions each round to figure out what the maximum movement is per action.

Don't try to figure fractions. Just break up the movement as evenly as possible. If a character can move 8 yards in a round and draws 3 cards, he could move 3 on the first card, 3 on the second, and 2 on the last.

You can't get extra movement by playing a cheat card. If you have actions left in the round when you play a cheat card, just split your remaining movement as evenly as possible. If you have no actions left when you play a cheat card, your hero can't move during that action.

Running

A character can double his Pace during any particular action by running. The downside is that characters who do so incur a -4 penalty to any tasks they attempt that action.

Chases

We use the phased movement described above because characters have variable numbers of actions per round. Occasionally, this makes no sense, especially if a quick hero with several actions is chasing some bad guy with only 1. In these cases, the Marshal should let both characters break up their move however they want. The downside is that the Marshal has to decide if any of the characters should incur the -4 running penalty for any particular actions.

Pickin' Up the Pace

If your hombre *really* needs to skedaddle, he can "pick up the Pace." This means she goes as flat-out fast as he possibly can. The cost is an Action Card and a little fatigue, represented by Wind.

Your character can pick up the Pace on any action. This is a short task, so he can't do anything else that action. All that extra effort makes it too hard to bark orders or squeeze off shots.

The extra movement your hero gets can be found on the Gitalong Table below. Add that many yards to the character's movement for that particular action. The number listed under "Wind" is the amount of Wind the cowpoke takes each time for pushing himself so hard.

A rider can make his mount pick up the Pace by making a Fair (5) *ridin'* or *teamster* roll. In this case, the animal takes the Wind.

Picking up the Pace on a vehicle requires a Fair (5) *drivin'* roll. Vehicles don't take Wind (naturally), but they might suffer a breakdown after being pushed for a while, if the Marshal feels it's appropriate.

Teller still hasn't escaped the muties, so he picks up the Pace. He gets two actions this round. On the first, he gets four extra yards of movement but takes 1 Wind. On the second, he gets two extra yards and takes another Wind.

Gitalong

Here's a handy table to help you keep all this movement business straight.

Your hero can't "run" (double his movement) when swimming or climbing, though he can still pick up the Pace.

Action	Pace	Pickup	Wind	Max
Walkin'	*Nimbleness*	—	—	—
Runnin'	2 × *Nimbleness*	d4	1	—
Climbin'	2+*climbin'*	d2	1	8
Swimmin'	*swimmin'*	d2	1	5
Ridin'	Varies by animal	d10	1	—

Pace is the base movement rate for the entire turn. For swimming and climbing, use your character's Aptitude levels in *swimmin'* and *climbin'* as the base number.

Pickup is the type of die you roll to get extra movement by "picking up the Pace." Don't roll again on Aces for this kind of roll. It's not a Trait or skill check or a damage roll.

Wind is the amount of Wind your character takes when he picks up the Pace.

Max is the maximum your character can move due to his Aptitude level in climbing and swimming. Supernatural bonuses or equipment may raise the total beyond the maximum, but raising the Aptitude higher doesn't.

Carrying a Load

No, we don't mean the one in your pants. That's a personal problem. What we're talking about is the fact that a scavenger trying to haul a box of ammo away from a horde of slavering muties isn't going anywhere fast.

The load is an estimate of the character's, critter's, or vehicle's capacity to carry stuff versus the weight of the load in pounds. If and when such a thing matters, you and the Marshal need to figure out how heavy a load is. A strong character carrying a *scrawny* companion probably has a light load. Two horses pulling a wagon have an average load. If the wagon is full of ghost rock or metal salvaged from a ruined city, it would be heavy for even six horses. If you don't have exact weights, guess.

The maximum weight for each level of load is listed under "Weight" in pounds. *Strength* refers to your character's *Strength* die type. After that is how much that load reduces his Pace by. Round any fractions down.

Don't figure up loads if there's no reason to. Use these rules only when it adds some drama or tension to the scene.

Loads

Load	Weight	Pace
None	Up to 3 × Strength	—
Light	Up to 6 × Strength	75%
Medium	Up to 10 × Strength	50%
Heavy	Up to 20 × Strength	25%

Syker Jon Grissom finds a box of priceless 9mm ammo in an old Northern Alliance bunker. Unfortunately, he gets caught by a band of muties looking for meat. He has to run for it, but he doesn't want to drop his valuable prize.

Jon has a *Strength* of 2d8. He can carry up to 24 pounds easily, 25–48 pounds at 75% Pace, 49-80 pounds at 50% Pace, and 81-160 pounds at 25% Pace. Anything over that brings him to a dead stop. The ammo box weighs around 50 pounds, so Jon's in big trouble.

His normal Pace of 10 is reduced to 5.

Blowin' Things All to Hell

Tests o' Will

When most folks think of combat, they think of yanking triggers and beating things to a pulp. That's a lot of fun, but sometimes it's just as much fun to stare down some lily-livered wastelander and send him running home to his radioactive momma.

Bluff, overawe, and *ridicule* are tests of will that can be used to break an opponent's nerve or concentration. *Persuasion* is also a test of wills, but it isn't generally used in combat.

A test of wills is an opposed roll versus one of the target's Aptitudes. If the test is being made against a group, use the leader's Aptitude.

Initiating a test of wills is a short task. Resisting one is an automatic simple task.

Each raise over an opponent's total has its own special effect, as shown to the right. Note that these are "raises." Beating someone by 1-4 points is a success but has no effect. You have to get a raise for a special effect.

Remember that, since this is an opposed roll, the fellow who started the test of wills must get at least a Fair (5) success. If he doesn't, the target automatically wins the contest.

Tests o' Will

Test Aptitude	Opposed Aptitude
Bluff	Scrutinize
Overawe	Guts
Ridicule	Ridicule

Raises	Effect
1	Unnerved
2	Distracted
3	Broken

Unnerved

Your character's stern gaze or cruel taunt angers or upsets your opponent. The target suffers -4 to her next action. This includes any defensive Aptitudes like vamoosin' or resisting further tests of wills. The penalty is not cumulative should the character be unnerved more than once, even if unnerved by different characters.

Distracted

The target is distracted by your hero's jibe, trick, or surly stare. She is unnerved and also loses her highest Action Card. If she's got a cheat card up her sleeve, she loses that instead.

Broken

You've broken the bad guy's will—for the moment at least. He's unnerved and distracted and might even run if he can. Even better, you get to draw a Fate Chip from the pot!

Tasha finds herself in the arena of the S-Mart Overlord. Her opponent is a veteran pitfighter armed with a buzzing chainsaw. Tasha screams in rage at her savage opponent, making an *overawe* attack.

With 1 raise, Tasha unnerves the chainsaw warrior, giving him -4 to his next action, which is likely an attack.

With 2 raises, Tasha distracts her opponent. Besides suffering the -4 penalty, he also loses his next highest Action Card.

With 3 raises, the pitfighter is at -4 and loses his next Action Card, and Tasha gets a draw from the Fate Pot. The pitfighter would probably run—if he wasn't trapped in a 5-foot-deep hole. It sucks to be him!

Blowin' Things All to Hell

Shootin' Things

There often comes a point when you need to turn some dastardly villain's head into mulch. This section tells you how to do just that.

Weapon Speeds

Every weapon in *Deadlands* has a Speed score, usually of 1 or 2. That's how many actions it takes to cock the weapon and fire it.

Automatic pistols and other weapons have a Speed of 1 and can be fired every action once cocked. Double-action revolvers don't need to be cocked.

Weapons that must be cocked between every shot, such as single-action pistols, bolt or lever-action rifles, pump shotguns, and the like, take 1 action to cock and 1 to fire (though there are ways to speed this up, as we'll show you later in this chapter).

Also, double-action and automatic pistols must be cocked the first time they're fired or reloaded, so they're effectively Speed 2 weapons until they've been cocked, the safety's taken off, the battery's engaged, or whatever. Smart survivors usually ready their firearms before the fight starts. Make sure you tell the Marshal your hombre cocks his gat before the action breaks down into rounds. It can make a world of difference.

The Shootin' Roll

Once you've figured out how many actions it takes to operate your hombre's hogleg, you simply make a *shootin'* roll versus the appropriate Target Number. If your roll comes up equal to or higher than the TN, you've hit.

Rate of Fire

When a weapon is ready (cocked), it can fire up to its "Rate of Fire" each action. Semiautomatic weapons fire once an action.

Fully automatic weapons (such as Gatlings, assault rifles, and the like) fire three or more shots per action. We'll tell you how these work under **Automatic Weapons** on page 91.

Some shotguns have a "Rate of Fire" of 2 because you can fire one or both barrels on a single action. Roll separate *shootin'* totals for each shot. We'll tell you more about shotguns under **Shotguns,** also on page 91.

Check the **Gear** list in Chapter Four to find out a weapon's Rate of Fire or "ROF."

Range

The Target Number you're looking for is Fair (5) plus the range modifier. To figure the modifier, count the number of yards between the shooter and the target, then divide it by the weapon's Range Increment, rounding down as usual. The number you get is added to Fair (5) to get the base TN.

The Shootin' Irons Table in Chapter Four lists a whole mess of firearms' Range Increments (as well as all their other statistics).

Modifiers

Now that you've got your TN, you might have to add or subtract a couple of modifiers to your *shootin'* roll. These things come up often in a gunfight, so be sure to keep track of them. Sometimes even stranger things can happen. Then it's up to the Marshal to figure out a modifier for that particular situation.

Shootin' Modifiers

Situation	Modifier
Firer is running	-4
Firer is mounted	-2
Firer is wounded	Varies
Size	Varies
Target is moving fast	-4
Target is hidden	-8 to -4
Night, full moon, twilight	-2
Night, half moon	-4
Night, quarter moon	-6
Blindness, total darkness	-10

Firer is Moving

It's a lot harder to hit a target when you're on the move. As you might remember from our little discussion on movement, any turn in which your character runs, he suffers a -4 penalty to any other things he might try to do—like shooting whatever's chasing him.

Target's Size

If a target is half the size of a man, subtract a penalty of -1. If it's one-quarter the size of a man, subtract -2, and so on, to a maximum penalty of -6.

The opposite is also true. A target that is twice as big as a man gives the character a +1 bonus, a target three times the size of a man has a +2 modifier, and so on, up to a maximum of +6.

Blowin' Things All to Hell

Target is Moving Fast

Any time a target is moving faster than a relative Pace of 20, subtract -4 from your *shootin'* roll. "Relative" means you need to take into account how fast the target and the shooter are moving in relation to each other. If a mutant on a motorcycle is chasing a posse in a pickup, for instance, no penalty for speed applies. If they're going in opposite directions, however, the penalty applies to both parties.

Target is Hidden

Use the **Cover** rules (page 96) and the Hit Location Table when a target is partially concealed (explained later in this chapter). Use this modifier if a target is completely concealed (hiding) but an attacker has a pretty good idea where the target is. Subtract -8 from the total if the cover is about four times the size of the target hiding behind it. Use -6 if the concealment is twice as large.

Lighting

It's hard to shoot something you can't see. Apply these modifiers based on the available light.

Shootin' Summary

The base TN to shoot something is Fair (5). It is modified by range and other circumstances.

The range modifier is figured by counting the total range from the shooter to the target in yards, then dividing it by the Range Increment (round down). Add this number to the base TN of Fair (5).

Add any bonuses or penalties to the current TN.

If the *shootin'* roll equals or exceeds the modified TN, the shot hits. Otherwise it misses.

Special Maneuvers

Gunslingers use all kinds of tricks and techniques to make sure they get their man. Here's how to handle some of the most common.

Called Shots

Occasionally you may run across some critter that just doesn't want to die, even after you've turned it into Swiss cheese. Hopefully it's got a weak spot somewhere, like an eyeball or the brainpan.

Hitting a specific spot on a target is a "called shot," and of course, it comes with a penalty. The smaller the target, the bigger the penalty. The table below is for targeting people, but it should give you an idea for blasting parts off nasty critters as well.

Note that the heart or other vital organs count as a "gizzards" hit. Don't assume because your hombre makes the shot that he actually hits the target's heart—obviously the poor schmuck would be dead if he did. It just means he hit in the general area. If the damage is really high (and kills the sucker), he probably did hit it. Hence the twitching corpse. The damage and your all-knowing, all-wise Marshal decides *exactly* what gets hit if it really matters.

Called-Shot Modifiers

Size	Penalty
Guts	-2
Legs, arms	-4
Heads, hands, feet	-6
Heart	-10

Drawing A Bead

A normal shot assumes your cowpoke aims his smokewagon only for a heartbeat before squeezing off a round. If a character spends an entire action "drawing a bead," she can add +2 to her *shootin'* roll in the next action.

Every action spent drawing a bead adds +2 to the hero's next *shootin'* roll, up to a maximum of +6. The modifier carries over to the next round if needed. Performing anything other than a simple task while drawing a bead negates the modifier.

Gun-toting survivors can never *draw a bead* when fanning or firing bursts. Lead showers are just too erratic.

Blowin' Things All to Hell

Fannin' the Hammer

Veteran gunslingers sometimes "fan" their sidearms. Fanning simply means holding the trigger down on a single-action pistol and slapping the hammer repeatedly with the palm of the other hand. This puts a lot of lead in the air fast, though it isn't very accurate.

And no, there aren't a lot of single-action pistols in the Wasted West, but there are a few. Some traditions die hard out here.

Fanning requires the *shootin': pistol* Aptitude. The fanner needs one free hand and a single-action revolver in the other.

The rate of fire is 1 to 6—your choice on how many bullets you want to waste. Even if a gun holds more than six rounds, that's the most a survivor can fan in one action. Fanning one shot isn't really worth while, but it can be done.

To resolve the attack, pick a target and figure out the TN based on the range and any other modifiers. Fanning a pistol isn't very accurate, so the shooter has to subtract -2 from his roll for slapping his gun around like a redheaded stepchild. This is on top of the "shooting from the hip" modifier (see page 90), so the total penalty is -4. Each success causes a bullet to hit. The firer chooses which targets he hits, though any after the first must be within 2 yards of the last target hit.

A shooter can't draw a bead when fanning, though he can make a called shot—on the first bullet only. Figure the TN for the first shot. Any raises after that hit random locations as normal.

Jessie, a Law Dog whose father was a Texas Ranger, now continues his tradition. She uses her pappy's old, single-action Colt Peacemaker to dispense her particular brand of justice.

Jessie's *shootin': pistol* is 3d10, and she needs to gun down three goons in a hurry. She decides to fan three shots. The first goon has an assault rifle, so she calls her first shot to his brainpan (the noggin, friend).

The range is negligible, so the base TN is 5. Fannin' carries an automatic -4, and the called shot to the head is -6, for a total TN of 15. She rolls and gets a 22 for two successes!

The first thug catches a slug in the head, the next gets hit in a random location. Her third shot (which missed) goes wild.

Quick Draw

Drawing a weapon takes an action, as does cocking and firing. What if you don't have that kind of time? A skilled gunslinger can whip out his pistol, cock it, and plug a mutie in the eye all in one action.

How can someone pull that off? Easy. The *quick draw* skill not only lets you draw a weapon as a simple task, it also lets you cock it if needed. The TN to draw or draw and/or cock a weapon as a simple task is shown on the table below.

If the roll is made, the weapon is drawn—or drawn and cocked if needed. If you roll a 5 while trying to draw and cock a weapon, the gun is drawn but not cocked. You're going to have to spend another action to get that gat smoking.

Quick Draw

Task	TN
Draw	5
Cock	5
Draw and cock	7

Blowin' Things All to Hell

Reloadin'

Sooner or later, your piece is going to run out of ammo smack in the middle of a firefight. It happens to the best of us. So many brainers; such small magazines. Fortunately, it only takes a little reloading to get the bad guys dying in bloody droves again.

It takes one full action to put a single bullet into a pistol or rifle, or a single shell into a shotgun.

In magazine-fed weapons, reloading a single bullet in a pistol, rifle, or shotgun is a short task and takes an entire action. In clip-fed weapons, reloading an entire clip is a short task. (Now you can see why survivors use guns with clips!)

Reloading any kind of weapon can be hastened with the *speed-load* skill (see Chapter Three). A skilled *speed-loader* can get his hogleg smoking again much faster than some other brainer fumbling through his spare "change" for just the right size bullet.

Once you've got some lead loaded, remember that most weapons must be cocked again. This is a short task unless the user makes a *quick draw* roll like we just told you about on the last page.

The Rifle Spin & One-Handed Pump

There are still a few lever-action rifles lying around the wastes, and well-traveled survivors know it pays to be able to pump a shotgun with only one arm (usually so you can hold your innards in with your other hand).

Generally speaking, you need two hands to work a lever or pump a shotgun, but if you're good you can do it with only one. (Oh, grow up, and stop snickering out there.)

Lever-action rifles can be cocked by spinning the rifle by its lever. Shotguns can be pumped by holding the weapon by the pump and jerking it up then down. (We said calm down, brainer.)

If you really need to try this manly but difficult maneuver, it requires a Fair (5) *Strength* check and an action. If your hero fails, the gun isn't cocked. Try again, bunkie.

Shootin' from the Hip

Sometimes a glowing, three-eyed, liver-eating mutie isn't going to wait for you to ready your weapon and take a shot at him. They're rude that way. If not, you have to shoot from the hip.

Single-action revolvers, rifles, and other weapons with a Speed of 2 can fire faster (making the Speed 1) by sacrificing a little aim. This is called "shooting from the hip" and subtracts –2 from the firer's *shootin'* roll.

The Two-Gun Kid

Some folks have too much ammo and like to fire two pistols at once. They usually don't hit much, but they sure make a lot of noise.

A character firing two guns suffers –2 to each attack. Any action taken with an offhand is made at an additional –4 (for a total of –6 with that hand). A survivor can fire with each hand up to the weapons' usual Rate of Fire. Roll each weapon separately as usual.

Two-Handed Weapons

Small weapons like pistols and SMGs only require one good arm. Heavier firearms like rifles, shotguns, and machine guns, and hand weapons like big axes and chainsaws, need a good, two-handed grip, but sometimes you just can't manage that.

Anytime your character is forced to use a two-handed weapon with one hand, subtract –2 from the attack roll. Your hero also loses any Defensive Bonus the weapon offers.

Blowin' Things All to Hell

Special Weapons

Here's how to handle things like shotguns and automatic weapons.

Automatic Weapons

Automatic weapons spray the air with lead at the expense of accuracy. To make things easy, we don't roll for every bullet. We roll for each burst of three bullets. That's why automatic weapons have Rates of Fire of 3, 6, 9, 12, and so on. A character must fire all three shots of a burst. He can't choose to fire only two shots, though all full-auto weapons allow the shooter to switch to single shots as a simple task.

The character's *shootin'* roll determines how many rounds from each burst actually hit. Make one *shootin'* roll per burst. Every success means one of the three bullets hits its target. Additional raises are lost.

When firing on full-auto, the weapon uses the lower of its two Range Increments (see the weapon listings in Chapter Four).

A character firing bursts can draw a bead and make called shots on his first burst in an action only. Just add or subtract the modifiers to the usual TN and figure raises from there.

Multiple Targets

Multiple targets can be hit by a single burst. Like normal, each raise means another bullet finds a target.

Here's how. Choose a primary target. The first bullet hits this unfortunate fellow. A raise could hit a second victim up to 2 yards away, and another raise could hit a third target 2 yards away from the second.

To hit targets further than 2 yards from the first target requires a second burst. Determine each round's hit location and damage separately.

The player must assign his hits before rolling damage or resolving a second burst. In other words, roll all your attacks, assign hits to targets, then go back and roll hit location and damage for each. That way you can't see if the first bullet in a burst kills some poor fool before assigning your second or third.

Recoil

Firing off a hail of automatic fire is hard to control. Each burst fired after the first in a single action suffers a –2 recoil modifier. This is cumulative, so the third burst in an action suffers a –4, and so on, to a maximum of –6.

Braces

A good brace such as a sling or a bipod reduces the recoil penalty to –1 or even 0. Lying prone and using the ground as a brace reduces the recoil to –1 per burst.

Explosives

There are few things as much fun as blowing stuff up. Here's how to handle what happens to all the brainers unfortunate enough to be nearby something that goes boom.

Everyone within the first "Burst Radius" of an explosive takes full damage. After that, the damage of the explosion drops by a die each time it crosses a Burst Radius.

Most explosives have a Burst Radius of 10. See **More Pain & Sufferin'** on page 102 to find out how to disperse the wounds.

If you're wondering where a grenade that missed its target goes, keep reading. The **Deviation** rules are coming right up.

Shotguns

Shotguns and scatterguns unleash a hail of tiny balls, filling the air with lead. This makes them ideal for unskilled shooters, though they cause less damage as the buckshot spreads.

Anyone firing a shotgun adds +2 to her *shootin': shotgun* roll. Its damage decreases the further it travels, as shown on the table below.

By the way, "touching" means the shotgun is smack up against the target, such as in a hostage situation.

Shotguns & Scatterguns

Range	Damage
Touching	6d6
1–10	5d6
11–20	4d6
21–30	3d6
31+	2d6

Slugs

Both shotguns and scatterguns can also fire slugs, which are basically huge, self-rifled hunks of lead.

Slugs subtract –2 from the attacker's roll because of their poor rifling. On the plus side, they do 6d6 damage regardless of range. That's a big can of whup-ass. They're very rare, so your scavenger should use them wisely if he finds a few.

Throwin' Things

Grenades are dangerous things. Most folks can't throw them farther than their Blast Radius anyway. You'd better at least make sure you put the thing in the right place.

The *throwin'* skill works just like *shootin'* for most weapons. Your survivor makes a *throwin'* roll and compares it to the TN. Add in Range Modifiers and any situational modifiers and you're set.

Unless the weapon says otherwise, most thrown weapons have a Range Increment of 5. Check the weapon lists in Chapter Four if you're not sure.

The maximum range a character can throw an average size weapon (1-2 pounds) is her *Strength* die type times 5 yards.

Tasha's *Strength* of 3d10 lets her chuck a hubcap 50 yards. At her maximum distance of 50 yards, the TN to hit a normal creature would be (base TN of 5 plus [50 yards divided by the Range Increment of 5 is] 10=) 15.

Deviation

When most ranged attacks miss their target, you can usually forget about them. If you're really worried about who might be in the way, you can use the **Innocent Bystander** rules in the next column.

For some weapons, however, like grenades, missiles, or even area-effect spells that have a chance to miss their target, you need to know just how far the shot deviates.

First determine the direction by rolling a d12 and reading the result as a clock facing. Thrown missiles deviate 1d20 yards in that direction.

Projectiles fired from a launcher of some sort deviate 10% of the total range plus 2d20 yards in the direction indicated by the d12. If the shot deviates backward, it still goes at least half the distance from the shooter to the target. On a bust, the round jams or is dropped and detonates at the shooter's feet.

Teller fires a grenade launcher at a target 100 yards away and misses. The Marshal rolls a d12 and gets a 3. Then he rolls 2d20, gets a 17, and adds it to 10% of the range (10 yards). The grenade lands 27 yards due right of its target.

Innocent Bystanders

First things first. No one over walking age is innocent in the Wasted West. Some folks just aren't guilty *yet*.

Sometimes you want to know if a missed shot could hit someone near or along the path of the target. This isn't a situation that crops up all of the time, but sometimes it does, and these rules can help you figure out which brainer catches the stray rounds.

Don't keep track of where all those missed shots go if it's not important. If a hero is jumped by radrats, though, and his trigger-happy buddy cuts loose with a burst of his SMG, you definitely want to check.

You should almost always use these rules when someone fires on full-auto and there are other characters in the line of fire. That makes spraying an SMG, assault rifle, or other automatic into a crowd of people very dangerous—as it should be. The character may likely hit with a round or two from his *shootin'* roll, but the missed rounds have at least a chance of slamming into something anyway.

Using Hit Locations

If a bystander is within a yard of a target and directly between it and the shooter—as in the classic hostage pose—you can use the Hit Location Table (which we'll tell you all about in just a few pages). If the bystander was covering up the part of the target that was hit, she gets hit instead. You have to figure out where the bystander gets hit based on the situation or another roll.

Random Shots

If the bystander isn't blocking the target, you can use this simple system. For single shots that miss their target, a bullet has a 1 in 6 chance of hitting anyone within 1 yard of the bullet's path. Start at the bystander closest to the shooter and roll a d6. If it comes up a 1, he's hit. Roll hit location and damage normally. If the roll is anything but a 1, check any other bystanders in the path until you run out of bystanders, don't care anymore, or the bullet finds a home.

A spray of lead fired from a shotgun is wilder and has a greater chance of going all the wrong places. These hit bystanders on a 1 or 2.

If you're using the awesome *Deadlands* miniatures—and we don't know why you wouldn't be—you should have a very clear picture of who's likely to get hit by a stray shot.

Blowin' Things All to Hell

Fightin'

Bullets being as scarce as they are, your hero's going to find himself in hand-to-hand combat more often than you'd like. So whip out your chainsaw, and let's teach you how your hero can carve up some mutie-meat.

Making *fightin'* Aptitude rolls is a lot like making *shootin'* rolls. First figure out the concentration that matches the weapon your hero's using. Some basic *fightin'* concentrations are *knives*, *swords*, *whips*, and *brawlin'*. The last one, *brawlin'*, covers clubs, hammers, and any other improvised weapons. Chainsaws, garrotes, and weird weapons like that are always their own concentration.

The Target Number of the attack is Fair (5) plus the opponent's *fightin'* Aptitude level for whatever weapon is currently in his hand. A cowboy gets his *fightin': brawlin'* skill if he is empty-handed or has some sort of "club" in his hand—like a bottle or even a pistol. If he's using a weapon he's not skilled with, he can still use his *brawlin'* level. It's easy to just keep jumping out of the way instead of trying to parry with a sword he's not skilled with, even if he occasionally tries to hack with it as well. Make sure your character has the all-purpose *brawlin'* concentration if you want to keep his brainpan attached to the stump.

As with *shootin'* maneuvers, a *fightin'* attacker can make "called shots" if he wants (see earlier in this chapter, bub).

Weapon Speeds

Most hand-to-hand weapons have a Speed of 1, so the fighter can make one attack each action. A few weapons—like lariats—are really slow and have a Speed of 2. These take an action to ready before they can strike (but see **Rushing an Attack**).

Defensive Bonuses

Certain weapons make it hard for an opponent to get in close. A road warrior armed with a knife has a hard time getting close enough to jam it in the heart of a Templar with a sword. The reach advantage or parrying ability of certain weapons is their "Defensive Bonus."

The Defensive Bonus is applied directly to the attacker's TN when he makes his *fightin'* roll. See Chapter Four for a list of these.

Long clubs and rifles (when they're used as such) have a Defensive Bonus of +2.

Hand-to-Hand Maneuvers

We don't want to deprive those of you who like your fighting up close and personal from all the fancy maneuvers those gunslingers use. So here's a list of hand-to-hand maneuvers.

Rushing an Attack

Every now and then, when knocking some zombie's cranium off its carcass with a golf club, you just don't have time for a decent follow-through.

As with guns which a wastelander can "shoot from the hip," Speed-2 hand weapons can also be used faster, effectively making them Speed 1. The trade-off is the same. Your hombre isn't as accurate when forced to hurry. Subtract -2 from rushed strikes.

Two Weapons

If your brainer has a nickname like "Cuisinart," it's probably because he uses two knives, swords, or hatchets for his wasteland dance o' death. And if he's got two of those nifty mini-chainsaws, folks had best call him "Sir!"

A character with a weapon in each hand can make two attacks during one action. Each of these are rolled separately with a penalty of -2 to each attack.

A weapon in the offhand attack subtracts an additional -4 penalty as well, so that attack suffers a total penalty of -6.

Whips & Lariats

Besides making big red welts, whips and lariats can be used to entangle and trip a fellow too. Doing either is an opposed roll of the attacker's *fightin': whip* or *fightin': lariat* skill versus the opponent's *Nimbleness*.

A character can break out of an average whip or lariat with an Incredible (11) *Strength* roll, ruining the weapon in the process. Otherwise, she has to just plain wriggle her way out of it. This is an opposed *Nimbleness* roll versus the attacker's skill with the weapon.

The Marshal should feel free to apply modifiers according to the situation. Obviously, if your lassoed character is being dragged behind a motorcycle (ouch!), it's going to be a bit tougher to break free than it might normally be.

Blowin' Things All to Hell

Vamoosin'

It's not much fun getting shot, stabbed, or bitten by some rabid mutie with an overbite. When the horse apples are really about to hit the hover fan, you might want to duck.

The TN to hit a character already assumes he's doing a decent job of being where the fangs, bullets, or rusty blades aren't. But if he wants to, a brainer in need can try a little harder not to get hit. This is an "active defense" as opposed to your hero's normal "passive defense." That sounds kind of technical though, so in typical *Deadlands* style, we call it "vamoosin'."

After your character's been hit, but before damage is resolved, you can throw away your highest remaining Action Card to vamoose. If you've got a card up your sleeve, that's your highest. Otherwise, this is the only time an Action Card lets you act before it's your turn.

Now make a *dodge* or *fightin'* Aptitude roll. *Dodge* is used against ranged attacks, and *fightin'* against hand-to-hand. The TN for the bad guy to hit you is now the greater of either his normal TN or your *dodge* or *fightin'* roll.

The aggressoid who made the attack can't spend chips or do anything else to affect your hombre's vamoose. Once your hero's made his attack, spent any Fate Chips (see Chapter Six), and used any special abilities, that's his total. Your vamoose must then beat that total. If it does, whoosh. If it doesn't, welcome to a world o' hurt, friend.

To make up for breaking our precious rules, your character actually has to do something to represent the vamoose. If he's dodging, he needs to jump behind cover or throw himself to the ground. In hand-to-hand combat, a vamoosin' character has to give ground by backing up 1 yard, or he must subtract –4 from his roll.

A cannibal with an ax wants to hack Teller into two hunks of meat. He swings, gets a whopping 15, and pegs Teller smack in his blonde beanie.

Teller's player, Jay, thinks about it for a moment, cleverly weighing the odds, and decides to try a vamoose. Jay rolls Teller's *fightin'* and gets a 16. Teller gets a hair cut, but fortunately not the kind that bleeds and leaves him a vegetable!

Hit Location

Before you can start rolling handfuls of damage dice, you need to see where the attack actually hit (as in what body part, brainer, not what burnt-out town the poor schmuck's standing in). You also need to know if the area you pegged was covered by anything, like a wall, a table, or armor. Fortunately, we handle all this with one simple roll on the Hit Location Table.

Roll 1d20 on the table below whenever the Marshal tells you you've scored a hit. Roll another die when arms or legs are hit. An odd roll tags the left limb, and even hits the right. Simple, huh?

The Hit Location Table works best with humans and things that like to think they're human, but it can also be used for critters with a little tinkering for extra arms, legs, heads, or whatever. The Marshal may use a special chart for really weird varmints, but this one works most of the time.

Gizzards are all the target's vital parts, by the way, like the all-important groin, heart, lungs, liver, and all those other messy parts the body needs to keep walking and talking. Consider the gizzards part of the guts when applying wounds and wound modifiers. Hits here just cause extra damage (keep reading, friend).

Hit Location

1d20	Location
1-4	Legs
5-9	Lower Guts
10	Gizzards
11-14	Arms
15-19	Upper Guts
20	Noggin

Modifiers

Here are a few modifiers to make attacks hit just where they ought to. Apply these directly to the hit location roll.

Modifiers

Modifier	Situation
+1/-1	Per attack-roll raise
+2	When *fightin'*
+2	Height advantage when *fightin'*
+2	Point blank when *shootin'*

Raises

Every raise on an attack roll lets the shooter adjust the hit location by ±1 point up or down. This way, a good shooter is more likely to get a killing blow to the guts or noggin. Sometimes you don't want to add the bonus because it might actually make you miss due to cover. You don't have to use the bonus if you don't want to.

Fightin'

The really nifty thing about this chart is that it starts at the legs and works its way up. Adding +2 to the die roll puts most hand-to-hand hits in the guts, head, or arms where they should be.

Height

You can also add +2 to the roll if one character has a height advantage over another in a fight, such as if one fellow is on a horse taking a saber swing at some sodbuster on foot.

Point-Blank Range

Point-blank range is used when one character is holding a gun on another, using him like a shield, holding him hostage, or shooting over a table they're both sitting at. In general, the gun should be only a few feet away to count this modifier. This means that when a hostage tries to break free, his captor is more likely to shoot the victim in the guts or his flailing arms than in the pinky toe. Occasionally you might want to subtract this modifier—such as when someone shoots somebody *under* a table.

Hit Locations and Goons

180

The Marshal usually only keeps track of wounds for really nasty cretins and important bad guys. She uses a simplified system for keeping track of hordes of goons, as we explain in her supersecret, ultra-neato portion of the book you can't read.

Head & Gizzard Hits

We'll tell you more about the head and gizzards later on, but we like to repeat things. No, really, we like to repeat things.

Hits to the head let the attacker roll an extra 2 damage dice. Hits to the gizzards give 1 extra die. These are added to his final damage total just like any other damage die.

Cover

Smart survivors get behind things when a firefight breaks out. Barrels, boxes, and other cover don't scream as much as a gunslinger who catches a 10mm round in the kneecap.

Deadlands uses the Hit Location Table to figure out whether an attack hits the hero or the cover he's hiding behind.

How, you ask? Easy, we say. Simply roll the attack normally. If it hits, roll on the Hit Location Table to see where. If that part of the target's body is covered by something, it hits the cover instead. If it's ambiguous, the Marshal should roll a die. Odd, the body part was covered. Even, it wasn't.

Using cover is very important to staying alive in *Deadlands*. That's why it's important you tell the Marshal *exactly* what your character is doing, so he can figure out if the hero should get the benefits of cover or not. If your brainer is hiding behind a corner and exposing only his head and arm, tell the Marshal. That way when some scav takes a potshot at him, the round might hit the wall instead of your hero.

Upper & Lower Guts

Since the torso is so large, the Hit Location Table is broken up into lower and upper guts, even though both locations count as one area for purposes of wounding (explained later). This way, if your character is behind a bar and a shot hits his lower guts, you know it's going into the bar instead of his innards.

Gizzards

When "gizzards" is rolled on the Hit Location Table, it means the victim got hit somewhere important.

Since gizzards could be anywhere in the torso, a hit there counts if either the upper or lower guts was unprotected. Only if both are covered does a hit to the gizzards hit the cover.

Prone Targets

A biker lying on his beer-belly is much harder to hit than a zombie standing in the street.

When you make a successful attack roll against a prone target, roll hit location normally. Unless the attack hits the arms, upper guts, or noggin, it's a miss.

Blowin' Things All to Hell

Armor

Armor blocks or reduces the damage a round does. That's why we cleverly grouped weapon damage values by die types.

For characters, Traits above the human norm go from a d12 to a d12+2, then d12+4, and so on. Damage dice work a bit differently. After a d12, the next die type is a d20. This lets us assign weapon damages to general categories as shown on the table below.

Damage Steps

Die Type	Weapon Types
d4	Light clubs, small knives
d6	Arrows, heavy clubs, pistols, large knives
d8	Rifles, sabers
d10	Sniper rifles, flamethrowers
d12	Small artillery
d20	Grenades, cannon rounds

Reducing Damage

When bullets, knives, or anything else go through an obstacle, they lose some of their energy. The thicker and tougher the obstacle, the more damage is absorbed. These obstacles have a rating that tells you how to handle an attack that hits it.

Positive numbers represent heavier armor. Each level reduces the die type of damage by one step. An attack that uses d20s (like dynamite) is reduced to d12s by a single level of Armor. Two levels of Armor drops the damage to d10s, and so on.

If the die type is dropped below a d4, drop the number of dice instead. An attack reduced to 0d4 does no damage.

A 3d6 bullet that goes through something with an armor value of 1, for instance, is reduced to 3d4. A 3d6 bullet that hits something with an armor of 2 is reduced to 2d4.

Light Armor

A negative number such as -2 means the armor is light protection such as leather hides or thick winter clothes. Armor -4 is heavier, such as boiled leather. Deduct this number directly from the damage total.

For instance, a 14 point attack that hits a savage wearing thick leather (-4) does 10 points. Get it? Good.

Deflection

If there's a little space between a target and the cover, such as a hero behind a wall, roll a die. Even, the round is deflected and doesn't hit the character. Odd, it hits the hero but reduces the damage as we just described.

Armor in Hand-to-Hand

Against hand-to-hand attacks, reduce the weapon's die type (not the character's *Strength*) when determining armor effects. If a character or critter isn't using a weapon, reduce the damage dice of its claws or teeth just as if they were weapons.

In the rare cases a critter has no additional damage dice besides its *Strength*, it simply cannot penetrate anything with an Armor value of 1 or more. Occasionally, the Marshal may rule big creatures can cause nonlethal *brawlin'* damage, even to heavily armored targets.

Armor-Piercing Ammunition

"Armor-piercing" ammunition reduces the Armor level by its value. Thus a weapon with AP 3 ammunition reduces a target with 6 levels of Armor to level 3. Reducing armor to a negative number has no additional effect on damage.

AP ammo doesn't expand and cause as much damage as regular bullets against unarmored targets, however. When used against targets in light or not armor, reduce the damage by one die (not die type).

Common Armor Levels

The table below lists some obstacles and their Armor levels. Armor levels higher than 6 are common on military vehicles. Weapons must use AP ammunition to penetrate these targets.

Armor

Armor	Material
-2	Light leather, heavy cloth
-4	Thick leather, hides
1	Wood less than 1" thick
2	1-3" of solid wood, tin
3	4-6" of solid wood, thin metal
4	A small tree, bricks, a pan
5	A large tree, armored boxcar
6	Inch-thick steel plate
7	Ghost steel
8+	Thick metal, 21st-century steel

Blowin' Things All to Hell

Bleedin' & Squealin'

Once you've hit your target, you need to know how big a hole you put in it. Whether you sank an artillery shell into some ornery critter or buried your battle-ax in its backside, figuring damage is handled in the same way.

Once you've figured out where an attack hits, it's time to roll the damage dice. Every weapon in *Deadlands* has a listing for "damage." This is the number of dice you roll whenever you score a hit.

Don't read this roll like a normal Trait or Aptitude check. Damage dice are always *added* together. You can still reroll any Aces and add them to the final total, however.

Firearms have fixed damage, such as 3d6 for large-caliber pistols. When you've hit your target, roll this many dice.

Weapons that rely on muscle—like arrows, spears, or knives—have fixed damage dice to which you add the result of a regular *Strength* check. Roll the weapon's dice and add them to a normal *Strength* roll. This way a character with 4d6 *Strength* should usually do more damage than one with 1d6 *Strength*.

Tasha rams her spear through a zombie's thigh. She does her *Strength* plus the spear's damage. Her *Strength* is 3d10. Her spear does 2d6.

She gets a 4, 5, and 9 on her *Strength* roll for a total of 9 (it's a normal Trait roll, remember?) Her 2d6 roll is a 6 and a 1. She rerolls the Ace and gets another 5 for a total of 12. The spear's damage (12) and her *Strength* roll (9) is 21. Ouch! Zombie on a stick. Tastes like chicken!

Noggins & Gizzards

A hit to a vital spot causes more trouble than a hit to the little finger.

Whenever a character is hit in the gizzards, add 1 extra die to the damage roll. A hit to the noggin adds 2 extra dice.

The die type is the same as whatever other dice you're rolling. For hand-to-hand weapons, use the weapon's die type.

Tasha puts a hubcap into a mutie's melon. Her *Strength* is 3d10, the hubcap's damage is 1d6. She scores a hit to the head, which increases her damage to her *Strength* roll plus 3d6.

Size Matters

(Ahem.) Once you have your final damage total, tell the Marshal. For every full multiple of your target's Size you do in damage, your attack causes 1 wound. As always, remember to round down any fractions.

Most humans have a Size of 6, but critters vary considerably. Unless you've taken the *scrawny* or *big 'un* Hindrance, or the *brawny* Edge, your character has a Size of 6 as well.

Wounds

Everyone—scavvies, critters, and mutants alike—can take the same number of wounds in each body area: five to be exact. How much damage it takes to cause a wound is another matter.

Most survivors can shrug off a single wound, but more than that starts causing a whole lot of trouble. Check out another of our famous tables to get a better picture of what we're talking about.

Wound Severities

Wound Level	Description
1	Light
2	Heavy
3	Serious
4	Critical
5	Maimed

Light wounds are bruises, shallow but irritating cuts, and muscle strains.

Heavy wounds are sprains, deep but nonthreatening cuts, or multiple bruises.

Serious wounds encompass fractured or broken bones or deep and bloody cuts.

Critical wounds are compound fractures, internal bleeding, or life-threatening cuts across major arteries.

Maimed is, well, maimed. If a character's wounds reach the maimed mark in his guts or noggin, he's kicking buckets, pushing daisies, buying farms, and the like. You get the idea. If a leg or arm becomes maimed, it's severed, crushed, burned to a charred stump, or whatever. Another wound level beyond maimed to a limb means it cannot be healed by medicine or even magic. It could be *replaced* by very powerful technology or magic, however. Such wonders are rare, but they do exist—as does resurrection, or so it's rumored.

Blowin' Things All to Hell

Marking Wounds

Deadlands character sheets make it easy to track wounds. Attach colored paper clips to your sheet to keep track of wound levels. The clip's color tells how bad the wound is in each area.

Wound Key

Type	Clip Color
Light	White
Heavy	Yeller
Serious	Green
Critical	Red
Maimed	Black

For Wind, slide a single clip down the chart until you hit 0. If the Wind is negative, just slide the clip back up the other way to keep track.

Wound Effects

Now things get a little trickier. You need to keep track of damage in six different locations: head, guts, right arm, left arm, left leg, and right leg. Wounds taken to the gizzards and upper and lower guts go to the guts area. We break them up only to help figure extra damage (for the gizzards) and hit locations. The character sheet on pages 62 and 63 has an area for you to keep track of your hero's pain and suffering.

Wounds are only added together when they're taken in the same location. For instance, a character who takes a light wound to the right arm in one round and a heavy wound in the same arm later would then have a serious wound in that arm. If a character takes a light wound to the head and then takes a heavy wound to his leg, they aren't added together.

A character can't be killed by wounds to the arms or legs. She can take enough Wind to put her out of action, but she can't die until she bleeds to death or someone plugs her in the head or guts.

Blowin' Things All to Hell

Wound Modifiers

Wounds really aren't much fun, especially if you're on the receiving end. Blood drips in your eyes, broken fingers make it hard to yank triggers, and crunchy ankles make it a real pain to run from angry varmints.

As you might have guessed, the pain and suffering that result from wounds can really affect a character's dice rolls. The exact penalties for each level of wounds are shown on the table below.

Wound penalties are never subtracted from "effect" totals such as damage or magic effects, but they do apply to everything else, including *Quickness* checks and *Strength*-based damage rolls.

Wound Effects

Wound	Modifier
Light	-1
Heavy	-2
Serious	-3
Critical	-4
Maimed (limbs)	-5

Wound penalties aren't cumulative. The modifier depends on the highest-level wound your hero has suffered. If he has a light and a serious wound, for instance, subtract the penalty for the serious wound (-3) from all his action rolls.

Maimed Effects

Where the wound is doesn't really matter for penalty purposes unless it's a maimed result. A maimed arm can't hold or use a weapon or any other device. Go figure.

A single maimed leg reduces the character's Pace to half. Two maimed legs means the character can only crawl a single yard per round (and maybe it's time to retreat, friend).

Maiming wounds to the head or torso mean the hero's dead. Thanks for playing.

Tasha takes a heavy wound to her arm and a light wound to her leg. She would normally suffer a -2 to her action totals. Fortunately for her, she has the *thick-skinned* Edge, meaning she can reduce her penalty by -1 level. She must only subtract -1 from her rolls.

Blowin' Things All to Hell

Stun

Another word on all this pain and suffering business. Whenever a character takes damage, there's a chance he might miss the next action or two kissing his missing finger or holding in his entrails. It's funny what massive amounts of pain can do to even the hardest hombres.

When your hero takes damage, he has to make a "stun" check. Stun checks are made by rolling the character's *Vigor* against the wound's level, as shown on the combined Stun and Recovery Table. Don't forget to apply your hombre's wound penalty as well.

If you make the roll, nothing happens. If you fail, your character's stunned and can only limp a few yards and cry like a baby until he makes a recovery check (see below).

Unless he's already stunned, your character needs to make a stun check every time he takes a wound. Taking another wound while you're already stunned has no further effect as far as stunning goes, though it may make recovery harder if the wound is greater than one suffered previously.

Recovery Checks

Your hero must try to recover from being stunned. He can't choose otherwise. This is called a "recovery check," and it takes an entire action. A recovery roll is made just like a stun check, except the difficulty is your highest current wound level.

One last thing. Your character goes unconscious immediately if you go bust on any stun check. He stays down 1d6 hours or until someone makes a Fair (5) *medicine* roll to revive him.

Stun & Recovery

Wound Level	TN
Wind	3
Light	5
Heavy	7
Serious	9
Critical	11
Maimed	13

Tasha rolls to avoid being stunned by her heavy wound. She needs a 7, and must subtract -1 from her *Vigor* roll (remember, she's *thick-skinned*). She gets an 8—just enough—and keeps on fighting.

Wind

It just keeps getting better.

Every time your character takes a wound, she also takes Wind. Wind is shock, fatigue, and—in the case of wounds—trauma associated with losing bits and pieces of your favorite body parts.

For every wound level your character suffers, she also takes 1d6 Wind. Like damage, this roll is open-ended. That means it's possible for a shot that only causes minor damage (a light wound) to actually put your hombre down for a while because of an unlucky Wind roll.

Gettin' Winded

When a character is reduced to 0 Wind or lower, he becomes "Winded." This doesn't necessarily mean he passes out, but he does feel like crawling into a hole and dying, or curling up into a ball and whining like a baby.

Winded characters might lose consciousness for a few minutes, fall to the ground, trying to catch their breath, or collapse from sheer fatigue and exhaustion. It really depends on the situation. Most of the time, characters Winded from wounds simply collapse into the nearest corner and vainly try to stop their bleeding and spurting.

Winded characters get no cards and can't perform any actions unless the Marshal feels like letting them whisper or crawl a short ways at the end of the round. On the plus side, Winded characters generally fall by the wayside and don't get beaten on anymore.

Characters who continue to take Wind after they run out of it might die. This is usually caused by things like bleeding or drowning.

Every time a character's negative Wind is equal to his starting Wind level, he takes another wound to the guts. A character with 12 Wind, for example, takes a wound when his Wind reaches -12, another when it reaches -24, and so on.

Tasha's taken a heavy wound with 7 Wind. She starts with 16. Another hit to her arm, though it only causes a light wound, ends up causing 9 Wind. Tasha curses as her Wind hits 0. She falls down, holding her arm in pain, and crawls out of harm's way. She stays there until someone comes and helps her or she recovers at least 1 point of Wind.

Blowin' Things All to Hell

More Pain & Sufferin'

There are lots of ways to buy the farm. What follows are a few more ways to maim and dismember the bad guys—and probably a few good guys as well.

Massive Damage

Before you go reading about falling, burning, and blowing up, here's how to handle damage that affects several body areas at once.

First, figure out how many total wounds a victim takes, then roll hit location for each wound. Wounds applied to the same locations add as usual.

Since attacks that cause massive damage don't generally penetrate well, head and gizzard hits are ignored. Massive damage that might penetrate all those juicy parts (like shrapnel) is described in the weapon's special rules.

Each Armor value reduces a wound level. Say a brainer takes 5 wounds to the head. If he's wearing a helmet with an Armor value of 2, he only takes 3 wounds.

For light armor, roll a d6. If the d6 roll is less than the protection the armor provides, 1 wound is eliminated. A fellow with light armor on his head (Armor value -2) has to roll a 2 or less on a d6 to soak 1 wound.

Only after all damage has been assigned can a character cancel the wounds with Fate Chips.

Bleedin'

Serious damage is likely to start a fellow bleeding like a sieve. Whenever a character takes a serious wound, he begins bleeding, losing -1 Wind per round. Critically wounded characters bleed -2 Wind per round. Severed (maimed) limbs bleed -3 Wind per round.

Every time a character's negative Wind total is equal to a multiple of his starting Wind level, he takes another wound to the guts. See **Healin'** (page 104) to find out how to stop that messy arterial spray from getting in your eyes.

Explosives

Concussion damage from explosions is treated as massive damage. Worn armor which is completely sealed, or armor due to cover which completely shields the target from the blast (like a wall) reduces the damage die type normally before wounds are applied.

Brawlin'

Certain kinds of attacks, like *fightin': brawlin'*, can be used to put someone down without killing them. When one fellow hits another with his bare hands or a light club such as a chair leg or a bottle, he rolls his damage dice (usually *Strength*, plus 1d4 if he's using a light club). The target then makes a *Vigor* roll. If the attacker wins, the victim takes the difference in Wind.

Heavy clubs like pistol butts, ax handles, or entire chairs allow the attacker to choose whether she would like to cause lethal or nonlethal damage. If she just wants to cause Wind and try to knock her opponent out without causing serious injury, she can do so. Or she can bash the other fellow's brains out to her heart's content.

Drownin'

It's a lousy way to go, but it happens.

Every round a character swims in rough water, his first action must be a *swimmin'* roll. The TN depends on the water as shown below. If the swimmer doesn't make the TN, he takes the difference in Wind.

A character without the *swimmin'* Aptitude is in big trouble. When he's in *any* kind of water over his noggin, he has to go through the steps above.

Drownin'

Water	TN
Swift creek	3
Rapid river	5
Rough ocean	7
Stormy seas	9

Fallin'

If it's tall, folks are going to want to climb it—and they're probably going to fall too.

A character takes 1d6+5 damage for every 5 yards fallen, up to a maximum of 20d6+100. Wounds are applied like we told you under **Massive Damage** above, though armor doesn't protect unless it specifically says otherwise.

Landing in water reduces the damage by half or cancels it entirely if the character makes a Fair (5) *Nimbleness* roll. With an Onerous (7) *Nimbleness* roll, landing on something soft reduces the damage by half. (Be reasonable here. Falls from great heights are just plain fatal.)

Blowin' Things All to Hell

Fire

Things burn: buildings, fallout shelters, forests, and heroes too stupid to stay out of those things when they catch fire. Characters in dense smoke have to make an Onerous (7) *Vigor* check during their first action each round. A wet cloth over the mouth and nose (or similar makeshift protection) adds +2 to the roll.

If the character fails the *Vigor* roll, she takes the difference between her roll and the Target Number in Wind. Should she happen to fall unconscious, she continues to lose Wind in this way every round until she dies.

The damage applied to a character who is actually on fire depends on just how big the flames are. A small fire, such as a burning sleeve, causes 1d10 damage at the beginning of every turn to the area on fire. A larger fire causes 2d10 to the affected areas. Use the **Massive Damage** rules if you're not sure which parts are on fire. A character totally consumed by flames takes 3d10 damage, with the wounds applied to every area at once.

Sticky fire like napalm burns for 1d6 minutes and can usually only be put out by depriving it of oxygen. Good luck!

A brainer can put himself out by smothering the fire with cloth or by doing the old "stop, drop, and roll" tango. Putting out a normal fire takes an Onerous (7) *Nimbleness* roll. Sticky fire has a TN of Incredible (11).

Ghost Storms

The ghost-rock bombs devastated everything within their blast radii when they first fell on September 23, 2081, leaving phenomena know as ghost storms behind. Most of the storms have abated now, except for a 10-yard thick "wall" surrounding ground zero, the 5-mile radius around the impact point of a bomb.

From ground zero out to 30 miles or so causes radiation poisoning (see **Radiation**).

Passing through the walls of the remaining storms is more dangerous. Whenever a character does so, the Marshal pulls a card. The value of the card (check the Traits & Coordinations Table on page 28 for this) is the amount of spiritual damage the character takes. The Marshal rolls the damage, and the character makes a *Spirit* roll. The difference is read as actual damage to the guts. Armor does not protect against this.

On a red Joker, the Marshal rolls no damage. On a black Joker, the Marshal rolls 5d12 damage, and the character develops a mutation.

Radiation

It's a Doomsayer's best friend, but that warm glow coming from the ruined cities is a sure killer for everyone else.

Here are some quick rules for low-level "background" radiation. Remember that the bombs dropped in *Deadlands: Hell on Earth* were made of irradiated ghost rock, so the energy produced is a weird mix of supernatural and radioactive power. That means you may see much stranger things than these simple rules in certain blast zones.

A character must make a *Vigor* roll every hour spent in a radioactive area. Within 5 miles of ground zero the TN is 9, and between 5 and 30 miles is a TN of 5. Lesser sources, such as crossing a stream that runs through a blast zone, have a TN of 3.

If the roll is made, the character suffers no harmful effects. If the roll is failed, the hero loses 1 Wind that cannot be recovered except by magic or a day after a scrubbing shower in clean water. On a bust, the character has radiation poisoning and picks up a bad case of the glows. That's the *ailin': chronic* Hindrance, brainer.

Blowin' Things All to Hell

Healin'

A fellow using his intestines as a belt probably ought to see a sawbones. With a little luck, a good doctor can shove his squirmy insides back in his gut and sew him shut in time for chow.

Sawbones

Wind loss is easy to get rid of. On a Foolproof (3) *medicine* roll of any kind, someone can bandage scrapes or give the sufferer some water, restoring all lost Wind. This takes about a minute.

Real wounds are trickier. A *medicine* roll can be made up to one hour after an injury. Sawbones call this the "golden hour."

A character with the *medicine: general* Aptitude can heal light and heavy wounds. Only a sawbones with *medicine: surgery* can heal more severe wounds.

The doctor has to roll once for each area wounded in the golden hour. If successful, the roll reduces the area's wounds by one level. The TN and the time it takes to heal someone

depends on the wound level. Maimed limbs cannot be healed by normal means, but the doc can still try to stop the bleeding.

If the treatment isn't started within the "golden hour," a wound can only be healed by time (or certain arcane processes). Doctors really can't do a whole lot for a broken bone that's surrounded by swollen tissue, or a gash that's already started to heal on it's own.

Going bust when trying to heal a wound or Wind causes an extra wound level to that area.

Natural Healin'

Heroes recover Wind naturally at the rate of 1 per minute of rest. That means they have to sit, drink a little water, and put some bandages on their scrapes.

A wounded character makes a healing roll every 5 days by making a *Vigor* roll against the difficulties listed on the Healing Table. Add +2 if under a doctor's care.

If the roll succeeds, the wound improves by +1 level. The *Vigor* roll is made for each area. A character with wounds to an arm and his guts would roll twice, possibly improving the condition of each location by +1 step.

Remember that both upper guts, lower guts, and gizzards all count as the "guts" area. Roll once for the entire guts, but roll for each wounded arm or leg separately.

Healin' Difficulties

Wound Level	TN	Time
Wind	3	5 minutes
Light	5	10 minutes
Heavy	7	20 minutes
Serious	9	1 hour
Critical	11	1d6 hours
Maimed (limbs)	13	1d6+1 hours

Teller is caught in an explosion and suffers a heavy wound to the head and a light wound to the arm. He also loses 8 Wind.

Doc Bose comes around within the "Golden Hour" to lend aid. Doc needs a 7 to heal Teller's head. He gets a 9, and the wound is reduced to light.

Doc needs a 5 to patch up the light wound to Teller's arm, but he goes bust, so our hero's light wound becomes a heavy.

Doc lets Teller recover Wind naturally.

Blowin' Things All to Hell

Driver's Ed

Now you know how to shoot, stab, drown, and blow up your fellow human beings. Let's focus all that destructive energy on vehicles.

Given all the nasty critters roaming the wastes, hoofing it from place to place is not the brightest of ideas. Although it's been 13 years since civilization went down the toilet, there are still a good number of vehicles in service. Most are held together with baling wire and a generous application of duct tape, but they move. We're going to show you how to drive them and, when need be, blow them up.

A vehicle moves on the Action Cards of its driver. Divide the vehicle's Pace as evenly as possible between the driver's cards. This works best for situations where many of the characters are on foot. If you are playing out a chase, it's easier to have each vehicle move its full Pace on the driver's first Action Card.

All ground vehicles may make one turn of up to 45° each round. Each turn made after that requires a *drivin'* roll and is a short task. The TN for this roll is the vehicle's Turn number, a measure of how maneuverable the rig is (see the gear list). A driver can attempt to turn again, but each turn after the second in the same round adds +2 to the TN. A hot dog can try a single turn of up to 90° but this adds +4 to the TN.

If the roll is failed, the vehicle moves ahead its normal Pace for that action and skids half that distance in the direction opposite the attempted turn. If the driver goes bust, the vehicle is out of control and may even flip (Marshal's call).

The Marshal should feel free to adjust these TNs to fit rain, difficult terrain, and the like.

Do You Know How Fast You Were Going?

Unlike pedestrians, vehicles can't go from a dead stop to their full Pace in a single round. A vehicle's Pace is broken up into four brackets: Dead Stop, Quarter Speed, Half Speed, and Full Speed.

These are exactly what they sound like. Dead Stop means the vehicle isn't moving, Quarter Speed covers any movement up to one fourth of the vehicle's full Pace, and so on. The Paces listed for vehicles in the Chapter Four are maximum Paces.

Vehicles can accelerate +1 Pace bracket per round and decelerate up to -2 Pace brackets. The driver can change the vehicle's Pace bracket on any of his actions, but he may only change it once per round.

Driving Modifiers

Condition	TN Modifier
Quarter Pace	–2
Half Pace	0
Full Pace	+2
Each turn after the second	+2
90° turn	+4

Crashin'

Every once in a while, a rig whacks into something it shouldn't have. When this happens, the vehicle takes 1d6 damage for every 5 miles an hour (12 Pace) it was moving. If the collision is between two moving vehicles, use their relative speed to figure the damage. Two buggies moving 24 yards per round collide head-on for a relative speed of 48 and 4d6 damage.

Armor works differently in collisions. Instead of reducing the die *type*, it reduces the number of dice. Subtract -1d6 for each level of Armor.

Kaboom!

Vehicles have Durability ratings instead of wounds. This is a measure of how much punishment they can take before they stop working. Damage to a vehicle is subtracted directly from this number, and when it reaches 0 it's time to put the rig up on cinder blocks.

There's a catch though. Unlike people, vehicles have a lot of empty space in them that a bullet can pass through without hurting anything. To reflect this, damage from small-arms fire (pistols, rifles, shotguns, most machine guns) is divided by 10 (round down) before being subtracted from Durability. A shot *can* do no damage. If so, it just doesn't hit anything vital.

Damage from explosives and large caliber weapons like a 30mm auto-cannon is just subtracted directly from Durability. All damage, regardless of size, is adjusted by a vehicle's armor rating.

You may have noticed the vehicles in Chapter 4 have two numbers listed for Durability. The first is the vehicle's total Durability. The number after the slash is its "damage increment." As the vehicle accumulates damage, a modifier of -1 is applied to all *drivin'* rolls for each multiple of this increment the rig has taken. A vehicle with a 50/10 Durability for instance, takes 50 points of damage to destroy. If it takes 20 points of damage, all *drivin'* rolls made for it suffer a -2 penalty.

Posse: 106

Chapter Six:
Fate Chips
& Bounties

Fate is a fickle bitch. Sometimes she smiles on you, and sometimes she spits the nastiest thing you've ever seen right on your head.

In *Deadlands,* characters can store up a little fate to save their kiesters in dire situations. Fate, in this case, is represented by poker chips.

The Marshal starts the first game session with a pot of 10 blue, 25 red, and 50 white chips. The mix doesn't change, except under very special circumstances which we'll tell the Marshal about later on.

At the start of each game session, every player gets to draw three Fate Chips at random from the pot. (That means no looking. Got it?) The Marshal also gets to draw three chips that he can use for all the extras and bad guys.

Players also get rewarded with Fate Chips during play. We'll tell you all about that next.

Chips can be saved between game sessions. Just write down how many your character had at the last game and get them out of the pot before anyone draws their new ones next time.

One last rule. You can never have more than 10 chips at one time. If you earn a chip and you already have 10, you can discard a lower-value chip to keep the new one if you want. Otherwise, you have to discard it.

Earning Chips

Let's talk specifically about how you earn precious Fate Chips. The Marshal's going to toss them to you when you do one of three things: roleplay, solve problems, or make him chuckle.

Roleplaying

This is where your Hindrances start to shine. Sure you get points for them when you make your character, but no one's going to *make* you roleplay or suffer from those Hindrances later on. The Marshal might if she thinks of it, but truthfully, running a roleplaying game occupies enough brainpower that she may often forget about all your character's problems. So we're going to make *you* remember.

Roleplay your Hindrances, and you get chips. The more severe your disadvantage, the higher-value chip you get. It's that simple.

Say your Templar has taken a vow to kill every one of Throckmorton's goons he can get his sword into. If he hears about Black Hats nearby, he has to go do something about it. The Marshal should

More on Roleplaying

Sometimes you might roleplay something that isn't covered by one of your Hindrances. Maybe your Doomsayer isn't particularly brave or heroic, but when he hears a weeping mother's tale of her child being abducted, he feels he must act.

That's okay. The Marshal should still reward you just as if your character actually had the *heroic* Hindrance. The reward is for roleplaying, after all, and that might not always fit the Hindrances you chose. It's best if it does, but don't feel too confined by them. Don't decide your hero can't be a hero just because he isn't *heroic*.

If it becomes a habit—your hero is always running off to save folks—then you should pick up the *heroic* Hindrance and make it official. Otherwise, just accept that the rules don't always fit the situation and that your Marshal wants to reward you for helping create an interesting and memorable story.

Problem Solving

The Marshal also rewards those who overcome the many obstacles in *Deadlands*. This includes defeating monsters, solving puzzles, and even working out the inevitable complications that arise when a bunch of hardened warriors with different attitudes adventure together.

Again, the chip the Marshal rewards you with depends on how great a problem you solved or clue you found. Find a journal that holds a few key clues, and you can expect a white or red chip. Help a town ward off a biker raid and you can expect a blue chip to fall from the sky.

The Marshal's Whim

The last occasion a Marshal might give you chips is (drum roll, please): whenever he feels like it. Maybe he likes the way your gunslinger stylishly met his opponent in the street at high noon, grumbling a cool line in an *overawe* attempt. Or maybe you said something that's got the whole group in stitches.

Sometimes your character just does something clever, like duct-taping a flashlight to his assault rifle when exploring a dark ruin. That's worth a white chip the first time someone does it.

When these things happen, maybe, just maybe, chips could fall from the sky, just for helping everyone have a good time.

And *that's* what it's all about.

chuck a white chip your way. When your Templar finds the goons and realizes he's hopelessly outnumbered, you earn a red chip for talking the rest of the posse into sticking around at their own peril. Finally, when it looks like your posse is losing, the hero might net a blue chip for not running away, even when death is imminent. The more inconvenience it causes you and your companions, the greater the reward.

Abusing Hindrances

Here's the sweet part: You can't. If you never play a Hindrance, you never get chips. It's okay if you got points for it earlier. That was really just built into the system anyway.

The other extreme is if you milk a Hindrance for all it's worth. Say your Law Dog has a *hankerin'* for alcohol, and you say he drinks constantly so you can beg for chips.

The Marshal might fall for this trick a few times, but she's only supposed to reward you when your character's Hindrance is truly an inconvenience. If your Law Dog gets drunk, who cares? If he's drunk when the scavvies attack, you might get some chips just before your hero bites the dust. Congratulations!

Fate Chips & Bounties

Calling on Fate

Great. So now your gunslinger's suffering from chronic tuberculosis, you figured out how to kill the blast shadow, and the group's rolling around on the floor, laughing like idiots. You've got a stack of chips in front of you. What do you do with them? We'll tell you.

A character can use his Fate Chips in one of three ways: to improve Trait and skill checks, to save his skin by canceling wounds, and to trade them in for Bounty Points (keep reading).

Trait & Aptitude Checks

White Fate Chips give the character +1 extra die per chip spent, just as if he had an extra point of Aptitude or Coordination. The player can spend these chips one at a time until he's happy with the result or decides not to spend any more (or runs out of chips).

Red Fate Chips let you roll a bonus die and add it to your highest current die. The downside is that using a red chip for a Trait or Aptitude check gives the Marshal a draw from the Fate Pot. Only one red Fate Chip can ever be spent on a single action.

Blue chips are just like red chips, except they don't give the Marshal any draws. Good deal, huh? Only one blue chip may ever be spent on a single action.

Spending Chips on Damage

You can't spend chips on damage, but there's a slight loophole you can use. See, damage in hand-to-hand combat is a weapon's fixed dice *plus* a regular *Strength* Trait roll. You can use chips on the *Strength* part of the roll (but not on the weapon's dice). The point is, whenever your character can exert a little extra will, you can spend a chip on his Trait or Aptitude roll.

Upping the Ante

When you use chips to improve a Trait or Aptitude roll, you must spend any white chips you care to use first, then a red if you want, and then a blue. You can't spend a red chip and then spend a white to reroll it if you don't like the result. You also can't spend a blue chip and then go back and spend a red or a white. Once the stakes are raised, there's no going back.

Just to be perfectly clear, you can jump right to a blue chip on a roll. You just can't go backward and spend a white or red chip after the blue's been spent.

Going Bust & Fate Chips

There's one big catch to spending chips. You can't spend Fate Chips on a Trait or Aptitude roll once you go bust, even if you have *luck o' the Irish*. Fate turns its back on even the most heroic souls from time to time.

Legend Chips are an exception. You'll find out about these once you adventure for a while. When you do, remember that if you have one of those rare prizes, you can spend it to pick up all your dice and start over from scratch.

By the way, you can't go bust on the *Strength* part of a *fightin'* damage roll. You just add nothing to the weapon's regular damage.

Savin' Your Skin

Fate Chips can also be used to avoid getting your character's noggin or other important parts of his anatomy blown off. Spending a Fate Chip doesn't make wounds "heal" or stop an attack. It just reduces the effect or makes it so it never happened in the first place.

Whenever your character takes damage, you can spend chips to negate some of it. This applies to damage from a single attack. If your hero's shot twice in the same round, you have to reduce each attack separately.

These wounds are negated before any Wind is rolled. If you need to negate Wind (after taking damage from bleeding, drowning, brawling or something else), each level of Fate Chip negates 5 points of Wind as shown below.

Fate & Damage

Chip	Wounds Negated	Wind Negated
White	Up to 1	5
Red	Up to 2	10
Blue	Up to 3	15

Trading Chips

A player can give another player Fate Chips, but it's expensive. The giver has to put one like-colored chip in the pot for every chip he gives another player. The giver should also explain how his hero helps his friend, whether it's by distracting a bad guy or simply offering a few colorful words of encouragement in time of need.

Fate Chips & Bounties

Bounty Points

After your hero tussles with the creepy inhabitants of the Wasted West, he's likely going to get either a whole lot smarter or a whole lot dead. This experience and savvy is represented by Bounty Points. You can use these to raise your character's abilities.

Between game sessions, you can convert your Fate Chips into Bounty Points and use or save them to improve your character. Whites are worth 1 Bounty Point, reds 2, and blues 3. Chips are usually the only way you get Bounty Points, so don't blow them all in the game if you can help it!

Spending Bounties

It's time to tell you how to spend those hard-earned Bounty Points to raise your survivor's Aptitudes, Coordinations, or Traits.

It doesn't take your character any particular amount of time to do so, other than the rate you can acquire and spend your points, but no ability should be raised more than +1 level between game sessions.

Raising Aptitudes

New Aptitude levels cost whatever the new level is. If you want your character's *shootin'* to go from 3 to 4, it costs 4 Bounty Points. You can't "skip" a level and buy level 5 without first buying level 4. Nice try, brainer.

Once an Aptitude gets to level 5, your hero is considered an expert, and it costs twice as many points to raise it again. A level 6 skill costs 12 Bounty Points, level 7 is 14, and so on.

Raising Coordinations

Raising your hero's Coordination in a Trait costs two times the new level. So to go from 4d6 *Strength* to 5d6 would cost 10 points (2 x 5=10). As with Aptitudes, you can't skip a level.

Raising Traits

Traits can be raised as well. The cost is equal to three times the die type of the new level. To go from a d4 to a d6 costs 18 Bounty Points. No skipping die types in between, friend.

You don't have to, but it makes for a better story if you say exactly how your character gets stronger or smarter. Maybe he spends his off hours lifting engine blocks or studying.

JAMES FRANCIS

Fate Chips & Bounties

New Concentrations

You can purchase a new concentration in an Aptitude for 3 Bounty Points. You can't (and wouldn't want to) raise a second concentration as a whole new skill. That would be far more expensive, so this trick saves you a bundle.

Gaining New Aptitudes

So what if you want to buy a new Aptitude after you've made your character?

No problem. You can buy a new Aptitude with Bounty Points. It just costs you 1 point to get the first Aptitude level in that skill as usual.

Most Corporeal Aptitudes don't require training to pick up and start using right away, but some mental Aptitudes do. Use common sense. Your hombre can learn to *scrutinize* on his own, but he can't pick up *professional: law* without some kind of formal training (or a lot of time in front of a Law Dog!). That's when the Marshal might also come up with some time requirements for you. Learning the basics of *ridin'* can be done in a single lesson. If you want to learn to be a junker, you can, but it's going to take a few *years* of study.

The Marshal should judge each request on a case-by-case basis. Don't beat her up over it.

Buying Off Hindrances

Sometimes your character can overcome his sordid past. Maybe he started out a *kid* and now he's full-grown. Or perhaps something made your *one-armed bandit* whole again (don't you hate it when that happens?). Maybe your hero's quest for vengeance against the bandits who murdered his family is finally over. Or you decide a Hindrance you took when you created your character just doesn't fit any more.

No sweat, muchacho. We've got you covered.

A character can buy off a Hindrance by doing two things. The first thing she must do is figure out why or how the Hindrance goes away. The Marshal has to approve of your rationale, and she might require you to buy it off gradually or right away. You and your Marshal need to decide these things based on the storyline and the Hindrance itself.

Once the roleplaying conditions have been met, the character must pay back double the original cost in Bounty Points. From this point on, your character shouldn't usually receive Fate Chip awards for roleplaying the Hindrances.

That's all there is to it. Do you feel all better now? Good. Now let's talk about picking up new personality flaws.

Gaining New Hindrances

Gaining new Hindrances is easier. Lose an arm tussling with a dust devil, and your hero's a *one-armed bandit*. The bad news is your character doesn't gain any points when he acquires it. The good news is she starts receiving Fate Chip awards for roleplaying the handicap immediately.

You can actually choose to pick up new Hindrances, but keep it reasonable. If your hero gets a *hankerin'* for whiskey after a few journeys into the Wasted West, who can blame her? We don't recommend letting a hero *choose* more than 5 points worth of "extra" Hindrances. If things just happen that way (such as phobias from failed *guts* checks), that's another matter.

Gaining New Edges

So you've got a ton of Bounty Points, and you want to buy an Edge. How do you do it?

Normally, the only way to gain new Edges is if something fantastic happens during play. Say your heroine gets a sidekick, or she comes into possession of a valuable piece of hardware, like a hover tank. These events don't cost a thing. They're the reward of playing and surviving.

But say your gunslinger has been hanging around a syker for a while and wants to learn his tricks. He can do it, but it's going to take some time and Bounty Points.

It's tough to make a hard and fast rule for this kind of thing. It might take someone a few weeks to become *keen,* while developing a good *voice* might only take a couple of days. Becoming a syker or Templar should take years. Becoming a Doomsayer really requires only a few months and lots of radiation!

So here's the deal. You can take a new Edge if you have a good roleplaying rationale for it, and your Marshal approves. After that, you have to pay triple the Edge's cost in Bounty Points, and you can only put 1 point per "game week" into the Edge as you develop it. The Marshal might decide to change the time it takes to 1 point per game day, month, week, or whatever she feels makes the most sense. Once you've paid the Bounty Points, the Edge is yours. If you change your mind while investing, too bad. You can't get the points back, but they're still there if you change your mind.

New Powers & Abilities

If your hero has an unusual power, check out the proper section to learn how to improve her abilities or gain new ones.

Puttin' It All Together

Here's how everything works once a fight breaks out. The game is broken down into rounds of 5 seconds each. Each round is composed of a variable number of "segments," represented by Action Cards.

Before the Fight: Everyone who has a chance to be surprised makes a Fair (5) *Cognition* check. Characters caught totally unaware roll against an Incredible (11) TN. Those who fail cannot take actions this round, but may attempt a Fair (5) *guts* roll at the beginning of each new round.

Action Cards

1) Every player makes a *Quickness* check at the beginning of each round. Draw one card for free and another for every success over a TN of 5, up to 5 cards.
2) A black Joker is discarded along with any card held up your sleeve. A red Joker can be used at any time in the round.
3) The Marshal counts down from Ace to Deuce. Each card is called a segment. Order of suits is Spades, Hearts, Diamonds, Clubs. Ties are simultaneous.
4) Your hero can act on each of his Action Cards.

Actions

Actions are either simple, short, or complex. Simple actions effectively take no time and can be performed in conjunction with a short or complex task. Short tasks require one Action Card (Speed 1). Complex tasks require 2 or more (Speed 2 or higher).

Cheat Cards

When an Action Card is called, you can save it for later instead of using it. It can be used at any time in this round or another. You may only have one cheat card. Discard any other Action Cards you do not use.

Interrupting Actions

Cheat cards and red Jokers can be used to interrupt another person's action. With a red Joker, success is automatic. With a cheat card, both characters roll a contest of *Quickness*. The character who gets a raise over the other acts first. If a character fails, he's last. If both characters make the roll but there is no raise (they roll within 1–4 points of each other), the action is simultaneous.

Jokers

If a player draws a red Joker, he gets a draw from the Fate Pot. With a black Joker, the Marshal gets a draw.

Movement

A character divides his Pace over each segment. He can double his movement each segment by running, but this subtracts –4 from any skill rolls made that segment.

Attacking

The TN to hit a target with a ranged weapon is Fair (5) plus the range modifier. The range modifier is found by dividing the range to the target by the weapon's Range Increment and rounding down.

So, TN=5+(Range÷Range Increment).

Hand-to-hand attacks are equal to a TN of 5 plus 1 for each level the opponent has in *fightin'*, plus the weapon's Defensive Bonus if it has one.

So, TN=5+Opponent's *fightin'* Aptitude level+weapon's defensive bonus.

Damage

Damage dice from ranged attacks are added together.

Hand-to-hand damage is the result of a normal *Strength* roll (take the highest die), added to the weapon's damage dice (which are added like ranged attack dice).

Fate Chips and Damage

Any number and combination of Fate Chips can be used to reduce damage. Blue chips eliminate 3 wounds, red chips 2, and white chips 1.

No Man's Land

Chapter Seven:
Doomsayers

In the name of the twisted,
In the image of the deformed,
In the fury of the atom,
In the glow of the bomb,
The new age arose.

So goes one of the canticles of the Cult of Doom, a group of wackos who think the Apocalypse heralded a new breed of humanity.

How did this come to pass? Good question. As with most cults, it centered around one certifiable nutjob who managed to convince a bunch of other nutjobs that he was some kind of prophet.

The story began in 2083 with a wanderer named Silas Rasmussen. He was once a young physics professor at MIT. Unfortunately for the rest of the world, he survived the Apocalypse and staggered around for a few years, trying to get over the whole "the world just got stepped on by the Four Horsemen" concept.

When Silas finally stopped wandering, he realized he'd picked up a fast-moving case of the "glows." That's radiation sickness to you and me, friend. The former professor shrugged his shoulders, decided to make the best of it, and walked smack into the nearest radioactive ruins he could find—in this case, Las Vegas, Nevada.

There Silas found a huge tribe of mutants. Most were bald, missing teeth, deformed, or deranged from the hot zone they called home, but they weren't dying. After a tense first encounter, Silas was welcomed into the community and quickly learned that some of the mutants even had incredible powers. In fact, many of them could absorb radiation as a tasty after-dinner snack to supplement their normal diet of, well, mystery meats.

Silas decided being a mutant with incredible powers was better than being a glowing corpse, so he started experimenting on his new friends. After a few short months (and a few secret dissections), Silas developed powers of his own.

Maybe he's a lunatic, maybe he's deranged from rad sickness, or maybe—just maybe—he's right, but Silas believes mutants are the forerunners of a new race—the next evolution of humanity.

Oh, and he's more than a little mad as well.

Grendel

The ruins of Las Vegas are a Deadland just like most every other city in the world. And in a Deadland, there are more monsters than you can shake a rocket launcher at.

The one most feared by the muties in Las Vegas was a glowing, green, scaly humanoid that lived in the ruined arboretum of the old Tropicana Hotel and Casino. The locals called it Grendel, after the mythical monster that stole from its lair to eat men's flesh—which is just what this monster did too.

Doomsayers

One night, just as his new family was beginning to think Silas was a little too crazy, even for pus-oozing muties, Grendel emerged and cut a bloody swath through a mob gathered to complain about Rasmussen.

Grendel chased the flock through the streets of Las Vegas until Silas emerged and, to everyone's surprise, fired a bolt of sizzling, green energy from his palm. Grendel reeled from the blow, and Silas blasted it again. This time, the blast was so strong it popped the creature's arm like a mouse in a microwave. Grendel howled in pain and retreated to his lair.

Silas blew the smoke off his finger and grinned at the muties. He was their master now.

The Mutant King

The former professor now had tenure with the muties. The powers he developed were incredible. He could blow things up, cook them, make them glow, and so on. Silas also learned to "eat" radiation, cure those with radiation sickness, and even heal flesh.

Silas proclaimed himself the Mutant King and Prophet. It was his duty, he told his subjects, to lead and protect mutants from the "norms" and usher in a new age of humanity. The muties of Las Vegas, who were mostly simple folks thrown out of their old settlements because of their disfigurement, disease, or derangement, liked what they heard and bowed down to their new king. A few thought this was nonsense and mistakenly said so. They stopped doubting Silas' power when their heads exploded.

Over the next few years, Silas declared his teachings and followers the "Cult of Doom." The "doom" business refers to the doom of normals and the rise of mutants. At first, it didn't mean the cult would actually *cause* the doom, just that the "poor" norms were heading down the evolutionary exit ramp.

Silas made the most powerful and intelligent mutants his high priests. Others were sent out as "Doomsayers," missionaries tasked with finding enclaves of mutants and teaching them the ways of the cult. They also recruit any mutants with particularly incredible abilities and send them back to Las Vegas to be studied, used, or made into Doomsayers.

During this time, Silas shared his abilities with his followers. Soon, most every member of the Cult of Doom could fire blasts of radiation, warp metal, heal wounds, and wield many other strange and amazing powers.

Theology

Silas and his Doomsayers worship the powers of radiation and the Apocalypse. Individuals may or may not believe in God. They just think that after the Apocalypse, supernatural radiation is the true master of humanity's destiny.

Marie Curie, Dr. Darius Hellstromme, Albert Einstein, Robert Oppenheimer, and others who worked with radiation, bombs, and irradiated ghost rock are something like revered apostles. The Doomsayers don't worship them, but they do respect them. They're especially excited about the disappearance of Hellstromme. They think he's on a pilgrimage somewhere, and when he returns he'll share some startling and apocalyptic revelation with them.

The Temple o' Doom

Any good cult needs a really big temple. The less gifted mutants of Las Vegas were put to work restoring the old Luxor Hotel and Casino, a mammoth pyramid like those of the ancient Egyptians. Work was completed in 2084, and only a few hundred mutants gave their lives cleaning it of monsters and rebuilding the ruins.

Those who have been to the place say it glows inside and out, and its electrical devices are powered by the cult's strange mastery of radioactive energy.

Once Silas had his temple, he felt it was time to show the rest of the world who the new king of the wastelands was.

Virginia City

By 2085, Silas' cult boasted hundreds of priests and thousands of followers, both in Las Vegas and across the country. His mutants had phenomenal powers, equipment scavenged from cities no one else dared enter, and a whole lot of anger against norms who shunned them.

Then, after several Doomsayers were murdered preaching to the norms of nearby Virginia City, Silas decreed there would be retribution. He assembled a horde of mutants and Doomsayers and attacked. The norms, all hard-bitten survivors of the Apocalypse, fought back much harder than Silas had ever imagined and made the horde look just a little bit silly. Enraged, the Mutant King gathered even more forces and threw them up the steep, desert slopes to the spiked walls of the norm settlement. After a long and bloody month-long siege, the town finally fell to a massive assault.

Doomsayers

The Schism

The slaughter on both sides was incredible. The bodies of scores of norms and mutants lay baking in the hot Nevada sun, waiting for the circling buzzards to pick their corpses clean. Not surprisingly, Virginia City became a Deadland.

Silas, furious and more insane than ever, declared that Virginia City was only the beginning of a new and bloody crusade. It was now the Cult of Doom's mission to destroy all norms.

A handful of Doomsayers refused to take part in the crusade. They believed all that business about mutants being the next evolution of man, but they didn't want to kill those "poor" norms who were doomed anyway—especially when half of Silas' new mutant hordes were flesh-eating, violent lunatics instead of misunderstood outcasts looking to save the world.

In any event, Silas eventually rounded up the "heretics" and tortured them until they saw things his way or kicked the depleted-uranium bucket. Most did not survive the "Inquisition," but in 2086, a group of priests led by a woman known only as Joan escaped.

The Harbinger

Joan and the others fled to an old missile silo somewhere in southwestern Nevada. There they established a secret base and sent word to others who felt as they did to come there. While waiting for other heretics, Joan experienced an incredible vision.

She dreamed that the dawn of the next generation would be heralded by a mutant known as the Harbinger. This mutant would be known by its pale skin and "blazing-red third eye." Through this third eye, the Harbinger could see the future and lead humanity to a brilliant and peaceful new age. Most importantly, the Harbinger would replace Silas, the "false prophet," and become the new leader of the mutants.

Joan had thought to use her small army to attack Silas directly, but the dream of the Harbinger changed all that. She knew that if her handful of Doomsayers lost their battle, there would be no one left to protect the Harbinger. Worse, once Silas found out about the Harbinger, he would make sure it did not replace him—by slitting its frail throat.

Doomsayers

The Pact

Joan and her inner circle gathered the other heretics and tasked them with a mission. They were to venture out and carry the word of the true Doomsayers to the world.

Their first goal is to find and protect the Harbinger. Joan doesn't even know if it's been born yet, but she believes the future depends on making sure it survives long enough to replace Silas and usher in a new age.

The second goal is to show norms the Doomsayers are not their enemies—Silas is. Though all Doomsayers believe norms are doomed to extinction, they have no desire to hurry the process along. In fact, if norms aren't made to accept "good" mutants (generally those who aren't trying to eat you), they may actually wipe them *all* out.

Of course, the deranged, violent mutants might also wipe out those with warm, fuzzy mutations, so the "evolutionary failures" must be culled by whatever means necessary. That means violent muties: bad; peaceful muties: good. Heretical Doomsayers protect mutants who aren't doing any harm, but they're the first to wade into a den of the bad kind and start blasting. Any muties allied with Silas are first preached to, and if they don't see the light, the Doomsayers nuke 'em 'til they glow.

The heretics also prove themselves by doing good deeds for benevolent mutants and norms. They protect villages, cure rad sickness, heal the wounded, and—most importantly—lead the resistance against mutant attacks. It's a brilliant public relations move, and so far, most settlements welcome Doomsayers in purple robes (the bad kind of Doomsayers wear green, and fortunately the insane zealots rarely switch robes and infiltrate their heretical brothers and sisters—that wouldn't be "righteous").

Doombringers

215

Silas' legions prowl the wastes looking for heretics. The worst are the Doombringers, relentless, rabid zealots who are more than willing to raze an entire town just to ferret out one hidden heretic. When they find one, they torture him to find out where other heretics are, or the location of Joan's secret base (fortunately, most don't know).

Playing a Doomsayer

So you want to play a Doomsayer? Okay. First off, unless you have the Marshal's permission to play a mutie-loving bad guy in some weird, "we're all out to make the world even worse" campaign, your hero is one of the heretics. She either rebelled against Silas several years ago, or she has been recruited by a heretical Doomsayer since. In any event, she openly wears a purple robe to show people her allegiance. Doomsayers don't disguise themselves like Templars. It's hard to show people the benevolence of your order if they don't know you belong to it.

Initiation

Heretical Doomsayers are "ordained" by Joan or a select few of her original companions. Other Doomsayers must be ordained by Silas or one of his high priests.

Once ordained, a Doomsayer is granted a robe emblazoned with the symbol of the cult: a stylized, three-legged mutant dancing in the fires of the Apocalypse. (Silas claims it's an "Alpha to Omega" symbol, but most folks still think it looks like a three-legged mutie.)

Mutation

An integral part of initiation is that a new Doomsayer gains a mutation (even if he already has one of his own!) Fortunately, most of the church's mutations are good. Tell the Marshal to draw three mutations and give you the best. (He can let you choose if he's feeling generous.)

198

Hindrances

Your hero starts with an awesome *enemy:* Silas and the Cult o' Doom. Most any "bad" muties (and there's a lot of them) and loyal Doomsayers try to kill heretics on sight.

For most heretics, this is a 3-point Hindrance. If your character is actively hunted by the cult, it might be worth 4 or even 5 points.

Your hero also has a 3-point *oath* to fulfill Joan's Pact. Specifically, Doomsayers must find the Harbinger and prove the goodness of the true Cult of Doom to norms. The latter means healing the sick, curing them of yummy radiation, and laying waste to any bad muties they cannot convert. It's a lonely job, but somebody's got to do it.

Using Powers

Enough bad stuff. We wouldn't send your hero off into the wastes without a few tricks up his irradiated sleeve.

A Doomsayer knows one power for every level of his *faith.* The first power he learns is *tolerance,* which lets him soak up rads like a cockroach. *Tolerance* must be your character's first miracle. Other miracles can be chosen from those in this book.

Learning New Powers

After character creation, raising *faith* does not grant additional miracles. Instead, new miracles must be learned by study and meditation. Each new power costs 5 Bounty Points. The only time requirement is how fast your character can accumulate Bounty Points.

Strain

Channeling supernatural radiation through one's body is stressful. When successfully used, a power causes an amount of Strain. An easy way to keep track of your Doomsayer's current Strain is by sliding a paper clip up the Strain scale on the side of your character sheet.

When a Doomsayer's Strain reaches the breaking point (equal to his *Vigor* die type), he can no longer use his powers.

Reducing Strain

Strain is reduced by quiet rest and meditation. Every hour the rad priest rests allows him to reduce his Strain by 1 point. By "rest," we mean no physical or mental exertion.

Faith

Doomsayers channel their abilities through mental discipline and *faith* in their quasi-religion. To use a power, simply choose the power and make a *faith* roll. If the roll is equal to or greater than the miracle's TN, the priest takes the power's Strain. Then the power takes effect. If the roll is failed or the power's Strain would take the Doomsayer beyond his breaking point, nothing happens. Failed powers don't cost Strain.

Playing around with all this radiation has a price. Anytime a Doomsayer goes bust on his *faith* roll, the radiation courses through his body and causes a random and instantaneous mutation.

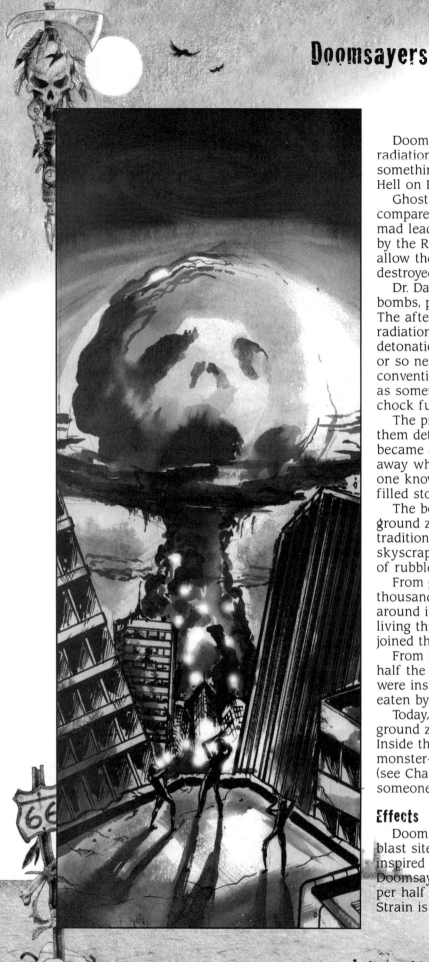

The Power of the Atom

Doomsayers are truly at home in areas of high radiation. To understand why, you need to know something about the bombs used to bring about Hell on Earth.

Ghost-rock bombs are relatively low-yield compared to traditional nuclear weapons. The mad leaders of the world, perhaps whispered to by the Reckoners, decided these weapons would allow them to eventually occupy the lands they destroyed.

Dr. Darius Hellstromme, who perfected the bombs, proved his theory in isolated explosions. The aftereffects caused dangerous levels of radiation only for a decade or so after detonation, much better than the thousand years or so needed to detox a place hit with a conventional nuke. Think of ghost-rock bombs as something like weird neutron bombs. Oh, and chock full of angry manitous.

The problem came when a few million of them detonated at once. That's when the Earth became a Deadland and the aftereffects didn't go away when they were supposed to. In fact, no one knows when or if the murderous, spirit-filled storms will ever go away.

The bombs killed in one of three ways. At ground zero, one mile in diameter, there was a traditional explosion. We're talking craters, skyscrapers reduced to two- or three-story piles of rubble, and so on.

From ground zero out to another five miles, thousands of damned souls (manitous) raced around in an incredible hurricane of death. Every living thing in this zone was killed and quickly joined the growing spirit storm.

From five miles out to another 30 or so, about half the folks died and half lived. Most who lived were instantly warped or mutated. The rest got eaten by the new mutants. Lucky stiffs.

Today, the storms continue to rage around ground zero, forming a wall about 10 yards thick. Inside these walls is a highly irradiated, monster-filled area of otherwise relative calm (see Chapter Five for what happens when someone tries to pass through the wall).

Effects

Doomsayers draw on the radioactive energy of blast sites to reduce the Strain of their nuclear-inspired powers. Within 5 miles of a ghost storm, Doomsayers reduce Strain at the rate of 1 point per half hour. Within a ghost storm, 1 point of Strain is reduced every 10 minutes.

Powers

Below are the powers available to Doomsayers. Those funny lines just before the description are the miracle's important mechanics.

TN is the Target Number the Doomsayer needs to make the power work.

Strain is the amount of Strain the power causes when successfully used.

Speed is the time or number of actions it takes to complete the miracle.

Duration is how long the power stays in effect. If the miracle's duration is 1 round, it lasts until the beginning of the next round. "Concentration" means the power stays in effect as long as the rad priest does nothing but take simple actions (such as walking or talking). A number listed here means the caster can take that much Strain each round (or other time period) to keep the power in effect.

Range is the maximum distance at which the power takes effect.

Atomic Blast
TN: 5
Strain: 1
Speed: 1
Duration: Instant
Range: 20 yards/*faith* level

The first power Silas manifested was this tremendous burst of irradiated energy. This miracle is handy for keeping unarmored mutants and the like in line. When they need a bigger boom, Doomsayers use *nuke*.

Atomic blast causes a sizzling green bolt to fly from the priest's palm. The Doomsayer must direct the blast, so compare his *faith* roll to the TN of the miracle as well as the TN to hit the target (with a Range Increment of 10). If the miracle succeeds *and* hits the target, it inflicts 1d10 damage for every success over the miracle's TN (not the TN to hit the target).

Latrelle, a Doomsayer in the Texas area, lets loose with an *atomic blast* at a mutant 36 yards distant. The TN to hit the mutie is (base 5 plus [36 divided by the Range Increment of 10 is] 3=) 8. The Doomsayer gets a 17. That hits and is 2 raises over the miracle's TN of 5 (not the TN of the shot). The blast does 3d10 damage.

Latrelle takes 1 Strain. His breaking point is 10, so he's got a lot of juice left for more hungry muties.

EMP
TN: Special
Strain: Special
Speed: 1
Duration: 10 minutes/success
Range: 10 yards/*faith* level

It stands for "electromagnetic pulse," and it's what knocks out all the electronics when a nuke goes off. Doomsayers with this power are pure trouble for Throckmorton's goons and any others who rely on technology.

The TN, Strain, and Duration all depend on how good the electronics are. Check the table, brainer. When *EMP* works, the item is knocked out and can't function for the power's duration.

If used on a device already ruined by an EMP, this power fixes it for the duration instead.

EMP

TN	Strain	Item
3	1	Cheap digital watches
5	1	Handheld electronics
7	2	Home Computers
9	3	Light military equipment, industrial computers
11	4	Military computers, shielded electronics, cyborgs, junker device
13	5	Heavily shielded electronics, automatons

Flashblind
TN: 7
Strain: 1
Speed: 1
Duration: 1d10 rounds
Range: 10 yards/*faith* level

If a brainer's lucky, a Doomsayer blinds him because he doesn't want to kill him. Otherwise, he's just been neutralized for a slower demise.

Flashblind creates a brilliant flash of radiation in front of the target. This has a chance of blinding him for a while. Victims see nothing but a brilliant, skull-shaped mushroom cloud for the duration of the power.

Every character within 10 yards of the flashpoint must make a *Vigor* roll versus the Doomsayer's casting total. Targets who win are unaffected. Everyone else suffers -2 to any action that requires vision. Every raise the priest gets over the miracle's TN (not the target's roll) increases the modifier by another -2.

Doomsayers

Geiger Vision

TN: 5
Strain: 1
Speed: 5 seconds
Duration: 10 minutes/1 point of Strain
Range: 50 yards/*faith* level

Geiger vision allows a priest to see radiation. In game terms, the Marshal should tell the hero if there is dangerous radiation nearby, and what the TN to resist it is. With a raise on the roll, the Doomsayer gets a clue about any weird effects the radiation might have as well.

With a raise, the Doomsayer can also sense trace radiation well enough to see in the dark up to the power's range. Most everything has at least a few rads and appears as a vague, luminous-green outline, but only in darkness. Give the rad priest a +6 to spot most normal *sneakin'* figures at night, underground, in dark rooms, and so on. Occasionally, a really clean figure might not give off any radiation. If so, the figure, object, or whatever is actually invisible to a Doomsayer using *Geiger vision*.

Finally, if used to gauge the intensity of a ghost storm, this power works only for 1 segment (one Action Card if in rounds) and costs +1 additional point of Strain (whether it's being maintained or not). The Marshal should draw a card for the storm (see page 103) and tell the Doomsayer its value. If he doesn't go through the wall that segment, the chaotic storm changes and another card is drawn should he use this power again or enter the storm later.

Molecular Bonding

TN: 5
Strain: 1
Speed: 1
Duration: 1 round/1 point of Strain
Range: Touch

Doomsayers don't like pain any more than anyone else. While this miracle might not keep them from getting shot, it does help to reduce the effects of things that make them go "ouch."

The power works by bonding the very molecules of the target's flesh on the subatomic level. This makes the flesh tough as leather.

Each success on the Doomsayer's *faith* roll allows him to ignore up to 2 points of damage (like Armor −2). This is cumulative with other forms of armor, so a shot that gets through a rad priest's Kevlar vest must then subtract this damage from whatever dice are rolled.

Mutate!

TN: Opposed (*faith* versus *Vigor*)
Strain: 5
Speed: 1
Duration: Special
Range: Touch

Mutate is one of those miracles that make even the hardiest survivors of the Wasted West shudder with horror. Besides being deadly, it's just plain disturbing. Read on, and you'll see why.

This wicked miracle causes scores of rapid and deadly mutations in its victim. The unfortunate brainer grows extra digits, eyes, tumors, cancers, and all kinds of other nastiness in an instant. Not surprisingly, most victims can't handle having an armbone shoot up through their brain, or an extra limb grow out of their ear. It's not a pretty sight.

The range of the power is touch. A success causes the priest's *Spirit* in damage, added together just like damage from a firearm. Each raise the priest gets on his *faith* total versus the target's *Vigor* raises the damage roll by another step. Apply the resulting wounds as massive damage (see Chapter Five).

Victims who take even a single wound are automatically stunned as their bodies wrench, twist, and warp uncontrollably. They can recover normally on their next action.

The Doomsayer must be able to touch the victim for the power to work. He doesn't have to touch bare flesh, so regular clothes and most armor don't protect against the power. If the target is protected by thick armor, though, such as hardened leather or a battlesuit, the power is useless.

Mutate works only on living beings. It has no effect on inanimate objects or undead. It's the Marshal's call as to whether it works on weird critters.

Should a victim of *mutate* live through the attack, the warped bones and puss-filled sores slowly snap back to normal or fade as he heals. The effects are permanent only if a maimed result is reached in a leg or arm. (Remember, maiming wounds to the head or guts mean the victim's dead.) In that case, the limb does not heal, and the deformity causes a −4 to rolls requiring its use. The only way to heal the defect is to be healed by a Doomsayer.

If this power is ever used against an important character like one of the posse or a major extra, the Marshal needs to describe the mutations in a fair amount of detail. Feel free to be as gross as the players can handle.

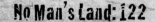

J·ROSEN

Nuke

TN: 5
Strain: 5
Speed: 2
Duration: Instant
Range: 20 yards/*faith* level

When *atomic blast* just isn't enough, a Doomsayer can roll up his sleeves and try *nuke*. Due to the high Strain, it's likely to knock even the most faithful priest on his robed butt, but it can also do exactly what its title implies.

Nuke works just like *atomic blast* in that the Doomsayer uses his *faith* roll to get the miracle off and put it on target. It has a Range Increment of 10. If the Doomsayer achieves the TN of the miracle but misses the spot he was aiming for, it deviates 2d20 yards. Use a d12 like a clock facing to determine direction. If the shot deviates backward, it still ends up at least half the distance from the priest to the target. That way it can't come back on the Doomsayer unless he fires it *real* close.

Wherever it lands, *nuke* causes an explosion with a Burst Radius of 10 yards. The damage at ground zero is 3d20 plus 1d20 for every raise over the miracle's TN (not the targeting TN). This counts as "massive damage" (see Chapter 5).

One other minor difference is that *nuke* has a Speed of 2. During the first action, the Doomsayer begins to gather glowing radiation about his body, an effect visible to anyone who can see him. That's a good time for them to run away and hide.

Latrelle spies an automaton coming at him, and he knows he has to whip out the big guns. He casts *nuke* and waits for the carnage.

He tries to center the miracle smack on top of the automaton, 50 yards away. The range makes the TN to put the blast on target a (base 5 plus [50 divided by 10 is] 5=) 10.

Latrelle gets a 9 *faith* total. That means he gets the power off (TN 5) but misses his target (TN 10). The blast deviates just enough to put the automaton in the second burst ring. Since Latrelle didn't get a raise over the miracle's TN, the damage at ground zero is 3d20. The damage in the second burst ring (see **Explosives** in Chapter Five) is 2d20. That's one angry automaton.

Doomsayers

Powerup

TN: Special
Strain: Special
Speed: 1 minute
Duration: 1 hour/1 point of Strain
Range: Touch

There's a lot of old junk lying about the wastelands. Some of it can come in handy if you can just get it working again. For gadgets that need power, Doomsayers use this trick.

Powerup allows a rad priest to draw on his *faith* to activate any device that requires electricity. To power a device "zapped" by an EMP (caused by either a Doomsayer or the Apocalypse), he has to use the *EMP* power as well.

Powerup

TN	Strain	Item
3	1	Battery power
5	2	Computer
7	3	Generator
9	4	Electric car
11	5	Hover tank

Sustenance

TN: 5
Strain: 1
Speed: 10 minutes
Duration: Permanent
Range: Self

Doomsayers travel far and wide in their quests. Besides mutants, gangs, and ravening monsters, one of their most dangerous challenges is finding enough food to cross the wastelands. *Sustenance* allows them to draw nourishment from radiation instead of food.

Each casting fulfills the Doomsayer's need for food and water for one entire day. The miracle does not provide radiation, however, so a priest must have a significant source nearby to draw from. A pound of irradiated material is usually good for one casting. A priest in the ruins of a city can forget about food for a long time.

Even Doomsayers need real food once in a while though. Each time *sustenance* is used, the Doomsayer loses 1 Wind that cannot be replaced until he eats a reasonable-sized meal. Doing so alleviates all Wind suffered from *sustenance*.

Finally, the miracle allows a Doomsayer (not his companions) to eat irradiated food and drink irradiated water with no ill-effects. The food or water provides normal nourishment (and tastes just like momma's home-cooking!).

Tolerance

TN: 5
Strain: 1
Speed: 1
Duration: 24 hours
Range: Touch

Doomsayers must frequently venture into heavily irradiated areas, like ruined cities. This is suicide for most folks, but Silas' priests quickly developed this miraculous power to protect themselves and their followers from the deadly touch of sacred radiation.

Tolerance allows the subject to ignore the effects of low-level radiation for an entire day. Even once the subject has passed from the irradiated area, his flesh and gear are "clean" and present no further harm (unless they were irradiated already).

Certain areas of extremely high radiation (much higher even than that at ground zero) may exist. Those areas often require some sort of test to avoid damage, mutations, or other effects. *Tolerance* doesn't block those effects, but it does provide a +2 bonus to whatever Trait or Aptitude is used to resist them.

Doomsayers

Touch of the Doomsayers

TN: Special
Strain: Special
Speed: Special
Duration: Permanent
Range: Touch

Silas learned to heal wounds by very slowly and carefully manipulating flesh on a molecular level. Unfortunately, when a Doomsayer heals someone, it leaves the skin discolored or covered with hideous boils.

After the schism, Joan and the other heretics knew healing would be one of their greatest tools in proving themselves to norms. Joan knew norms would not tolerate being mutated, so she developed a new healing miracle with no side-effects. She got close.

Whether a Doomsayer is a heretic or loyal to Silas, the procedure for healing is the same. The rad priest places her hands over the area to be healed and waits until both her palms and the injured flesh begin to glow with irradiated light. Next, the priest makes a *faith* total versus the TN of the wound level, as shown on the table below. If successful, the priest heals the wounds in that particular area. Failure when trying to heal a maimed limb means it's a permanent wound.

The bad news is loyal Doomsayers always warp the flesh. The patient is forever after *ugly as sin* (–1) if that area is visible. Heretical Doomsayers don't warp flesh unless the wound level is critical or maimed. Even they can't halt the effects of that much radiation.

In any case, going bust on the *faith* roll means the patient suffers a mutation. Have the Marshal pull a card immediately.

Touch also cures the glows (radiation poisoning), but it doesn't heal other types of diseases (that's the Templars' job). The TN is Hard (9). Remember that if an attempt to heal an ailment by supernatural means is failed, it can never be healed (see *ailin'* in Chapter 3).

Touch of the Doomsayers

Wound Level	TN	Strain	Speed
Wind	3	1	1 minute
Light	5	1	2 minutes
Heavy	7	2	3 minutes
Serious	9	3	4 minutes
Critical	11	4	5 minutes
Maimed	13	5	10 minutes

Doomsayer Powers

Power	TN	Strain	Speed	Duration	Range	Description
Atomic Blast	5	1	1	Instant	20 yards/ *faith*	Blast foes with nuclear beam.
EMP	Special	Special	1	10 minutes/ success	10 yards/ *faith*	Knock out electronics.
Flashblind	7	1	1	1d10 rounds	10 yards/ *faith*	Blind foes with radiation.
Geiger Vision	5	1	5 seconds	10 minutes/ 1 Strain	50 yards/ *faith*	Detect radiation; see in the dark.
Molecular Bonding	5	1	1	1 round/ 1 Strain	Touch	Turn skin to leathery armor.
Mutate!	*faith* vs. *Vigor*	5	1	Special	Touch	Hurt foes with mutations.
Nuke	5	5	2	Instant	20 yards/ *faith*	Blow up foes with radiation.
Powerup	Special	Special	1 minute	1 hour/1 Strain	Touch	Instant power.
Sustenance	5	1	10 minutes	Permanent	Self	Food.
Tolerance	5	1	1	24 hours	Touch	Ignore radiation.
Touch of the Doomsayers	Special	Special	Special	Permanent	Touch	Heal wounds with radiation.

No Man's Land: 126

Chapter Eight:
Junkers

Junkers, also known as "junkmen," are the techno-wizards of the Wasted West, picking clean the skeleton of the society which collapsed during the Last War. They can rebuild old technology and, with the help of the spirit world, build new devices of incredible power. They depend on the spirits for both inspiration and raw energy, but while manitous inspire and power their arcane gadgets, junkers still need the remnants of prewar technology to construct their infernal devices. Unfortunately, these things just aren't manufactured anymore, so when a junker spots a piece of hardware which looks like it might prove useful, he quickly adds it to his collection. Most of these techno-mages wander the wastes weighed down by heavy packs full of assorted junk.

Junkers tend to keep to themselves. Some by choice, but most because many survivors of the Last War don't want anything to do with them. The devastation wrought by ghost-rock bombs has made anyone who still willingly uses the stuff suspect. Many people use ghost rock for fuel, but to knowingly consort with the spirits inside and walk the path of Hellstromme seems dangerous and foolhardy to the average survivor.

The junker's typically bizarre appearance only adds to many folks' distrust. Most junkers wear techno-talismans made from discarded bits of machine innards and often have arcane schematics recorded on their clothing or tattooed into their skin. Slap on top of that the fact that some of them have been mutated by faulty devices, and this suspicion is understandable. Of course, misgivings often vanish when a junker shows up with some incredible device people just can't live without—like a spirit-battery-powered beer cooler.

Mad Science

The arcane science of the junkers is fairly new to the world. Before the junkers, there were mad scientists.

In the years following the Reckoning in 1863, a new form of science appeared in the world. Its practitioners liked to call it "new science" but most non-eggheads referred to it as "mad science."

The second name was a good description of it for two reasons. First, the products of this science often seemed to defy reality and sometimes appeared almost magical. The things these gizmos could do when they worked were spectacular. (The results when they didn't work were spectacular too!) Second, those who dabbled in this science often became stark raving lunatics.

Ghostly Visions

What the early practitioners of mad science didn't realize was that their flashes of inspiration had supernatural origins. The Reckoners sent their manitous to touch the minds of those with the skill and imagination to turn their dreams into reality. These spiritual messengers filled the scientists' thoughts with dimly-seen visions of future technologies and arcane rituals. These ghostly visions loosened the inventors' grip on reality and eventually drove them mad.

Mad scientists were common throughout the 20th and 21st centuries, but as conventional technology increased, their prominence decreased, though a few still grabbed an occasional headline with a spectacular device. Although mad science was no longer the quick path to fortune and fame it had been, there were still many who practiced it. The urge to create the things whispered about by the voices from beyond was too great to resist.

What Changed?

In the late 20th century, the world's most famous mad scientist, Dr. Darius Hellstromme, discovered that irradiated ghost rock could be used as a nuclear fuel.

It was found that when ghost rock was burned as a nuclear fuel, it gave off large amounts of spiritual energy in addition to heat. This arcane energy has the same effect on spirits—including the human soul—that radiation has on living flesh. This energy became known as G-rays (ghost rays).

Hellstromme's experiments with irradiated ghost rock inevitably led to the development of nuclear ghost-rock bombs. The first of these bombs was detonated on April 9, 2045.

And the Reckoners rejoiced.

Although Hellstromme Industries developed the first bombs, it wasn't long before other companies and nations stumbled onto the secret of their creation—and their awesome power. A new arms race began as each country worked to expand its ghost-rock arsenal. The ownership of ghost-rock deposits on Earth and Faraway became matters of national security that determined the leaders of the new world order.

Ghost-rock bomb technology was refined, and the bombs grew bigger and more reliable. On July 3, 2063, Hellstromme Industries unveiled its new City-Buster ghost-rock missile.

The Sound of Silence

That night, scientists the world over slept undisturbed for the first time in 200 years. When they awoke, the projects they had been feverishly working on only the day

before appeared to be so much hogwash. Disillusioned inventors abandoned their work in disgust. Some even took their own lives.

The Reckoners' plan was complete.

The world now possessed a ghost-rock arsenal capable of destroying humanity and terrorforming the entire world into a Deadland. All that was needed was a spark to touch it off.

All the Wrong Places

Not all the mad scientists gave up their work. Some went looking for answers. Most of these were members of the Sons of Sitgreaves, a movement which could trace its roots back to 1876 and R. Percy Sitgreaves, the first mad scientist to discover the awful truth about the source of his inspiration. The SOS were outcasts among mad scientists, most of whom refused to believe their scientific genius came from anywhere but themselves.

When the manitous stopped their whispering, some of these scientists went and paid them a house call. A few were hucksters in addition to being mad scientists, and they were able to get the information they needed from the spirits after a few torturous mental duels.

What they discovered meant the end of mad science as they knew it. The manitous would no longer willingly aid mad scientists in their work, and even when forced to talk they had nothing new to contribute. The aid the manitous had given in the past was based on their knowledge of future technologies. This knowledge had been granted to them by the Reckoners and did not extend past July 3, 2063. The scientists themselves now had a far better idea of what the future held for science than the manitous did.

The scientists did discover something useful however. It was still possible to use arcane energy (what layfolk would loosely call "magic") to fill in the gaps in otherwise impossible contraptions. The SOS continued their research in this area and found that it was possible to replicate and sometimes even improve existing technology in this way. Unfortunately, this method of inventing was possible only by those scientists who were also skilled hucksters, because these devices could only be powered by the arcane energy available in the Hunting Grounds.

The SOS continued to develop this new form of inventing, but the level of skill needed to perform it kept the number of fledgling techno-mages low.

Junkers

The G-Ray Collector

The process became much easier once Ridley Velmer invented the first G-ray collector. Based on the technology used in ghost-rock reactors, this new device allowed any scientist equipped with one to capture a portion of the spiritual energy given off by burning ghost rock and store it in specially prepared spirit batteries. Using a collector meant the inventor no longer had to battle with a manitou for energy, only the occasional tidbit of information—something the manitous were willing to part with a bit more easily.

Velmer shared his discovery with many of his colleagues, and the new science of technomagic was born. Using this new device, any scientist with a knowledge of the appropriate occult rituals could build hi-tech gizmos run by spiritual energy. Velmer's G-ray collector sparked a new wave of invention which was cut short by the start of the Last War.

The full limits of this new technology had yet to be explored when the Last War began. A few junkers were drafted by the military, but their contributions to the war effort were too little, too late.

Playing a Junker

It ain't easy being a technologically minded soul in a post-Apocalyptic world. A junker must have the *arcane background: junker* Edge and at least 1 point in *academia: occult* and 3 points in *science: occult engineering*.

The upside is that junker devices are built by infusing them with arcane powers. Each power is learned separately. Your hero begins play with two powers of your choice. (These are listed on the following pages.)

Junker heroes can begin play with any one of the occult-engineering devices listed in this chapter, or if your Marshal allows it, you can design a number of devices for your hero with a combined cost of 150 points. Each device comes with a spirit battery with a charge equal to 10 times its most expensive Drain.

Also, what would a junker be without some junk? Your hero can buy device components as part of his starting equipment. Structural components cost $2 each, mechanical components cost $5 each, and electronic parts cost $10 each. We'll explain these in a moment.

Junkers

The Junkmen Cometh

In the Wasted West, scrounging has become a way of life. Most people simply scrounge for what they need to get by. Others, though, are looking for a little more.

Junkers can't conjure devices out of thin air. They need some physical components to serve as the basis for their techno-magical miracles.

Parts is Parts

To make things easy on you, we've broken the spare parts junkers collect into three big categories (you can thank us later).

Structural: These are the pieces upon which the rest of a machine hangs. They can be anything from an I-beam to a fender panel to a computer casing to a shelf bracket. Just so you know how much junk your hero is lugging around (and it's relative value), the average structural component weighs about 3 pounds and is worth about $2.

Mechanical: These are all the little fiddley bits that make things go. This category includes things like gears, electric starters, fan belts, and watch mechanisms. Most mechanical parts average about a pound in weight and are worth around $5 each.

Electronic: These parts are all the electrical goodies that put the high in high-tech. This includes circuit boards, computer processors, modems, etc. These pieces weigh in at about 8 ounces to a pound and are worth $10 each.

Note that the prices listed for these components are for people who have a use for them, like junkers. The average joe with no technical skills isn't going to give you a spent shell casing for them.

Finding Parts

So, how do you get your grubby mitts on these parts? Listen up, because they're not going to rain down from the sky. As your character travels the Wasted West, she needs to keep her eyes peeled for *scroungin'* opportunities. This could be a wrecked car, a hardware store, or a battlefield.

Whenever your junker spots a likely prospect, he gets to work. Tell the Marshal what sort of component your junker is looking for. It's possible to get multiple types of components from a single source, but each requires a separate *scroungin'* roll.

If the Marshal decides any of the component types are present, he sets the TN for the *scroungin'* attempt. If your hero succeeds, she finds 1d4 components. Each raise on the *scroungin'* roll adds +1 to this die roll.

Each *scroungin'* attempt takes 30 minutes plus 5 minutes per component recovered.

Scroungin' Guidelines

First off, most electronic components within 10 miles or so of a bomb crater have been fried by the bomb's EMP. Any obvious source of components near a major population center or a major highway is going to be fairly well picked over after 13 years. The TNs for these sources should start at Incredible (11) and upward.

Larger sources should lower the TN. It's easier to find multiple components on battlefields littered with disabled vehicles than to find the same number on a single burned-out hover tank.

G-Ray Collectors

The last piece of equipment your junkman gets for his *arcane background* points is a G-ray collector. A collector consists of a ghost-rock furnace and a converter-coil assembly. Ghost rock burned in it releases G-rays which are trapped by the converter coils. This energy can be stored in spirit batteries for later use.

Any junker with the proper components can build a collector in a day. This requires an Onerous (7) *science: occult engineering* roll. The collector burns a single pound of ghost rock at a time, but it's not necessary to burn the entire pound in a single session.

Conventional G-Ray Collector
Components:
Structural: 5
Mechanical: 3
Electronic: 0
Ghost Rock: 2 pounds
Power Output: 50 GR per pound of ghost rock

A conventional collector weighs about 10 pounds and is roughly the size and shape of a small gas grill. The collector's furnace puts out a large amount of heat while burning ghost rock. Most are equipped with hoses which can draw water from a nearby source to cool the furnace.

When operating with a water supply, the collector remains cool enough that it's safe to approach, although it's still hot (some junkers cook their meals on their collectors). Without a source of coolant, the furnace operates at such a high temperature that anyone within 10 yards of it suffers 1d6 Wind per minute.

It takes about an hour to extract the energy from a single pound of ghost rock. The typical collector can charge one spirit battery at once.

Making a Spirit Battery

Junkers store the power generated by their collectors in special receptacles known as spirit batteries. These are much lighter than the collectors and don't generate any heat, nor can they power electrical devices.

All junkers know how to make these devices. Making a battery requires an ounce of ghost rock and 1 structural component for each 10 points or portion thereof that the battery stores. Assembling a battery requires a *science: occult engineering* roll against a TN of 5, plus the battery's power rating divided by 10. Round normally. It takes 10 minutes, plus 1 minute per point stored, to complete.

A 75-point battery requires 8 ounces of ghost rock, 8 structural components and a *science: occult engineering* roll against a TN of 13 (5+8). It takes 85 minutes to build.

Recharging Batteries

Newly-made and drained batteries must be charged by hooking them to an operating spirit collector. A battery absorbs energy as fast as the collector it's hooked to can generate it. When recharging multiple batteries, divide the power generated evenly between them.

Making a Device

This is the fun part, where your junker hero gets to show off and whip up some killer gadgets from the junk in her pack.

There are five steps to building a device:
1. Concoct a theory
2. Determine the powers
3. Buy the powers
4. Assemble the components
5. Build it

Concoct a Theory

The junker character's *player* must come up with a theory as to how the device works. It doesn't have to be complicated (if your character is making a radar set, just say, "my character's building a radar set") or even 100% scientifically accurate (we don't expect our players to have a doctorate in physics) but it must at least sound somewhat plausible. No theory, no device. The Marshal has the final say on what works and what doesn't.

Coming up with a theory helps define what the device can and can't do and gets you ready for the next step.

Determine Powers

Once you've cooked up a theory, it's time to figure out which arcane powers your junker needs to build into the device. Look over the power descriptions and see which ones match the functions you're looking for.

At this step, it's a good idea to look at what the device can do and to determine which functions need to be built through junker science and which ones you might be able to rig up using conventional technology. Sure, you can build a tripod-mounted smart gun that tracks and fires on its own using the *sensor*, *trait*, and *damage* powers, but if you have an old machine gun laying around, using that for the gun portion of the device instead of *damage* reduces the components and batteries needed and the risk of backlash.

Buy Powers

Now that you know what powers you need, it's time to buy them. This is probably the most complicated step, and you may want a calculator handy, but if you take it slow, you shouldn't have any problem.

Every power description lists the cost for different levels of it, as well as what cost modifiers apply to it. Each power a device possesses is bought separately. Read the power's description and determine what level is needed for the device you're designing. Record the required cost. This is the power's base cost.

Next, look over all the modifiers which might apply to the power. Write down each modifier which applies, and the percentage listed. Once you've found all the applicable modifiers, add them all together. This is the power's total cost modifier. (It can't offer more than a 50% discount however.)

Multiply the power's base cost by the power's total cost modifier. Add the result to the base cost of the device. This is the final cost for that power. If the device has more than one power, repeat these steps to find the final cost for each.

Junkers

Assemble Components

You can't build a device without parts. Most places in the Wasted West have stopped making them, so your junker has to go out and find them. For more details, check out the special junker *scroungin'* rules later on in this chapter.

Each power description lists the types and number of components needed to build a device with that power. To find the number of components you need to complete your junker's device, multiply the power's final cost by the fraction listed in each category. This gives you the number of each component type needed. Do this for each of the device's powers.

Total up the components needed by all of the device's powers. The junker must have these components to construct the item. If he doesn't have them, he has to go out and find them. In rare circumstances the Marshal may allow substitutions, but this should increase the TN needed to assemble the device.

Either way, going out to scrounge up components for a device the junker really wants (or needs) to make can be the basis of an adventure (or several adventures) all by itself.

Drain

Once you know the final cost of the device's powers you can also figure out how much energy is needed to run it. Each power has a Drain rating listed for it. Divide each power's total cost by the listed Drain number to determine how much arcane energy it requires (measured in G-rays (GR)). Round normally. The minimum Drain for any power is 1 GR.

The arcane energy provided by spirit batteries works differently than electrical energy. Whenever a power is activated it burns its full Drain off the battery, even if it is deactivated before its duration expires. A device which uses 3 GR an hour uses up 3 GR even if it's only switched on for 10 seconds.

Build It

Once all the needed components are found and the final costs of all powers are computed, it's time to put the whole shebang together. The junker must make a *science: occult engineering* roll for each power included in the device. The TN for this roll is found by comparing the power's final cost against the Device Construction Table below.

This table also shows the time needed to add that power to the device. Roll to see how much time is needed. If the *science: occult engineering* roll is successful, the time is spent, and the device is built. Each raise on the construction roll lowers the time needed by the increment listed. If the listed time is 1d6 days, each raise lowers the time by one day. The time needed can never be less than 1 increment.

If the roll is failed, the time spent is wasted. The junker can try again however. If he goes bust, the components for that power are destroyed in the process, and he must gather new ones.

Device Construction

Cost	Time	TN	Cards
1–25	2d20 minutes	5	1
26–50	3d20 minutes	7	1
51–100	2d6 hours	9	2
101–150	2d20 hours	11	2
151–200	2d6 days	13	3
201–250	2d4 weeks	15	4
251–300	2d6 weeks	17	5
301–350	2d12 months	19	6
351+	2d6 years	21	7

Junkers

Backlash

203

Junkers must contact manitous for information while designing and building their devices, and that can mean trouble.

Each time a junker tries to put a power in a device, he must pull the number of cards indicated on the Device Construction Table. If any of these is a Joker, he suffers some backlash from the spirit world. The Marshal has the details.

The Powers

Junker devices are made possible through the arcane powers built into them. Without these powers, the contraptions junkmen build would be exactly that: junk. Different powers require different arcane trappings and rituals, so each one must be learned separately. The exact effects of each power depend on the desires of the junker and the technology upon which he chooses to build it.

Each power description spells out what the power can do and explains any special modifiers which apply specifically to that power. Each power also has some standard information:

Mods lists all the modifiers which may apply to the power. Not all modifiers always apply. Read each description and apply them on a case-by-case basis.

Components lists the types and number of components needed to build a device with a particular power. Multiply the final cost of the power by the listed ratio to determine the exact number of components needed. Round up here.

Drain is the amount of energy the power drains from the device's spirit battery each time it's activated. Multiply the power's final cost by the listed ratio to determine its Drain.

Learning New Powers

Your hero can learn a new power from another junker or by wrestling the information from the manitous. Either way takes a full day of study, a successful *science: occult engineering* roll against an Onerous (7) TN, and 5 character points. If the roll fails, the time is lost, but the junker can try again later.

Browbeating a new power out of the spirits is dangerous. The manitous really don't like giving this sort of information to junkers, because they know the more powers a junker knows, the more often he calls on them. When learning a power from the manitous, draw a card for each power your hero already knows. If a Joker is pulled, the manitous try to nip your hero's inventing career in the bud. He takes 4d10 damage to the guts from a coordinated spiritual ambush.

The powers listed here are just to get your techno-mage rolling. More will appear in later *Hell on Earth* supplements. Feel free to invent your own, as long as your Marshal approves.

Damage

Mods: Ammo, area effect, armor piercing, damage type, duration, range increment, ROF, speed

Components:
  Structural: 1/20 points
  Mechanical: 1/25 points
  Electronic: 1/50 points

Drain: 1 GR/50 points/shot (/round for melee weapons)

The *damage* power is used to build weapons. It gives the device some damage-dealing potential. It can be used to make powered melee weapons or a wide assortment of missile weapons.

The first thing you must do when buying this power is set the damage it does. Melee weapons do *Strength* plus the dice purchased. Missile weapons do the dice purchased in damage. To purchase the basic power, simply pick a die type and pay the listed cost per die. The Marshal may limit the damage a weapon does based on both the theory and type of weapon. A sword which does STR+3d20, for instance, had better have a good rationale behind it.

Damage Mods

The *armor piercing* mod drops the target's Armor level by –1 for each level of *armor piercing* the weapon possesses.

The *rate of fire* mod sets the number of shots a ranged weapon can fire per action.

The cost of a weapon is heavily influenced by its ammo requirements. Weapons which require some sort of ammo, be it bullets, napalm, or what have you, are easier to build than those which generate ammunition. Most energy weapons like plasma pistols, lasers, etc., fall into this second category. Ammunition modifiers only apply to ranged weapons.

The type of damage the weapon inflicts is important. Basic weapons inflict damage through physical means, either a slug, shrapnel, or explosion of some sort. More

Junkers

advanced weaponry causes damage through energy-based attacks like lasers or plasma bolts. The most advanced weapons use the arcane power of the spirit battery to actually inflict spiritual damage on a target. This works normally against physical targets, but it can also damage creatures which are normally only affected by magic.

Some weapons actually fire pure supernatural energy. This works normally against living and supernatural creatures, but it has absolutely no effect on inanimate objects. Purely spiritual attacks ignore things like normal armor and cover.

One-use weapons like grenades and bombs are much cheaper to build.

Damage

Die Type	Cost/Die
d4	10
d6	15
d8	20
d10	25
d12	30
d20	35

Damage Mods

Mod	Cost Modifier
Armor piercing:	+10%/level
Generates ammo:	+50%
Physical damage:	+0%
Energy damage (electricity, laser)	+25%
Spiritual damage:	+50%
Spiritual damage only:	+100%
Wind damage only:	−25%
One-use weapon:	−50%
ROF:	
1	0
2	+25%
3	+50%
6	+100%
9	+150%
12	+200%

Sensor

Mods: Active/Passive, ECM, Range
Components:
　Structural: 1/50 points
　Mechanical: 1/25 points
　Electronic: 1/10 points
Drain: 1 GR/50 points/hour

The *sensor* power gives the device the ability to scan its surroundings. The basic level gives the device senses equivalent to a normal human. More advanced powers give the device the ability to detect a wide number of energy types.

Each sense must be bought separately. If the device is something which depends on its user to spot things (night-vision goggles are a good example), you only need to purchase the basic sense. If the device needs to detect things on its own, like a radar set, you need to buy a *sensor* rating also.

Just select a die type and number of dice and pay the listed cost. This rating is used just like a character's *Cognition* for all rolls used to detect things with that sensor. No sensor may have more than 5 dice.

It's not necessary to roll to detect every little thing, only things which might be missed or are actively trying to avoid detection. A radar set, for example, automatically detects all aircraft within range, flying at normal cruising altitudes. Detecting a chopper flying nap-of-the-earth requires a roll. The TN is up to the Marshal.

The *spirit sight* ability allows the device to see the energy given off by spirits and other supernatural creatures which are present in the physical world.

Active versus Passive

Sensors can be active or passive. Passive sensors rely on detecting energy given off by objects around them, like an eye detecting light.

Active sensors transmit energy and build a picture of their surroundings by detecting reflected energy. A radar dish, for instance, beams radio waves out and then detects the ones which are reflected back.

Some sensors may be bought (separately, of course) as either active or passive. Radar can be an active sensor giving your device the ability to detect objects. As a passive sensor, it has the ability to detect other operating radar sets.

Sensors can be bought with the *electronic countermeasures (ECM)* mod. This makes it a system which defeats other sensors of the same type. Buying basic sight with the *ECM* mod gives the device the ability to fool other visual sensors. This could be an ability which allows the device to blend into its surroundings.

When an ECM-equipped device is scanned by a sensor of the same type, the scanning sensor must win a contested *sensor* roll to detect it.

Sensor

Sense	Cost
Basic sight, hearing, smell	10
Night vision, infrared	20
Radar, sonar, energy	30
Spirit sight	40

Die Type	Cost/Die
d4	5
d6	10
d8	15
d10	20
d12	25
d20	30

Sensor Mods

Mod	Cost Modifier
Active sensor	0
Passive sensor	Reduce Drain by 50%
ECM	+20%
Scan area:	
Beam	-25%
45°	0
90°	+10%
180°	+25%
360°	+50%

Trait

Mods: Size (physical only)
Components: (Physical—Mental)
 Structural: 1/10 points—1/50 points
 Mechanical: 1/10 points—1/50 points
 Electronic: 1/20 points—1/10 points
Drain: 1 GR/100 points in Trait and associated Aptitudes/day

This power allows you to give a device a character Trait. Once a device has a Trait, you can then purchase Aptitudes for the device which use this Trait. No Trait or Aptitude may have more than 5 dice.

Not all Traits and Aptitudes are suitable for devices (*Mien* and *persuasion* come to mind, although it might be possible for an advanced AI to possess these). The Marshal has final say.

Trait

Die Type	Cost/Die
d4	10
d6	20
d8	30
d10	40
d12	50
d20	60

Aptitude Type	Cost/Die
Mental	20
Physical	10

The Devices

Here are a few devices to get you rolling. As mentioned above, new junkers can begin play with any one of these devices. They can also serve as examples of roughly what kinds of devices junkers can tackle.

Chainsword

Drain: 3 GR/round

Many of the denizens of the Wasted West like to play up close and personal, so lots of junkers like to have something to keep them at arm's length. If your hero has a chainsword, he can hack off an offending arm if his playmates get too close.

The chainsword has a thick blade around which runs a chainsaw. This blade has an added kick to it: a current of arcane energy runs through the chain, allowing it to damage creatures which are normally only harmed by magic.

Junkers

The chainsword also has a small gyro built into the handle, which assists the wielder in recovering the heavy blade after each stroke. This makes for a surprisingly quick weapon, despite its cumbersome look.

Weapon	Speed	Defensive Bonus	Damage
Chainsword	1	+2	STR+3d10

Motion Detector

Drain: 1 GR/hour

The considerable junk collections most of the Wasted West's inventors have assembled are tempting targets for the less-than-scrupulous. Since junkers often travel alone, they've learned to trust their tech to watch their backs.

The motion detector is a passive sensor that samples the noise around its position thousands of times per second and then compares the samples using triangulation and Doppler shifts to pinpoint the source of these noises. This information is displayed on a small screen on the top of the device. The detector only displays the estimated distance and direction to a noise source. It can't identify what's causing the noise.

Under normal conditions, the detector automatically detects any noises above a whisper within 250 yards of its position. Anyone trying to move undetected through this area must win a contested roll of *sneak* versus the detector's *sensor* rating of 3d8 each round.

The Marshal should feel free to modify the detector's rolls under conditions that may interfere with its performance. These include things like high winds, loud noises which might overload the sensor or cover other noises (like explosions and gunfire), and caves, canyons, and other areas with odd acoustics. The scanner works best when stationary. When moving, apply a cumulative –2 modifier to all scanning rolls for each 10 m.p.h. of speed.

The sensor can give an alarm if a new noise source enters its scanning area.

Junkgun

Drain: 2 GR/shot

Ammunition is scarce in the Wastes, so some enterprising junkman devised a way to make his own.

The junkgun is a large backpack-like weapon. Attached to the pack is a magnetic collector tube. This acts just like a giant vacuum cleaner, except that it only works on metal. When activated, it uses powerful magnetic pulses to suck up any metallic junk within a few inches of the tube. The tube is roughly 6" in diameter and can handle any object smaller than that, weighing up to 3 pounds.

Scrap metal picked up by the tube goes into a hopper at the top of the pack and then feeds down into a miniature electric furnace which slices the metal up into uniform-sized chunks. The chunks drop down into an ammo storage container and remain there until fired.

A second, smaller tube reverses the process and uses magnetic pulses to fire the processed chunks out in a devastating spray of jagged metal. This creates a shotgun-like effect.

Firing a junkgun is its own concentration of *shootin'*. In combat, the junkgun gets a +2 to hit due to the large spread of its shot. Because it fires a long stream of projectiles, it doesn't lose damage with range like a shotgun.

The ammo hopper can hold 30 shots worth of scrap metal. If there is suitable metal debris in an area (Marshal's call), this can be replenished in combat. Spending an action to run the collector tube gathers enough metal to replace 1d6 shots, and it burns off 1 GR of power. It's possible to run the collector while firing the gun, but this imposes a –4 penalty to hit, because it normally requires two hands.

When not in combat, it's possible to open the scrap hopper and feed in large hunks of metal too large for the collector tube to handle.

Weapon	Speed	ROF	Damage	Range Inc
Junkgun	1	3	3d10	10

Plasma Pistol

Drain: 3 GR/shot

The plasma pistol is a small gun with a big punch. You don't have to be overly accurate with it. As long as you get your shot in the general area, your target's going to have a really bad day.

The pistol uses a small piece of irradiated ghost rock as its ammo source (this one-ounce chunk needs to be replaced every 100 shots or so). When the gun is fired, arcane energy washes over the ghost rock and breaks part of it down into superheated plasma. This is propelled down the barrel by powerful magnetic fields.

The plasma bolts are extremely powerful. Each bolt does 3d8 damage and explodes on impact with a 1-yard Burst Radius. Due to this Burst Radius, you need to know where missed shots go. Use the standard grenade deviation rules for shots that don't connect with the target.

Weapon	Speed	ROF	Damage	Range Inc
Plasma pistol	1	1	3d8	10

Junkers

General Modifiers

The modifiers listed here are general modifiers which may apply to several powers.

At the moment, some of these modifiers apply to only a single power listed in this chapter, but this is certainly bound to change as more and more powers are added in the course of the development of *Deadlands: Hell on Earth*.

Area Effect

This modifier allows certain powers to extend over a larger area than a single point. The most common use is of this modifier is for weapons. Any weapons with an explosive effect must purchase this modifier. The modifier used sets the explosion's primary Blast Radius.

The cone area of effect is for weapons like flamethrowers and such, which spray things in a cone. The listing sets the weapon's maximum range and is used instead of the *range* or *range increment* modifier. (There are no range penalties at any range.) A 30° cone is half as wide as it is long.

Circular Area

Radius	Modifier
1 yard	+10%
5 yards	+20%
10 yards	+30%
15 yards	+40%
20 yards	+50%

30-Degree Cone

Range	Modifier
1 yard	+5%
5 yards	+10%
10 yards	+15%
15 yards	+20%
20 yards	+25%

Pace

This modifier applies to vehicles and other self-propelled devices. Stationary objects (things with a Pace of 0) don't have to worry about these modifiers.

Pace

Speed	Modifier
5 m.p.h.	+10%
10 m.p.h.	+25%
20 m.p.h.	+50%
40 m.p.h.	+75%
80 m.p.h.	+100%
160 m.p.h.	+125%
320 m.p.h.	+150%
640 m.p.h.	+200%
Mach 1	+225%
Mach 2	+250%

Range

The *range* modifier applies to powers which can have effects over long distances (like lights, radar dishes, etc.). This modifier *is not* used for weapons. They use Range Increments instead. For more details on how to handle those, check the top of the next column.

Range

Range	Modifier
Touch	-10%
1 yard	+5%
5 yards	+10%
10 yards	+25%
25 yards	+50%
50 yards	+75%
100 yards	+100%
250 yards	+125%
500 yards	+150%
1,000 yards	+175%
1 mile	+200%
5 miles	+225%
10 miles	+250%
25 miles	+275%
50 miles	+300%
100 miles	+325%

Range Increment

The *range increment* mod sets a weapon's basic Range Increment. Melee weapons that aren't thrown too have a Range Increment of 0.

Range Increment

Increment	Modifier
5	±0%
10	+10%
15	+20%
20	+30%
50	+100%
100	+200%

Size

The cost of many powers is dependent on the size of the device or the size of the object the device is used with. Bigger things cost more.

Size

Size	Modifier
Baseball	-25%
Dog	-10%
Human	±0%
Motorcycle	+10%
Car	+25%
Bus/tank	+50%
Jet fighter	+100%
Airliner	+200%
Oil tanker	+300%

Speed

This modifier sets the Speed with which a device's power can be used in combat (in other words, how many actions it takes to do so).

Speed

Speed	Modifier
Instant	+50%
1	+20%
2	+10%
3+	±0%

No Man's Land: 138

Chapter Nine:

Sykers

The governments of the world learned much from their long and deadly study of the Reckoning. In America, Pinkertons and Rangers captured numerous creatures, studied countless hucksters, and eventually even learned something of the blessed, shamans, the Hunting Grounds, and mad science. They and other agencies around the world looked for ways to tap directly into this power and create a new breed of "super soldiers."

The magic of the blessed proved useless because they preferred to heal rather than to destroy. That wasn't much fun for the military.

Hucksters were more eager to unleash their power, but their reliance on insane manitous caused a number of tragic if somewhat amusing disasters.

The answer to the dilemma came from studying Asian priests and martial artists. These individuals had learned to tap into the power of the Hunting Grounds directly. No manitou or deity was involved. Their power was channeled solely through their psyches and shaped by mental training.

Both the USA and CSA taught a few "volunteers" these techniques and first put them to use in World War I. The famous Sergeant York was a "syker." The papers said he captured a hundred Germans all by himself. What he and his government kept secret was that York had used his powers to make himself look like a whole company.

Later, folks like Sergeant York were studied, probed, and dissected (posthumously—mostly). By WWII, the sykers were used as spies and commandos. These fledgling agents developed their powers under fire, and few remained to share their knowledge after the war. Those who did hid themselves in top-secret bases around the world and started refining their existing powers and creating new ones.

After the war, low-level conflicts and cold wars made a perfect environment for sykers. Thousands of recruits were pushed through stressful five- and 10-year programs around the world. They infiltrated bases, stole secrets, and assassinated leaders. The most famous incident took place in 2016, when a terrorist posed as one of the United States' President's many mistresses and, in the privacy of the Oval Office, dropped his illusion and gutted the lech like a trout.

The next 20 years saw bigger wars with bigger guns. Laser satellites were accurate enough to burn a pimple off an ass, guided missiles could weave through an office building and hit a rat hiding in the basement, and hover tanks could cross oceans to blow up and invade a country before CNN could interrupt Larry King's virtual call-in show. Sykers were no longer so important.

The military machines kept a cadre of their best sykers around for "black ops," but the young recruits just cost bucks the generals wanted for more hover tanks.

Sykers

Faraway

The most recent chapter of the syker's history was written in, of all places, a whole other world. In 2044, Hellstromme Industries opened the "Tunnel" in space. It was a doorway between our system and another, which Hellstromme himself named "Faraway."

Soon after the Tunnel was opened, probes were sent through, and a planet inhabitable by humans, Banshee, was discovered. Incredibly, Banshee was already inhabited by a race of aliens called the "anouks." Hellstromme's marines only killed a few hundred before they confirmed the anouks were friendly.

At first, only a few scientific colonies were founded. Within the decade, however, ghost rock and other precious metals were discovered, and the rush to Faraway was on.

For the next 30 years, the human colonists lived and worked beside the anouks, slowly culling more resources from Banshee. Just like the old Indian Wars of North America, conflicts between the two races were usually short and savage, followed by "peace treaties" and other agreements broken by both sides in later years.

The Faraway War

Though there were few major conflicts, the anouks developed a genuine dislike for their pasty-skinned visitors during this time. The colonists who rushed to Faraway were by definition the greediest of the bunch, and there were too few law officers to keep the worst of the colonists in line.

In 2074, after a series of unfortunate and violent incidents, a coalition of rebellious humans and anouks attacked the scattered colonists in an attempt to chase them from the planet. The rebels weren't genuinely concerned about the exploitation of the anouks. They were mostly pirates, terrorists, and hordes of trapped colonists who had lost their jobs for one reason or another and now wanted the precious resources for themselves. The anouks did not care for their human allies, but they weren't foolish enough to turn down such well-armed help.

Reinforcements were slow in coming because colonists from different countries had mingled so freely on Faraway that individual nations squabbled over who was responsible for them. The United Nations was asked to step in.

No Man's Land: 140

Sykers

General Warfield

The human and anouk horde was beaten back under the strict command of Major General Paul "Overkill" Warfield, a United States marine in the service of the UN. Warfield didn't believe in economy of force in the face of such a simple enemy. He carpetbombed anouk cities, annihilated their heavy cavalry with hover tanks, and rained artillery down on any large concentration of the reeling aliens.

Then the "skinnies" appeared. Everyone knew the anouks used "life magic" for simple tasks, but rarely had it affected a battle. The skinnies were different. Scores of these ancient and mysterious sorcerers struck across the planet. Using their incredible powers of mind control, the skinnies took over military officials and had them blow up their own troops. They also forced pilots to fly their bombers into mountainsides, and they instigated bloody riots among the colonists. Other skinnies acted as shocktroops, blasting key defensive installations with incredible energy vampirically drawn from prisoners and slaves.

Enter the Sykers

Warfield decided to fight fire with fire. He asked for sykers from the UN member nations and got them. Over 1,000 young recruits with no usefulness on Earth were pressed into service on Faraway. There they were organized into the United Nations Syker Legion, though everyone simply called it, "the Legion."

The Legion was further broken down into troops of around 20 members each. The troops were numbered but came to be known by their nicknames and their symbols, usually emblazoned on a clasp on their uniforms.

The troops were stationed around Banshee and even in certain areas offworld. Their mission was to protect colonists, root out human sympathizers, and—most importantly—protect Warfield's troops from the skinnies.

The Legion learned the power of the skinnies under fire. The anouks thought nothing of sending entire waves of their warriors into certain death just to protect the skinnies blasting away from the rear. The atrocities the sykers saw—and were forced to commit themselves—are still a sore point among those brooding veterans who survived them.

The grueling battles eventually produced a corps of talented sykers who could resist the skinnies. By 2076, the rebels had retreated into the hills, jungles, and canyons of Banshee.

The Red River Campaign

One of the rebels the Legion chased was known as Kreech, a female warrior from the human-named "Red River Canyon." Ground troops sent after the guerilla and her horde literally killed themselves as Kreech's skinnies took over their minds, detonated their armaments, and drove their commanders insane.

Warfield responded with sykers, but the first troop sent into the valley was later found skinned and hanging from the jungle canopy. The second and third troops fared even worse.

Humiliated, General Warfield assembled the entire Syker Legion and threw it into the meatgrinder that became Red River. The sykers rampaged through the enemy camps, searching for Kreech and the skinnies, but they found mostly unarmed innocents trapped between the two armies. Unfortunately, these "innocents" harbored saboteurs, spied for the rebels, and kept the enemy's location a secret, so the Legion was once again compelled to use their overwhelming power on the wrong foes.

In the end, the Legion's ruthless tactics proved efficient, though more than a little merciless. They trapped the skinnies, Kreech, and the last of the rebels and their families in a mountaintop fortress known as Castle Rock. The final assault was an incredible battle between the sykers, the skinnies, and hundreds of fanatic human and alien rebels who would not surrender. Kreech and her followers were wiped out, though they took a great number of the Legion and thousands of support troops with them.

Most sykers do not speak of the Red River campaign and the things that happened there.

Exodus

Morale among the Faraway forces was low when the Last War began on Earth in 2078. The nations of Earth first recalled their conventional forces, hover tanks, planes, artillery, and infantry. It was several months before they recalled their commandos, leaving the Legion to fight a renewed wave of rebel enthusiasm in the wake of Red River and the UN withdrawal.

The months passed slowly. Every day required more acts of violent desperation on the part of the Legion, just to survive in the collapsing vacuum. Finally, the nations of Earth recalled their sykers, creating a mass exodus from Faraway and leaving the colonists behind to stave off the angry anouks and traitorous humans.

Sykers

The *Unity*

The sykers gathered at the UN space station and were placed on one massive transport: the *Unity*. On the way home, these people who had come to rely on each other as no others ever had, vowed that members of the same troop would never willingly cause harm to another, regardless of nationality. It was a foolish vow, and many no doubt later regretted it, but most sykers honor it.

The *Unity* entered Earth-space on November 23, 2082. To their dismay, there was no answer from the ground. The world they had left behind was already dead. The Apocalypse had come during their transit from Faraway.

Suddenly, disaster struck. Something had come through the Tunnel with them. Civilians traveling on the *Unity* reported horrid things destroying the ship. Some sykers stayed. The rest boarded an escape shuttle preprogrammed to land at the UN safe port at Houston, Texas.

There they got their first glimpse of their ruined world. The grim veterans wished their comrades good luck and vanished into the howling wastelands to seek out what remained of the world.

Earth Sykers

The older sykers who had remained on Earth during the Faraway War had a far different experience than their comrades. At first they did what they had always done, serving as commandos, saboteurs, and assassins.

Near the end, in the last months of the war, desperate generals threw them into doomed battles in last-ditch attempts to gain some temporary victory or hold some meaningless piece of ground. Though their powers were great, the lives of the sykers were ultimately squandered. On the battlefield, their powers of infiltration and subversion were no match for the machine guns, laser-guided bombs, and hovertanks of the armies. Even their ability to cloud minds meant little when faced with mindless warbots crawling across the blasted battlefields.

After the war, only a handful remained, and only a few of those survived until 2094. The few "Earth sykers" still stalking the Wasted West are older, more experienced, and more powerful, and they care nothing for their starspanning, younger counterparts who "had it easy fighting a bunch of savages."

Playing a Syker

Sykers focus mental energy and use it to create telekinetic and mind-altering effects. Their powers don't have the scope of true magicians like hucksters of old, but neither must they deal with crafty manitous.

Sykers can use their telekinetic powers to move things on molecular levels, but it's difficult. They can heal wounds, change the shape of an item, and so forth, but only by expending much time and energy. Sykers are also masters of manipulating thoughts. They can cloud a person's mind, create minor illusions, or even take over a subject's will.

None of these powers come easy. The supernatural energy is strong enough to burn the hair from sykers' heads and even fry their brains. The discipline it takes to handle that kind of force takes years to learn, and even then, a syker doesn't use his power foolishly.

If a syker is attacked by a horde of mutants, he uses his machine gun before he resorts to *brain blasts*. If he has to hide from a horde, he crawls beneath a sheet of rusted iron before he uses *chameleon*. If you want to play a syker, realize that this phenomenal power can drain your hero quickly. Use your abilities wisely.

Background

Your character is a syker who served in the Faraway War. Earth sykers are old bastards we'll tell you about in a later sourcebook.

Your hero learned her trade in a government training facility of some sort. In both the USA and the CSA, syker training takes about 5 years. That means your hero has to be at least 35 years old.

There are a good number of foreign sykers stalking about the Wasted West as well. They were trapped in North America when the *Unity's* shuttle landed in Houston. Most are looking for a way back to their own countries, but some know their homes are in no better shape than the American West and have decided to remain here.

Attitude

The vast majority of Faraway sykers had a really bad time on Banshee. This isn't mandatory, but most have an *intolerance* for any kind of authority, especially military authority. General Throckmorton is especially hated.

Most sykers also honor their vow not to harm another from their old troop. This is an *oath* worth 1 point when you first create your hero.

Syker Powers

Sykers call using their abilities "blasting." Powers are learned through hard work and practice, and they use a new skill called *blastin'* (a *Knowledge* Aptitude). Your syker must have *blastin'* at level 3 or better.

Some powers use the syker's *Spirit* to power the effect, but it's skill and training that controls the arcane energy they channel through their bald heads.

Strain

All these fantastic abilities cause Strain, the stress and fatigue that builds up in the syker's brain whenever he uses his powers. We told you in the Aptitudes section in Chapter Two how to figure out what your syker's maximum Strain is, but in case you forgot, it's equal to his *Vigor* die type.

Every power has a Strain cost listed with it. When successfully used, it causes this amount of Strain. An easy way to keep track of your syker's current Strain is by sliding a paper clip up the Strain scale we so cleverly put on your character sheet.

When a syker's Strain reaches the breaking point (his maximum Strain), he can no longer use his powers.

Reducing Strain

Strain is reduced by quiet rest and meditation. Every hour the syker rests allows him to reduce his Strain by –1 point.

Blastin'

To use a power, the syker declares the power he wants to use and makes a *blastin'* roll. Assuming the syker makes the roll, he then marks the Strain, and the power works as described. If the power's Strain would take him beyond his breaking point, the ability doesn't work, and no Strain is suffered.

All supernatural energy comes from the Hunting Grounds. While sykers have developed ways of channeling that power, sometimes things go wrong.

If the syker goes bust on a *blastin'* roll, he suffers a raw power surge to the brain and takes damage to his noggin. The Marshal should tell you how much this hurts.

203

Sykers

Learning New Powers

Before the Big Bang, sykers learned their powers in government-funded academies. They had teachers, learning machines, and a mental ruler across the knuckles every time they did something wrong—to make sure they got it right the next time.

Your syker went to an academy like this, and so he starts the game with one power for every level in his *blastin'* ability. If he has *blastin'* at level 5 (as most well-trained sykers do), he has five powers.

After the bombs, things aren't so easy. Sykers develop new powers only by lots of concentration, experimentation, and practice.

The cost to learn a new power is a flat 5 Bounty Points. As soon as the bounty is paid, the syker can start blasting.

The time it takes to learn a power is fairly short: sometimes minutes, sometimes a few days. Characters can only purchase new powers in between sessions (like with any new skill), but they are otherwise limited only by the time it takes them to earn enough Bounty Points to pay for their new power.

Fortitude

The sykers on Faraway learned a valuable if dangerous lesson from the skinnies. The alien sorcerers could tax their bodies far beyond the normal limits (as defined by Strain), and some sykers learned a way to mimic the effect. In essence, they can draw the life energy from their own bodies and use it just like power from the Hunting Grounds.

For 1 point, sykers may purchase an Edge called *fortitude*. Only characters with *arcane background: syker* who had contact with the skinnies on Faraway (or learned it from another syker who did) may acquire this ability.

Here's how it works. A syker can continue to use powers up to double his normal Strain. The moment he exceeds his breaking point, however, he takes a like amount in Wind, and he must make a Fair (5) *Vigor* check on that action, and the first action he draws in each subsequent round (check every 5 seconds if not in combat). If he fails, he instantly loses 1d20 Wind. If the syker goes bust on a *blastin'* roll while using *fortitude* (his Strain is beyond its breaking point), the power fails, he takes damage as usual, and he loses 1 point of Strain permanently.

Sykers

Powers

Below are the powers available to sykers. Here's a description of just what all the junk beforehand means.

TN is the Target Number the syker needs to make the power work. "Opposed" means the syker must compare his roll to one made by his opponent. Remember that in an opposed roll, the minimum TN is still a 5. A *blastin'* roll less than that is a failure, even if the opponent rolls less.

Strain is the amount of stress the syker suffers for using the power. A syker never suffers Strain if he fails his *blastin'* roll.

Speed is the number of actions or time it takes to complete the power.

Duration is how long the power stays in effect. If the duration is 1 round, it lasts until the beginning of the next round, regardless of when the power was first enabled in the previous round. "Concentration" means the power stays in effect as long as the syker does nothing but simple actions. A number means the syker can take that much Strain at the start of each round (or time period) to keep the power working.

Range is the maximum distance at which the power takes effect. Unless a power says otherwise, the target of a blast must be in sight of the syker.

Arson

TN: 7
Strain: 3
Speed: 1
Duration: Instant
Range: 10 yards/*blastin'* level

"Burn it to the ground."
—General Warfield after the fall of Castle Rock, 2078

Arson is pure "pyrokinesis," the ability to create and manipulate fire and flame. It's great for cooking hot dogs, s'mores, and all those angry muties who think you should share.

Arson creates a fiery burst with a diameter equal to the syker's *Spirit* die type in yards. Targets within this burst take 2d10 damage and catch fire if they take a single wound. Burning targets take 2d6 damage at the beginning of each round thereafter, though the Marshal might raise or lower this amount if the bad guys are particularly dry or wet. See **Fire** in Chapter Five (page 103) for information on dispersing fire damage and how a victim can put himself out.

Brain Blast

TN: 5
Strain: 1
Speed: 1
Duration: Instant
Range: 20 yards/blast level

Most every syker learned to rely on *brain blast* in the Last War. The surge of energy it produces can destroy flesh, break bricks, and rend metal with but a thought.

Brain blast is a tremendous beam of energy that streams like a laser from the syker's head to the target. The blast does not "home in" on the target, so the syker must actually hit to inflict damage.

The attack roll is equal to the *brain blast* roll. Simply compare the *blastin'* roll to the TN to hit the target. This is a purely physical attack, so figure in cover and any other negative modifiers due to range, wounds, running, and so on.

Brain blast has a range increment of 10 and a ROF of 1. It affects both animate and inanimate targets. Raises allow the syker to modify the hit location as normal.

Once a target is hit, the syker should roll his *Spirit* as damage. (Add the dice together just like a firearm, and reroll Aces.) Add bonuses due to supernatural levels of *Spirit* to the total. Hence a *Spirit* of 4d12+2 would add +2 to the final damage total, not each die rolled.

Chain Brain

TN: Opposed (*blastin'* versus *Spirit*)
Strain: 1
Speed: 1
Duration: Instant
Range: 20 yards/*blastin'* level

Chain brain strings a bunch of minds together and slaps them silly. It's not particularly dangerous, but it feels like it is. Sykers use this one to stun guards or race through a room of losers they don't have time to kill.

The syker picks a single target in range and treats his *blastin'* roll as an opposed roll against the target's *Spirit*. If the syker wins (and beats the power's TN), the victim is stunned and must make an Onerous (7) *Spirit* roll to recover. If the victim's already stunned, he rolls against the higher TN.

With a raise on the opposed roll, the syker can immediately make a second strike against another target within the power's range of the first (20 yards per blast level). If the syker gets another raise, the power jumps again, and so on.

Sykers

Chameleon

TN: 9
Strain: 1
Speed: 1
Duration: Concentration
Range: Self

If you can't beat 'em, hide and blast 'em from behind. So say the sykers who use this power.

Chameleon manipulates an opponent's mind to "edit out" the syker's image. It's a very difficult power to use, since the syker must contact his opponents' minds, blur out his own image, and even make sure the shadows in his mental illusion are just right. This requires absolute concentration, so the syker can't move, use a power, or even whisper without ending *chameleon's* effect.

Characters who aren't actively looking for the syker don't even get a chance to see him. Those who are make a *search* roll as usual, though the syker adds +6 to his *sneak* roll. Once someone actually spots the syker, that target can see the syker normally. Others can see the syker only when they win their own opposed *search* versus *sneak* roll, or once the syker stops his concentration.

Fleshknit

TN: Special
Strain: Special
Speed: Special
Duration: Permanent
Range: Self

A syker with this power can take a lickin' and keep on tickin'. *Fleshknit* allows him to heal his worst wounds, even when a sawbones would start cutting the syker up for parts.

Fleshknit is mind over matter to the extreme. The syker sits and "listens" to the pain coming from one particular area. Then he speeds up his metabolism, hastening clotting, helping white blood cells kill infection, and knitting the flesh itself back together. This requires complete synchronization of mind and body, so sykers can't heal anyone other than themselves with *fleshknit*.

The TN, Strain, and time required to piece wounds back together again is shown below. Each success reduces the wound level of a single affected area by –1. Roll and pay the Strain of each area knitted. Failure when trying to heal a maimed limb means it's a permanent wound.

Note that unlike most healers, sykers cannot heal Wind with this power.

Note that sykers use their minds to heal themselves, not their hands. Even if bound or otherwise restrained, they can heal themselves.

Also, *fleshknit* doesn't do crapola for poisons, diseases, or the glows. Use *purge* for that job.

Fleshknit

Wound Level	TN	Strain	Time
Light	5	1	1 minute
Heavy	7	2	5 minutes
Serious	9	3	15 minutes
Critical	11	4	30 minutes
Maimed	13	5	1 hour

Rosey is a grim veteran of Faraway who made the mistake of signing on to guard a caravan. Sure enough, it gets jumped by muties, and in the course of fighting them off, the syker catches a rusty shiv in the belly.

Rosey has a serious wound to the guts. She must make a *blastin'* roll of 9 or better. Rosey meditates for 15 minutes and rolls a 15. That's a success and one raise, meaning her wound goes down –2 levels to light, at a cost of 3 Strain.

Sykers

Mindrider

TN: Opposed (*blastin'* versus *Smarts*)
Strain: 1
Speed: 2
Duration: Concentration
Range: 100 yards/*blastin'* level

Sykers were used primarily as spies up until their mentors realized how great they were at assassination. That's where *mindrider* came from. It's a lot like "clairaudience" and "clairvoyance" all rolled up in one.

The syker first establishes a link with his target by touch. At that point, he makes his *blastin'* roll versus the victim's *Smarts*. If he's successful, he gets in the target's mind and can see and hear everything the victim does, as long as he pays 1 Strain every 10 minutes.

A character with a *mindrider* in his cranium gets a Hard (9) *Smarts* roll on contact and every 10 minutes thereafter to notice something is wrong. Once he does, the victim gets the feeling he's being watched and subconsciously (or consciously if he's familiar with sykers) tries to eject the rider from his cranium. This requires a raise on an opposed *Smarts* roll (not *Smarts* versus *blastin'*), which may be attempted once every 10 minutes.

Mindwipe

TN: Opposed (*blastin'* versus *Smarts*)
Strain: 3
Speed: 10 minutes
Duration: Permanent
Range: 5 yards/*blastin'* level

Sykers never get embarrassed. Why? If they do something stupid, they just scramble your memories around and make you forget it. That's if they don't just kill you, brainer.

Mindwipe causes a target to forget the last few minutes. The power can't make new memories, only create a "blackout" in which the target remembers nothing.

To use this power, a syker makes an opposed *blastin'* roll versus his opponent's *Smarts*. With a success, the target forgets the last five minutes. Every raise extends the blackout another five minutes.

Most subjects don't seem to notice the blackout. They don't even know something's missing. If the Marshal feels the victim would be suspicious (like all his buddies are dead, or his beer got warm), he gets a Fair (5) *Smarts* roll to realize something's up, though only someone who knows the ways of a syker might know just what happened.

Purge

TN: Special
Strain: 3
Speed: 10 minutes
Duration: Permanent
Range: Self

Only sykers use a healing power to kill. An old syker assassin's trick is to poison a drink, then pour both himself and his unsuspecting victim a glass from the same bottle, canteen, or other container. Then the syker uses *purge* to flush out the poison while his victim lies gurgling in the dirt.

That was the old days. In 2094, sykers don't have too many folks to assassinate. There's still plenty of people who need killing, but real assassinations are few and far between. The real use for *purge* these days is to flush out diseases, poisons, radiation, and other nastiness before it sets in and makes itself at home.

A syker can *purge* most toxins within 12 hours of the time they get into his system without harm. After that, or in less time if the syker's blood has been pumping faster than usual, the toxin has set in, and the poor fellow's out of luck.

The TN to *purge* poisons, diseases, radiation, and other toxins is shown on the table below. In the case of radiation, a successful *purge* returns all Wind lost due to radiation poisoning (see Chapter Five). Like all ailments, once someone attempts to heal it by supernatural means and fails, it's permanent.

Purge

TN	Toxin
3	Colds, most nonfatal poisons
5	Common viruses
7	Most natural poisons (such as snake venom), infections
9	Radiation, chronic infections
11	Tough viruses such as ebola or AIDS
13	"Supernatural" diseases such as tummy twisters, the touch of a faminite, or any plague started by Famine

Rosey got stabbed by a rusty piece of metal and got tetanus. The Marshal decides that's a chronic infection, so Rosey needs a 9 on her *blastin'* roll to get it out of her system. If she fails, the infection can't be cured by magic.

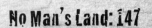

Sykers

Shh!
TN: 5
Strain: 2
Speed: 1
Duration: 10 minutes/1 point of Strain
Range: 10 yards/*blastin'* level

Every now and then, despite a syker's best efforts, someone spies her going about her dirty business and decides to be a tattletale. *Shh!* shuts the blabbermouth up quick.

Unlike *silence*, which actually creates a field that dampens sound, *shh!* locks up a target's mouth and vocal folds by sending neural impulses from the brain to the victim's jaws and throat. This prevents him from speaking, grunting, or making any sort of intelligible sound from his throat. It's frustrating and quite deadly when some flunkie can't tell his commanding officer what he wants to know, and he can't even explain why he sounds like a wounded seal.

Of course a victim can still write, point, draw pictures, or play charades, but by the time such a message is conveyed, the syker commando is usually long gone.

Shh! has one additional perk. For every raise on the syker's *blastin'* roll, she can affect one other person within range.

Silence
TN: 5
Strain: 1
Speed: 1
Duration: 10 minutes/1 point of Strain
Range: Self

Commandos, assassins, and saboteurs are sneaky types for one simple reasons: Every nation on Earth executed special operatives when they were caught. Needless to say, the sykers quickly learned how to hide (thus the *chameleon* power) and sneak. The problem, however, was that most of the things the sykers did once they got in position made loud bangs. That's where *silence* comes from.

Silence cloaks the syker in a field of absolute silence. He can run, shout, fire a weapon, or otherwise perform any action that would normally produce noise, but in absolute silence. When the syker's *sneakin'*, an opponent relying solely on sound has no chance of detecting him. If the opponent has a chance of seeing the quiet commando, the power simply adds +4 to his *sneak* rolls.

If he suddenly needs to shout for help, the syker can end the power at any point.

Skinwalker
TN: Special
Strain: 3
Speed: 1
Duration: 1 hour/1 point of Strain
Range: Self

Nearly 200 years ago, during the Great Rail Wars, a Rail Baron named Simone LaCroix captured a number of hideous creatures called "skinwalkers" and used them against his foes. The governments of both the North and the South studied the shapeshifting dopplegangers, but never could figure out their secrets. When sykers created this power, their mentors named it after the old horrors (some of which might still sit starving but immortal in secret underground labs, by the way!).

Skinwalker allows a syker to take on the form, image, and voice of someone else. To use the power, the syker merely beats the TN and pays the cost in Strain. The TN depends on how much the syker knows about the person he's imitating, as shown on the table.

The syker can only alter his appearance, not create complex illusions. That means that even if the duped person is carrying a rifle, the hero does not have one unless he has something to disguise as a rifle, like another rifle or a stick. The Marshal must decide what elements the syker can disguise and what he cannot, but in general, physical features, clothes, hair, and the like are included in the illusion.

Characters who recognize the target don't usually notice the disguise and have no chance to notice the illusion unless the syker does something out of the ordinary. Characters who know the target well automatically get once chance to see through the disguise, and another after any unusual action, such as the target doing something out of character or not knowing some bit of trivia the target should have down cold.

Seeing through the disguise is an opposed *scrutinize* versus the syker's *blastin'*.

Skinwalker

TN	Familiarity
3	Intimate
5	Close friend
7	Friend
9	Acquaintance
11	Someone met once or twice
13	Someone seen on video

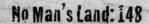

Slow Burn

TN: 7
Strain: 1 per Armor level
Speed: Special
Duration: Instant
Range: 100 yards/*blastin'* level

Sykers were rarely expected to duke it out with a tank, but their teachers wanted them to have a big can of whup-ass if they did, so this is the power they came up with.

Slow burn allows a syker to take out even the most-heavily armored targets, though it requires a little time and risk. To do so, the syker "probes" the target with a visible beam of crackling energy, determining the strength of its armor, and then releases an armor-piercing (AP) bolt of psychic energy to take it out.

The target must have at least 1 level of Armor (not light armor) to be affected. The power's Speed is equal to the Armor value of the target. On the last action of concentration, the syker makes his *blastin'* roll against the power's TN and the TN to hit the target with a Range Increment of 20. The syker adds +1 to the attack roll (not the *blastin'* roll) for each action spent probing, up to the target's Armor level.

If both rolls are successful, a blast of psychic energy streaks from the syker's head. This blast has an AP value equal to the target's Armor, and it causes xd6 damage, where x is the target's Armor.

A syker can make a called shot with this power by applying the modifier to her attack roll (but not her *blastin'* roll).

Tattletale

TN: Opposed (*blastin'* versus *Spirit*)
Strain: 2
Speed: 5 minutes
Duration: 5 minutes
Range: 5 yards

Commandos rarely have time to stage elaborate interrogations. *Tattletale* allows a syker to drag information from a foe's mind without the poor schmuck realizing he's been violated.

A syker who engages his opponent in conversation and uses this power can get the target to talk about things he ordinarily would not. Even better, the target remembers the talk, but he forgets he revealed anything.

This is an opposed *blastin'* roll versus the target's *Spirit*. The syker gets some information with each success. The Marshal says how much.

Syker Powers

Power	TN	Strain	Speed	Duration	Range	Description
Arson	7	3	1	Instant	10 yards/*blastin'*	Sets fires.
Brain Blast	5	1	1	Instant	20 yards/*blastin'*	Damages foes.
Chain Brain	*blastin'* vs. *Spirit*	1	1	Instant	20 yards/ *blastin'*	Hurts several foes.
Chameleon	9	1	1	Concentration	Self	Hides syker.
Flesh Knit	Special	Special	Special	Permanent	Self	Heals syker.
Mindrider	*blastin'* vs. *Smarts*	1	2	Concentration	100 yards/ *blastin'*	Uses foe's senses to spy on him.
Mindwipe	*blastin'* vs. *Smarts*	3	10 minutes	Permanent	5 yards/ *blastin'*	Makes foe forget things.
Purge	Special	3	10 minutes	Permanent	Self	Heals diseases.
Shh!	5	2	1	10 minutes/ 1 Strain	10 yards/ *blastin'*	Silences other people.
Silence	5	1	1	10 minutes/1 Strain	Self	Silences self.
Skinwalker	Special	3	1	1 hour/1 Strain	Self	Disguises self.
Slow Burn	7	1/AV	1/AV	Instant	100 yards/	Fires an AP blast.
Tattletale	*blastin'* vs. *Spirit*	2	5 minutes	5 minutes	5 yards	Pries secrets from foes.

No Man's Land: 150

Chapter Ten:

Templars

Simon Mercer was an accountant in Boise, Idaho. He had a family, a house, a car, was a member of the local Freemasons, and even a Boy Scout Master—a nice, average fellow.

He was on a business trip when the bombs fell. His entire life vanished in a skull-shaped mushroom cloud.

Simon returned to Boise and confirmed what he already knew: His family was gone. From there he wandered the West for over a year, shambling from town to town, working for food while wrestling with severe depression.

One day, Simon was enjoying tainted milrats somewhere in Colorado when General Throckmorton's goons showed up and demanded their "tithes." The town paid up, and Simon watched as the people went hungry over the next several weeks.

Then a tough female Law Dog showed up, and the town begged her for help. She agreed and set off after the Black Hats.

A few days later, she came riding in from the wastes on a motorcycle. She screamed for the townsfolk to let her in and help fight Throckmorton's goons hot on her heels, but to Simon's horror, they refused, saying that if they let her in, the soldiers would destroy them all.

The Ranger cursed and screamed but stood her ground anyway, trying to protect the ungrateful town, as was her sworn duty. She never had a chance. Simon thought it poetic justice the Black Hats overran the town anyway.

Simon managed to escape the carnage and return to Boise. During the trip, his depression slowly turned to anger. The Ranger had been one of the good guys, and she had thrown her life away for those who wouldn't even fight beside her to protect their own homes.

When Simon reached Boise, he wandered into the ruins and went to his old Freemason's Temple. A deep fever took hold as he lay in the dark, stone building for days, staring at the pictures of the Knights Templar, an order within the Masons' secretive organization. His delirious mind dreamed of the knights of old and watched the pictures of their battles come to life.

When Simon Mercer finally awoke, he knew what he must do. He would become the first of the new Templars, a heroic figure who would protect the weak. He would draft others worthy of the title to join him, and they would bring order and compassion to this dark world.

But these new Templars would not make the same mistakes as the noble but foolish Law Dogs. The Templars would not throw their lives away on lost causes. Nor would they die for those that did not deserve their efforts. Thus he would cull the guilty and preserve the righteous.

Simon took an ancient, ceremonial sword from its display case, then made a tabard from an old sheet. Upon the tabard he painted the red Maltese cross—symbol of the Knight's Templar.

Templars

Crusade

Within a year, Simon had recruited scores of followers. A few were simply after the power he promised to deliver to them, but those were quickly rooted out by Simon and his most-loyal inner circle.

Gradually, the incredible supernatural energies of the world embraced Simon and his Templars. They began to develop minor but important powers. Templars do not blast foes like Doomsayers or sykers, but they do benefit from lesser supernatural benefits rewarded by whatever forces of goodness still watch over this ruined world. Some believe their benefactors are the spirits of the Knights Templar; others say it is God. A few believe their holy rewards come from the spirits of all the heroes who have fought evil and wickedness in the past.

Regardless of where this power comes from, Templars gain rewards after achieving important goals. Experienced and pious Templars have numerous such gifts that help them heal, fight, and elude their foes.

Today there are several hundred Templars crossing the Wasted West, looking for wrongs to right. They do not offer their services lightly, but when they do, even Throckmorton's heavily armed and armored Black Hats take note.

The Temple

With so many Templars, Simon eventually realized that there needed to be some sort of central headquarters for communication and support. In 2088, he returned to the Temple in Boise and declared himself "Grandmaster." A trio of other Templars serve as his permanent council, and a few squires attend to the building itself.

Since the building is inside the ghost-rock storm over Boise, there are few visitors. It is a plain building decorated with a single, large white flag marked with the red cross of Malta.

Templars are expected to visit the Temple once per year. There they meet with Simon and inform him of their deeds and the state of the world. For this reason, Simon knows much about the Wasted West.

Civilian petitioners are heard daily. They may ask the Templars for help, and if they seem worthy, Grandmaster Simon might assign a single visiting Templar to accompany them home. That Templar may still do as he wishes—including refuse aid—once he is on the case.

Initiation

New Templars must spend a year of their life in the service of another Templar. They are called "squires" until they either die, leave the side of their mentor, or are brought before Simon to be made Templars themselves. Squires wear no special uniforms, nor are they issued equipment. Many carry makeshift swords they've made themselves, for they must learn hand-to-hand combat before their mentor can recommend their advancement.

Each Templar may only have one squire at once. Simon feels training more than one at a time wouldn't allow the mentor to properly teach them not only *how* to be a Templar, but *why*.

Once the year is up, and if the mentor thinks his student has learned well, he presents his squire to Simon in Boise. The Grandmaster meets with the petitioner, asks him about his adventures, and—if he is satisfied the squire demonstrates the proper intelligence, humbleness, and piety—Simon awards the squire a Templar's sword and tabard. If not, the squire returns to his mentor's service for another year.

Being a Templar

Templars are a strange lot. They turn their backs on entire villages one day, then give their lives for a single child the next. Their philosophy centers around worth, piety, and the greater good. They protect those who they feel benefit the world with their lives. Those who do nothing to help civilization, and who might even harm it, are not to be defended. They don't help the wicked and don't have any compunction about "blackmailing" a settlement or individual into changing their ethics in return for their help.

Some have called them selfish, and there is a certain truth to it. Templars believe their lives are valuable to the future of humanity, and they don't risk them without a good reason.

Disguise

A Templar's primary tool in deciding whether or not a person, family, or village is worthy of their efforts is to visit them disguised as a mutant, an outcast, a diseased soul, or some other pitiful wretch. If those in need treat him poorly, he usually leaves before they even know they were on the brink of salvation. If, instead, they are sympathetic and compassionate to the disguised Templar, he may choose to reveal himself and pledge his sword to their cause.

Templars

Oaths

Templars and their squires are bound by two oaths: poverty and blood.

The Oath of Poverty states that a Templar must gather only those goods and provisions necessary to carry out his duties and survive. A Templar may own a vehicle to help him travel quickly across the wastelands, but such wealth often makes it hard to disguise oneself so vehicles are often hidden outside of town before a Templar approaches a community.

The second vow is the Oath of Blood. Simon has tried to rescind the powers of a few Templars he felt did not uphold the ideals of the order, but without success. Once granted, it seems, their rewards are permanent. For those who seriously abuse their power, through theft, murder, or cowardice, Simon's only recourse to protect the honor and integrity of his order is to send other Templars out to hunt down the errant knights and kill them

When time and distance prohibit Simon's judgment, Templars are expected to judge their brothers and sisters for themselves and slay any who grievously violate their oaths. This is the Oath of Blood.

Swords

All Templars start with a "free" sword awarded to them by Simon himself. The weapon serves as a symbol of their station and as a useful backup when bullets are scarce.

Templars consider hand-to-hand combat a sign of bravery, but they don't hurl themselves into a fray when a gun serves them better. They generally use their swords to save precious bullets, when they want their foe to taste the fear of retribution before they perish, or when they face overwhelming odds and want to go down swinging.

Partly due to Simon's blessing and partly because Templars live with a sword in hand, they add +1 to their *fightin': sword* and *quick draw: sword* rolls. The *quick draw* bonus applies only to the Templar's sword and not any other weapons he carries.

Templars don't like to lose their swords. If one is ever taken, they vow to get it back. They also revere their brothers' and sisters' swords. When one falls, other Templars eventually come to claim his sword. These are then taken to the Temple in Boise and hung in a place of honor.

Templars

Playing a Templar

To be a Templar, your character must be at least 18 years old and purchase *arcane background: Templar*. She must also have certain skills that allowed her to pass from squire to full Templar, as shown below. Your character must also be relatively good-hearted. No cannibals or raving lunatics need apply.

Templar Skills

Skill	Minimum Level
Academia: occult	2
Faith	3
Fightin': sword	4
Medicine	2
Survival	2

Religion

Note that your character must have *faith*. Simon has not made religion an official part of the order, though Christianity was integral to the old Knights Templar and the Freemasons as well. Simon is a Christian himself, but he knows in this day and age, there are many other religious beliefs, and most all denominations believe God has forsaken the world anyway.

What *faith* represents in this case is the Templars' belief that some "good" presence still watches over the world. There are many theories within their ranks, but the most common is that the Templars are rewarded by the spirits of fallen heroes of the past. These spirits are commonly called the "Saints."

Simon has not shared this with anyone, but a few years ago he learned about the Harrowed known as Stone and his true role in bringing about Hell on Earth. Since then, Simon has come to believe his order's Saints are those heroes who defeated the Reckoning the first time around but were murdered by Stone when he went back into the past and changed history. An intriguing mystery for a later date.

Oaths

As you might guess, your hero must take the Templar's Oath, which includes a vow to help the worthy, the Oath of Poverty and the Oath of Blood. All together, this is a -5 point *oath* Hindrance. All Templars have this *oath*. Those who violate it—and are caught—quickly gain a -5 point *enemy* instead.

Rewards

Templar magic isn't nearly as spectacular as that of Doomsayers or sykers. Most of their "gifts" are small blessings that affect only the Templar himself. Offensive gifts don't strike enemies down. They augment the Templar's own prowess or perhaps deliver some sort of additional effect when a Templar smites a foe himself. Defensive powers aren't glowing shields able to keep out tank rounds. They're small improvements in the Templar's own body that help him resist shock and heal slightly faster than usual.

Rewards are measured in levels from 1 to 5 (they don't go any higher). The higher the level, the more powerful and beneficial the reward.

A beginning Templar receives 5 levels divided between any two rewards, though *lay on hands* must be chosen as one of these two rewards.

Gaining & Improving Rewards

A new reward can be bought at level 1 for 5 Bounty Points. This takes the Templar a full day of meditation.

Improving a reward costs double the new level and requires a like number of hours in meditation. Thus, raising *lay on hands* from level 1 to 2 costs 4 Bounty Points and requires four hours of meditation. As with Traits and Aptitudes, only 1 level in a power can be raised between game sessions, no matter how many Bounty Points the hero might have.

Greater Rewards

After a Templar reaches level 5 in a particular reward, there is one extra perk to be gained: the greater reward.

Greater rewards are obtained by completing noble and important quests. Your Templar may automatically choose a greater reward for any power he has at level 5 when he or his posse receives a Legend Chip. There is no Bounty Point cost for this reward.

The powers on the following pages all list their greater reward. When one is granted, the Marshal must figure out exactly how the new blessing manifests itself—no bathing in golden rays of light. Greater rewards usually manifest in subtle and humble ways, such as a dream, a sudden revelation, or—as in the case of *beast friend*—a critter that suddenly shows up and takes a liking to your hero.

Templars

Armor of the Saints

The Saints look after their own.

Each level in *armor of the Saints* reduces any damage the Templar takes by a like amount. At level 5, for instance, 23 points of damage is reduced to 18 points of damage.

Greater Reward: The Templar gains 1 point of real, honest-to-God armor. If the hero also wears any other type of armor, it adds to it. A Templar in a Kevlar jacket, for example, has an Armor level of 3: 2 for the jacket and 1 for his Greater Reward. And yes, he still subtracts –5 (–1 for each level in *armor of the Saints*) from whatever damage manages to get through as well.

Beast Friend

Beasts can sense fear and other human emotions. Templars are a stoic lot, and those with this gift seem a little less "human" to normal animals.

A Templar with this reward gains +1 per power level to all *ridin'*, *teamster*, and *medicine: veterinary* rolls.

Greater Reward: the Templar can "bond" himself to a particular creature. The animal isn't supernatural, though it does become a little smarter than the average dog, horse, bear, hawk, or whatever once bonded. The animal can understand the Templar's commands and obeys them to the best of its ability.

The statistics for several common animals can be found in Chapter 17. The Templar can usually choose which beast to bond himself to, and if he wants he can even wait until he finds that particular creature before declaring his bond.

Celerity

By clearing their thoughts of distractions and exercising their incredible wills, Templars can increase their effectiveness in stressful situations, such as combat. Each level in *celerity* allows a Templar to discard one of his Action Cards in combat and draw another in its place. Jokers may not be discarded, but any other card, high or low, may be.

Greater Reward: The Templar gains one additional Action Card in combat. This allows him to have 1 more than the usual maximum of 5 cards in a single round.

Templars

Command

Templars are stern taskmasters. When one says jump, most folks do it.

Command doesn't turn a person into the Templar's puppet, but it can make a scavvie drop his gun, or a mutie run for the hills.

Each level of *command* adds +1 to the Templar's *leadership*, *overawe*, and *persuasion* rolls.

Greater Reward: The Templar can gain temporary but powerful control over a single individual. He can issue a single command as an action by making an opposed roll of his *faith* versus any human target's *Spirit*. This reward has no effect on creatures without a human spirit (so walkin' dead are immune, but Harrowed are not!). If the Templar succeeds, the target loses an action. With a raise, the victim must carry out a single, short instruction.

Victims of the *command* can still refuse to do anything to directly injure themselves, but they can be made to harm others, including their close companions. In rare cases, such as *commanding* a victim to harm a loved one, the victim should get a second chance to resist the *command*.

Guise

Templars often disguise themselves to watch those they are thinking of aiding. Only if those folks seem honest and compassionate does a Templar reveal herself and provide service.

This gift helps the Templars remain incognito. Each level adds +1 to the hero's *disguise* skill. The bonus only works when the Templar is attempting to blend into a crowd or, more often, appear as an afflicted beggar or mutant. *Guise* never helps a Templar pretend to be a specific person. It could be used to look like just another bandit in a large gang of road warriors, but not to slip into one of Throckmorton's 20-man patrols, because they all know each other.

Greater Reward: The Templar's *guise* actually becomes an illusionary ability he can adapt at will (Speed 1). No props, clothes, makeup or other "special effects" are required. His bonus to *disguise* is still +5 (+1 for each level he now has in *guise*), but most folks don't even attempt to *scrutinize* the Templar unless they have good reason to.

Inner Strength

"The power of righteousness lends great strength."

—Simon Mercer, 2088

Simon's words must be true. Each level of *inner strength* adds +1 to the Templar's *Strength* rolls, including those made to cause damage.

Greater Reward: The Templar's *Strength* actually raises a step permanently. Remember that if your hero already has a d12 in *Strength*, one additional step raises it to d12+2.

Lay on Hands

The first lesson a Templar learns is how to heal. Only after this ability is mastered and the Templar's *faith* and compassion are proven does Simon invest the hero with more sacred power.

To use this power, the Templar makes a *faith* roll against the TN of the victim's highest wound level, as shown on the table, adding +1 for each level in this reward.

If he makes the roll, every area on the victim improves +1 level. If the Templar fails the *faith* roll, the victim is not healed, and the hero cannot attempt to aid him again until 24 hours have passed. Failure when trying to heal a maimed limb means it's a permanent wound.

A Templar can use the power on any particular victim only once per day. He can also use his power on himself.

Templars

Lay on Hands

TN	Wound Level	Time
3	Wind	1 minute
5	Light	5 minutes
7	Heavy	10 minutes
9	Serious	15 minutes
11	Critical	20 minutes
13	Maimed (limbs)	30 minutes

Greater Reward: The Templar gains the ability to cure ailments too. The TN of his *faith* test depends on the severity of the toxin.

Curing

TN	Toxin
3	Colds, most nonfatal poisons
5	Common viruses
7	Most natural poisons, such as snake venom; infections
9	Radiation, chronic infections
11	"Supernatural" diseases such as tummy twisters or any plague or illness started by Famine or his minions

Survivor

Templars are hard to kill. This reward proves it.

Immediately after a Templar dies, he may draw from a fresh deck a number of cards equal to his level in this power, plus another for every point of Grit.

If a red Joker comes up, the Templar clings to life. Maybe he lies in the desert for hours or days before a band of nomads finds him and nurses him back to health. Maybe he drags himself into an old cave and lays in delirium for a week. Perhaps a seemingly terminal fall deposits him in a snowdrift. Or maybe he just hangs on to life by the slimmest thread until help finally manages to arrive.

A black Joker means he's coming back from the Great Beyond in a different way. Marshal, this reward replaces the usual Harrowed draw. Don't do it twice. No Joker equals death.

Greater Reward: Even after a Templar has suffered a maiming wound to the head or guts, he can keep fighting as long as he makes an Incredible *(11) Vigor* roll on his first action of each round. Afterward, he drops to the ground like any other brainer and can start drawing cards as described above.

Templar Powers

Power	Description	Greater Reward
Armor of the Saints	Reduces damage by the number of levels in this power.	Adds 1 point of Armor.
Beast Friend	Adds +1 to *ridin', teamster,* and *medicine: veterinary* rolls per level.	The Templar can bond himself with an animal.
Celerity	For each level, the hero can discard an Action Card and draw a fresh one.	The Templar gets +1 Action Card every turn.
Command	Each level adds +1 to the hero's *leadership, overawe,* and *persuasion* rolls.	The Templar gains temporary control over an individual.
Guise	Add +1 to the Templar's *disguise* for each level.	The disguise becomes an illusion.
Inner Strength	Add +1 to the hero's *Strength* die rolls.	Add +1 step to the hero's *Strength.*
Lay on Hands	Can actually heal others.	Can cure ailments too.
Survivor	Helps the hero hang on to life.	Can fight on, even with a maiming wound to the head or guts.

Chapter Eleven:

Beyond the Pale

There's nothing worse to a gunfighter than having to scratch a notch *off* his pistol. In *Deadlands*, however, it just might happen. You see, death isn't always the last you might hear of a really tough hombre.

What you're about to learn lends a whole new meaning to the word "survivor." The Marshal should let you read this chapter only after your character kicks the bucket and digs himself out of his hole.

Strong-willed individuals sometimes come back from the grave. These individuals are given "unlife" by manitous, evil spirits looking for a joyride in the host's mind and body. When this happens, the host becomes an undead being called a "Harrowed," which means "dragged forth from the earth."

A manitou in an undead host is slain if the brain is destroyed (one of the few ways these malicious spirits can truly be destroyed), so they only risk their otherwise eternal souls on individuals with exceptional abilities. Weak or infirm mortals are only possessed when it suits some truly diabolical purpose.

Becoming Harrowed

Whenever a player character dies in the game and her body is mostly intact (especially the head), she draws 1 card from a fresh deck of cards, plus 1 additional card for every point of Grit she's got.

If the player draws a Joker of either color, her character is coming back from beyond the pale. Otherwise, the manitous are not interested in her spirit, and it passes unmolested through the Hunting Grounds to the Great Beyond.

Most Harrowed stay in the hole 1d6 days. It takes a while to fight for the hero's soul and then another 10-12 hours to dig herself out—assuming she was buried properly. Some come back quicker; some take longer—especially if the body was mangled worse than usual.

Very few characters come back from the dead, so you shouldn't go catching bullets hoping to come back with all kinds of cool powers. Unless your character has a lot of Grit, odds are you're wormfood.

Dominion

Manitous need the energy of a mortal soul to survive in the physical world. This means they must keep their host's soul around. When they inhabit an undead host, they constantly fight with the soul for control.

When the manitou has "Dominion," the human soul loses all contact with the outside world. It has no memory of anything the manitou does while it's in charge. The manitou can still draw on the host's memories, however. It uses these to pass itself off as the mortal while it causes mischief and mayhem.

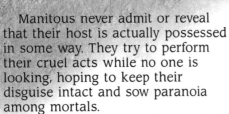

Manitous never admit or reveal that their host is actually possessed in some way. They try to perform their cruel acts while no one is looking, hoping to keep their disguise intact and sow paranoia among mortals.

Occasionally, the manitou wriggling around inside your Harrowed hero is going to take control. Bet on it.

The Nightmare

Manitous first battle for Dominion moments after snatching mortal souls as they pass through the Hunting Grounds. This spiritual test of wills manifests as a horrible nightmare drawn from your character's own past. That's why we had you fill in the "worst nightmare" box on the back of your character sheet.

The Marshal draws on this information when she's ready to put your stiff through Hell, so try to be fairly detailed. That means you'd best have a history built up for your character by the time she kicks the bucket.

The Unlife of the Harrowed

So what's it like being undead? It's definitely a mixed blessing. A walking corpse is a tough hombre in a fight, but he doesn't have an easy time making friends.

The first few hours an undead crawls back into the world aren't pleasant. His last memories are of whatever caused his death, and then he usually finds himself waking up in a grave or some other strange place. Whatever wounds the brainer died of don't seem as bad as they should, but he bears a scar or some other evidence of his death wound that *never* goes away.

The Harrowed's body doesn't adjust to its new state quickly. At first, rigor mortis causes the character seizures, and his mind is fuzzy as well. For the first 2d6 hours after returning from the dead, the Harrowed's Traits (both Coordinations and die types) are halved.

Things aren't much better once the fog clears a bit. The character still doesn't know why he thought he died but is still walking around. Even more confusing, if he listens for a heartbeat, he hears one, though it sounds more like a pregnant flutter than a heartbeat (that's the manitou wiggling around inside). If he tries to cut himself, he bleeds, but the blood is thick and dark and clots quickly.

Powers

After a while, the Harrowed figures out he's undead. Eventually, say when someone blows out his midsection and he keeps on fighting, he might decide being a stinking corpse ain't all bad.

Harrowed have two types of powers: common and personal. Read on, and we'll tell you more, friend.

Common Powers

As you already know, all Harrowed are born back into the world in a similar state of undeath. The manitous inside them just have to do a few things in certain ways to keep the stiff walking and in good condition (relative to a walkin' dead, that is). This gives the Harrowed a slew of common powers they share with the rest of their grisly kinsmen.

Here's a quick rundown on the various innate abilities a Harrowed gets just for being a living corpse.

Death Wounds

As you'll see in a bit, Harrowed regenerate. Gut one like a trout, and he's fine in a few days. The exception to the rule is the hero's "death wound." It heals, but it never "sets" quite right. A survivor who was hanged might have a long, crooked neck. A Doomsayer hacked up by muties has scars like a jigsaw puzzle. No one's likely to notice these details unless they're looking for them, but they can be a dead giveaway to someone who's wise to the ways of the living dead.

Most Harrowed go out of their way to cover up as much of their wounded flesh as they can get away with. In the Wasted West, where most folks wear dusters and rags to keep the fallout off, they blend in just fine.

Of course, some means of death leave scars that can't be covered up. Get fragged by a plasma gun and you're going to look pretty gross no matter how many bandages someone slapped on afterwards. When you're thinking about how your character died, try to take all of this into account, and describe his wounds in some detail on the back of your character sheet.

Decay

Undead characters have pale, sallow skin. They don't rot, since the manitous inside them sustain their bodies with magical energy, but they don't exactly smell like roses either. Up close and personal (say dancing or getting frisky), another character gets a Fair (5) *Cognition* roll to sniff rotten meat. Whenever an undead drinks a quart or so of alcohol, the difficulty of detecting his undead state by smell goes up to Incredible (11) for the next 24 hours. By that time, the rotgut seeps out his rotten innards and any other holes he might have in his carcass. In the meantime, he just smells good and liquored up.

Animals always react poorly to a piece of rotting meat that has the audacity to walk around on two legs. They can detect something's wrong with a Harrowed up to several yards distant. All *ridin'*, *animal wranglin'*, and *teamster* rolls are made at -2.

Drugs & Alcohol

Harrowed can never be poisoned, catch non-supernatural diseases, get drunk, or be affected by drugs.

Some of them *think* they can get drunk or high, and they act accordingly, but it's all in their heads. Even the undead have "issues."

Food

Strangely, the undead do need to eat—at least if they want to repair any damage their carcasses have taken. Theirs is a diet of meat: fresh or long-dead, it doesn't matter. The manitous draw energy from the meat and use it to rebuild the flesh of their hosts.

A Harrowed who hasn't eaten at least a pound of meat in the last 24 hours can't make a healing roll. This is why Harrowed are sometimes mistaken for ghouls by those with just enough knowledge of the occult world to be dangerous.

Harrowed don't need water, but a little whiskey can keep the stench of death down (see **Decay**).

Grit

Becoming a member of the walking dead hardens the mind. Seeing a horde of radrats eat your best friend is still unnerving, but a fellow who can shoot himself in the heart and keep on laughing learns to accept these things.

Add +1 to your character's Grit after returning from the grave.

Pain

Undead don't suffer greatly from pain, but they still can't shoot as well if half their shooting hand is blown off. They can ignore 2 levels of wound modifiers per area. In other words, only if the Harrowed sustains a serious or greater wound does he suffer a "pain" modifier. Lesser wound modifiers are ignored. This is cumulative with any other abilities that allow the creep to ignore pain, such as *thick-skinned*.

One last perk. The Harrowed never make stun checks caused by physical damage (magical effects that cause stun checks work normally).

Regeneration

Besides keeping the Harrowed's skin soft and smooth (relative to the average cadaver, of course), the manitous also rebuild their hosts' flesh from damage—as long as they have some other meat to replace the undead flesh (see **Food,** above). Unlike living heroes who only make natural healing rolls every week, the Harrowed may make healing rolls once per day.

If the Harrowed can't get meat, he can't make any healing rolls. A Harrowed who's been dismembered and can't find anyone to feed him food is still alive. He's just not

real mobile (and maybe a little embarrassed when the next scavvie comes along). This can be a unique kind of Hell if the Harrowed is trapped in this way for any length of time. Remember, the only thing that can kill a Harrowed is for its brains to be destroyed. They can even survive a beheading (though they *really* hate that).

The brains are the motivator of the Harrowed's body. A body part that's amputated doesn't work any more. If the Harrowed was somehow decapitated, the head would still work fine, but its control over the rest of its body would cease. Someone would have to sew the head back onto the body and feed the head some meat so it could start healing. Then the Harrowed would eventually be as good as new.

If the Harrowed's digestive tract is destroyed, that's okay. She just puts the meat in her innards, and her body absorbs it.

A body part that is totally removed or destroyed cannot be regenerated (unless the hero has the *reconstruction* power). A Harrowed can sew cosmetic body parts back on (such as an ear or a chunk of flesh), but hands, eyes, and the like don't start working again right away just because they've been stitched back on.

It takes time to heal severed body parts, but this can be done normally (roll once per day for each wounded area). Once the wound is healed from maimed to critical, the damaged limb can be used again, and the stitches (or whatever) that were holding the limb on can be safely removed.

Finally, the undead can never benefit from any form of healing that regenerates living flesh. This includes medicine as well as supernatural means. Even a syker with the *fleshknit* power can't heal reeking meat.

Sex

It just can't happen. Without getting into any gritty details, undead males can't get their gats out of their holsters, if you catch our drift. And even if they do somehow manage to find some way to draw, they shoot blanks. This doesn't mean they might not try. They are still men after all. They're just doomed to failure.

Female Harrowed can fake it a little better than males, given some preparation. A gal "working" her way across the Wasted West might even be a little better at her job, given a lot of perfume.

Beyond the Pale

Sleep

A manitou needs a few hours of "downtime" every night to keep its host from rotting away. For this reason, a Harrowed must "sleep" for 1d6 hours out of every 24.

If the Harrowed doesn't voluntarily crawl under a rock for a few hours of shut-eye, the manitou may well shut everything down for him. The demon isn't going to zonk his host out in the middle of a firefight, but it may well do it while he's supposed to be on watch. Who cares about the rest of the posse anyway?

When the manitou decides it's time for some maintenance (usually at the same time normal folks sleep), but the Harrowed wants to fight it, the hero and the Marshal should make an opposed *Spirit* roll every hour. If the demon wins, it's bedtime for bozo. Otherwise, the Harrowed manages to stay awake.

Fighting the manitou like this is exhausting work. The undead subtracts 1d4 Wind for every 24-hour period he doesn't go dormant. When he finally does shut down and lets the manitou do its work, he regains 1 of these lost Wind for every hour of shut-eye. A Harrowed who drops to 0 Wind in this way falls to the earth like— well, like a corpse. Once the body returns to at least 1 Wind, then the manitou puts him to sleep for 1d6 hours as usual.

Sleeping Harrowed aren't entirely unaware of their surroundings, by the way. The manitou always keeps one eye half-open for trouble. Should someone sneak up on the hero, allow her a *Cognition* roll versus the opponent's *sneak*. Add any modifiers for *light sleepers* as well.

Undeath

The undead can ignore bleeding and Wind caused by physical damage, drowning, or other indirect damage that affects the body's organs. The Harrowed still take Wind caused by magical or mental strain, such as failed *guts* checks or supernatural powers, however.

More importantly, though they take wounds normally, Harrowed can't be killed except by destroying the brain. The manitou needs that to make the body function.

If the noggin takes a killing blow (is maimed), the undead and the manitou inside it are destroyed. In fact, this is the only way to ever actually destroy a manitou.

Killing blows to the guts area put a Harrowed down until the manitou inside heals the damage back to critical or less. Then they just get up and start looking for whoever put 'em down.

Personal Powers

The manitou crawling in your hero's innards is a powerful critter. With talent, practice, and more than a little luck, your survivor can tap into its power and make it his own. These abilities manifest as extensions of the Harrowed's own personal background. What follows is a short list of some of the most common. There are tons more in *Book o' the Dead*.

When choosing powers, try to find ones that fit your survivor's Hindrances, Edges, background, and personality as a whole. A character with a nasty disposition, for example, could raise her *Strength* or grow *claws*.

Most powers have 1 to 5 levels. Harrowed don't start with any powers, but you can buy a new power for 10 Bounty Points, which gives your character that ability at level 1. Additional levels are bought with Bounty Points for 2 times the value of the new level. Raising a level 1 power to level 2, for example, costs 4 points.

Power Descriptions

Each power has only two elements: Speed and Duration.

Speed is the number of actions it takes to activate the power. Some powers, such as *supernatural trait*, are always on and don't require any kind of activation.

Duration is how long the power lasts. "Concentration" means the power ends if the hero does anything other than simple tasks. If a number is listed, the Harrowed must expend that much Wind per round (or other time period) to keep the power active.

Dispositions are Edges, Hindrances, and backgrounds that tend to lead to these powers. Your hero doesn't have to have one of these to get the power. Just consider them guidelines on what types of Harrowed might learn these powers.

Claws

Speed: 1
Duration: As desired
Dispositions: *Two-fisted, all thumbs, bloodthirsty, grim servant o' Death, one-armed bandit, ugly as sin, vengeful*
A lovin' woman can leave vicious scratches down a fellow's back, but that's nothing compared to what a Harrowed can do. These claws can slice through a spine like a hot knife through a toxic zombie.

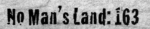

Beyond the Pale

The character's hands turn into cruel claws at will. The higher the level, the bigger the claws. The damage of the claws is added to the character's *Strength* roll whenever she hits using *fightin': brawlin'*, just like the claws were a hand-held blade.

The Harrowed can extend or retract the claws by simply thinking about it, and this simple act can pierce even leather gloves (if worn). Keeping them out or in requires no concentration on the Harrowed's part.

Claws

Level	Damage
1	+1d4
2	+1d6
3	+1d8
4	+1d10
5	+1d12

Dead Man's Hand

Speed: 2
Duration: Concentration
Dispositions: *Curious, one-armed bandit, sneak*

Harrowed with this power can continue to control their own severed limbs for short periods of time. The undead creep could cut off his hand and let it run around a room on its own, or give an eyeball to a compadre so the Harrowed can spy on what's going on when he doesn't happen to be around. Pretty creepy isn't it? Creepy, but useful.

If a Harrowed attempts to attack with an animated severed limb, he uses his own statistics, but he must subtract –4 from the *fightin': brawlin'* roll. The damage from an animated hand, by the way, is half the character's normal *Strength* total, read as nonlethal damage. These limbs are much better at opening jail cells and causing distractions than beating the living Hell out of someone.

The undead typically remove their hands or eyes for use with this power. It just doesn't make much sense to slice off your foot and send it after someone.

The duration the body part can be controlled while separated from the owner depends on the user's power level. After that, the parts rot like normal dead flesh unless reattached. Only one of the hero's body parts can be manipulated at a time.

Anyone seeing an animated limb must make a Hard (9) *guts* check.

Dead Man's Hand

Level	Duration
1	1 Wind/round
1	Concentration
3	Concentration or 1 Wind/round
4	10 minutes
5	1 hour

Marked for Death

Speed: 1
Duration: Variable
Dispositions: *Arcane background, grim servant o' Death, vengeful*

The dead are a merciless bunch of bastards. Get one riled up enough, and he might sacrifice his own flesh to make sure yours gets cooked.

Marked for death works simply. The Harrowed nominates a target within sight, makes a gesture the victim can see, and rolls a contest of *Spirits*. The Harrowed adds his power level to the roll.

Should he win, the target is *marked for death* and cannot spend Fate Chips to negate damage. The drawback is that as long as the power's in use, the Harrowed is *marked for death* too.

A Harrowed can only ever have one victim *marked for death* at one time, though he can drop the mark as an action as long as he can see the victim and reverse whatever gesture he made the first time around (no roll is required).

Relic

Speed: Special
Duration: Special
Dispositions: *A trademark piece of equipment, belongin's, a junker*

Some folks invest more than money in the equipment they use. They put a little piece of their soul into their favorite belongings as well. Sometimes the item even becomes part of the hero's legend and develops a history of its own.

A relic is just that: an item charged with supernatural energy. These come into being when they are bound closely to an event of momentous importance. The death of a hero and her subsequent resurrection as a Harrowed is frequently more than enough cause to give rise to a relic. A gunslinger who used nothing but his trademark Buntline, for example, is due for an upgrade should he come back from the grave.

The exact power of the relic is always up to the Marshal. There's no way we could cover every possibility, so we're leaving it up to you and your Marshal's imagination.

Beyond the Pale

As your hero gains levels in this power, his relic becomes more and more powerful, useful, or helpful as well. Again, the Marshal must determine exactly what that means, but here are a few pointers.

First, a relic sometimes merely mimics another power, spell, or ability. If it resembles another Harrowed power, the relic's power level corresponds to the levels of the imitated power.

Gunslingers and their prized weapons, a long tradition in the West, are prime targets for this power. Each level might add another die of damage to bullets fired from the favored gun. Or the power might add accuracy in the form of +1 to hit per level.

Not all relics need be weapons. Maybe a tale-teller has found an old mini-cam, and when he comes back from the dead, it gains the ability to show ghosts or other spirits. Or maybe someone who's about to die appears in black and white. The creepier the power, especially when it comes to things other than weapons, the better!

The possibilities are endless. If you have a good idea for your Harrowed's relic, talk it over with your Marshal. Together, the two of you should be able to come up with something that is powerful and useful, but still balanced enough that it doesn't ruin the campaign and, more importantly, doesn't overshadow your character's *personal* accomplishments. A creep with a gun that automatically hits and kills anything might be fun for a while, but who couldn't win with a gimmick like that?

Of course, one major drawback with relics is that they can be lost or stolen. Worse yet, they might even be used against the hero. And for some strange reason, a relic can always kill the person it was empowered by, regardless of immunities or the normal damage rules for Harrowed (treat your hero just like a normal brainer). A pistol that shot its Harrowed maker in the gut, for instance, could kill him again, even though it's not a head shot.

Such is the way of the mad Hunting Grounds, where the powers of these awesome artifacts are forged.

If the relic is ever truly lost, the Marshal should allow you to work on recreating it somehow. The best way is for your hero to pick up a similar item and start using it constantly. Eventually, the gadget attunes itself to your hero, and you're back in business. The Marshal has the final call, but by and large, a replacement relic gains +1 power level per month until it reaches your hero's former level.

Spook
Speed: 1
Duration: Instant
Dispositions: *Mean as a rattler, "the stare," veteran o' the Wasted West, "the voice," ugly as sin*

This power gives a Harrowed's target a glimpse into the twisted corridors of his dark soul, and it ain't a pretty sight.

The Harrowed draws upon the power of the manitou within to add a creepy element to her voice, appearance, and sheer presence. This is an opposed test of wills between the Harrowed's *overawe* and the target's *guts*.

Besides any normal test-of-wills results, a target who loses this contest must also roll on the Scart Table (tucked away in the Marshal's Handbook). The level of the Harrowed's power determines the number of dice the victim must roll on the Scart Table.

Spook

Level	Scart Dice
1	1d6
2	2d6
3	3d6
4	4d6
5	5d6

Supernatural Trait
Speed: Always on
Duration: Permanent
Dispositions: Any

A gunslinger with supernatural *Quickness* can be deadlier than a chaingun, and a savage with heightened *Strength* can put a sharpened hubcap through a cinder block.

This power raises any one Trait (chosen when the power is purchased) by +1 step per level. The power is tied to a particular Trait, though a character can have multiple *supernatural traits*.

The trait raised should somehow reflect the character's personality or past. A Templar would probably gain supernatural *Strength* or *Quickness*, for example, while a syker's *Knowledge* or *Vigor* might be affected.

One way to figure out what Trait might be affected is to look at the hero's highest Trait. That's most likely the one he uses all the time. If so, that's the one that ought to get raised. A Doomsayer wants the biggest *faith* total he can get, so bump up the stiff's *Spirit* and watch him grin.

No Man's Land: 166

Chapter Twelve:
The Power o' Fear

Soiled pants. Shaky nerves. Stark, raving madness. These are the end results of sheer terror. It is said the mysterious Reckoners feast on the fears of mortals.

Now that your hero has had some experience with the minions of the Reckoners, it's time you learned a few of their secrets. The Marshal should let you read this section if your hero has *academia: occult* at level 3 or greater.

Abominations

One of the first things a veteran of the Wasted West learns is that there are far more dangerous things out there than outlaws and mutants. There are also monsters, real monsters pulled from humanity's worst nightmares or born in the terror-drenched Deadlands.

183

A hero who's been around a while might also discover that the nastiest of these creatures sometimes have powerful supernatural essences that can be absorbed after their death. This is called "counting coup" and results in your hero gaining some strange new ability. Before the Apocalypse, only Harrowed could count coup, but now anyone near the fiend as its essences "bleeds" off can do so. The Marshal has full details on how this is done. Just make sure your hero isn't too far away when a really wicked beast goes down.

Fear Levels

Don't laugh at the power of fear. It's turned most of the world into a Deadland, so it is very, very real. It took the Reckoners over 200 years and a little cosmic cheating to make it happen, but as any brainer can see, it worked.

There's two ways an area can become a Deadland. The traditional way is for some horrific creature to go about its terrible business in an area. Assuming no hero steps up to slay the thing, it eventually (and unconsciously) "terrorforms" the land in fear by its very actions.

The second way a place gets turned into a Deadland is by ghost rock bombs. Unless the description says otherwise, all cities in the Wasted West are Deadlands.

Most towns and the wastes in between them are slightly less steeped in terror. We rate the "Fear Level" of a place on a scale from 0 to 6, with 6 being a Deadland and 0 being a quiet town in 20th-century America.

185

Any sort of supernatural evil gets advantages as the Fear Level rises. The Marshal has the details, but you should know that fighting the walkin' dead on their home turf is much worse than fighting them out on the open prairie somewhere (unless that stretch of prairie got turned into a Deadland as well).

The Power o' Fear

Fearmongers

The worst of the abominations are the "fearmongers," powerful creatures responsible for creating the most fear in an area. Defeating one of these suckers comes with a lot of rewards (see **The Big Payoff**), but first you need to know a little more about just what a fearmonger is and isn't.

Fearmongers are not common, and they're not easy to defeat. A servitor of the Reckoners, such as a hunger spirit, is almost always a fearmonger. It's the biggest, baddest thing in an area. An ancient vampire, liche, or other powerful monster is usually a fearmonger as well.

Sometimes a fearmonger is a group of horrors instead of a single monster. A pack of wormlings terrorizing an area might be the fearmonger instead of a single powerful individual. Of course, if they're led by an ancient rattler, they're just its minions, and the rattler is the fearmonger.

The threat has to be one that locals fear and dread more than anything else in the area, and even then, the threat must break a certain threshold. If the locals are scared to death of pink flowers, they're just wacky (unless we're talking about carnivorous flowers slowly growing towards their town, and then they're just really observant wackos).

Finally, don't expect every adventure to even have a fearmonger. If you're fighting muties or an outlaw biker gang, they're probably just bad guys. They might be plenty dangerous and even scary, but they're not *horrific*. These fights are great ways to build your character's skills and abilities for the real threats, however.

The point is that a fearmonger must be very powerful, supernatural, and horrific. Lesser threats certainly contribute to the overall Fear Level, but defeating the local bully just isn't a big enough deal to lower an entire Fear Level. Even fending off Throckmorton's goons is inspiring, but doing so can't cause a Fear Level to drop because you're not fighting against *that* kind of fear. Still, such tasks are a great way to get warmed up for tougher foes.

In any event, your Marshal determines what's a fearmonger and what's not, so you don't really have to worry about it. We just wanted you to have some idea what's worth getting killed over and what you should probably run screaming from.

The Big Payoff

Fearmongers are nasty sorts, and they're never alone. Don't expect to walk in on the King Rattler sleeping. Your posse is going to go through Hell just to find out the thing is responsible for the local disappearances, let alone where it's lairing, how many minions it has, and—most importantly—how to kill it.

But when you do, the rewards are great. We're talking real "save the world" stuff here. Specifically, putting a fearmonger away has three rewards: lowering the Fear Level by telling the tale, gaining Grit, and winning Legend Chips.

Tale-Tellin'

The heroes are at the front line in the battle against the Reckoners and their minions. Destroying abominations saves lives and has an immediate effect, but the heroes can only truly exploit their successes by telling others about the defeat of evil.

The folks in Omaha might appreciate your posse clearing it of flesh-eating slugs, but by telling the tale elsewhere, even more folks can start to gain hope that they can defeat whatever evil confronts them.

This makes the *tale-tellin'* Aptitude the greatest weapon the heroes have against the Reckoners. When heroes defeat nefarious evils, they can tell the masses of their victories and attempt to reduce the Fear Level of an area. If the overall Fear Level of the world is reduced enough, it just might be possible to one day defeat the Reckoners.

Soon after the defeat of a fearmonger, usually at the climax of the adventure, someone in the posse should tell the tale. Taletellers, Templars, and Doomsayers are the most likely candidates.

The tale-teller needs to speak to at least half the community that was affected by the fearmonger, or at least some influential portion of it. At the conclusion of the tale, the speaker makes a *tale-tellin'* Aptitude roll against the TN of the Fear Level in the locale in which the fearmonger was defeated, as shown on the table below. If the speaker is successful, the Fear Level drops by 1 immediately. Further tales have no effect on the area until another fearmonger is defeated or a certain amount of time passes (known only to the Marshal).

The downside is that if the speaker goes bust on a *tale-tellin'* roll the audience hears only the grisly details of whatever horror your hero's

Do I Have to Save the World?

Some characters may not care about all this Reckoning business. They're more interested in gaining fame and fortune. That's fine. As long as *someone* tells of their deeds, the world still benefits from their victories.

This means every adventure that takes place in *Deadlands* matters, no matter how insignificant it might seem on the surface. Better still, your posse isn't forced into saving the world time and time again. It just happens naturally as long as your group continues to defeat evil.

Feel free to save one little girl. Or go into a ruined city looking to kill monsters and take their stuff. Anything goes, and you'll *still* be fighting the Reckoners.

described. They may not acknowledge their fears, but they're not likely to grab their pitchforks and shovels to help out either. This *raises* the Fear Level by +1 point (to a maximum of 6).

Sometimes, it's rumored the Reckoners' most persuasive minions spread tales like this on purpose. Pretty sneaky, huh?

Tale-Tellin'

Fear Level	TN
1	3
2	5
3	7
4	9
5	11
6	15

Modifiers	Reasons
+1	Each "lesser" threat dealt with (maximum of +5).
-1	Each hero who died in the process (maximum of -5).
-1 to -5	Sacrifices made by the locals due to the posse's efforts.

The Power o' Fear

Charge!

Does that mean all the heroes ought to charge into the highest Deadlands—the cities? Not really. Two reasons.

First, the vast majority of the world hovers between Fear Level 4 and 5, and there's a whole lot more of these areas than there are Deadlands. It's just simple math. If the survivors of the Wasted World can reduce the overall Fear Level to somewhere between 3 and 4, a few savvy folks—like the Prospector—think the Reckoners may die. Of course, it is a worldwide effort, but the American West is where everything started, and it seems to be the center of the Reckoners' power.

The second reason not to go charging off into the cities is kind of a catch-22. Sure, each Deadland that gets "healed" is a real pain to the Reckoners, but because of the sheer number of horrors lurking around such a place, and the advantages the Deadland itself gives them, heroes who spend a lot of time in cities are likely to just wind up dead. And the death of a true hero hurts the cause more than anything. Just ask that bastard Stone, if you can find him these days.

Grit

"Grit" is a measure of your hero's willpower and his exposure to the sinister power of the Reckoners. After he's battled bloodwolves and walkin' dead, he gains some resistance to fear and terror.

Every time your character defeats (or takes part in the defeat of) a fearmonger, his Grit goes up by +1 point to a maximum of +5. Every point of Grit adds +1 to the character's *guts* checks, steeling him against any horrors the Reckoners have to offer. That doesn't mean the walkin' dead don't put a chill up even a veteran survivor's spine. He's just not as shocked as someone who's never seen them before.

No one has to tell the tale or sing your hero's praises for him to gain Grit. As soon as the fearmonger goes down, the character realizes he's fought a creature beyond imagining and won. This gives him the strength to keep fighting the next time his posse encounters the horrors of *Deadlands.*

Legend Chips

There's one last benefit to be gained from defeating a fearmonger. When you successfully lower a Fear Level, the Marshal places a special chip into your posse's Fate Pot. This is called a "Legend Chip," and since it's special, you're going to need some way to distinguish it from all the other chips. The easiest way to do this is for the Marshal to just color an extra poker chip with a marker.

The Legend Chip represents a bit of the legacy your posse leaves in its wake. Fate smiles on those who persevere against the odds, so Legend Chips can be used for special purposes above and beyond the norm.

The Legend Chip can be played as a blue chip and has a value of 4 when reducing wounds or being converted into Bounty Points. In addition, the Legend Chip can be used to let you completely reroll a Trait, Aptitude, or damage roll from scratch—even if you've already gone bust or spent other chips. You can also give it to another player without sacrificing any other chips (see Chapter Six).

The only problem with a Legend Chip is after it's used, you must roll a die. Odd, it's gone for good. Even, all that good karma sticks around (put it back in the Fate Cup). Use them wisely.

The Marshal never gets to use a Legend Chip. Should she draw a Legend Chip, she must return it to the pot and draw again.

The Marshal's Handbook

Marshal: 172

Chapter Thirteen: The Reckoning

Now that you've read the dirt we fed those gullible player types, it's time to let you Marshals in on the real secrets of *Deadlands: Hell on Earth*.

Let's start with a little prehistory.

There have always been monsters in the world. All cultures have their bogeymen, night terrors, haunts, spirits, werewolves, vampires, ghouls, and zombies. And they *are* real—don't let yourself think otherwise.

Such abominations dwell in the physical world. In the spirit world—the Indians call it the Hunting Grounds—nature spirits and manitous are most common. Nature spirits are generally good or at least neutral toward the affairs of humanity. Manitous are downright evil.

Manitous drain fear and other negative creations the abominations spawn, and they channel them back to a special place in the Hunting Grounds called the Deadlands. That's where the ancient and mysterious Reckoners once dwelled.

The manitous live only to serve up death and destruction in large helpings. They aren't aware why, nor do they really care. What the spirits do know is that the Reckoners tap the energy the manitous bring to the Hunting Grounds. Most of it is used to sustain their unnatural existence on Earth, but some small sparks are still hurled back into the physical world to bring new abominations to life. These abominations then create new fears to feed the manitous, who carry it back to the Hunting Grounds, and so on.

It's an ongoing, vicious cycle with razor-sharp teeth, and it's been going on since the dawn of time. As you can imagine, matters got out of hand, and things were looking bad for the home team—right up until the end of the Middle Ages.

The Great Spirit War

That's when the Old Ones—the elder shamans of various Indian tribes in the American East—called a council deep in the mountains of New England. There they discussed the state of the Earth and the increasing number of horrors that walked upon it. Their people suffered as no others, having little in the way of technology, arms, or armor to protect them.

The Old Ones knew there was no way to banish all evil from the land at once. The abominations would have to be defeated one at a time. If the manitous were gone, however, they reasoned, far fewer new abominations would be born.

So it was that the Old Ones asked the spirits of nature to war against their evil cousins, the manitous. The spirits agreed, but their price was high. The Old Ones would have to enter the Hunting Grounds and join them in their war.

The Old Ones traveled to an ancient Micmac burial ground and performed an arduous ritual. When they were through, a portal to the Hunting Grounds stood open.

The Reckoning

The shamans stepped through and began their long fight. The "Great Spirit War" raged for hundreds of years. The Old Ones eventually tracked down and defeated their foes, but found that the manitous, being spirits, could not truly be destroyed. The best the Old Ones could do was defeat them and hold them to a sacred bond: As long as the Old Ones remained in the Hunting Grounds, the manitous could not meddle with humanity.

The Old Ones were trapped (seemingly forever) with the malignant spirits they had defeated, but the horrors of our world abated and began to dwindle. The price the shamans paid was high, but they had won.

A Tale of Vengeance

Centuries later, in 1763, a young Susquehanna shaman named Raven was completing his studies. He was a great student, devouring his lessons as if each was his last meal.

One summer day, he sat on a high mountain in the colony the white men called Virginia. As he meditated, his conversation with the nature spirits was cut short by the sounds of musketry near his village far below.

Raven climbed down the mountain as fast as he could, the cruel din of battle mocking his every step. His feet felt as if they were made of stone, and the miles seemed like leagues. When he finally arrived, he saw a band of whites butchering his family. They had been the last band of the Susquehanna.

Now he was the last son.

Raven Reborn

Soon after the massacre of every human being he had ever held dear, Raven left the valley he had always called home and wandered the land looking for ways to increase his own power and exact vengeance on those who had murdered his people.

The shaman learned many secrets of the world during his travels among both the Indian tribes and the towns of the white men. The first was that of long life. Though born in 1745, Raven looks no more than 50 years old today.

The most important secret he learned, however, was that the Old Ones had left the long-forgotten door to the Hunting Grounds wide open, unaware they would not be able to return.

Between 1861 and 1863, Raven visited all the other tribes he could find and spoke solemnly of the massacre of his people at the hands of whites. He said he was the last of his tribe, the "Last Son," and he was searching for other braves who shared his blind anger.

The Last Sons

Other shamans often sensed Raven's long quest for vengeance had consumed him with evil. Most banished him, but sometimes a vengeful youth adopted by the tribe would turn his back on his new family and follow Raven. These young men understood his sorrow and his rage. They were the last of their tribes, families, or villages as well.

They were the Last Sons.

Raven told his followers their troubles were caused by the coming of the whites. In some cases, it just happened to be the truth. In others, it was yet another gross misunderstanding between two different peoples.

In either case, Raven told the Last Sons he knew how to defeat their common enemy. He would release the manitous from their old bond. And there would come a Reckoning.

Raven told the braves who chose to take up with him and follow his ways that the manitous were their peoples' protection against the white

The Reckoning

man's invasion. The Old Ones were fools for their actions. They had condemned the tribes to a long and painful road that could only end in their extermination.

Raven told the Last Sons it was their sacred duty to travel to the Hunting Grounds and return the spirit world to its natural order. But there was only one way to accomplish their task. The Last Sons would have to enter the Hunting Grounds and destroy the Old Ones.

The Hunt

The Last Sons began their long trek from the southwestern deserts and plains to the wooded mountains of New England early in 1863. The group reached the old Micmac burial ground in which the Old Ones' gate was hidden on the first of July of that year. With little ceremony, the Last Sons stepped through the open gate and into the Hunting Grounds.

The battle with the Old Ones took many weeks as time is reckoned in the Hunting Grounds. In that strange place, the Last Sons committed one atrocity after another, all in the name of vengeance.

The Last Sons emerged from their war for retribution on July 3, 1863, at the end of America's greatest and bloodiest battle of the Civil War—Gettysburg—and just scant hours before America's Day of Independence. Many of the Last Sons had not returned from their battle, but they had been successful in their quest.

The Old Ones were dead, their blackened spirit-blood forever staining the hands of their slayers.

The manitous were free.

The Reckoners Awake

The Reckoners had turned their attentions to other places when the manitous ceased bringing them delectable morsels of fear from Earth. Now a flood of energy washed over them, feeding the mysterious beings and waking them from their centuries-old malaise.

The Reckoners reveled in the feast and realized the mistakes of their past. They would no longer horde their power. They would return bits of it to Earth, spawning more abominations and creating even more fear.

The mortals below would bleed pure terror. When there was enough fear to sustain them, when the Earth was finally terrorformed after their own Deadlands, the Reckoners would descend and walk upon it.

The Story Begins

The grand story of *Deadlands* spans over 200 years and more than one world. Here's a brief overview of events.

The Weird West

The Weird West takes place in 1876, 13 years after the Reckoning began. The reign of terror infested every desert, canyon, town, and hollow with fearful beasts born of nightmares. Things went the Reckoners' way for a while. Site after site fell to their evil desires and became a Deadland.

Amazing events occurred. California was sundered and became a labyrinth of towering sea canyons. The Civil War, which should have ended in 1865, dragged on until 1876 and beyond, neither side able to gain an advantage due to the horrors that followed in the wake of any battle. Salt Lake City became the capital of a new state, Deseret, and the western territories between the North and South became a lawless frontier known as the Disputed Lands.

Perhaps most importantly, a new superfuel called "ghost rock" was discovered. What no one knew was that this new mineral had been planted across the world by the Reckoners as part of their grand scheme. It triggered incredible discoveries. Steam-powered ornithopters soared over the prairies, and deadly flamethrowers immolated terrible horrors. These and thousands of other odd devices gave birth to "mad science."

Unfortunately, the incredible value of the new mineral also gave way to violence. The Great Rail Wars started as the railroads tried to be the first to reach the Great Maze in California, one of the richest sources of ghost rock in the world. Thousands died in this terrible conflict, and in the end, only the Reckoners truly won.

Things went according to the Reckoners' insidious plan for a long while, but these ancient beings hadn't counted on the stubborn heroes of the West. Lone gunslingers, courageous buffalo gals, wily hucksters, mad scientists, fierce braves, wizened shamans, and—perhaps most importantly—the Pinkertons and Texas Rangers, all fought the horrors inflicted on their world, with more determination than the Reckoners ever dreamed possible from the human race.

These heroes won. Almost 200 years later, the Reckoners' presence on Earth was all but wiped out.

The Reckoning

Hell on Earth

With the last of their influence on Earth, the fading Reckoners did something they had never attempted before and—because of the energy it took—knew they could never do again. They ripped a hole in the Hunting Grounds and sent one of their most faithful servants back in time to the Weird West. He emerged from a secret portal hidden deep in Devils Tower and set out on his unholy mission at once.

This grim, undead gunslinger, known only as Stone, had lived through the Reckoners' defeat and is one of the few who remembers the "Lie." This traitor quietly assembled a pack of bloodthirsty assassins to hunt down heroes like rabid dogs. They were all too successful.

Boot Hills across the West filled with heroes' bones. With few there to stop them, the monsters of the Weird West grew unchecked. Slowly, Deadlands formed, each creating a climate of fear that sparked even more pain and suffering for humanity.

This time, the Reckoners won.

The Reckoners' secret plan to seed the world with ghost rock succeeded. Two hundred years later, the Last War broke out because of it.

Bombs made from irradiated ghost rock covered the world, but worse than the nuclear carnage, they were also filled with angry manitous. Once released on the planet, the devastation was followed by an incredible maelstrom of evil spirits and arcane energy.

The bombs destroyed most of the world. Toxins, plagues, famines, and war destroyed almost all that was left. The incredible carnage and rush of energy from the Hunting Grounds completed the Reckoning. Earth became a Deadland. The Reckoners manifested as physical beings in the American West, showing their true form as the Four Horsemen of the Apocalypse. They rampaged through the few survivors and eventually stalked off East. No one knows where they are today, but most believe they will return once the Wasted West has rebuilt.

It is now 2094. The Reckoners have won, but they're trapped here on Earth. If the Wasted West's heroes can reclaim the land, the Reckoners might be destroyed once and for all.

The Reckoning

Lost Colony

Long before the Last War, Dr. Darius Hellstromme invented something called the "Tunnel," a giant ring in Earth's orbit that opened a doorway to another system. Hellstromme dubbed it "Faraway."

Probes returned pictures of a distant system of many planets, at least one of which was inhabited. Humanity was not alone.

Hellstromme's marines were sent to greet the aliens, and after a few brief conflicts, humanity breathed a sigh of relief when they were welcomed with open arms. The "anouks," as they called themselves, proved friendly.

Years later, ghost rock was discovered on the anouks' home planet, Banshee, and the rush was on. Millions of Earthers headed for Faraway to seek their fortunes.

Things went well for several decades, but then human agitators began to tell the anouks they were being exploited. The aliens cared little at first, but slowly, the agitators—most of them wanting Banshee's wealth for themselves—got their way. Some of the most violent anouks turned to raiding isolated mining outposts. When the colonial marines responded heavy-handedly, the anouks banded together against their common foe. The Faraway War broke out, but the marines had far superior technology and gave the more primitive anouks a bloody lesson in modern warfare.

Then the Last War broke out on Earth. The colonial military forces splintered and fought among themselves as well. The anouks regrouped and began a new offensive, this time with the aid of their ancient shamans, the "skinnies." The colonists still managed to hold out, especially with the aid of the Syker Legion, but eventually most of the human forces were recalled to aid their home nations on Earth.

Shortly after the military withdrew, the Tunnel collapsed. The colonists were on their own. Munitions were limited, food was scarce, and the settlements were stretched thinly across Banshee and other outposts in the Faraway system. The war began anew, but this time the natives had the advantage. Between the humans' dwindling supplies and numbers and the sabotage of the agitators, the tide began to turn.

That's when someone noticed the Tunnel was still active. Ships could enter Faraway, but they could not leave. But what was coming through had not come from Earth's solar system. This was something entirely new—and terrifying.

No More Secrets

When we first published Deadlands, we promised to reveal its "Big Secret" in August of 1998. Now you've seen it, and we hope you think it was worth the wait.

Now we have a new surprise for you, but no more big secrets. *Deadlands: Hell on Earth* will be followed by *Deadlands: Lost Colony* in 2000.

The game will use the same rules, and you'll be able to play your old characters from either *The Weird West* or *Hell on Earth*, plus a few new types as well.

Okay, so we might have a few secrets we don't want to give out just yet. Just trust us that *Deadlands: Lost Colony* is a whole new setting with a whole new feel—and terrors the likes of which you've never seen.

Stick with us, compadre. This story ain't over yet.

Changing the Story

Do the heroes of the Weird West face a hopeless future? Are the inhabitants of Faraway doomed? Absolutely not.

If the heroes of *The Weird West* continue to thwart the abominations of the Reckoning and eventually destroy Stone, the Reckoners might be defeated, and *Hell on Earth* and *Lost Colony* won't take place. Or they might take place but with slightly or dramatically different details.

There's lots of ways this can happen, but of course the most obvious is dealing with Stone. Be careful, because if the heroes put him down for good, the future could turn out different.

So what if your posse goes back to *The Weird West* and kills Stone? Can you still play *Hell on Earth*? Of course you can. (It's just a game, silly!) Officially, there are still ways for the heroes to lose. The first time through wasn't easy, even without Stone. If continuity is important to you, just assume some other heroes somewhere screw things up royally, maybe by going bust on a few too many *tale-tellin'* rolls or just getting themselves killed.

These are questions only you can answer.

Runnin' the Game

Marshal: 178

Chapter Fourteen:
Runnin' the Game

You're the Marshal.

Remember that. You're the fellow who makes all the decisions and keeps things moving. It's your job to make the posse afraid of the dark while still dying to know what's in it. You have to run scenes full of high action and drama, then turn around and do a little romance, a little terror, and even a pinch of comedy. You need to know enough rules to get you by, and you'll probably wind up paying for more pizza and soda than anyone else in the room.

You have to come up with adventure ideas, write down enough detail to run them, and handle your friends when they think they got a raw deal. You're also going to have to beat them sometimes. *Deadlands: Hell on Earth* is a game about heroes, but victories are hollow if the players don't know the possibility of defeat—and death for their characters—is real.

It's a tough order to fill sometimes. That's why we've made things easier on you. This chapter shows you how.

This chapter is all about the rules of the game. We start with tricks to help run all those muties and other bad guys. Then we tell you how to structure adventures and award those Fate Chips we talked about in Chapter Six. The power of fear is up next, followed by a discussion on coup powers. We've dropped hints to the posse about these things, but now it's time to get into the details.

Hang on to your hat, Marshal. Here we go.

The Real Handbook

Let's start with something simple that new Marshals sometimes overlook: a notebook.

When you start a campaign, get a notebook and write down a bit about each of the heroes in the posse. You should know some of their background, like whether or not they have *enemies,* mysterious pasts, or *veteran o' the Wasted West* drawbacks. Write these down, and you can refer to them as you need to later on.

You should also keep a log of any towns or important extras the group might run into. If you said Busterville's got a Sheriff named James Hitchcock one week, you don't want to say the law is now Town Marshal Jerry Page the next.

Also make room for a couple of saloon names. You'd be surprised how often those come up in an adventure where the posse's looking for information. Maybe someone's set up a whisky-joint in the ruins of an old McDonalds. What's the bartender's name? How about the waitress? You don't want to make up everyone in Busterville, but you'd best have a few notes on the extras the posse is most likely to run into.

Keeping a good notebook is often overlooked, but it can mean the difference between a rich campaign with memorable extras and one in which the heroes can't remember their girlfriends' names.

Runnin' the Game

Marshal's Shortcuts

Deadlands has a lot of detail for player characters. Tons of Traits and Aptitudes, complex combat maneuvers, and a detailed wound system. They need rules like these because they're trying to "win." You're the Marshal. You win by making sure everyone has a good (and challenging) time. You sometimes have hundreds of things to keep track of at once, so you don't really want all this detail all the time. That's great, because we've got several shortcuts for you. This way you can worry about the game and the story instead of the rules.

Traits & Aptitudes

You've set up a notebook, let's talk a little about the extras recorded inside it.

Player characters have 10 Traits and tons of Aptitudes, Edges, and Hindrances. They want and need lots of detail because they're the heroes. They only have one character to keep track of.

You, on the other hand, don't need to be so picky with the vast number of extra characters (or just extras) you've got to handle. Instead, you can base the Traits and Aptitudes of common extras on averages or the Action Deck.

Average folks have 2d6 in most Traits and sometimes 2d8 in things they depend on every day (like a blacksmith's *Strength*).

In Aptitudes, average folks have 3 levels in skills relating to their main profession, 2 levels in common Aptitudes like *drivin'* and probably one *shootin'* skill, and 1 level or nothing in everything else. If you think a particular extra should have a higher or lower score, go ahead and give it to him.

If you suddenly need to know a Trait or Aptitude and don't care to figure out what it should be, draw a card from your Action Deck. The value of the card tells you a die type to use, and the suit can tell you the Coordination or Aptitude level. Check the Traits and Coordination Table on page 28 for all you need to know.

You only have to draw for the Trait or Aptitude you need at that moment, not the entire range that you'd need for a major character. This has the advantage of giving some variety, but it can be fairly extreme.

You get complete statistics for major extras in published *Deadlands* sourcebooks and adventures, but you can use the guidelines above to determine the skills of incidental extras your heroes run into.

Combat Shortcuts

Sometimes there are a lot of bad guys. You don't want to keep track of 15 scavvies' *Quickness* totals, wounds, Wind, and wound modifiers when you're trying to describe the scene and help the heroes resolve their actions. You've got better things to do.

We've got something for you here too.

Actions

Of all the tricks we give you, the Action Deck is the niftiest. You don't have to roll an "initiative" number for each bad guy and then try to remember it. You just lay down a few cards behind your screen and wait until they come up in the round. Then the bad guy takes his action, and you move on.

Roll *Quickness* totals for major bad guys and important critters. For numerous extras, deal one card for each "group." It's your call as to what each group is, though usually it's each set of bad guys that have the same statistics. If the group is really fast (usually extras with *Quickness* of 3d8 or better), give them two or more cards to act on. You could even roll *Quickness* totals once for the entire group each round if you want. It's your call.

If a group gets a Joker, pick one of its members to get its effects, and deal another card for the rest of the group.

The downside for the bad guys is that they only get one card. The upside is they all get to go together like one big, happy, mutated family. It all balances out in the end.

Wounds

As Marshal, you need an easy way to keep track of wounds for lots of bad guys with *no* bookkeeping. Our radioactive mommas told us to always do our darnedest to keep our best customers happy—that's you, of course, Marshal—so here's an easy way for you to keep track of wounds for tens or even hundreds of bad guys—without ever touching a piece of paper. You will have to use miniature figures, however, or something else to represent the heroes and the bad guys.

Besides letting you use this Marshal's "cheat," minis help your players understand the scene better—especially important in a big fight. This gives everyone a good tactical sense of what's going on and encourages them to visualize and use the environment instead of just saying "I shoot it" every action.

Runnin' the Game

Pinnacle makes a bunch of minis for just this purpose. If you're gun-shy about minis, use dice, coins, tokens from a game ("I'm the shoe!"), or even pieces of paper with the heroes' names on them. Place the minis on a map of some sort with the terrain sketched in to complete the scene. Big sketch pads work great, and good hobby shops have erasable "battle mats" as well.

There's the pitch for using minis. We won't ram it down your throat. We'll give you the cheat soon, promise, but first a disclaimer: *Don't* use this shortcut for important bad guys or really unique monsters. You should use the more-detailed wound system for anything that spectacular. You should also use the regular wound system if there are only a few thugs involved in a fight.

Okay. Enough disclaimers and preaching about miniatures. Here's the shortcut.

Marking Wounds: Whenever a player character makes a successful attack, go ahead and let her roll hit location to determine the effects of cover and see if she gets any extra dice for a hit to the gizzards or noggin. Use the damage total to determine how many wounds the opponent takes, then place a chip under the miniature's base to mark its wound levels. See the table below for what color chips to use. Assume all the hits go to the thug's guts area. Now everyone knows at a glance which bad guys are fresh and which ones are on their last legs.

Wound Penalties: The chips also tell you what kind of penalty to assess the bad guy when it makes an attack. Again, check the table.

Make the Posse Work: The best part? You can even tell the players their opponent's Size and let them "chip" your bad guys for you. That way you can keep even a really huge combat moving faster than a three-legged toad by letting the players do some of the work for you.

Here's a quick table to sum everything up in one easy-to-reference spot. Note that the last color chip is "blue+white." This works fine if you've only got the standard three colors of chips. If you got a fourth, use that instead.

Wounds & Chips

Wound	Chip	Penalty
Light	White	–1
Heavy	Red	–2
Serious	Blue	–3
Critical	Blue+White	–4

Wind

So you're thinking, "Okay, smart guys. But some attacks only do Wind damage. What about that?" We got you covered. Treat Wind just like damage. Every increment of the bad guy's Size in Wind raises the Wound level a notch just like any other damage. It all balances out when taken together with the Wind the victim should be taking with any "real" wounds (which you shouldn't bother rolling for).

Stun

You might not want to keep track of stun for all the bad guys. Don't worry. The rules are as complete as we could make them, so you can dig into the details when it matters. You don't need to all the time. When you do, this cheat can help you keep track of stunning as well.

Place a stunned opponent's figure on its back *on top* of its wound chip. That reminds you to have the creature make a stun check on its next action. If it makes the roll, stand the sucker back up on top of its wound chip.

How do you tell the stunned figures from the dead ones? Take the chip out from under them.

Runnin' the Game

Adventures

An adventure is basically one story. It has an introduction, a middle riddled with plot twists, and a climax. String several of these adventures together into a sort of "serial" and you've got what we call a campaign (or saga). The adventures in your campaign are played out over "sessions." Most folks get together once a week and play for four to six hours, so that's what we call a session.

Published adventures are usually designed to be played over one to four sessions. We've got a standard way of presenting them to help you figure out what's going on quickly and easily.

A *Deadlands: Hell on Earth* adventure starts with "The Story So Far," the introduction to the adventure. The next section is "The Setup," which tells you how to get the posse involved in the adventure. The meat of the adventure is broken down into individual "Chapters." After the last chapter is "Boot Hill," in which all the bad guys and critters the posse is likely to fight are summed up.

Here's a little more information on each of these sections.

The Story So Far

The introduction describes the backstory that sets everything in motion. You're likely the only one that's going to read it, but establishing a solid background is vital.

Posses being what they are, things can happen that you hadn't counted on during the course of your adventure. If you've got a detailed background, you can figure out the answers to questions you hadn't thought of and determine how the extras react to the posse's schemes.

The Setup

The point at which the posse gets involved is called "The Setup." This is where you figure out how to rope the heroes into the shenanigans that are about to occur.

There are lots of ways to pull the player characters into your adventures. The most common is to have someone hire them to do a job or solve some problem. Remember to keep the posse poor. Wealthy characters aren't likely to go chasing dangerous outlaws, after all.

Another good way to get the group together is to let the players tell you why their characters are involved. Even if the characters have been hired by someone, the players should still have a good reason why they are each interested in the offer. This is also good because it often lets the player work some of his character's background into the story.

Chapters

Now you're ready for the meat of the adventure. Each chapter describes a location and the events that occur there.

This is where you find complete statistics for important extras and monsters, as well as the skinny on what's supposed to happen in this location.

You should generally get through one or two chapters each game session, but this can vary if the group does a lot of roleplaying (or arguing).

Bounty

At the end of each chapter is a section entitled **Bounty**. Here you'll find guidelines for giving out Fate Chips, "money", and other goodies the posse gets for accomplishing the chapter's goals.

Remember when giving out money or goods that part of the fun of *Hell on Earth* is fighting for every last bullet. Keep 'em poor, Marshal.

Runnin' the Game

Rewards

Now let's talk about the things that make the players love you—Fate Chips and coup powers.

Fate Chips

The guidelines on Fate Chips in Chapter Six don't need to be repeated. What you might need to know a little more about is just how often to award chips.

In *Deadlands: The Weird West*, Marshals award Bounty Points as well as Fate Chips. We've changed that for *Hell on Earth*, and will eventually do so in *The Weird West*.

That means you really need to be on your toes about awarding Fate Chips. An average player who gets an equal amount of time as the rest of the posse should probably get a couple of whites and one red in a night. With luck, he should be able to convert 2-4 Bounty Points worth of Fate Chips each session.

Sometimes a player spends all he gets. This usually happens if there's a big fight in a session with not a lot of roleplaying.

If there's tons of roleplaying and hardly any combat, he'll get a stockpile.

It's up to you to judge how freely to distribute Fate Chips, but don't feel bad holding back if there hasn't been much to "bleed them off" in a while. By the same token, don't be too stingy, or your posse may never advance, and the players may feel cheated.

Coup

There's another reward besides Fate Chips you can give your posse when they defeat a powerful abomination: coup.

Coup powers are creepy, supernatural effects gained from absorbing the essence of something creepy and supernatural. (Go figure.) The nastiest creatures we feature in *Deadlands: Hell on Earth* products have coups already listed in their descriptions.

To count coup, a hero needs to be within a few yards of the abomination when it expires. Everyone present then makes a *Spirit* roll. Have each player roll and spend any Fate Chips on it secretly so that only you, the Marshal, know everyone's totals until everyone's finished.

The character with the highest *Spirit* total gets the coup. No Bounty Points are needed. The power is free. Of course, the rest of the heroes might be a little upset they lost out.

Creating Coups

You're going to need to create all-new coups when making your own monstrous abominations. For that, you might need a little guidance.

In general, the coup should be derivative of the monster it came from. A hero who slays a liche, for example, might learn a dark spell. Put down a king radrat, and maybe the character becomes more radiation-tolerant. Check the monsters in the last chapter of this book for more examples.

Minor coup powers—such as +1 to *survival* rolls made to resist cold (for killing some kind of snow beast)—are often always on. Also they rarely cause the hero any trouble.

If the coup's powerful, it should have a taint. Often, whatever was evil about the monster it came from rubs off on the hero as well. Kill some kind of snake-man, and maybe the hero sssstartssss talking like thisssssss. If it's difficult to figure out a taint, maybe the hero simply has to spend Fate Chips to use his coup. The cost really just depends on how often you want the character to use it. Just try to keep it balanced, fun, and creepy!

Runnin' the Game

The Power o' Fear

The Reckoners thrive on fear. Some poor soul wets himself, and they gobble his terror down like candy. The incredible energy it produces sustains the Reckoners and allows them to stomp across the Earth, causing War, Pestilence, Famine, and Death.

Their minions, the thousands of abominations walking, crawling, and slithering across the planet, are by and large unaware of their own origin or the source of their power.

A wendigo stalks the wintery north because it is hungry and evil. It has no idea it serves the Reckoners, or even that such creatures exist. It also has no idea its actions increase the Fear Level and make itself stronger. Only manitous and a few truly aware abominations know the truth.

The biggest, baddest thing in an area is responsible for raising the Fear Level. We call it a "fearmonger." This is often the main creature or creatures behind the tale of horror the Marshal has spun. This is the creature that best serves the Reckoners' ends and creates the most terror in an area.

Fearmongers might have minions, but they have no special control over other abominations. In fact, the monsters of the Reckoning almost always work alone. Maybe the radrats stay out of the pool where the toxic zombies lurk, but only because the undead eat the rats, not because they're all in on some sweeping conspiracy.

Several powerful abominations may all exist in the same area—and in fact, you can count on it in cities and other Deadlands—but only the most wicked is the fearmonger. And it and any other horrors in the area only work together if they're clever or otherwise motivated to make some kind of pact.

Together, these monsters create an atmosphere of fear in an area when they do their dirty work. Usually this is a forest, a cave, a section of a ruined city, a town where folks have been disappearing, and so forth, but the location isn't necessarily a geographic area.

Sometimes an abomination inhabits an arcane artifact or haunts a particular group of people, such as a family with some ancient curse. In essence, the Fear Level of an abomination encompasses everyone who lives in its shadow on a day-to-day basis.

Marshal: 184

Runnin' the Game

Fear Levels

Let's talk a little about what each Fear Level should feel like. This should help you describe areas as the posse travels through them.

Fear Level 0: This is happy land, folks. Think of a small town in 20th-century America, complete with picket fences and smiling neighbors. Trees are green, the sky is blue, and you can walk the streets at night. Okay, these places don't really exist in *Deadlands*, but it's a nice thought.

Fear Level 1: Some folks believe monsters exist, but for whatever reason, they haven't seen any here. The trees are still green, and the sky is blue, but you should walk the street at night in pairs—just in case.

Fear Level 2: There are rumors of radrats in the old sewers, so no one goes there—or in the supposedly haunted houses either. The land looks about the same, but the shadows are just a bit darker. It's not really safe to go out at night alone, but lots of folks still do.

Fear Level 3: Things are starting to get a little weird. There's an occasional disappearance, and probably more than a few weird creatures live close by. Don't go out at night without a weapon and a friend, in that order.

Fear Level 4: There are mysterious disappearances followed by reappearances—but the unfortunate victim is found in bits and pieces. The land starts to look creepy. Maybe the shadows on the rocks look like leering faces, and the boughs of trees look like reaching arms. Venturing out at night without some heavy firepower is not a good idea.

Fear Level 5: There's no doubt something's strange. Most folks have seen monsters and are terrified of them. Most flowers are dead, but weeds have no problem growing in the dark shadows of the land. Don't go out at night without an armed posse.

Fear Level 6 (Deadland): This is it: a full-blown landscape right out of your worst nightmare. Monsters run rampant, rocks look like skulls, trees have groaning faces, and anyone who goes out at night is meat.

Fear Effects

The posse suffers penalties to its *guts* checks, depending on the Fear Level. As if that weren't bad enough, abominations also gain Fate Chips whenever the Marshal draws certain cards from his Action Deck (see the Fear Effects Table for details).

Level	Effects
0	None.
1	–1 to *guts* checks.
2	–2 to *guts* checks.
3	–3 to *guts* checks.
4	–4 to *guts* checks. The Marshal draws a Fate Chip when One-Eyed Jacks are dealt from his Action Deck.
5	–5 to *guts* checks. The Marshal draws a Fate Chip when One-Eyed Jacks or Suicide Kings are dealt from his Action Deck.
6	–6 to *guts* checks. The Marshal draws a Fate Chip when One-Eyed Jacks or Suicide Kings are dealt from his Action Deck. The fearmonger draws an extra card from the Action Deck every round.

One-Eyed Jacks are the Jack of Spades and the Jack of Hearts. The Suicide King is the King of Hearts. If you don't understand the names, take a look at the cards. You'll get it.

Raising the Fear Level

Abominations can raise a Fear Level by +1 once a month or so, assuming they cause considerable mischief and don't go overboard. That's a *very* rough guideline, Marshal. Some critters are far more subtle, taking years to work their dark magic. Others barge in and start rending, driving the Fear Level up in a week.

Abominations that get too wild can actually stagnate a Fear Level. The unknown is the greatest horror of all. A rumor of a wolflike creature on the prowl for young maidens strikes fear into the hearts of everyone. A bloodwolf that wades into a survivor settlement and starts eating people certainly makes for some wet crotches, but then it becomes just something else to waste good bullets on.

Lowering the Fear Level

An area slowly returns to Fear Level 1 on its own if nothing particularly nasty happens there. When the local fearmonger is inactive or defeated, the Fear Level drops by –1 every two months or so.

A faster way to spank the Reckoners is for a hero with a big mouth to do a little *tale-tellin'* (see Chapter 12). If successful this immediately drops the Fear Level by –1.

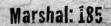

Terror

The mortal mind can't easily handle all the horrors of the Wasted West. Even hardened souls who've been around a while can never get used to the horror of a pouncing wormling or the shock of watching a close friend get torn to pieces by it.

The more startling or frightening something is, the more difficult it is for a character to get over his shock and get to shooting. When a hero spots a horrible, supernatural creature or gruesome scene, he must make a *guts* check.

Don't forget to modify this roll by the character's Grit and the Fear Level.

The TN depends on the Terror score of the abomination, scene, or event. The creatures listed in this book already have Terror scores. You need to assign your own Terror score to any new abominations you create or scenes the posse comes across.

Here are some helpful guidelines for you, along with the number of dice you should roll on the Scart Table if a character fails his *guts* check. Add an extra 1d6 to the roll if he goes bust, by the way.

Terror

TN	Dice	Description
3	1d6	A terrifying but otherwise normal creature, like an angry grizzly or a rattlesnake.
5	2d6	Something slightly strange and disturbing, but not immediately dangerous, like a radrat.
7	3d6	A bizarre but almost plausible creature, such as a croaker; a gruesome corpse.
9	4d6	An undeniably supernatural creature or a gruesome abomination such as a walkin' dead; a sickening scene, such as a dismembered or mutilated corpse.
11	5d6	A unique and overwhelming horror like a wormling; a nauseating scene of mass carnage.
13	6d6	A creature that defies the imagination; grisly carnage that serves some arcane and evil purpose "man was not meant to know."

No Guts, No Glory

Failing a *guts* check is a "bad thing." Usually it means something a character can't defeat anyway just got some extra time to beat on him. Most results cause a character to stand staring with her jaw hanging open, drooling like an idiot. Sometimes it means those milrats are coming up for a second taste, especially if the cause of the *guts* check was a particularly gory scene. Get really unlucky, and the old ticker might pop.

Roll the dice listed on the Terror Table then read the results on the Scart Table on the next page. Like with skill and damage rolls, add in any Aces you get.

If a character went bust on her *guts* check, add an extra die to the roll on the Scart Table, just for fun.

Experience

Once a character has seen something strange and made a *guts* check, the Marshal shouldn't usually make him roll again. The first time a hero finds the victim of a toxic zombie, he should roll. If he later finds more victims, he should only roll if something new, unique, and disgusting presents itself. Just use your own judgment, Marshal. We trust you.

LOSTON

Runnin' the Game

Scart

Roll	Effect

1-3 Uneasy: The character stops and stares for a moment at the grisly scene. For his hesitation, he loses his next Action Card.

4-6 Queasy: The victim stares in horror at the scene, loses his next Action Card, and subtracts -2 from any Trait or Aptitude rolls made the rest of the round.

7-9 The Willies: The character staggers back and stares in horror, missing his turn for the round. Just have him toss in all his Action Cards, including anything he might have up his sleeve. He takes 1d6 Wind, and his actions are at -2 until he makes a *guts* check, which he may attempt once per action—once this round is over and he again has cards to use.

10-12 The Heebie-Jeebies: The character turns white as a sheet and loses his entire turn and 1d6 Wind. Again, he should simply toss in all of his Action Cards, including anything up his sleeve. All actions suffer a -2 penalty for the rest of the encounter.

13-15 Weak in the Knees: The victim loses 1d6 Wind. At grotesque scenes, he loses his lunch and staggers away, choking the entire way. At terrible scenes, he puts his tail between his legs and gets the Hell out of Dodge. In either case, he is completely ineffectual until he makes the *guts* check that caused this result. (He can try this on any action.) He suffers a -2 penalty to any Trait and Aptitude rolls for the remainder of the encounter. A white Fate Chip negates this penalty once the *guts* check is successful.

16-18 Dead Faint: The character takes 3d6 Wind. If she's reduced to 0 or less, she faints dead away until she recovers. Chips can be spent to reduce Wind normally. If the character has *faith*, she must make an Onerous (7) *faith* total immediately. If she fails, the horrors of the Deadlands cause her to lose 1 level of *faith* permanently.

19-21 Minor Phobia: The character goes *weak in the knees* and gains a minor phobia (a 2-point *loco* Hindrance) centered around the event. When affected by this irrational fear, he suffers a -2 penalty to any actions.

22-24 Major Phobia: The character goes *weak in the knees* and gains a major phobia (a 5-point *loco* Hindrance) focused on the event. This is the same as above, except the penalty is -4, and the victim must make a Hard (9) *guts* check to directly affect the object of his fear.

25-27 Corporeal Alteration: The character gains a *minor phobia* and suffers a physical defect of some kind, such as a streak of white hair, his voice box contracts and he can only speak in whispers, etc. Whatever it is, it immediately lets people know that this poor soul has had a brush with unspeakable horrors that has left an indelible mark on him. He may never be the same.

28-30 "The Shakes": The survivor gets a *major phobia* and must make a Hard (9) *Spirit* roll or reduce her *Deftness* by -1 step permanently due to constantly shaking hands. If the *Spirit* roll is made, the terrible nervous condition is only temporary, and her *Deftness* is only affected for the next 1d6 days.

31-35 Heart Attack: The poor sap's heart skips a beat. He must make a Hard (9) *Vigor* roll. If made, he suffers 3d6 Wind and gains a *major phobia*. If failed, he suffers 3d6 Wind, his *Vigor* is permanently reduced by one step, and he must make a second Hard (9) *Vigor* roll. If failed, he has a heart attack and dies unless someone else makes an Incredible (11) *medicine* or healing roll within 2d6 rounds. If his *Vigor* ever falls below d4, the victim automatically dies.

36+ Corporeal Aging: The character has a *heart attack* and ages 1 year—if he survives.

The Harrowed

Marshal: 188

Chapter Fifteen:

The Harrowed

At some point, you're going to end up having to kill some of your player characters. It's okay. *Deadlands* has a high character turnover rate compared to most games. But don't let your players start ripping up their character sheets too fast. Their characters just might come back from the dead.

We already told you how to find out who comes back in Chapter 11. Now you need to know some of the details. Let's start by learning something about the little buggers responsible for all this madness.

Manitous

Manitous are the spirits of the damned. Other than a few ancient spirits, manitous were humans sent to Hell for their sins. Many of them now serve the forces of destruction, the Reckoners. These creatures cannot affect the physical world without a mortal shell of some sort. The three forms they use to do so are living hosts, soulless undead, and the Harrowed.

Living Hosts

Some manitous have the ability to enter living beings, but these are few. When "exorcised," they are simply ejected from the host and released back into the world. These are the spirits responsible for the tales of "demonic possession" common to most religions. (Come on, you saw the movie.)

Soulless Undead

Most any manitou can enter a corpse. If the shell is empty, the manitou simply crawls inside, animates as much flesh and bone as it can, and starts its dirty business. This is where walkin' dead and other "soulless undead" come from.

In these cases, most manitous use the brain as a focus. (It's easy to "energize" it to control the rest of the body.) Some have more control and can use other body parts, like the heart, a hand, and so forth, but those are rare. In any case, if the manitou's focus or corpse is destroyed, it's simply ejected with no harm done.

The Harrowed

A Harrowed is special. In this case, the soul is still in the shell. This is the only way the manitou can get control of all the things that make a hero more than just a corpse. When the demon has control, it can use a gunslinger's incredible skill, a syker's amazing blasts, or the simple luck and gusto of a true hero.

The danger here is that to gain this kind of control the manitou must bond with the body permanently. If the Harrowed's brain is destroyed, the manitou is slain forever. In fact, this is one of the few ways in which these spirits can *ever* be destroyed. It's a great risk for the demon, but a hero's soul has much greater potential for sowing chaos.

The Harrowed

More on Manitous

Manitous are bound by a few limitations while inhabiting physical forms. First, they can only use the powers and abilities of their host—even Harrowed powers. If the host hasn't developed any powers, the manitou can't use them either (or develop any on their own).

Manitous can see and hear while the Harrowed character is in charge, although the reverse isn't true. This makes it nearly impossible to fool a manitou into revealing its true identity unless it wants to.

Second, if a manitou is trapped and somehow forced to speak, it proves a clever but ignorant spirit. Manitous know they serve the Reckoners, but they do not know what their true purpose is, nor do they particularly care. They also know that while they are in spirit form they gather fear from mortals and take it back to the Hunting Grounds. How the Reckoners get the fear they leave there is a mystery to them. They aren't privy to secret information about abominations or their motives either.

So what exactly do manitous do when they're in charge? Whatever they can. Their goal is chaos and mischief, not necessarily death. They never make an outright attack—unless they've got one of the Harrowed's companions in an inescapable and precarious position. Say a junker friend of the Harrowed stands looking over the edge of a radioactive pit. No manitou could resist giving him a little shove.

Time to Play

So when should the manitou come out to play? Basically, whenever you want it to. The main thing to remember about manitous is that they tend to be subtle in their methods. They're crafty spirits, always looking for ways to spread fear, but content to wait for the right moment to make their move. Most of all, they do not want to be caught. Tough as they are, they can be killed, but they're entirely determined to stay alive.

The Marshal should use the manitou as a plot device and a grueling Hindrance for the Harrowed *and* his companions.

What is its purpose exactly? Simple. To cause mischief, mayhem, confusion, and—above all—ice-cold fear. If the demon sees a chance to cause trouble, it takes it. If the creature has an opportunity to kill someone who's doing a little too much good, it does so with relish.

This doesn't mean the manitou struggles for Dominion every time its host draws a gun. If the fiend interferes too often, others are going to catch on and find a way to kill it. Those who already know but have to live with the manitou—such as a Harrowed's companions—usually put up with it as long as their friend does them more good than harm (at least as far as they know). If the Harrowed gets out of hand, they may be forced to put him down once and for all.

Manitous know this and so keep their existence and, most importantly, their *actions*, secret from interfering mortals.

Strength

You need to know the *Spirit* of each Harrowed's manitou to determine the Dominion tests we're going to tell you about next. To do so, draw a card and consult the table below.

Manitou's Spirit

Card	Spirit
2	Legion
3-8	Spirit is equal to the character's
9-Jack	Spirit is same die type but +1 higher Coordination
Queen-Ace	Spirit die type is +1 higher and Coordination is +2 higher
Joker	Greater manitou

Legion

The hero is inhabited by a horde of lesser manitous, collectively calling themselves "Legion." Whenever you need to know Legion's *Spirit*, draw a card and compare it to the Traits and Coordination Table on page 28.

Legions are far more chaotic and destructive than other manitous. They make overt attacks more often, use their powers more blatantly, and basically flaunt all the guidelines on subtlety we've been telling you about.

Greater Manitous

These ancient manitous are some of the baddest hombres in the Hunting Grounds. When they grab a mortal shell, it's for keeps.

Greater manitous have a *Spirit* of 3d12+4. They're something like hunting dogs for the Reckoners, sent specifically to hunt down heroes who kill one too many of the Reckoners' pets. They're very subtle, but once unleashed, they hold nothing back and absolutely destroy everything in their path.

The Harrowed

The Nightmare

The next section shows you how the manitou takes control. It does so by battling for something called "Dominion." Before you learn more about Dominion, however, you need to know how many Dominion points a hero starts with. That's where the nightmare comes in.

When a character dies and attracts the attention of the manitous, she immediately wages her first battle for Dominion. There are two ways to resolve this spiritual battle. The first way is faster and best if you are playing for only a single night. The second way, the nightmare scenario (see below), is creepier but takes a little extra work.

The Fast Way

After it's determined a character is coming back, she has to make an opposed *Spirit* plus Grit check versus her manitou for each Dominion point. A character has a number of Dominion points equal to her *Spirit*, and each of these are going to be fought over, tooth and nail.

The winner of each check gets that Dominion point. Unless the hero loses every contested point of Dominion, the Harrowed comes back in control—but not entirely. We'll get to that soon.

The Nightmare Scenario

The second way to determine the result of the nightmare is to actually play it out like you would any other adventure. This is a lot more fun and horrific, but it takes some work on the part of the Marshal—certainly more than simply rolling some dice. Still, it might just be one of the coolest and creepiest adventures you've ever designed.

The back of each character sheet has an area in which the player is supposed to describe his character's worst nightmare. The Marshal should use this to construct a nightmare scenario when it's determined a character is coming back from the dead. That's why we put it there, after all.

Running a solo nightmare takes some time. Plan ahead, and do this alone with the character's player before your group's next play session. If a character becomes Harrowed in the middle of a game, leave him buried till the end of this session (it takes 1d6 days to come back anyway). That way you can take the time to resolve the scenario when everyone else isn't waiting on you.

If several characters die and come back at roughly the same time (perhaps they were hanged together), the manitous might absorb several of them into a collective nightmare. If this is the case, you can construct a longer scenario that encompasses all of the characters' nightmares in one, long, horrific tale.

Milestones

The goal of the adventure is to overcome several "milestones." These symbolize the hero's mental duel with the manitou. The results determine who has Dominion when the character returns.

You need to set a number of milestones equal to the character's *Spirit* die type. Every milestone he conquers, defeats, or negotiates gives him a Dominion point. Every challenge he cannot manage to overcome gives the manitou a point of Dominion.

During the nightmare, the hero is in charge, regardless of who's been winning more Dominion at any particular point. This battle takes place in the Hunting Grounds. While it might seem to take days or weeks, it passes quickly in reality.

The Harrowed

Dominion

"Dominion" represents the constant struggle for control over the Harrowed's body and mind between the manitou and its host. On occasion, the manitou takes over. When this happens, the mortal "blacks out." He can't see, hear, or have any idea what the demon is up to while it's running the show.

The battles of this war are most often fought when the Harrowed shuts down to rest. While the manitou rebuilds and regenerates the body, the mortal soul is subjected to terrible nightmares. Perhaps the host dreams of the grisly deeds the manitou committed the last time it took control. Or perhaps he witnesses horrible images dredged from the worst parts of the Hunting Grounds.

To reflect those occasional nightmares in which the mortal mind caves in to the manitou's torment, Dominion tests are made at the start of each play session. As you learned in the nightmare section, Harrowed characters have a number of Dominion points equal to their *Spirit*. The more Dominion the character or demon has, the easier it is to gain control of the body.

To make the test, both the hero and the devil inside make opposed *Spirit* tests, each adding their current Dominion to their rolls. The winner takes 1 point of Dominion for each success.

Taking Over

When the manitou wants to take control, the Marshal must first pay a Fate Chip. We want you to be able to play your undead friends at will, so draw yourself an extra chip at the beginning of each game session for every Harrowed in your posse. Of course you don't have to use it on the Harrowed, it's just a little extra help to counter all that power the undead have.

Once you spend a chip to try to take over a Harrowed hero, make a *Spirit* test for the manitou. The TN is Fair (5) plus +1 for every point of Dominion the character currently has.

The Fate Chip is not applied to the roll. It's simply the cost the manitou must pay to wrest control of the Harrowed's reins for a while. You can spend additional chips on the roll, but you get no bonuses to the roll for the chip you spent to initiate the test. If the manitou is successful, the amount of time it gets control depends on the color of the first chip you spent.

Lost Control

Chip	Duration
White	1 minute
Red	10 minutes
Blue	1 hour

If you need the manitou to have a little more play time, you can simply pay additional chips. You don't have to roll again or spend chips to initiate another takeover attempt.

If a manitou lets its control lapse early, it can take over again without another roll, as long as it's within its original time period.

Total Dominion

If a manitou ever controls all a hero's Dominion points, it takes over for a good, long while. Some Harrowed have been lost in this way for years. When they finally do come around, they discover they have a lifetime's blood on their rotting hands.

The only time the mortal soul gets to fight back is when the manitou is affected by certain magic spells, relics, or arcane procedures. The Marshal might also give the hero a chance to fight back in particularly unusual circumstances, such as if the demon is about to kill someone close to the host. Then it might be time to give the poor schmuck stuck inside another chance to fight back.

Breaking Away

Sometimes, a hero's will is so strong that it can overthrow a manitou's Dominion and keep it from doing something positively atrocious, at least for the moment.

These kinds of checks should be extremely rare because almost everything the manitou does is downright despicable. But even a subjugated hero might be able to fight back if his manitou is about to cause direct harm to a very close companion.

When the Marshal feels such an occasion is about to occur, he can let the Harrowed's player make an opposed *Spirit* test versus the manitou. With a raise, he regains control instantly. Any remaining time the manitou had coming to it is lost.

Letting a player character attempt to break Dominion should be a rare occurrence that happens only under special and unique circumstances.

Dominion Summary

Here's a quick look at how you should handle all this Harrowed business. Don't worry, it's simpler than you think. Mess with your heroes a few times and you'll get the hang of it.

- At the start of each play session, the Marshal gets to draw one extra Fate Chip for every Harrowed hero in the posse.

- The Harrowed and the manitou make a *Spirit* test at the start of every game session, each adding their Dominion points.

- The winner of the Dominion test gets 1 Dominion point for a success, and another for every raise over his opponent.

- When the Marshal wants the manitou to take over, he must first spend a Fate Chip.

- After spending a chip, the Marshal rolls the manitou's *Spirit* against a TN of 5 plus the number of Dominion points controlled by the Harrowed.

- If successful, the amount of time the manitou remains in charge depends on the color of chip spent.

- Additional chips can be spent to extend the duration of the manitou's control as long as you like (or your chips hold out).

- The hero has no memory of what occurs while the manitou is in charge.

Marshal: 194

Chapter Sixteen:

Arcane

Happenin's

The world of *Deadlands: Hell on Earth* is filled with weirdness. Horrible monsters stalk the irradiated plains, crazed mutants war with norms, junkers make priceless gizmos out of the stuff everyone else throws away, the dead walk, and the Four Horsemen of the Apocalypse themselves ride the Earth.

Sometimes a little of this weirdness rubs off on a hero. If he's lucky, it gives him some new advantage to help keep his heart pumping and mouth drooling. The not-so-lucky ones end up jinxed, missing limbs, haunted, or even dead.

This is the chapter where we give you, the Marshal, the skinny on all those weird things we've been hinting at.

First there are mysterious pasts and mutations for those unfortunate souls who drew Jokers when they were making their characters. After that is a table of mishaps for suckers who took the *veteran o' the Wasted West* Edge. Then there's a short section on syker's brain burn and how much channeling the power of the Hunting Grounds through your noggin can really hurt. Finally, we give you some tools to trash junkers with.

Everybody has a fair chance of getting screwed here in the Deadlands.

Mysterious Past

Many folks have been affected by arcane weirdness in their lives. Some don't even know it—yet.

When a player draws a red Joker during character creation, she has a mysterious past of some sort. You can either make something up on your own or use the Mysterious Past Table. We recommend talking to the player and getting some background on his character first. If you have a good idea for her mysterious past, use that. If you don't, draw a card from your own Action Deck and see if the result on the table makes sense or can be tailored to the individual character.

We know you've heard this a thousand times, but we really mean it: Don't use the table if you've got a better idea. It's far better for you to tailor a mysterious past for a character than to make one of these fit. The table is here for some inspiration and as a backup if the character doesn't have a particularly unusual background.

On a black Joker, the character has a Mutation. Check the table on page 198 for all the grisly details.

Arcane Happenin's

Draw

Deuce: Curse

The character is cursed in some way. Figure out when and why it happened by sorting through the hero's past, looking for someone he may have wronged.

The character has the *bad luck* Hindrance until he resolves whatever issue caused the curse. If the character winds up also having *bad luck* in some other way (like by purchasing it during character creation), the curse proves doubly catastrophic.

Three: Sworn Enemy

The character has an enemy in her past that she doesn't know about. Look over the character's background and pick an enemy or a group of enemies that are looking for the hero. The nature of the enemy and the frequency of its occurrence is entirely up to you.

Four: Doppleganger

The hero looks eerily like some other well-known person. A red card means the other person is someone who is generally considered good, like a Law Dog, a Templar, or a Doomsayer. A black card means the character looks like a wanted bandit or someone else with a bad rep.

Five: Kin

A family member or close companion gets involved in the adventure every now and then. The relative tries to help but can't really take care of himself, so he generally ends up getting in the way more often than not. He also tends to make a great hostage should one of the character's enemies ever get wind he exists.

The hero occasionally benefits from the relative's actions, but she usually just winds up rescuing him. In the Wasted West, not too many families survived the Apocalypse, so the "kin" might be more like a godchild or another kind of dependent than a blood relative.

Six: Sixth Sense

The character has an uncanny sixth sense that sometimes warns her of danger. Whenever a hidden danger or ambush is about to occur, make a secret Onerous (7) *Cognition* check.

Add a +2 bonus if the hero is suspicious. Subtract –2 if she is seriously distracted in some way.

Seven: Blackouts

The character has "holes" in his past and can't quite remember certain periods of his life. He probably doesn't even know he can't remember them.

What happened to him during these "blackouts" is entirely up to you and the needs of your game. The character might occasionally experience glimpses into his mysterious past. These visions eventually make sense, but they just confuse and confound him until then, when the past finally catches up with him.

Eight: Ancient Pact

The character's ancestors made a pact with a manitou some time in the distant past, before the Great Spirit War. The power of that pact still traces through the family's bloodlines.

The character gains a power of the Harrowed at level 1. The level cannot be raised unless the hero someday becomes Harrowed.

You should decide which power to grant the character. You can base the ability on her personality if you choose, or you can choose an ability at random since the power was chosen by a distant ancestor instead of the hero.

Nine: Arcane Background

Though the character doesn't know it, she has the ability to tap the supernatural power of the Hunting Grounds. Some strange and obscure event in her past granted her this talent.

Choose a power from Chapter Nine and assign it to her at level 1. She can improve the power at a cost of double the new level in Bounty Points.

Ten: Favor

Someone owes the character a favor of some sort. Perhaps a Law Dog was saved by the hero's mother long ago, or maybe it turns out that one of Throckmorton's lieutenants is the character's father. Whatever the circumstance, the indebted extra can occasionally bail the hero out of some dire situation.

Jack: Haunted

A ghost of some sort haunts the character. No one else can see or hear the being, but it is always lurking nearby. Draw another card, and check the color to get the details.

In either case, you should put some thought and personality into the ghost's identity. Perhaps a beneficial spook is the ghost of a dead relative. A malevolent specter could be the ghost of someone who died because of the character.

Arcane Happenin's

Red: The ghost is beneficial. Once per session, it warns the character of danger or provides him with useful information. The phantom shouldn't be too powerful, but useful.

Black: The character is haunted by a malevolent ghost. It appears at the most inconvenient times to frighten and confuse the hero. At least once per adventure, the ghost shows up and messes with him.

Queen: Animal Hatred/Ken

Animals react strangely in the hero's presence. The hero may have been this way from birth, or perhaps she gained the attention of the nature spirits through a kind or thoughtless misdeed. Draw another card, and check the color.

Red: Animals love the hero. They never attack her unless provoked, and she can add +2 to any *animal wranglin'*, *teamster*, or *ridin'* rolls. If the hero rides a horse, the animal should be especially intelligent and well-trained after spending any time at all in the hero's care.

Black: Animals hate the character. Dogs always growl and sometimes bite. Horses complain constantly and buck whenever the character goes bust on a *ridin'* roll. The character always suffers –2 to any *animal wranglin'*, *teamster*, or *ridin'* rolls.

King: Relic/Cursed Relic

The character has in his possession an artifact once owned by someone else. It is valuable or perhaps even magical. Draw another card, and check the color.

Red: One of the character's possessions is a valuable or arcane relic of some sort. Perhaps he has a high-tech weapon or the legendary and magical pistol of a famous Law Dog.

Black: The artifact is cursed or comes with trouble. Perhaps the hero's knife was once used in a heinous murder, or someone famous died in his cursed body armor. The effects of the curse depend on the item. At the very least, a cursed weapon should secretly fire at –2, while a mundane item quietly causes the hero *bad luck* until he figures it out and rids himself of it.

Ace: Destiny

The hero has an epic destiny or quest of some sort. Perhaps he's been sent to find a water filtration device for his village before it runs out of water, or he's the son of the Governor of Texas, looking to reclaim the state.

You have to work this one out with the player based on his character's background.

Either way, destiny makes the character incredibly resistant to dying until his quest is complete. Whenever he would otherwise die, draw a card from an Action Deck. If it's a red card, he lives somehow. If the card is black, he's lost, left for dead, and takes months to heal, but eventually recovers. Only a Joker sounds the death knell for this hero, and he can't come back Harrowed. The manitous refuse to touch this soul. Its destiny might bring about their downfall.

Joker: Harrowed

The character is dead and just hasn't figured it out yet. Make up some recent event that took place in the character's past in which he was left for dead but somehow "survived." Shuffle the deck, and draw another card to determine Dominion.

Red: The hero starts with a 2-point advantage in Dominion.

Black: The manitou starts with a 2-point advantage in Dominion.

Red Joker: The hero has total Dominion.

Black Joker: The manitou has total Dominion.

Arcane Happenin's

Mutations

A character who draws a black Joker during character creation has a mutation caused by exposure to the arcane energy of irradiated ghost rock. Doomsayers also start with a mutation, and sometimes their powers cause them as well. This table should give you lots of ideas to warp your posse's minds and bodies, but as always, you should feel free to come up with your own.

Anytime a mutation imitates an Edge or a Hindrance, it *is* cumulative with other Edges and Hindrances, including the ones they mimic.

The energy causing all this madness is supernatural, by the way, so it can affect the Harrowed as well.

Clubs

2♣: Violence solves everything. Your hero is a deranged lunatic and a *grim servant o' Death*. Worse, his friends often suffer for his love of carnage. Anytime he misses with a shot or a hand-to-hand attack and there's a chance it can hit a friend, it does.

3♣: A bad case of the glows gave your hero thick, balloon-like veins and a supernaturally fast heart rate. If he ever takes a maiming wound to a limb, it literally explodes like a blood sausage, killing him instantly.

4♣: If your hero was born before the Apocalypse, she had the bad luck to be looking at a distant city when it was hit by a ghost rock bomb. The image of a skull-shaped mushroom cloud is forever burned into her eyes. She can see, but must always look slightly askance to focus. This makes her more than a little weird to talk to, and gives her the *bad eyes* Hindrance at level 3. If she was born after the bomb, radiation caused cataracts with the same effect.

5♣: The hero has "Methuselah Syndrome." Every year that passes counts as five.

6♣: Your hero ages far faster than he should. Every year that passes counts as two.

7♣: The hero gives off weird radiation that kills plants and small animals (rabbits and smaller). Most plants wilt after a few minutes of contact with the hero. Animals run away. If they can't, they take 1d6 damage every minute they're within a yard of him. (Sentient plants—should your hero run across such a thing—take damage just like small animals.)

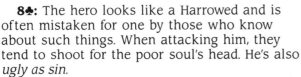

8♣: The hero looks like a Harrowed and is often mistaken for one by those who know about such things. When attacking him, they tend to shoot for the poor soul's head. He's also *ugly as sin*.

9♣: Your survivor has a few telltale signs of radiation poisoning, but there is no ill effect. This time.

10♣: Hello, hypersensitive-boy. Radiation-heightened senses gives your hero the *keen* Edge.

J♣: Your hero's toad-like skin is thick and rubbery. He's *ugly as sin* but has the *thick-skinned* Edge.

Q♣: Your hero's skin is tough and leathery, providing light armor. He subtracts -2 from damage he takes to any location.

K♣: The hero can store rads in his body and release them in short but lethal bursts. On physical contact (skin to skin), the mutant can choose whether or not he wants to release some of the strange radiation he stores inside him. If so, the target must make a Fair (5) *Vigor* roll. If she fails, her heart cooks, and she dies in 1d6 rounds.

A♣: Radiation covers the character from head to toe. He makes Geiger counters click like a baseball card set in the spokes of a speeding bicycle. Fortunately, radiation doesn't hurt him. He's immune to low levels of natural radiation, and he gets a +4 to resist more powerful radiation effects, including any spell cast by a Doomsayer.

Hearts

2♥: Your hero needs sunshine vitamins. He's *scrawny* and must go shirtless in the daytime or suffer a -2 modifier to all Trait and Aptitude rolls after one hour's time. He always suffers this modifier during the night (one hour after the sun goes down until one hour after it comes up).

3♥: Thirteen years without a toothbrush (and a bad case of the glows) has made your hero's teeth fall out. He can't chew anything and must subsist on liquids alone. He's *scrawny, ugly as sin*, and cannot have a *Strength* or *Vigor* die type greater than d8. If either Trait was previously at a d10 or higher, reduce it (or both of them) right now.

4♥: Radiation infects any food the hero touches. It becomes ruined and disgusting to anyone but him. Anyone who eats it must make a Hard (9) *Vigor* roll or upchuck. It never provides nourishment to anyone else, even if they manage to wolf it down.

5♥: The survivor's metabolism is so great he can never get enough to eat. He's *scrawny* and must eat twice as much as any other.

6♥: Food does not break down normally in your mutie's irradiated belly. It bloats up and makes constant and embarrassing gas. He's an *obese big 'un* with a bad flatulence and burping *habit*.

7♥: Freaky. Your hero has a potbelly and spindly legs. Subtract -2 from any *Nimbleness* based rolls made to jump, run, or maintain balance.

8♥: The hero is gaunt and thin to the point of strangeness. Some folks might even mistake him for a faminite, which isn't going to endear him to their hearts. He's also *ugly as sin*.

9♥: Your survivor has a few telltale signs of radiation poisoning, but there is no ill effect. This time.

10♥: The hero's body can't break down "cooked" meats. He now has a strange taste for raw meat. Even weirder, he ate an irradiated cat one time, and now he has the thing's eyes. (How they got into his face from his belly is anyone's guess, but there they are in all their glory.) They glow when hit by direct light, but they also allow him to see in all but complete darkness as if it were twilight.

J♥: The hero's fingernails grew into long, sharp talons, then turned black and died. He doesn't have to cut them, and they can't be replaced if lost (anytime you go bust on a *fightin'* roll in hand-to-hand you break a nail). As long as half the fingernails are left (not the thumbnail), they add 1d4 to your *fightin'* damage.

Q♥: Irradiated food is yummy! It doesn't seem to bother this brainer a bit. He can pass any kind of poisoned or irradiated substances through his system with no harmful effects (including the 4♥ mutation). He's not immune to radiation, but his digestive system is.

K♥: Your survivor has somehow gained the ability to draw nutrients from another's body. By touching someone's skin, he can sap her Wind at the rate of 1 per action (or every five seconds if not in combat rounds). If the mutie has lost Wind, the stolen energy replaces it. Once his Wind is restored, excess energy is lost, but he can keep draining his victim until she's dead or fights back.

A♥: Your hero's metabolism is as slow as molasses. He eats half as much as most folks and ages only one year for every decade that passes.

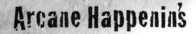

Arcane Happenin's

J·ROSEN

Diamonds

2♦: Your character's body is decaying rapidly with something like leprosy. The hero has the *ailin': chronic* Hindrance, and every time he goes bust on a *Vigor* roll at the beginning of a session, he loses some small piece of his body, such as a finger, a toe, a bit of ear, or so forth. After five such occurrences, the hero loses an entire limb.

3♦: Your character is where stories of "radiation vampires" come from. Radiation causes his blood to break down and run like water, so he bleeds at double the normal rate. Also, he must drink enough blood to replace his entire supply every week. Each day he goes without a half-pint or so, he suffers a –1 penalty to all Trait and Aptitude rolls. If the penalty ever reaches –7, he collapses. One day later, his body turns into a disgusting mass of gelatinous flesh. He's dead, and he can't come back Harrowed. (What kind of manitou wants to inhabit a jelly donut?)

4♦: Radiation has gotten into your hero's bones. The pain feels something like minor arthritis, giving him the *ailin': minor* Hindrance.

5♦: Disease and radiation have made the brainer a sickly, anemic creature. His Wind is equal only to his *Spirit*.

6♦: Your survivor was near a city when the bombs hit (or she was born near a blast site). Her body was burned and scarred horribly, making her *ugly as sin*. In addition, sand-laden winds and the sun's burning rays force her to keep her skin wrapped under layers of the softest cloth she can find. If she is exposed to the elements, she suffers a –2 to all her die rolls.

7♦: The blood in your survivor's veins is thin and doesn't clot right. He suffers twice the normal amount of Wind when he bleeds.

8♦: The hero has patches of hair, ugly boils, and other signs of the glows that make him *ugly as sin*.

9♦: Your survivor has a few signs of radiation poisoning, but there is no ill effect. This time.

10♦: Your hero has the regenerative capabilities of a lizard. She always succeeds at her natural healing rolls.

J♦: A mutant born after the bomb came out of her radioactive momma with huge flaps of skin between her arms and side. If she was born earlier, the flaps of skin grew while she was laid up in bed with radiation sickness for a month.

Arcane Happenin's

The bad news is your heroine is *ugly as sin*. The good news is she can now glide with these to a limited extent. She can't "take off," but if the heroine falls 10 yards or more, she can glide safely to the ground. Her arms must remain outstretched during this time, so anything heavier than a pistol in her hands must be dropped. The survivor can carry no more than a light load on her back due to the flimsiness of the "wing" membrane.

Q♦: Your hero's pheromones make roses smell like stinkweed. The opposite sex can't resist her. Add +6 to *persuasion* rolls made to seduce others in a calm situation (not in the middle of a firefight!).

K♦: Say hello to Typhoid Mary, circa 2094. Your mutie carries disease while rarely being affected by them herself. She adds +4 to any rolls she makes to resist the affects of disease or infection. In addition, once in contact with a disease, she can store it in her cells up to 24 hours. Then, if she can make contact with human flesh, she can release it into one person who immediately suffers its effects.

A♦: The hero is completely immune to natural poisons, infections, or disease. He's not protected from supernatural poisons and radiation however.

Spades

2♠: Your hero loves the smell of napalm in the morning. He's entirely deranged and *bloodthirsty*. He feels a need to lead others into battle and destroy the weak. Whenever there's a chance for conflict, especially violent conflict, he has to provoke it.

3♠: Radiation has caused your hero's nerves to be hypersensitive. He gets a +4 to *search* or *Cognition* rolls where touch is involved, but he doubles his normal wound penalties.

4♠: The character's entire body glows in the dark. Subtract –8 anytime he tries to *sneak* in dim light or darkness. On the plus side, he can see as if he was holding a small candle.

5♠: Your hero's pores ooze radiation, causing her to glow dimly in the dark. Subtract –4 anytime she tries to *sneak* in dim light or darkness.

6♠: Radiation has made the mutie's bones brittle. Anytime she takes a serious wound to a body area, something breaks. In the guts, this is usually a rib. In the noggin, it's a concussion. Increase the difficulty of healing serious or greater wounds by +2, both for natural and magical attempts.

7♠: The mutie's ears are supersensitive. He gets the *big ears* Edge with double the normal modifiers to hearing rolls. The downside is gunfire within 10 feet or so deafens him. He'd best get some earplugs or learn *fightin'*.

8♠: The hero scars easy. Impressive after a battle; not so fun on a date. He's *ugly as sin*.

9♠: Your survivor has a few telltale signs of radiation poisoning, but there is no ill effect. This time.

10♠: Your hero got lucky. Radiation caused his "flight" reflex to wither. He adds +2 to his *guts* checks and gains the *nerves o' steel* Edge. The downside is he must make a Hard (9) *Smarts* roll to run away from a fight.

J♠: The brainer has developed the uncanny ability to draw oxygen from water. If he was born after the Apocalypse, he has gills. Otherwise his physiology is just weird. Either way, he can breathe underwater like a fish.

Q♠: The bad news is your hero walked into a radstorm and got his synapses fused together. The good news is they fused in all the right places. Your hero is never surprised.

K♠: The touch of radiation has made your hero the perfect killing machine. His muscles and reflexes grow to incredible levels. Raise both *Strength* and *Quickness* by +2 die types.

A♠: When the adrenaline starts pumping, your hero's brain kicks into turbo. If you make a Hard (9) *Smarts* roll at the beginning of each round, you can swap any one of your character's Action Cards with any other Action Card on the table, including the Marshal's. The only thing you can't swap are Jokers or cards up your or another character's sleeves.

Jokers

Here's what happens if a player pulls a Joker when checking for his hero's mutation.

Red Joker

You can choose your hero's mutation from any on the list.

Black Joker

If this card was chosen during character creation, choose any Deuce as the mutation. It's bad, but you get some choice. If the card's drawn during play, the mutation's fatal. Your survivor now isn't. He might still come back from the dead as a Harrowed though.

Veterans o' the Wasted West

If a hero is a *veteran o' the Wasted West*, you need to check here for the price of all those free points. Remember that the hero does not gain any points for any Hindrances or other penalties she picks up here.

Veteran o' the Wasted West

Draw	Result
Deuce	**Jinxed:** Something you encountered cursed you. Your luck's fine, but your companions suffer minor mishaps constantly and act as if they had the *bad luck* Hindrance.
Three	**Hunted:** You didn't finish the job. A group of cultists, Black Hats, muties, or an abomination of some sort is looking for you.
Four	**Mutation:** You've spent a lot of time hunting monsters near old blast sites. That or a Doomsayer healed some really nasty wound on you. Draw three mutations and take the worst.
Five	**Addicted:** You'd like to forget the things you've seen out there. You have a severe *hankerin'* for alcohol or a drug.
Six	**Haunted Dreams:** Insomniacs get more sleep than you do. You have *night terrors*.
Seven	**Maimed:** One of your limbs is maimed or entirely missing. Roll a d6. On 1-2, you are *lame: limp*, on 3-4, you're *lame: crippled*, and on 5-6, you've lost your non-weapon hand and are a *one-armed bandit*.
Eight	**Disfigured:** An abomination you encountered tried to rearrange your face. You're *ugly as sin*.
Nine	**Insane:** Something you saw gave you a major phobia (see the Scart Table).
Ten	**Paranoid:** You've seen things you weren't meant to know. You're afraid of the dark, afraid to sleep alone, afraid to wander out of camp to relieve yourself, etc.
Jack	**Infected:** The last creature you tussled with left a mark that won't go away. You have some sort of strange wound that gives you the *ailin': chronic* Hindrance.
Queen	**Bollixed:** You've got a bad case of gremlins. Anytime you try to use a technological device with moving or electronic parts, including a gun, a grenade, whatever, roll a d20. On a 19, the device fails to work. On a 20, it self-destructs somehow. Computers fry their CPUs, guns backfire, etc.
King	**Forsaken:** Long ago, you did something horrid to survive your encounter with the supernatural. Ever since, the spirit world wouldn't aid you on a bet. No beneficial supernatural effect works on your character. Bad magic fries you normally.
Ace	**Cursed:** Your very soul was cursed by one of the insidious creatures you left in your terror-filled past. You draw only one chip at the beginning of each play session.
Red Joker	**Eternal Hero:** Fate chose your miserable soul to combat the forces of darkness across the centuries. You have lived in other lives and sometimes have flashbacks to them, and occasionally they're helpful. Whenever you are out of Fate Chips and about to die, making an Incredible (11) *Spirit* roll allows you to somehow survive the situation. This is often not without tragic consequences however. Perhaps a dear friend or loved one takes the bullet for you instead. Fate can be a cruel mistress.
Black Joker	**Damned:** Your hero crossed something that damned his mortal soul. At the beginning of each game, the Marshal must secretly draw a card. If it's your old friend the black Joker, your character is going to die by the end of the current adventure. A good Marshal can make sure you go out in style though.

Arcane Happenin's

Brain-Burn

When sykers go bust on a *blastin'* roll, draw a random card and use the Traits and Coordinations Table (page 28) to determine how much damage they take to the head.

Junker Mishaps

When a junker draws a Joker during device construction, use this table to put him in his place.

Junker Backlash

2d6	Result
2	**Fried Synapses.** The junker forgets all knowledge of the power he was building into the device.
3	**Scrambled Brains.** The junker loses 1 level in *science: occult engineering*.
4-5	**Attack.** The manitou causes 3d6 damage to the junker's guts.
6-7	**Energy Flare!** Roll a contest of *Spirits* between the junker and the manitou (determine its *Spirit* randomly). If the junker loses, he suffers the difference as damage to the guts.
8	**Side-Effect.** The power has an unintended side-effect of the Marshal's choosing.
9	**Arcane Leak.** The device's power system isn't shielded properly, allowing G-rays to leak. Each day the device is used, everyone who was within 10 yards of it while in operation must make a Fair (5) *Spirit* roll. If the roll is failed, the victim gains a mutation.
10	**Misinformation.** The manitou pulls a fast one and gives the junker bad information. The full construction time and components are spent, but the power does not work.
11	**Back Door.** The manitou builds itself a back door into the device. Once a session, it may use the power in the device for which this result was rolled.
12	**Ghost in the Machine.** A malicious spirit has been bound into the machine. It can use any of the device's powers at any time. If the device has any levels of *AI*, the spirit *is* the device's AI (which may make it smarter or dumber than intended—Marshal's call).

Marshal: 204

Chapter Seventeen:

The Bad Guys

The monsters of *Deadlands: Hell on Earth* have many fantastic powers and abilities. Your posse may encounter ghosts, vampires, werewolves, creatures mutated by radiation, and all manner of horrors. We want you to be able to concentrate on keeping the game moving, so we've come up with common descriptions of the most common powers used by the monsters and other bad guys of the wastelands.

After that, there are short entries for common varmints such as wolves, rats, and other normal critters. Finally, there's a handful of monsters and bad guys to get your game started.

You'll see more creatures in future products. When you do, their descriptions may often refer to powers discussed here. That way we don't have to repeat what *undead* means every time.

Powers

Armor

No self-respecting terror of the wastelands goes around unarmored.

The Armor value is listed directly after the creature's *armor* ability. This works just like the armor we told you about in Chapter Five. *Armor* –2 means the thing has light protection that subtracts 2 points of damage from every attack that hits it. *Armor* 2 means it has heavier armor that reduces an attack by 2 full die types.

Bolts o' Doom

Bolts o' doom covers any sort of missile attack the various horrors of the Wasted West might hurl at your posse. Some critters hurl poisonous quills, others throw things, and some might even projectile vomit. You never know.

Creatures use *shootin'* or sometimes *throwin'* to hit. For weird spellcasters, the attack roll for *bolts o' doom* is the same as their *faith* roll. All the usual rules and modifiers for shooting apply unless the description says otherwise. The statistics for the attack such as Shots, Speed, Rate of Fire (ROF), Range, and Damage follow the entry, just like we listed them for firearms in Chapter Four.

Cloak o' Evil

Armor is nice, but sometimes it's best not to get hit in the first place. *Cloak o' evil* does just that. It turns aside any sort of attack aimed directly at the user.

Right after *cloak o' evil* there's a negative number like –2 or –4. That's the penalty anyone attacking the critter must subtract from their *shootin'* or *fightin'* total.

Cloak o' evil doesn't protect the caster if he's caught in an area-of-effect attack, such as an explosion or spell not targeted specifically at him. If someone throws a grenade at the user, apply the modifier. If someone throws a grenade at the ground near the user, it doesn't apply.

The Bad Guys

Fearless

Some critters just can't be scared. Most soulless undead are like this (because the manitou inside has nothing to lose). Others are just too dumb to know when they're beat.

These kinds of monsters are *fearless*. They never make *guts* checks, even against a power or effect of supernatural origin.

Fearless creatures can be surprised for one round, but after that, they get over their shock and get to work. Deal *fearless* creatures in normally the round after they're surprised.

Immunity

Immunity simply means the character or creature can't be hurt by certain forms of attack. Anytime you see this, a description of the particular immunity follows.

One common *immunity* is to "normal weapons." You'll see a lot of the Reckoners' servitors, ghosts, and "spiritual" creatures with this power. In this case, normal weapons refer to any blade, bullet, or even fist that's not enchanted. Magical abilities, supernatural effects, and legendary weapons work normally unless the creature's description says otherwise.

To be absolutely clear, the weapon itself must be enchanted, not its user. Thus a *brain blast* could hurt this kind of creature, but a Templar with *inner strength* could not (though if his sword is considered enchanted, it could, and it would grant the benefits of *inner strength* as well!)

Another kind of *immunity* you might see is "All." That means this is one ugly critter and there's probably only one way to kill it. Check out its *weakness* to find out how.

Infection

Infection is the ability to turn a victim into something like the monster. Werewolves, vampires, and other creatures that can make more of their ilk have this ability.

The details are up to you. A bug-like horror might inject eggs that hatch inside its victim. A vampire bites someone and then forces him to drink of its own dark blood.

If the *infection* is spread through the blood, any wound, including a single point of Wind does the trick.

After the *infection* entry is a TN. That's the *Vigor* roll a character must beat to avoid the infection. If he fails that, he can only seek supernatural aid in resisting the inevitable results.

Poison

Poison does just what you think it does, though the way this kind of thing works in the profiles of the creatures of the Wasted West also applies to diseases, nonlethal poisons (such as paralyzers), viruses, and other toxins designed to get into the blood.

If the *poison* is delivered by fangs, claws, needles, blades, or other devices that have to hit the victim, it takes effect if the target suffers even a single point of Wind damage.

Once contacted, the victim must make a *Vigor* roll versus a TN based on the *poison's* power level listed in the creature's description. If failed, he suffers the effect listed.

Regeneration

Some critters heal faster than spit bubbles in a microwave. The exact rate of its *regeneration* follows the entry.

Stun

Some critters like to eat their prey while it's still warm or maybe even still breathing. That's a really bad way to go, friends. This power lets the bad guys *stun* their prey instead of hurting them, very likely saving them for a much more horrible fate than death.

Most creatures must touch their prey to stun them. In these cases, if the monster hits (usually whether it actually causes damage or not), the victim makes a *Vigor* check against the TN listed after this power. The victim can make recovery checks each action against this same TN to snap out of it.

Surprise

Creatures with this power are keen on catching their victims unaware. Some burrow up from below. Others swoop down from the sky.

Assuming the critter isn't detected, it starts the fight with one Action Card "up its sleeve" and makes its first attack at +4.

Undead

There are many different types of undead, from simple zombies and walkin' dead to ancient liches and vampires.

Those without any vestige of their mortal soul inside their rotting carcass are "soulless" undead. They are always inhabited and animated by a manitou. These are much less risky for a manitou to occupy because the demon simply escapes back to the Hunting Grounds when the shell is destroyed.

The Bad Guys

More powerful creatures like vampires and liches become undead because of ancient curses, a lifetime of evil, or by casting dark rites. They make a deal with the forces of evil and destruction (the Reckoners, though most don't know that) in exchange for awesome power, but in so doing they become irrevocably evil.

Harrowed are a special case of course. Their manitous share the shell with the mortal soul. We've already told you all about that in Chapters 11 and 15.

All these undead have many varied powers and abilities, but here are some common to all types:

Undead don't feel pain, but they still suffer from having their body parts blown off. They can ignore 2 levels of wound penalties and can never be stunned.

Undead ignore Wind caused by wounds or physical damage. Supernatural effects that cause Wind act as regular damage, since the spirit inside suffers the blow. (Since undead don't suffer Wind, halve damage if you're using the Marshal's trick we taught you for handling lots of lesser bad guys in Chapter 14.)

Soulless undead don't regenerate damage without a secondary power. Those with souls make natural healing rolls once per day unless they have a faster way to heal damage and regenerate their undead flesh.

Undead take full damage to their "focus." This is some area of the body the spirit inside uses to control the corpse. The most common focus is the brain, though a vampire's focus is usually the heart, and some very powerful creatures even remove their focus and hide it elsewhere for safekeeping. Unless the description says otherwise, assume the focus is the brain.

Finally, undead can only be destroyed by a maiming wound to their focus. That means horrors like walkin' dead (with the brain as a focus) keep fighting even if they receive a maiming wound to the guts.

Weakness

Creatures with a *weakness* are particularly susceptible to certain kinds of damage. A wendigo of the icy north probably doesn't enjoy fire. Similarly, a giant, mutated slug might dissolve if covered in salt.

Generally, attacking a creature with whatever it has a weakness of should cause double damage. If the weapon doesn't usually cause damage (such as salt, water, holy water, or so forth), the description tells you how much damage the weakness can cause the creature.

The Bad Guys

The Profiles

On the following pages are some of the Wasted West's common critters, monsters, thugs, and abominations. Each varmint has the standard Corporeal and Mental Traits and Aptitudes. After that is listed its *Pace*, with any special movement rates for flying, swimming, burrowing, or the like.

Next up is the critter's Size, Wind, and Terror scores. The latter is the TN of the *guts* check your heroes should make the first time they encounter this creature in a given scene. *Special Abilities* describes all the powers that make the creature unique (see the previous pages for common powers).

Animal Intelligence

A lot of the monsters loping across the irradiated plains have "animal intelligence." Like real animals, their *Knowledge* and *Smarts* Traits are relative to the animal kingdom—not human intelligence.

A gunslinger with a 1d4 *Knowledge* is still smarter than a shrak with the same score, though both might be as cagey in combat.

Common Critters

Before we get into the really bad stuff, let's get warmed up with some of the regular critters wandering around the Wasted West. (You can tell the meanest monsters are nastier 'cause we printed 'em in (un)living color!)

Bear

Corporeal: D:1d6, N:2d8, S:1d12+2, Q:3d10, V:2d12+2
Climbin' 3d6, fightin': brawlin' 4d8, sneak 2d8
Mental: C:2d8, K:2d4, M:2d10, Sm:1d4, Sp:2d6
Guts 4d6, overawe 2d10, search 2d8
Pace: 8
Size: 10
Terror: 3
Damage: Claw (STR+1d4), bite (STR+1d4)

Buffalo

Corporeal: D:1d4, N:3d6, S:2d12+4, Q:2d6, V:4d12+4
Fightin': brawlin' 3d8
Mental: C:1d4, K:1d4, M:1d6, Sm:1d4, Sp:2d6
Guts 2d6, overawe 3d6, search 2d4
Pace: 10
Size: 4
Terror: 0
Damage: Claw (STR), bite (STR+1d4)

Dogs (Big Dogs, Coyotes, Wolves)

Corporeal: D:1d4, N:3d8, S:3d6, Q:2d8, V:4d8
Fightin': brawlin' 3d8, filchin' 2d4, sneak 2d8
Mental: C:1d6, K:2d6, M:2d6, Sm:2d6, Sp:2d6
Guts 4d6, overawe 2d6, trackin' 6d6
Pace: 15
Size: 4
Terror: 0
Damage: Claw (STR), bite (STR+1d4)

Horse

These are the statistics for a standard horse. Faster, braver, smarter, and more aggressive mounts can occasionally be found or even bought.

For an extra $100 each, the animal can be: Brave (like the Edge), Fast (Pace 24), Smart (+2 to *ridin'* rolls), Strong (*3d12 Strength*), or Tough (2d12 *Vigor*). A good horse can command a high price, but if it saves your life, it's worth it. Of course, sticking a year's worth of scrounging into a critter that muties might find tasty might not be the smartest move.

Corporeal: D:1d4, N:2d8, S:2d10, Q:1d8, V:2d10
Fightin': brawlin' 1d8, swimmin' 2d8
Mental: C:2d6, K:1d6, M:1d6, Sm:1d6, Sp:1d4
Guts 2d4, overawe 1d6
Pace: 20
Size: 10
Terror: 0
Damage: Kick (STR)

Mountain Lion

Corporeal: D:1d4, N:3d10, S:4d6, Q:2d12, V:2d8
Fightin': brawlin' 4d10, sneak 4d10
Mental: C:2d10, K:1d4, M:1d8, Sm:1d4, Sp:2d4
Guts 2d4, overawe 2d8, search 2d10
Pace: 14
Size: 4
Terror: 3
Damage: Claw (STR+1d4), bite (STR+1d4)

Vipers (Rattlers, Cobras, Other Poisonous Snakes)

Corporeal: D:1d4, N:1d6, S:1d4, Q:4d12+2, V:2d4
Fightin': brawlin' 4d6, sneak 3d6
Mental: C:2d10, K:1d4, M:1d8, Sm:1d4, Sp:1d4
Guts 2d4, overawe 2d8, search 3d10
Pace: 14
Size: 2
Terror: 3
Damage:
Bite: STR
Poison: Most poisons range from TN 9 and damage of 3d6 (rattlesnakes) to TN 11 and instantly fatal (black adder).

The Bad Guys

Automaton

Dr. Darius Hellstromme created the first automatons way back in 1870 or so. Most believed they were "clockwork" men, propelled by an extremely complex combination of steam and gears. What no one could figure o

ut was how the automatons could *think*.

It took Hellstromme's rivals many years to finally crack the "secret of the automatons." It was actually dirt simple: the body was made of steam and gears, but the brain was that of the walkin' dead.

Both the USA and the CSA eventually figured out the secret. They experimented with their own automatons for a while, but their scientists weren't ruthless enough to "train" their new soldiers. Sometime during the Faraway War, though, those scientists went Hellstromme one better and created cyborgs: Harrowed with enough tech wedged in their undead bodies to take down an army.

For a long time, Hellstromme had little use for automatons—up until the Faraway War. His constant battles with the anouks forced him to resurrect the program. In 2076, he created the first of a new breed.

Where Hellstromme might be now is a mystery to all, but his automated factories in Denver continue to churn out automatons. The most powerful creations remain there, guarding the base and General Throckmorton until they're ready to take over the West. A few "recon" units have been sent out, however, to keep tabs on the outside world.

The model shown here is a standard type sent to find some important resource, track down some piece of information, or kill someone

thought to be a threat. Though they may look like robots, remember there's a zombie brain in charge—complete with a manitou straight from Hell. Automatons are mean, crafty, and full of tricks.

Profile

Corporeal: D:2d6, N:2d6, S:4d12, Q:3d6, V:2d12+4
Climbin' 2d6, dodge 2d6, fightin': brawlin' 3d6, shootin': MG 4d6, sneak 3d6

Mental: C:2d10, K:1d6, M:1d6, Sm:1d6, Sp:1d4
Overawe 5d6, ridicule 1d6, scroungin' 2d6, search 3d10

Pace: 6

Size: 8

Wind: NA

Terror: 9

Special Abilities:

Armor: 3

Auto-Targeters: +4 to *shootin'* rolls

Gear: Chain gun (Ammo: 12mm; Shots: 120 (stored in its chest); Speed: 1; ROF: 9; RI: 10/20; Damage: 5d8, AP 2). The automaton's iron arms act as a brace, allowing it to ignore recoil modifiers.

Grenade Launcher: (Ammo: Mini HE grenades; Shots: 20; Speed: 1; ROF: 1; RI: 20; Damage: 4d12; Burst Radius: 10) Grenades are fired from a tube in the automaton's shoulder and can be launched on the same action as it fires—with no penalty.

Fearless

Regenerate: Automatons don't actually *regenerate*, but they can heal themselves by scavenging for parts in ruins. Treat this as a normal healing roll made once per day of *scroungin'* against a Fair (5) TN.

Self-Destruct: When an automaton is put down, it explodes for 6d20 damage with a Burst Radius of 10.

Undead

Marshal: 209

The Bad Guys

Black Hat

The most common troops of General Throckmorton's Combine are collectively called the "Black Hats." They are bullies, thugs, savages, and murderers given the best arms available in the Wasted West by the robotic factories in Denver.

Even though they are all soldiers of the Combine, only hardware such as weapons and vehicles are issued to them. Clothing, most armor, and even their trademark hats must be scavenged from the wastes.

Black Hats travel in platoon-sized elements of 20-25 men and women. Since the group is so small, all the scum who enforce Throckmorton's know each other. That means donning a black hat and attempting to infiltrate them just gets you ventilated.

These platoons are filled with rabble and roam far away from Denver, scouting out and quelling resistance. They're preparing for the more-determined expansion of the Combine once Throckmorton feels the time is right.

Closer to Denver, Throckmorton's troops are more organized and disciplined. They wear different-colored hats to denote their various stations, and they're supported by automatons, hover tanks, and airborne attack craft, all manufactured in Hellstromme Industries' robotic factories.

Booby Traps

With thousands of human troops scouting the wastes for the Combine, Throckmorton knows it is inevitable that his troops may occasionally be defeated or even captured. He could care less about the loss of human life. What he's really afraid of is letting his ammunition, weapons, vehicles, and other valuables wind up in the hands of his foes.

For this reason, the Combine uses 10mm caseless ammo—completely unusable by any other pre-War weapon. Even more

frightening, every soldier of the Combine has a small chip inserted into his spinal column.

Should someone without one of these chips attempt to use a Combine weapon or vehicle, the device immediately detonates. This effect doesn't apply to items the Black Hats have taken or salvaged, only to their personal weapons and vehicles (those items issued by the Combine itself). Armor is not issued by the Combine.

Weapons generally detonate with a 1d20 explosive force. Vehicles detonate as if a grenade went off under the driver's seat (Damage: 4d12; Burst Radius: 10).

Profile

Corporeal: D:3d8, N:3d6, S:3d8, Q:3d6, V:2d8

Dodge 2d6, drivin' 2d6, fightin': brawlin' 3d6, lockpickin' 2d8, shootin': MG 3d8, sneak 3d6, speed-load 2d8, swimmin' 2d6, throwin': balanced, unbalanced 2d8

Mental: C:2d6, K:2d6, M:2d8, Sm:2d6, Sp:2d6

Academia: occult 2d6, area knowledge: Denver 2d6, artillery 1d6, demolition 2d6, gamblin' 4d6, guts 3d6, leadership (leader only) 2d8, medicine: general 2d6, overawe 2d6, scroungin' 3d6, scrutinize 2d6, search 3d6, survival 3d6, trackin' 3d6

Pace: 6

Size: 6
Wind: 14
Terror: NA
Special Abilities:
Armor: Scavenged Kevlar (AV 2)
Gear: Black Hats carry Hellstromme Industries Damnation assault rifles (Ammo: 10mm; Shots: 30; Speed: 1; ROF: 9; Range; 10/20; Damage: 4d8, AP 2). Most also have a large knife (STR+1d4) and a single frag grenade (booby trapped, of course).

Blast Shadow

It's said these rare and deadly abominations are the living shadows of those unfortunate souls caught at ground zero. Now they haunt the ruins like dark ghosts, longing for a physical form.

Blast shadows don't really attack. They simply "attach" themselves to a person, replacing his regular shadow. The person might not notice at first. In fact, it takes an Incredible (11) *Cognition* roll to figure out a character's shadow is lagging just a bit behind. Once the hero does notice this disturbing effect, he should make a *guts* check against the blast shadow's Terror score.

Once a blast shadow is attached, it slowly drains the hero's form away, making him more and more translucent as the shadow becomes darker and more substantial. Eventually, the hero fades away, and the shadow takes over his body. The blast shadow doesn't get to gloat for long, however, as the stolen form fades away after 1d6 days.

Blast shadows are tough to kill. They can't be harmed by physical or even magical attacks while in shadow form. The only way to destroy the shadow for good is to somehow create an environment with practically no shadows. Then the thing simply fades away and never returns. Standing under the sun at exactly high noon works, as does being in a room completely lit by artificial lights. It's your call as to when these conditions are met, Marshal.

Profile
Corporeal: In spirit form, a blast shadow has no corporeal Traits or Aptitudes. Once it has taken over a host, it has that person's abilities.
Mental: C:2d8, K:1d6, M:1d10, Sm:1d6, Sp:1d10
Search 3d6
Pace: 24 (matches user once attached)
Size: NA
Wind: NA (they ignore Wind as shadows)
Terror: 9
Special Abilities:
Life Drain: A blast shadow can attach itself to a victim automatically. Once it does, it drains 1 Wind per hour, slowly causing the victim to fade away to nothing but a shadow. When the host reaches 0 Wind, he dies and his soul is replaced by the blast shadow. A brainer killed like this never comes back Harrowed.
Weakness: A complete lack of shadow (while in spirit form) instantly destroys a blast shadow.

The Bad Guys

Bloodwolf

Ever wonder what you get when you cross a werewolf with a vampire? The answer is the unholy creature known as the bloodwolf.

This crimson-furred beast stalks the High Plains by the light of the full moon. Its bloodcurdling howl is enough to turn even the most stalwart hero's spine to ice. There are few folks—even among the hard-bitten denizens of the Wasted West—who can keep themselves from crawling into the nearest hidey-hole when they hear that savage call.

Most of the time, the bloodwolf's just a simple bloodsucker, a vampire who's biggest problem is finding a source of fresh blood in the wastelands. When the full moon rises, though, the silvery orb transforms the thing into a werewolf too, causing it to take its horrible bloodwolf form.

Before his disappearance, Dr. Hellstromme did some research on bloodwolves. His theory was that they were once normal folks who survived a werewolf attack and became kin to the things that preyed on them. After that, some kind of vampire got a hold of them and brought them into the bloodsucking fold as well. The result is something from humanity's worst nightmares.

Thankfully, the combination of the two afflictions seems to make them uninfectious. Theoretically, if someone was to survive a bloodwolf attack—which no one besides Hellstromme's automatons have done to date—she wouldn't have to worry about becoming a bloodwolf. Of course, when this beast's breathing down your neck, that's likely the least of your worries.

Profile (Vampire Form)

Corporeal: D:3d8, N:3d12, S:3d12+2, Q:4d12, V:2d10
Dodge 2d12, climbin' 4d12, fightin': brawlin' 4d12, sneak 5d10,
Mental: C:2d8, K:3d8, M:4d10, Sm:3d8, Sp:1d6
Academia: occult 3d8, area knowledge: Wasted West 2d6, guts 3d6, overawe 4d10, search 3d8, survival 3d8

Pace: 12
Size: 6
Wind: 16
Terror: 9
Special Abilities:
Undead
Damage: Claws (STR+1d4), bite (STR)
Bloodsucker: With a bite to the neck, the beast locks on. Every action after that, it drains 2d4 Wind. The bloody juicebox can only break free by winning a contest of *Strength* against the bloodwolf. The good news is the bloodwolf can't attack anyone else in the meantime.
Weaknesses: Wood weapons hurt normally, and a wooden stake through the heart (a called shot to the gizzards at -10) can paralyze one.

Profile (Bloodwolf Form)

Corporeal: D:3d12+2, N:3d12+4, S:3d12+6, Q:4d12+4, V:2d12+2
Dodge 2d12, climbin' 4d12, fightin': brawlin' 4d12, sneak 5d10,
Mental: C:4d10, K:1d8, M:4d12+2, Sm:2d6, Sp:5d10
Area knowledge: Wasted West 2d6, guts 5d10, overawe 4d12+2, search 3d10, survival 4d6, trackin' 6d10
Pace: 16
Size: 6
Wind: 24
Terror: 11
Special Abilities:
Undead
Damage: Claws (STR+1d6), bite (STR+1d6)
Bloodsucker: See above.
Weaknesses: The bloodwolf is immune to wooden weapons, but not silver.

The Bad Guys

Croaker

The creation of the Maze awakened several ancient races, many of them aquatic. The largest of these are the croakers, fishlike humanoids living in vast underwater communities across the Maze.

Although the croakers aren't abominations as such, they comprise a cruel and merciless race. Croakers worship a dark sea-goddess who demands frequent sacrifices. For several decades now, the high priests of their evil religion have claimed that the goddess demands human sacrifices. Victims are abducted from the many boomtowns around the Maze and given the ability to breathe water by injecting them with strange elixirs. Then they are pulled hundreds of feet below the surface and slowly murdered in the croakers' unholy rituals.

The details on croaker society and their strange cities will be revealed at a later date. In this entry, we'll concentrate on the standard croaker raiding parties that occasionally visit the surface world.

Typical raiding parties looking for sacrifices consist of 10–15 croakers armed with crossbows. A shamanic priest leads the school of warriors and lends support should the croakers encounter well-armed defenders. The group looks for small groups of humans and then attacks, killing all but one, who they then kidnap as described above.

Occasionally, croakers raid entire towns built too close to their lair. In this case, many raiding parties are put together, resulting in a massive force of several hundred warriors if need be. The croakers always try to outnumber their foes three to one.

Profile (Croaker)
Corporeal: D:1d6, N:2d6, S:3d6, Q:2d6, V:2d8
Dodge 2d6, fightin': brawlin' 3d6, shootin': crossbow 2d6, sneak 3d6, swimmin' 6d6
Mental: C:2d6, K:1d6, M:3d6, Sm:1d6, Sp:3d6
Faith 2d6, guts 3d6, overawe 2d6, search 3d6, trackin' 3d6 (in water only—by smell of blood)
Size: 7
Terror: 9

Special Abilities:
Armor: Blubbery skin -4
Damage: Claw (STR+1d4), bite (STR+1d4), crossbow (3d6)

Profile (Shaman)
Corporeal: D:1d6, N:2d6, S:3d6, Q:2d6, V:2d8
Dodge 2d6, fightin': brawlin' 3d6, shootin': crossbow 2d6, sneak 3d6, swimmin' 6d6, throwin': unbalanced 3d6
Mental: C:2d6, K:1d6, M:3d6, Sm:1d6, Sp:3d8
Faith 4d8, guts 3d8, overawe 2d6, search 3d6, trackin' 3d6 (in water—by smell of blood)
Pace: 6 on land, 10 in water
Size: 7
Wind: 16
Terror: 9
Special Abilities:
Armor: -4 (blubbery skin)
Damage: Claw (STR+1d4), bite (STR+1d4), crossbow (3d6)
Spells: Armor 2, bolts o' doom (Speed: 1; ROF: 1; RI: 10; Damage: 3d6), cloak o' evil -2 (can be cast on entire raiding party at Speed 2).

The Bad Guys

Dogs o' War

Following the Reckoning, War stomped across Kansas and the High Plains battling the Sioux and scattering bands of soldiers and other heroes. In War's wake followed a pack of baying, bloodthirsty hounds that came to be known as the "dogs o' War."

These beasts were raised from death by War to hound those who escaped his ravages. Several packs were left behind to continue chasing lone travelers and cull the weak. Today, they are most common to the High Plains where War once roamed.

The dogs o' War have a very simple and deadly form of attack. When they spy potential prey (anything that moves), the "alpha" (the pack's leader) gives off a mournful wail that unnerves all but the strongest souls. Then the rest of the pack bolts after the prey at a rush, not stopping until they or their victims are finished.

The alpha watches from a respectful distance. If his pack is destroyed, he leaves and forms another over the next 1d6 days. The alpha and its new pack have no special hatred for their old foes. In fact, if the group has no new "blood" in it and is spotted again, they ignore them, and even run away if attacked. Once someone new joins the posse, however, all bets are off, and the pack charges in again.

Profile (Dog o' War)
Corporeal: D:1d4, N:3d8, S:3d6, Q:2d8, V:4d8
Fightin': brawlin' 3d8
Mental: C:1d6, K:2d6, M:2d6, Sm:2d6, Sp:2d6
Trackin' 6d6
Pace: 15
Size: 4
Wind: NA
Terror: 5

Special Abilities:
Damage: Claw (STR), bite (STR+1d4)
Fearless
Undead

Profile (Alpha)
Corporeal: D:1d4, N:3d12, S:3d8, Q:4d10, V:4d10
Fightin': brawlin' 6d12, sneak 2d12
Mental: C:1d6, K:2d6, M:2d6, Sm:2d6, Sp:2d6
Guts 4d6, overawe 2d6, trackin' 6d6
Pace: 15
Size: 4
Wind: NA
Terror: 7
Special Abilities:
Damage: Claw (STR), bite (STR+1d4)
Fearless
Undead
Coup: The character never has to make *guts* checks while engaged in battle.

The Bad Guys

Doombringers

Silas has hundreds of Doomsayers in his service. Most look like the archetype we gave you earlier (though with the powers below).

Silas has many other troops at his disposal, from mutants to special priests. Among these are the Doombringers, ugly, mutated creatures more monster than human. They retain a feral human intelligence but are twisted and consumed by their hatred for norms, disloyal mutants, and especially heretics.

Even Silas doesn't want many of these wackos around, so he sends the worst of them off into the wastes to hunt down heretics. Even he doesn't know that the Doombringers have transcended their humanity and become undead abominations.

Listed below are the statistics for both Silas' loyal Doomsayers and the rabid but extremely powerful Doombringers at his disposal.

Profile (Doomsayer)
Corporeal:
D:2d6, N:2d6, S:2d6, Q:3d6, V:2d8
Climbin' 1d6, drivin': any 2d6, fightin': brawlin' 2d6, shootin': any 2d6, sneak 3d6, swimmin' 2d6, throwin': unbalanced 3d6
Mental: C:2d8, K:2d6, M:2d8, Sm:2d6, Sp:3d8
Academia: occult 2, area knowledge: Las Vegas 3d6, faith 4d8, guts 3d8, leadership 2d8, medicine: general 2d6, overawe 3d8, persuasion 3d8, science: nuclear physics 2d6, scroungin' 2d6, scrutinize 2d8, search 3d6, survival 2d6
Pace: 6
Size: 6
Wind: 16
Terror: None

Special Abilities:
Spells: Most Doomsayers have four to eight spells, usually including *atomic blast, mutate, nuke,* and *tolerance.*

Profile (Doombringer)
Corporeal: D:2d6, N:2d6, S:2d6, Q:3d6, V:2d8
Climbin' 1d6, drivin': any 2d6, fightin': brawlin' 4d6, shootin': any 2d6, sneak 3d6, swimmin' 2d6, throwin': unbalanced 4d6
Mental: C:2d8, K:2d6, M:2d8, Sm:2d6, Sp:3d8
Academia: occult 2, area knowledge: Las Vegas 3d6, faith 6d10, guts 5d10, leadership 2d8, medicine: general 2d6, overawe 3d8, persuasion 3d8, science: nuclear physics 2d6, scroungin' 2d6, scrutinize 2d8, search 3d8, survival 2d6
Pace: 6
Size: 6
Wind: NA
Terror: 7 (on close inspection)
Special Abilities:
Spells: Most have six to eight spells, usually including *atomic blast, EMP, flashblind, mutate, nuke,* and *tolerance.*
Invulnerability: Doombringers can be "killed," but even if they're disintegrated, their atoms reassemble in 1d6 days. The first thing most do when they return is hunt down their killers.
Undead
Weakness: Only Doomsayer magic that delivers a maiming wound to the guts or head can permanently destroy a Doombringer.
Coup: The character gets 1 point of Armor when resisting radiation-based attacks.

The Bad Guys

Lurker

Remember that abominations are often drawn straight from the fears of humanity. The lurker is the perfect example of such a creature.

Junkers and other scavengers forced to enter the cities in search of treasure cannot help but get creeped out by the eerie "blast architecture" caused by Deadlands. Girders look like twisted claws, building facades resemble leering skulls, and piles of debris look like corpses or monsters waiting to pounce on unsuspecting trespassers.

The lurker grew from such fears. It is a huge, hulking abomination made of metal beams and other scraps of rusted, jagged metal. It sits atop something of value, something it knows scavengers cannot resist, and it waits—immobile and patient—for sometimes months at a time.

When an unwary scavvie comes to collect bait, the lurker comes to life. Its metal body shrieks from the stress, and heavy, spiderlike arms of steel flash down in an attempt to impale the surprised victim.

Then the lurker drains its victim of its blood (presumably drawing out all its iron and other minerals) and moves on to another hunting site.

Profile

Corporeal: D:1d4, N:1d8, S:4d12+6, Q:4d6, V:3d10

Climbin' 2d8, fightin': brawlin' 3d8, sneak 10d8

Mental: C:2d6, K:1d4, M:1d8, Sm:1d6, Sp:1d6

Search 3d6

Pace: 12 (due to its long gait)

Size: 12 (usually about 15' tall, but spindly)

Wind: NA

Terror: 11

Special Abilities:

Armor: 4

Damage: Impale (STR+1d10) (Each of the thing's front four arms can attempt to impale a target every action. Roll each attack separately.)

Camouflage: The lurker's high *sneak* applies only when it is motionless. Once spotted, it has little hope of hiding again. Its prey can hear it creaking (if it moves) and can recognize its "parts" if it tries to look like a ruined frame again.

Fearless

Screeching Limbs: Once the lurker moves, the stressed metal of its body screeches so loudly that normal conversation is impossible. Those who yell can only be heard on a Hard (9) *Cognition* roll.

Immunity: Lurkers ignore Wind damage.

Coup: The character gains +6 to *sneak* rolls made when hiding in urban areas full of twisted metal and other debris. He just seems to blend in with the stuff.

Night Terror

Look! Up in the sky! It's a bird! It's a plane! It's the last thing you'll ever see!

Night terrors are hideous, harpy-like creatures that live on the tops of old, ruined skyscrapers. They range far and wide, looking for prey and dragging the soft bits back to their bone-covered lairs for the feast.

Night terrors are crafty creatures born from pure nightmare. Besides picking off lone travelers and scavengers in the streets below, they're not afraid to land on the wing of an aircraft and start ripping it to pieces. (They're *very* smart when it comes to aircraft for some reason.) When the flying prey crashes, the night terror simply lands and scoops up all the soft parts.

For ground-based prey, the night terror lets out an unearthly screech to stun it, then picks up the shocked victim and drops it from a great height.

Profile

Corporeal: D:3d8, N:3d10, S:3d6, Q:2d10, V:2d6
Climbin' 2d10, fightin': brawlin' 3d10, flyin' 4d10, sneak 4d10
Mental: C:2d10, K:2d6, M:2d8 Sm:2d10, Sp:1d8
Guts 2d8, overawe 3d8, search 3d10
Pace: 2 on the ground, 24 in the air
Size: 7
Wind: 14
Terror: 9

Special Abilities:
Damage: Claws (STR+1d4), Bite (STR+1d4)
Death from Above: Victims on foot (or sometimes in the back of open-topped vehicles) get picked up and dropped from great heights. To pick up a victim, the night terror must get a raise on an opposed *fightin': brawlin'/Strength* roll. Give the creature a +4 bonus if it strikes with surprise or the victim is stunned.

Drop: Each round a night terror hangs onto a victim, it rises another 10 yards, dropping its prey at 50 yards for 10d6+50 damage. If the thing is taking damage from a particularly stubborn piece of meat, it might be forced to drop him earlier. Anytime it takes a wound and is stunned, it drops its prey automatically.

Screech: The night terror's unearthly screech is used once the thing is close— within 10 yards or less. Anyone who fails a Hard (9) *Vigor* roll is stunned until he makes a recovery check against the same TN. The best way to use the ability is for a night terror to first put an Action Card "up its sleeve" and screech just before it attacks. Assume it already has a cheat card if it strikes with surprise.

Radrats

You've heard it said a thousand times: The only things that could survive a nuclear holocaust are cockroaches and rats. It was certainly true at ground zero, where everything else died.

Many of the rats that survived became radioactive and far more intelligent. Lucky humanity.

These nasty little buggers roam in packs of a hundred or more, stalking prey through ruined city streets, waiting for an opportunity to strike. At the first sign of weakness—a dropped weapon, a stunned or downed hero, or when a big weapon obviously runs out of ammo (we said they were smart)—they scramble from thousands of hidey-holes and swarm over the unfortunate victim.

Their claws rend, and their sharp teeth rip strips of flesh. Then suddenly, they retreat! What the victim may not know is that he's very likely contracted a severe form of radiation sickness that kills him in minutes. After that, the radrats move in for the easy meal. In the rush to beat their brothers and sisters to the gravy train, they often begin consuming the victim before he actually passes on.

Resolve their two-part attack like this. For the first rush, roll an attack, then apply the damage 1d6 times. (Treat each damage roll separately, don't multiply!). That's how many rats manage to get some meat that round. Once a victim takes a single Wind or wound, the rats sense the blood and retreat.

Should the victim go down, they rush in and finish him in the same manner.

During either rush, the only way to turn the pack back is to kill a substantial number of them, usually with fire or explosives. The stats below work for individual creatures. For massive-damage attacks against the entire swarm, assume every 15 points of damage kills 1d20 of the creatures. When half the swarm has been wiped out, the others retreat and go look for easier prey—though they may leave a few behind to watch the hated foes and look for a change in the situation.

Profile

Corporeal: D:1d4, N:3d8, S:1d4, Q:4d10, V:1d6

Climbin' 3d8, fightin': brawlin' 4d8, sneak 5d8, swimmin' 3d8

Mental: C:2d8, K:1d4, M:1d6, Sm:1d6, Sp:1d6

Guts 2d6, overawe 2d6, search 3d8

Pace: 15

Size: 3

Wind: NA

Terror: 5

Special Abilities:

Damage: Bite (STR+1d4)

Infection: 4. If the victim fails, he loses –1 Wind per round until he hits 0. At that point, he falls to the ground, too weak to move (though not strictly paralyzed). That's when the radrats move in to finish him.

The Bad Guys

Shrak

Rumor has it these horrid abominations were created by Northern Alliance scientists to drive the Confederates out of the Maze before the war. You've heard the tag line a thousand times: "They made the perfect killing machine. Now they've got to stop it."

Good luck. The shraks were created aboard the *Argos*, a military ship disguised as an academic research vessel in the Maze. The *Argos* suffered a horrible fate, one that will be fully explained in a future *Deadlands: Hell on Earth* adventure, but suffice it to say, the crew paid dearly for their attempt to play God.

Shraks now serve the croakers (see their description on page 213), acting as hunting dogs or "shock troops" for their frequent raids on human settlements. They can move on land as well as water, and they can even climb sheer walls by driving their claws into the rock.

That's bad when they're chasing you in water, because shraks have the noses of their shark parents and can smell blood from miles away, depending on the current.

When not hunting or raiding, shraks patrol the waters around their masters' vast lair. There are rarely any other fish where these voracious eaters roam.

Oh. The creature's name came from a famous typo published in the *Tombstone Epitaph*. Four miners near the boomtown of Mitch's Fortune were eaten by what witnesses thought was a real (if very aggressive) shark. It read: "Four Miners Eaten in Bizarre Shrak Attack!"

Profile

Corporeal: D:1d6, N:3d10, S:4d12+2, Q:4d10, V:3d10

Climbin' 3d10, dodge 3d10, fightin': brawlin' 4d10, sneak 3d10, swimmin' 5d10

Mental: C:2d10, K:1d4, M:3d10, Sm:1d4, Sp:1d6

Guts 6d6, overawe 5d10, trackin' 5d10 (in water)

Pace: 6 on land, 15 in water

Size: 9

Wind: 26

Terror: 9

Special Abilities:

Damage: Bite (STR+2d6)

Thick Skin: Armor −4

Coup: The character's teeth grow jagged, allowing him to cause STR+1d4 damage with them.

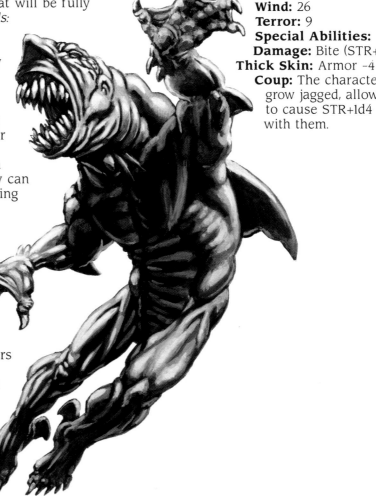

The Bad Guys

Toxic Zombie

It's amazing how much illegal dumping took place in the years before the Last War. After the Apocalypse, with no one around to put fresh loads of earth over the megacorporations' dirty secrets, many of these toxic dumps leaked into nearby ponds or created their own cesspools of deadly ooze.

Sometimes, desperate travelers in need of water give these ponds a try. Most of them drop dead within minutes of inhaling, touching, or drinking the sludge. Occasionally, they actually fall into the stuff and become toxic zombies.

These hideous creatures are human and sometimes animal corpses. Their stained flesh drips off them in soggy rivulets, and corroded, jagged fingerbones poke through what remains of their hands to form deadly claws.

Toxic zombies lurk just below the surface of these ponds and watch anyone who passes by to see if they die (whether by inhaling the fumes or drinking the water). If the travelers are too smart or somehow survive the pond, the zombies attack.

Toxic zombies rise from the water, magically buoyant, to gain surprise. Their rib cages hold globs of sticky, acidic goo pulled from the very bottom of the pond, and they can hurl up to six of these before having to return to the bottom to "reload" (which takes 1d4 actions).

If the prey runs, the toxic zombies give chase, but only up to 30 yards or so from their pond. They don't have much in the way of feet, and they don't want to be caught out of their hideout.

The water these creatures dwell in is always deadly. Folks inhaling the fumes (up close) must make a Fair (5) *Vigor* roll. If they fail, they take 3d6 damage. If they go bust, they drop dead on the spot. Increase the TN to Hard (9) and 4d10 damage should someone actually drink the stuff. These numbers work for most toxic ponds, but some are less dangerous, and some are far more so.

Profile

Corporeal: D:2d8, N:2d8, S:3d8, Q:2d10, V:2d8
Dodge 2d8, fightin': brawlin' 3d8, sneak 3d8, swimmin' 1d8, throwin': unbalanced 5d8
Mental: C:2d8, K:1d4, M:1d6, Sm:1d6, Sp:1d6
Overawe 2d6
Pace: 4, 2 out of their pond
Size: 6
Wind: NA
Terror: 9
Special Abilities:
Damage: Bite (STR), claws (STR+1d4)
Acid: Toxic zombies have an acidic touch that causes 1d20 damage to any location they hit with their goo-bombs, claws or teeth.
Fearless
Goo-Bombs: These are blobs of acid and other hazardous wastes scooped from the very bottom of their putrid homes. Goo-bombs have a Range Increment of 5 and a Speed of 1, and they cause 1d20 damage to whatever location they hit.
Undead: Toxic zombies are little more than skeletons. Roll a die for any bullets or other narrow, impaling attacks that hit. On an odd result, the attack passes through harmlessly. On an even result, the attack does normal damage.
Coup: If the entire lair is wiped out, there is no permanent coup, but all characters who attempted to count coup may drink from the sludge pond as if it were clean water for the next 1d6 days.

Marshal: 220

Trog

Trogs are the most pitiable mutants. They are lost souls who have become mutated beyond belief but are too stupid and stubborn to die. They do not breed, but simply wait for less-mutated souls to eventually succumb to the local ruins' warped embrace. Then they are ready to join the trogs' numbers.

Trogs gather in large groups of a hundred or more, bowing to the strongest and most fearsome of the lot. Ferocity is a commodity in their savage tribes. Settling things peacefully means screaming at the top of their lungs, beating their chests, or smashing rubble with their clubs (thus the high *overawe*). When that doesn't work, trogs fight to the death while the rest of the tribe gathers around and watches the carnage.

Silas uses trogs as expendable shock troops—absorbing the brunt of a resistant community's ammunition—before sending in his slightly more valuable mutants, then finally his own Doomsayers and other troops. Over 1,000 trogs live in the ruins of old Las Vegas. If not for Silas ordering them into suicidal charges, that number would be growing by the day.

Profile

Corporeal: D:2d6, N:3d6, S:3d10, Q:2d6, V:3d12

Dodge 3d6, fightin': brawlin' 4d6, swimmin' 2d6, throwin': unbalanced 4d6

Mental: C:3d6, K:1d4, M:2d8, Sm:1d4, Sp:2d6

Area knowledge: local 5d6, guts 3d6, leadership (leader only) 2d8, overawe 5d8, scroungin' 5d4, survival 5d5, trackin' 3d6

Pace: 4 (*big 'un*)

Size: 7

Wind: 18

Terror: 5

Special Abilities:

Big 'Un: Size 7

Thick-Skinned

Immunity: Radiation, and +6 to resist Doomsayer magic.

Damage: Trogs throw chunks of rubble (Shots: unlimited if in ruins, otherwise 1d6; Speed: 1; ROF: 1; RI: 5; Damage: STR+1d4). Most also carry a large club with nails driven through it (STR+1d6).

Walkin' Dead

There are a lot of corpses lying about the Wasted West. Don't be surprised when some of them get up and start chasing folks.

Walkin' dead are animated corpses temporarily inhabited by manitous. They're very common in ruined cities, creepy old graveyards, mausoleums, battlefields, or any other large concentration of bodies.

When the manitous inhabit a walkin' dead, it's either for fun or to serve some other evil being or creature they've taken a liking to. Sometimes, a "necromancer" forces a manitou into the shell of a human corpse. This suits the demons just fine. It's just another chance to sow horror and reap mayhem.

The first listing is for "civilian" undead. The second is for better stock, such as zombies raised from a battlefield, a military cemetery, or the like. Both forms are fast and mean. Sometimes they act like the slow, arms-out types, but that's only to fool folks into letting them close enough to bite.

Oh, and they love to eat brains. It helps the manitou control the corpse by regenerating its own rotting brain—and it puts a good scare into mortals to boot!

Profile (Walkin' Dead)

Corporeal: D:2d6, N:2d8, S:3d8, Q:2d10, V:2d8
Shootin': (any) 2d6, climbin' 1d8, dodge 2d8, fightin': brawlin' 3d8, sneak 3d8, swimmin' 1d8
Mental: C:2d10, K:1d6, M:1d6, Sm:1d6, Sp:1d4
Overawe 5d6
Pace: 8
Size: 6
Wind: NA
Terror: 9
Special Abilities:
Damage: Bite (STR)
Fearless
Guns: If the walkin' dead can get their hands on guns of any kind, they use them. And they're not concerned with saving ammo for later. If they get hold of a fully-automatic weapon, expect them to empty it before some do-gooder takes the opportunity to put them down and get all those bullets.
Undead

Profile (Veteran Walkin' Dead)

Corporeal: D:2d8, N:2d8, S:3d10, Q:3d10, V:2d8
Climbin' 2d8, dodge 3d8, fightin': brawlin' 4d8, shootin': any 4d8, sneak 3d8, swimmin' 2d8
Mental: C:2d10, K:1d6, M:1d6, Sm:1d6, Sp:1d4
Overawe 5d6, ridicule 1d6, search 3d10
Pace: 8
Size: 6
Wind: NA
Terror: 9
Special Abilities:
Damage: Bite (STR)
Fearless
Guns: Veteran dead are almost always armed unless they've just busted out of their graves. They often draw on old memories to remember where hidden caches of guns, ammo, armor, and grenades are as well.
Undead

The Bad Guys

Wormling

Wormlings are mysterious subterranean creatures first discovered over 100 years ago. No one knows their exact origin, but many scientists believe they are some sort of strange human/Mojave rattler hybrid because they possess the DNA of each. (Exactly how this crossbreeding took place is a mystery probably best left unanswered.)

This conclusion seems to be supported by the fact that wormlings generally appear in the same regions as their larger cousins—although some of these creatures have been spotted as much as 200 miles from the nearest Mojave rattler sighting.

The one thing that is known for sure is that wormlings are bad news. They normally hunt in packs of six to 10, and very few things can escape these ruthless predators. Most wormling "packs" stake out a territory as their hunting grounds and defend it against all comers, human, wormling, or otherwise.

These hunting grounds are studded with pit traps which the wormlings make by removing the earth from beneath a section of ground and lining the resulting hole with bits of jagged metal and sharp rocks. Anyone stepping on one of these weakened areas falls in and takes 2d6 damage to a random hit location. Spotting one of these traps requires a Hard (9) *search* roll.

In urban areas, wormlings sometimes set above-ground traps by using their acid to weaken a building's structural girders. Anyone placing any strain on these undermined buildings (say, by walking through them) causes them to collapse.

Profile

Corporeal: D:2d6, N:4d10, Q:3d8, S:4d10, V:4d8
Dodge 4d10, fightin': brawling 5d10, sneak 4d10, spittin' 4d6
Mental: C:3d6, K:2d6, M:3d4, Sm:3d6, Sp:2d8
Search 4d6, trackin' 5d6
Size: 7
Terror: 7
Special Abilities:
Acid: Wormlings produce a powerful acid which they can spray from their mouths. This is normally used when burrowing through rock, but it can be used as a weapon as well. The acid has a Speed of 1, Range Increment of 2, ROF 1, and does 3d10 damage.
Burrowing: Wormlings can move through soil (although not solid things like rock) at a Pace of 6). They like to use this to *sneak* up on prey and grab them from below.
Damage: Claws (STR+2d10; due to acid).

LOST COLONY

SUMMER 2000